C000217491

GHOSTS IN THE CLOISTERS

Ghosts in the Cloisters

Clerical Tales of Mystery and the Supernatural

Edited by Mark Bryant

Hodder & Stoughton

LONDON SYDNEY AUCKLAND

Introduction and collection copyright © 1998 by Mark Bryant

First published in Great Britain 1998

The right of Mark Bryant to be identified as the Editor of the
Work has been asserted by him in accordance with the
Copyright, Designs and Patents Act 1988.

10 9 8 7 6 5 4 3 2 1

British Library Cataloguing in Publication Data
A record for this book is available from the British Library

ISBN 0 340 71376 3

Typeset by Hewer Text Composition Services, Edinburgh
Printed and bound in Great Britain by
Clays Ltd, St Ives plc

Hodder and Stoughton Ltd
A Division of Hodder Headline PLC
338 Euston Road
London NW1 3BH

For Uncle Tom and Aunt Rita

Contents

Introduction

At the end of a quiet autumn day the old ruined abbey looks a picture of serenity. But as dusk falls and the clouds of night draw in, its more sinister character is gradually revealed. A sudden breeze rustles across the ivy-clad walls and disturbs the leaves of an ancient yew. Between the gusts a strange cry echoes down the valley end, as the darkness deepens, nocturnal creatures start to prowl. The clouds part and a cold an eery moonlight spreads slowly through the ancient cloisters, over the decayed medieval stonework and into the vaults. Then comes the sound of footsteps, uncertain at first, and a whispering in the walls. And as the clock chimes twelve in the sleeping hamlet below, a crouching shadow beings to stir in the tomb of the last abbot . . .

Ghosts, ghouls, spooks and phantoms have had a long and uneasy relationship with the Church since time immemorial. Indeed, readers of *Lord Halifax's Ghost Book* and other classic anthologies of apparently true supernatural tales will already be aware of the numerous well documented cases of hauntings, vampires, headless horrors and so forth which have been recorded over the centuries both in Britain and abroad, many of them by members of the clergy or their relations.

Such stories – whether real or imagined – have also inspired some of the finest works of literary fiction. This book is a collection of some of the very best of these clerical tales of mystery and the supernatural and includes contributions by some of the greatest short-sory writers of all time as well as two by practising priests (one of whom was also the son of a former Archbishop of Canterbury).

I have tried to make the anthology as balanced as the limitations of length and copyright availability have allowed, and it contains work by both men and women from the eighteenth century up to the present day. Among the spine-chilling tales there are also humorous ones and every aspect of clerical life is covered, from monks and nuns to bishops and saints – even the ghosts themselves are male and female! In addition, the settings for the stories range from the Middle Ages to modern times, in such various locations as Britain, Belgium, France, Crete and Switzerland, and feature all kinds of ecclesiastical buildings, from rectories, abbeys and cathedrals, to parish churches, chapels and a hermitage.

So whether you wear a dog-collar or a bow-tie, a surplice or a skirt, whether you live in a high-rise flat or a country mansion, turn the key in the door behind you, check all the windows are secure and settle down in a favourite chair with a comforting drink. Then let your imagination soar away into the darkest recesses of night and dream of ghoulish monks and restless souls, of unholy terrors and . . . ghosts in the cloisters.

The Cicerones

Robert Aickman

John Trant entered the Cathedral of St Bavon at almost exactly 11.30.

An unexpected week's holiday having come his way, he was spending it in Belgium, because Belgium was near and it was late in the season, and because he had never been there. Trant, who was unmarried (though one day he intended to marry), was travelling alone, but he seldom felt lonely at such times because he believed that his solitude was optional and regarded it rather as freedom. He was thirty-two and saw himself as quite ordinary, except perhaps in this very matter of travel, which he thought he took more seriously and systematically than most. The hour at which he entered the Cathedral was important, because he had been inconvenienced in other towns by the irritating continental habit of shutting tourist buildings between 12.00 and 2.00, even big churches. In fact, he had been in two minds as to whether to visit the Cathedral at all with so little time in hand. One could not even count upon the full half-hour, because the driving out of visitors usually began well before the moment of actual closure. It was a still morning, very still but overcast. Men were beginning to wait, one might say, for the year finally to die.

The thing that struck Trant most as he entered the vast building was how silent it seemed to be within; how empty.

Other Belgian cathedrals had contained twenty or thirty scattered people praying, or anyway kneeling; priests importantly on the move, followed by acolytes; and, of course, Americans. There had always been dingy bustle, ritual action, and neck-craning. Here there seemed to be no one; other, doubtless, than the people in the tombs. Trant again wondered whether the informed did not know that it was already too late to go in.

He leant against a column at the west end of the nave as he always did, and read the history of the cathedral in his Blue Guide. He chose this position in order that when he came to the next section to be perused, the architectural summary, he could look about him to the best advantage. He usually found, none the less, that he soon had to move if he were to follow what the guidebook had to say, as the architecture of few cathedrals can be apprehended, even in outline, by a newcomer from a single point. So it was now: Trant found that he was losing the thread, and decided he would have to take up the guidebook's trail. Before doing so, he looked around him for a moment. The Cathedral seemed still to be quite empty. It was odd, but a very pleasant change.

Trant set out along the south aisle of the nave, holding the guidebook like a breviary. 'Carved oak pulpit,' said the guidebook, 'with marble figures, all by Laurent Delvaux.' Trant had observed it vaguely from afar, but as, looking up from the book, he began consciously to think about it, he saw something extraordinary. Surely there was a figure in the pulpit, not standing erect, but slumped forward over the preacher's cushion? Trant could see the top of a small, bald head with a deep fringe, almost a halo, of white hair; and, on each side, widespread arms, with floppy hands. Not that it appeared to be a priest: the figure was wearing neither white nor black, but on the contrary, bright colours, several of them. Though considerably unnerved, Trant went forward, passed

2

the next column, in the arcade between the nave and the aisle, and looked again, through the next bay. He saw at once that there was nothing: at least there was only a litter of minor vestments and scripts in coloured bindings.

Trant heard a laugh. He turned. Behind him stood a slender, brown-haired young man in a grey suit.

'Excuse me,' said the young man. 'I saw it myself so don't be frightened.' He spoke quite clearly, but had a vague foreign accent.

'It was terrifying,' said Trant. 'Out of this world.'

'Yes. Out of this world, as you say. Did you notice the hair?'

'I did indeed.' The young man had picked on the very detail which had perturbed Trant the most. 'What did you make of it?'

'Holy, holy, holy,' said the young man in his foreign accent; then smiled and sauntered off westwards. Trant was *almost* sure that this was what he had said. The hair of the illusory figure in the pulpit had, at the time, reminded Trant of the way in which nimbuses are shown in certain old paintings; with wide bars or strips of light linking an outer misty ring with the sacred head. The figure's white hair had seemed to project in just such spikes.

Trant pulled himself together and reached the south transept, hung high with hatchments. He sought out *Christ Among the Doctors*, 'The masterpiece of Frans Pourbus the Elder', the guidebook remarked, and set himself to identifying the famous people said to be depicted in it, including the Duke of Alva, Vigilus ab Ayatta, and even the Emperor Charles V himself.

In the adjoining chapel, *The Martyrdom of St Barbara* by De Crayer proved to be covered with a cloth, another irritating continental habit, as Trant had previously discovered. As there seemed to be no one about, Trant lifted a corner of the cloth, which was brown and dusty, like so many things in Belgian cathedrals, and peered beneath. It was difficult to make out very much, especially as the light was so poor.

'Let me help,' said a transatlantic voice at Trant's back. 'Let me take it right off, and then you'll see something, believe me.'

Again it was a young man, but this time a red-haired cheerful-looking youth in a green windcheater.

The youth not only removed the cloth, but turned on an electric light.

'Thank you,' said Trant.

'Now have a good look.'

Trant looked. It was an extremely horrible scene.

'Oh, boy.' Trant had no desire to look any longer. 'Thank you all the same,' he said, apologizing for his repulsion.

'What a circus those old saints were,' commented the transatlantic youth, as he replaced the worn cloth.

'I suppose they received their reward in heaven,' suggested Trant.

'You bet they did,' said the youth, with a fervour that Trant couldn't quite fathom. He turned off the light. 'Be seeing you.'

'I expect so,' said Trant smiling.

The youth said no more, but put his hands in his pockets, and departed whistling towards the south door. Trant himself would not have cared to whistle so loudly in a foreign church.

As all the world knows, the most important work of art in the Cathedral of St Bavon is the *Adoration* by the mysterious Van Eyck or Van Eycks, singular or plural. Nowadays the picture is hung in a small, curtained-off chapel leading from the south choir ambulatory; and most strangers must pay to see it. When Trant reached the chapel, he saw the notice at the door, but, hearing nothing, as elsewhere, supposed the place to be empty. Resenting mildly the demand for a fee, as Protestants do, he took the initiative and gently lifted the dark red curtain.

The chapel, though still silent, was not empty at all. On the contrary, it was so full that Trant could have gone no further inside, even had he dared.

4

There were two kinds of people in the chapel. In front were several rows of men in black. They knelt shoulder to shoulder, heads dropped, hip-bone against hip-bone, in what Trant took to be silent worship. Behind them, packed in even more tightly, was a group, even a small crowd, of funny old Belgian women, fat, ugly, sexless, and bossy, such as Trant had often seen in other places both devotional and secular. The old women were not kneeling but sitting. All the same, they seemed eerily rapt. Strangest of all was their motionless silence. Trant had seen such groups everywhere in Belgium, but never, never silent, very far from it. Not a single one of this present group seemed even to be aware that he was there: something equally unusual with a people so given to curiosity.

And in this odd setting not the least strange thing was the famous picture itself, with its enigmatic monsters, sibyls, and walking allegories, and its curiously bright, other-world colours: a totality doubtless interpretable in terms of Freud, but, all the same, as dense as an oriental carpet, and older than Adam and Eve, who stand beside. Trant found the picture all too cognate to the disconcerting devotees.

He let fall the curtain and went on his way, distinctly upset.

Two chapels further around, he came upon the *Virgin Glorified* by Liemakere. Here a choir-boy in a red cassock was polishing the crucifix on the altar. Already he had thin black hair and a grey, watchful face.

'*Onze lieve Vrouw*,' said the choir-boy, explaining the picture to Trant.

'Yes,' said Trant. 'Thank you.'

It occurred to him that polishing was odd work for a choir-boy. Perhaps this was not a choir-boy at all, but some other kind of young servitor. The idea of being shortly ejected from the building returned to Trant's mind. He looked at his watch. It had stopped. It still showed 11.28.

Trant shook the watch against his ear, but there were no

recovering ticks. He saw that the polishing boy (he was at work on the pierced feet) wore a watch also, on a narrow black strap. Trant gesticulated again. The boy shook his head more violently. Trant could not decide whether the boy's own watch was broken, or whether, conceivably, he thought that Trant was trying to take it from him. Then, all in seconds, it struck Trant that, whatever else there was about the boy he certainly did not appear alarmed. Far from it. He seemed as aloof as if he were already a priest, and to be refusing to tell Trant the time on principle; almost implying, as priests presume to do, that he was refusing for the other's good. Trant departed from the chapel containing Liemakere's masterpiece rather quickly.

How much time had he left?

In the next chapel was Rubens's vast altarpiece of St Bavon distributing all his goods among the poor.

In the next was the terrifying *Martyrdom of Saint Livinus* by Seghers.

After one more chapel, Trant had reached the junction of the north transept and the choir. The choir was surrounded by a heavy and impenetrable screen of black marble, like a cage for the imperial lions. The guidebook recommended the four tombs of past bishops which were said to be inside; but Trant, peering through the stone bars, could hardly see even outlines. He shifted from end to end of the choir steps seeking a viewpoint where the light might be better. It was useless. In the end, he tried the handle of the choir gate. The gate had given every appearance of being locked, but in fact it opened at once when Trant made the attempt. He tiptoed into the dark enclosure and thought he had better shut the gate behind him. He was not sure that he was going to see very much of the four tombs even now; but there they were, huge boxes flanking the high altar, like dens for the lions.

He stood at the steps of the altar itself, leaning across the marble rails, the final barricade, trying to read one of the Latin inscriptions. In such an exercise Trant made it a matter of principle not lightly to admit defeat. He craned his neck and screwed up his eyes until he was half-dazed; capturing the antique words one at a time, and trying to construe them. The matter of the cathedral shutting withdrew temporarily to the back of his mind. Then something horrible seemed to happen; or rather two things, one after the other. Trant thought, first, that the stone panel he was staring at so hard, seemed somehow to move; and then that a hand had appeared round one upper corner of it. It seemed to Trant a curiously small hand.

Trant decided, almost calmly, to see it out. There must obviously be an explanation, and anything like flight would make him look ridiculous, as well as leaving the mystery unsolved. An explanation there was; the stone opened further, and from within emerged a small, fair-haired child.

'Hullo,' said the child, looking at Trant across the black marble barrier and smiling.

'Hullo,' said Trant. 'You speak very good English.'

'I *am* English,' said the child. It was wearing a dark brown garment open at the neck, and dark brown trousers, but Trant could not quite decide whether it was a boy or a girl. From the escapade a boy seemed likelier, but there was something about the child which was more like a girl, Trant thought.

'Should you have been in there?'

'I always go in.'

'Aren't you afraid?'

'No one could be afraid of Bishop Triest. He gave us those candlesticks.' The child pointed to four copper objects; which seemed to Trant to offer no particular confirmation of the child's logic.

'Would *you* like to go in?' enquired the child politely.

'No, thank you,' said Trant.

'Then I'll just shut up.' The child heaved the big stone slab

7

into place. It was a feat of strength all the more remarkable in that Trant noticed that the child seemed to limp.

'Do you live here?' asked Trant.

'Yes,' said the child, and, child-like, said no more.

It limped forward, climbed the altar-rail, and stood beside Trant, looking up at him. Trant found it difficult to assess how old it was.

'Would you like to see one of the other bishops?'

'No thank you,' said Trant.

'I think you ought to see a bishop,' said the child quite gravely.

'I'd rather not,' said Trant smiling.

'There may not be another chance.'

'I expect not,' said Trant, still smiling. He felt it was best to converse with the child at its own level, and make no attempt at adult standards of flat questioning and conventionalized reference.

'Then I'll take you to the crypt,' said the child.

The crypt was the concluding item in the guidebook. Entered from just by the north-western corner of the choir, it was, like the *Adoration*, a speciality, involving payment. Trant had rather assumed that he would not get round to it.

'Shall I have time?' he asked, looking instinctively at his stopped watch, still showing 11.28.

'Yes,' said the child, as before.

The child limped ahead, opened the choir-gate, and held it for Trant, his inscriptions unread, to pass through. The child closed the gate, and led the way to the crypt entry, looking over its shoulder to see that Trant was following. In the rather better light outside the choir, Trant saw that its hair was a wonderful mass of silky gold; its face almost white, with the promise of fine bones; its lips unusually full and red.

'This is called the crossing,' said the child informatively.

8

Trant knew that the term was sometimes applied to the intersection of nave and transepts.

'Or the narthex, I believe,' he said, plunging in order to show who was the grown-up.

The child, not unnaturally, looked merely puzzled.

There was still no one else visible in the cathedral.

They began to descend the crypt stairs, the child holding on to the iron handrail, because of its infirmity. There was a table at the top, obviously for the collection of the fee, but deserted. Trant did not feel called upon to comment.

In the crypt, slightly to his surprise, many of the lights were on. Probably the custodian had forgotten to turn them off when he or she had hurried forth to eat.

The guidebook described the crypt as 'large', but it was much larger than Trant had expected. The stairs entered it at one corner, and columns seemed to stretch away like trees into the distance. They were built in stones of different colours, maroon, purple, green, grey, gold; and they often bore remains of painting as well, which also spread over areas of the vaulted stone roof and weighty walls. In the soft patchy light, the place was mysterious and beautiful; and all the more so because the whole area could not be seen simultaneously. With the tide of centuries the stone-paved floor had become rolling and un-even, but agreeably so. There were occasional showcases and objects on pedestals, and there was a gentle perfume of incense. As Trant entered, all was silence. He even felt for a moment that there was something queer about the silence; that only sounds of another realm moved in it, and that the noises of this world, of his own arrival for example, were in a different dimension and irrelevant. He stood, a little awed, and listened for a moment to the nothingness.

The child stood too, or rather rested against a pillar. It was smiling again, though very slightly. Perhaps it smiled like this all the time, as if always happy.

Trant thought more than ever that it might be a girl. By this time it was rather absurd not to be sure, but by this time it was more than before difficult to ask.

'Bishop Triest's clothes,' said the child, pointing. They were heavy vestments, hanging, enormously embroidered, in a glass cabinet.

'Saint Livinus's ornament,' said the child, and crossed itself. Trant did not know quite what to make of the ornament.

'Animals,' said the child. It was an early book of natural history, written by a monk, and even the opened page showed some very strange ones.

The child was now beginning positively to dart about in its eagerness, pointing out item after item.

'Shrine of Saint Marcellus,' said the child, not crossing itself, presumably because the relic was absent.

'Abbot Hughenois's clothes.' They were vestments again, and very much like Triest's vestments, Trant thought.

'What's that?' asked Trant, taking the initiative and pointing. Right on the other side of the crypt, as it seemed, and now visible to Trant for the first time through the forest of soft-coloured columns, was something which appeared to be winking and gleaming with light.

'That's at the end,' replied the child. 'You'll be there soon.'

Soon indeed, at this hour, thought Trant: if in fact we're not thrown out first.

'*Via Dolorosa*,' said the child, pointing to a picture. It was a gruesome scene, painted very realistically, as if the artist had been a bystander at the time; and it was followed by another which was even more gruesome and at least equally realistic.

'Calvary,' explained the child.

They rounded a corner with a stone wall on the left, the forest of columns on the right. The two parts of a diptych came into view, of which Trant had before seen only the discoloured reverse.

'The blessed and the lost,' said the child, indicating, superfluously, which was which.

Trant thought that the pictures and frescoes were becoming more and more morbid, but supposed that this feeling was probably the result of their cumulative impact. In any case, there could not be much more.

But there were still many things to be seen. In due course they came to a group of pictures hanging together.

'The sacrifice of three blessed martyrs,' said the child. Each of the martyrs had died in a different way: by roasting on a very elaborate gridiron; by disembowelling; and by some process involving a huge wheel. The paintings, unlike some of the others, were extraordinarily well preserved. The third of the martyrs was a young woman. She had been martyred naked and was of great and still living beauty. Next to her hung a further small picture, showing a saint carrying his own skin. Among the columns to the right was an enormous black cross. At a little distance, the impaled figure looked lifelike in the extreme.

The child was still skipping in front, making so light of its disability that Trant could not but be touched. They turned another corner. At the end of the ambulatory ahead was the gleaming, flashing object that Trant had noticed from the other side of the crypt. The child almost ran on, ignoring the intervening sights, and stood by the object, waiting for Trant to catch up. The child's head was sunk, but Trant could see that it was looking at him from under its fair, silky eyelashes.

This time the child said nothing, and Trant could only stare.

The object was a very elaborate, jewelled reliquary of the Renaissance. It was presumably the jewels which had seemed to give off the flashing lights, because Trant could see no lights now. At the centre of the reliquary was a transparent vertical tube or cylinder. It was only about an inch high, and probably made of crystal. Just visible inside it was a short black thread, almost like the mercury in a minute thermometer, and at the bottom of the tube was, Trant noticed, a marked discoloration.

The child was still standing in the same odd position; now glancing sideways at Trant, now glancing away. It was perhaps smiling a little more broadly, but its head was sunk so low that Trant could not really see. Its whole posture and behaviour suggested that there was something about the reliquary which Trant should be able to see for himself. It was almost as if the child were timing him, to see how long he took.

Time, thought Trant, yet again; and now with a start. The reliquary was so fascinating that he had managed somehow almost to forget about time. He looked away and along the final ambulatory, which ran to the foot of the staircase by which he had descended. While he had been examining the reliquary, someone else had appeared in the crypt. A man stood in the centre of the passage, a short distance from Trant. Or not exactly a man: it was, Trant realized, the acolyte in the red cassock, the boy who had been polishing the brass feet. Trant had no doubt that he had come to hurry him out.

Trant bustled off, full of unreasonable guilt, without even properly thanking his child guide. But when he reached the boy in the cassock, the boy silently stretched out his arms to their full length and seemed, on the contrary, to bar his passage.

It was rather absurd; and especially as one could so readily turn right and weave a way out through the Gothic columns.

Trant, in fact, turned his head in that direction, simply upon instinct. But, in the bay to his right, stood the youth from across the Atlantic in the green windcheater. He had the strangest of expressions (unlike the boy in the cassock, who seemed the same dull peasant as before); and as soon as Trant caught his eye, he too raised his arms to their full extent, as the boy had done.

There was still one more free bay. Trant retreated a step or two, but then saw among the shadows within (which seemed to be deepening) the man in the grey suit with the vague foreign accent. His arms were going up even as Trant sighted him, but when their eyes met (though Trant could not see his face very well) he did something the others had not done. He laughed.

And in the entrance to the other ambulatory, through which Trant had just come and down which the child had almost run, bravely casting aside its affliction, stood that same child, now gazing upwards again, and indeed looking quite radiant, as it spread its arms almost as a bird taking flight.

Trant heard the great clock of the cathedral strike twelve. In the crypt, the tone of the bell was lost: there was little more to be distinguished than twelve great thuds, almost as if cannon were being discharged. The twelve strokes of the hour took a surprisingly long time to complete.

In the meantime, and just beside the reliquary, a small door had opened, in the very angle of the crypt. Above it was a small but exquisite and well preserved alabaster keystone showing a soul being dragged away on a hook by a demon. Trant had hardly noticed the door before, as people commonly overlook the working details of a place which is on show, the same details that those who work the place look to first.

In the door, quite filling it, was the man Trant believed himself to have seen in the pulpit soon after he had first entered the great building. The man looked bigger now, but there were the same bald head, the same resigned hands, the same multicoloured garments. It was undoubtedly the very person, but in some way enlarged or magnified; and the curious fringe of hair seemed more luminous than ever.

'You must leave now,' said the man kindly but firmly. 'Follow me.'

Ghosts in the Cloisters

The four figures encircling Trant began to shut in on him until their extended fingertips were almost touching.

His questions went quite unanswered, his protests quite unheard; especially after everyone started singing.

The Haunting of Shawley Rectory

Ruth Rendell

I don't believe in the supernatural, but just the same I wouldn't live in Shawley Rectory.

That was what I had been thinking and what Gordon Scott said to me when we heard we were to have a new rector at St Mary's. Our wives gave us quizzical looks.

'Not very logical,' said Eleanor, my wife.

'What I mean is,' said Gordon, 'that however certain you might be that ghosts don't exist, if you lived in a place that was reputedly haunted you wouldn't be able to help wondering every time you heard a stair creak. All the normal sounds of an old house would take on a different significance.'

I agreed with him. It wouldn't be very pleasant feeling uneasy every time one was alone in one's own home at night.

'Personally,' said Patsy Scott, 'I've always believed there are no ghosts in the Rectory that a good central-heating system wouldn't get rid of.'

We laughed at that, but Eleanor said, 'You can't just dismiss it like that. The Cobworths heard and felt things even if they didn't actually see anything. And so did the Bucklands before them. And you won't find anyone more level-headed than Kate Cobworth.'

Patsy shrugged. 'The Loys didn't even hear or feel anything. They'd heard the stories, they *expected* to hear the footsteps and the carriage wheels. Diana Loy told me. And Diana was

15

quite a nervy, highly strung sort of person. But absolutely nothing happened while they were there.'

'Well, maybe the Church of England or whoever's responsible will install central heating for the new person,' I said, 'and we'll see if your theory's right, Patsy.'

Eleanor and I went home after that. We went on foot because our house is only about a quarter of a mile up Shawley Lane. On the way we stopped in front of the Rectory, which is about a hundred yards along. We stood and looked over the gate.

I may as well describe the Rectory to you before I get on with this story. The date of it is around 1760 and it's built of pale dun-coloured brick with plain classical windows and a front door in the middle with a pediment over it. It's a big house with three reception rooms, six bedrooms, two kitchens and two staircases – and one poky little bathroom made by having converted a linen closet. The house is a bit stark to look at, a bit forbidding; it seems to stare straight back at you, but the trees round it are pretty enough and so are the stables on the left-hand side with a clock in their gable and a weathervane on top. Tom Cobworth, the last Rector, kept his old Morris in there. The garden is huge, a wilderness that no one could keep tidy these days – eight acres of it including the glebe.

It was years since I had been inside the Rectory. I remember wondering if the interior was as shabby and in need of paint as the outside. The windows had that black, blank, hazy look of windows at which no curtains hang and which no one has cleaned for months or even years.

'Who exactly does it *belong* to?' said Eleanor.

'Lazarus College, Oxford,' I said. 'Tom was a Fellow of Lazarus.'

'And what about this new man?'

'I don't know,' I said. 'I think all that system of livings has changed but I'm pretty vague about it.'

I'm not a churchgoer, not religious at all really. Perhaps that was why I hadn't got to know the Cobworths all that well. I used to feel a bit uneasy in Tom's company, I used to have the feeling he might suddenly round on me and demand to know why he never saw me in church. Eleanor had no such inhibitions with Kate. They were friends, close friends, and Eleanor had missed her after Tom died suddenly of a heart attack and she had to leave the Rectory. She had gone back to her people up north, taking her fifteen-year-old daughter Louise with her.

Kate is a practical down-to-earth Yorkshirewoman. She had been a nurse – a ward sister, I believe – before her marriage. When Tom got the living of Shawley she several times met Mrs Buckland, the wife of the retiring incumbent, and from her learned to expect what Mrs Buckland called 'manifestations'.

'I couldn't believe she was actually saying it,' Kate had said to Eleanor. 'I thought I was dreaming and then I thought she was mad. I mean really psychotic, mentally ill. Ghosts! I ask you – people believing things like that in this day and age. And then we moved in and I heard them too.'

The crunch of carriage wheels on the gravel drive when there was no carriage or any kind of vehicle to be seen. Doors closing softly when no doors had been left open. Footsteps crossing the landing and going downstairs, crossing the hall, then the front door opening softly and closing softly.

'But how could you bear it?' Eleanor said. 'Weren't you afraid? Weren't you terrified?'

'We got used to it. We had to, you see. It wasn't as if we could sell the house and buy another. Besides, I love Shawley – I loved it from the first moment I set foot in the village. After the harshness of the north, Dorset is so gentle and mild and pretty. The doors closing and the footsteps and the wheels on the drive – they didn't do us any harm. And we had each other, we weren't alone. You can get used to anything – to ghosts as much as to damp and woodworm and dry rot. There's all that in the Rectory too and I found it much more trying!'

The Bucklands, apparently, had got used to it too. Thirty years he had been Rector of the parish, thirty years they had lived there with the wheels and the footsteps, and had brought up their son and daughter there. No harm had come to them; they slept soundly, and their grown-up children used to joke about their haunted house.

'Nobody ever seems to *see* anything,' I said to Eleanor as we walked home. 'And no one ever comes up with a story, a sort of background to all this walking about and banging and crunching. Is there supposed to have been a murder there or some other sort of violent death?'

She said she didn't know, Kate had never said. The sound of the wheels, the closing of the doors, always took place at about nine in the evening, followed by the footsteps and the opening and closing of the front door. After that there was silence, and it hadn't happened every evening by any means. The only other thing was that Kate had never cared to use the big drawing-room in the evenings. She and Tom and Louise had always stayed in the dining-room or the morning-room.

They did use the drawing-room in the daytime – it was just that in the evenings the room felt strange to her, chilly even in summer, and indefinably hostile. Once she had had to go in there at ten-thirty. She needed her reading glasses which she had left in the drawing-room during the afternoon. She ran into the room and ran out again. She hadn't looked about her, just rushed in, keeping her eyes fixed on the eyeglass case on the mantelpiece. The icy hostility in that room had really frightened her, and that had been the only time she had felt dislike and fear of Shawley Rectory.

Of course one doesn't have to find explanations for an icy hostility. It's much more easily understood as being the

product of tension and fear than aural phenomena are. I didn't
have much faith in Kate's feelings about the drawing-room. I
thought with a kind of admiration of Jack and Diana Loy,
that elderly couple who had rented the Rectory for a year after
Kate's departure, had been primed with stories of hauntings
by Kate, yet had neither heard nor felt a thing. As far as I
know, they had used that drawing-room constantly. Often,
when I had passed the gate in their time, I had seen lights in the
drawing-room windows, at nine, at ten-thirty, and even at
midnight.

The Loys had been gone three months. When Lazarus had
first offered the Rectory for rent, the idea had been that
Shawley should do without a clergyman of its own. I think
this must have been the Church economizing – nothing to do
certainly with ghosts. The services at St Mary's were to be
undertaken by the vicar of the next parish, Mr Hartley.
Whether he found this too much for him in conjunction with
the duties of his own parish or whether the powers-that-be in
affairs Anglican had second thoughts, I can't say; but on the
departure of the Loys it was decided there should be an
incumbent to replace Tom.

The first hint of this we had from local gossip; next the facts
appeared in our monthly news sheet, the *Shawley Post*.
Couched in its customary parish magazine journalese it
said: 'Shawley residents all extend a hearty welcome to their
new Rector, the Reverend Stephen Galton, whose coming to
the parish with his charming wife will fill a long-felt need.'

'He's very young,' said Eleanor a few days after our
discussion of haunting with the Scotts. 'Under thirty.'

'That won't bother me,' I said. 'I don't intend to be
preached at by him. Anyway, why not? Out of the mouths
of babes and sucklings,' I said, 'hast Thou ordained strength.'

'Hark at the devil quoting scripture,' said Eleanor. 'They
say his wife's only twenty-three.'

19

I thought she must have met them, she knew so much. But no.

'It's just what's being said. Patsy got it from Judy Lawrence. Judy said they're moving in next month and her mother's coming with them.'

'Who, Judy's?' I said.

'Don't be silly,' said my wife. 'Mrs Galton's mother, the Rector's mother-in-law. She's coming to live with them.'

Move in they did. And out again two days later.

The first we knew that something had gone very wrong for the Galtons was when I was out for my usual evening walk with our Irish setter Liam. We were coming past the cottage that belongs to Charlie Lawrence (who is by way of being Shawley's squire) and which he keeps for the occupation of his gardener when he is lucky enough to have a gardener. At that time, last June, he hadn't had a gardener for at least six months, and the cottage should have been empty. As I approached, however, I saw a woman's face, young, fair, very pretty, at one of the upstairs windows.

I rounded the hedge and Liam began an insane barking, for just inside the cottage gate, on the drive, peering in under the bonnet of an aged Wolseley, was a tall young man wearing a tweed sports jacket over one of those black-top things the clergy wear, and a clerical collar.

'Good evening,' I said. 'Shut up, Liam, will you?'

'Good evening,' he said in a quiet, abstracted sort of way.

I told Eleanor. She couldn't account for the Galtons occupying Charlie Lawrence's gardener's cottage instead of Shawley Rectory, their proper abode. But Patsy Scott could. She came round on the following morning with a punnet of strawberries for us. The Scotts grow the best strawberries for miles around.

'They've been driven out by the ghosts,' she said. 'Can you

credit it? A clergyman of the Church of England! An educated man! They were in that place not forty-eight hours before they were screaming to Charlie Lawrence to find them somewhere else to go.'

I asked her if she was sure it wasn't just the damp and the dry rot.

'Look, you know me. *I* don't believe the Rectory's haunted or anywhere *can* be haunted, come to that. I'm telling you what Mrs Galton told me. She came in to us on Thursday morning and said did I think there was anyone in Shawley had a house or a cottage to rent because they couldn't stick the Rectory another night. I asked her what was wrong. And she said she knew it sounded crazy – it did too, she was right there – she knew it sounded mad, but they'd been terrified out of their lives by what they'd heard and seen since they moved in.'

'*Seen?*' I said. 'She actually claims to have seen something?'

'She said her mother did. She said her mother saw something in the drawing-room the first evening they were there. They'd already heard the carriage wheels and the doors closing and the footsteps and all that. The second evening no one dared go in the drawing-room. They heard all the sounds again and Mrs Grainger – that's the mother – heard voices in the drawing-room, and it was then that they decided they couldn't stand it, they'd have to get out.'

'I don't believe it!' I said. 'I don't believe any of it. The woman's a psychopath, she's playing some sort of ghastly joke.'

'Just as Kate was and the Bucklands,' said Eleanor quietly.

Patsy ignored her and turned to me. 'I feel just like you. It's awful, but what can you do? These stories grow and they sort of infect people and the more suggestible the people are, the worse the infection. Charlie and Judy are furious, they don't want it getting in the papers that Shawley Rectory is haunted. Think of all the people we shall get coming in cars on Sundays and gawping over the gates. But they had to let them have the cottage in common humanity. Mrs Grainger was hysterical and poor little Mrs Galton wasn't much better. Who told them to expect all those horrors? That's what I'd like to know.'

'What does Gordon say?' I said.

'He's keeping an open mind, but he says he'd like to spend an evening there.'

In spite of the Lawrences' fury, the haunting of Shawley Rectory did get quite a lot of publicity. There was a sensational story about it in one of the popular Sundays and then Stephen Galton's mother-in-law went on television. Western TV interviewed her on a local news programme. I hadn't ever seen Mrs Grainger in the flesh and her youthful appearance rather surprised me. She looked no more than thirty-five, though she must be into her forties.

The interviewer asked her if she had ever heard any stories of ghosts at Shawley Rectory before she went there and she said she hadn't. Did she believe in ghosts? Now she did. What had happened, asked the interviewer, after they had moved in?

It had started at nine o'clock, she said, at nine on their first evening. She and her daughter were sitting in the bigger of the two kitchens, having a cup of coffee. They had been moving in all day, unpacking, putting things away. They heard two doors close upstairs, then footsteps coming down the main staircase. She had thought it was her son-in-law, except that it couldn't have been because as the footsteps died away he came in through the door from the back kitchen. They couldn't understand what it had been, but they weren't frightened. Not then.

'We were planning on going to bed early,' said Mrs Grainger. She was very articulate, very much at ease in front of the cameras. 'Just about half-past ten I had to go into the big room they call the drawing-room. The removal men had put some of our boxes in there and my radio was in one of them. I wanted to listen to my radio in bed. I opened the drawing-room door and put my hand to the light switch. I didn't put the light on. The moon was quite bright that night and it was shining into the room.

'There were two people, two figures, I don't know what to call them, between the windows. One of them, the girl, was lying huddled on the floor. The other figure, an older woman, was bending over her. She stood up when I opened the door and looked at me. I knew I wasn't seeing real people, I don't know how but I knew that. I remember I couldn't move my hand to switch the light on. I was frozen, just staring at that pale tragic face while it stared back at me. I did manage at last to back out and close the door, and I got back to my daughter and my son-in-law in the kitchen and I – well, I collapsed. It was the most terrifying experience of my life.'

'Yet you stayed a night and a day and another night in the Rectory?' said the interviewer.

Yes, well, her daughter and her son-in-law had persuaded her it had been some sort of hallucination, the consequence of being overtired. Not that she had ever really believed that. The night had been quiet and so had the next day until nine in the evening when they were all this time in the morning-room and they heard a car drive up to the front door. They had all heard it, wheels crunching on the gravel, the sound of the engine, the brakes going on. Then had followed the closing of the doors upstairs and the footsteps, the opening and closing of the front door.

Yes, they had been very frightened, or she and her daughter had. Her son-in-law had made a thorough search of the whole house but found nothing, seen or heard no one. At ten-thirty they had all gone into the hall and listened outside the drawing-room door and she and her daughter had heard voices from inside the room, women's voices. Stephen had wanted to go in, but they had stopped him, they had been so frightened.

Now the interesting thing was that there had been something in the *Sunday Express* account about the Rectory being haunted by the ghosts of two women. The story quoted someone it described as a 'local antiquarian', a man named Joseph Lamb, whom I had heard of but never met. Lamb had told the *Express* there was an old tradition that the ghosts were of a mother and her daughter and that the mother had killed the daughter in the drawing-room.

'I never heard any of that before,' I said to Gordon Scott, 'and I'm sure Kate Cobworth hadn't. Who is this Joseph Lamb?'

'He's a nice chap,' said Gordon. 'And he's supposed to know more of local history than anyone else around. I'll ask him over and you can come and meet him if you like.'

Joseph Lamb lives in a rather fine Jacobean house in a hamlet – you could hardly call it a village – about a mile to the north of Shawley. I had often admired it without knowing who had lived there. The Scotts asked him and his wife to dinner shortly after Mrs Grainger's appearance on television, and after dinner we got him on to the subject of the hauntings. Lamb wasn't at all unwilling to enlighten us. He's a man of about sixty and he said he first heard the story of the two women from his nurse when he was a little boy. Not a very suitable subject with which to regale a seven-year-old, he said.

'These two are supposed to have lived in the Rectory at one time,' he said. 'The story is that the mother had a lover or a man friend or whatever, and the daughter took him away from her. When the daughter confessed it, the mother killed her in a jealous rage.'

It was Eleanor who objected to this. 'But surely if they lived in the Rectory they must have been the wife and daughter of a Rector. I don't really see how in those circumstances the mother could have had a lover or the daughter could steal him away.'

'No, it doesn't sound much like what we've come to think of as the domestic life of the English country parson, does it?' said Lamb. 'And the strange thing is, although my nanny used to swear by the story and I heard it later from someone who worked at the Rectory, I haven't been able to find any trace of these women in the Rectory's history. It's not hard to research, you see, because only the Rectors of Shawley had ever lived there until the Loys rented it, and the Rectors' names are all up on that plaque in the church from 1380 onwards. There was another house on the site before this present one, of course, and parts of the older building are incorporated in the newer.

'My nanny used to say that the elder lady hadn't got a husband, he had presumably died. She was supposed to be forty years old and the girl nineteen. Well, I tracked back through the families of the various Rectors and I found a good many cases where the Rectors had predeceased their wives. But none of them fitted my nanny's story. They were either too old – one was much too young – or their daughters were too old or they had no daughters.'

'It's a pity Mrs Grainger didn't tell us what kind of clothes her ghosts were wearing,' said Patsy with sarcasm. 'You could have pinpointed the date then, couldn't you?'

'You mean that if the lady had had a steeple hat on she'd be medieval or around 1850 if she was wearing a crinoline?'

'Something like that,' said Patsy.

At this point Gordon repeated his wish to spend an evening in the Rectory. 'I think I'll write to the Master of Lazarus and ask permission,' he said.

Very soon after we heard that the Rectory was to be sold. Notice-boards appeared by the front gate and at the corner where the glebe abutted Shawley Lane, announcing that the house would go up for auction on October the 30th. Patsy, who always seems to know everything, told us that a reserve price of £60,000 had been put on it.

'Not as much as I'd have expected,' she said. 'It must be the ghosts keeping the price down.'

'Whoever buys it will have to spend another ten thousand on it,' said Eleanor.

'And central heating will be a priority.'

Whatever was keeping the price down – ghosts, cold, or dry rot – there were plenty of people anxious to view the house and land with, I supposed, an idea of buying it. I could hardly be at work in my garden or out with Liam without a car stopping and the driver asking me the way to the Rectory. Gordon and Patsy got quite irritable about what they described as 'crowds milling about' in the lane and trippers everywhere, waving orders to view.

The estate agents handling the sale were a firm called Curlew, Pond & Co. Gordon didn't bother with the Master of Lazarus but managed to get the key from Graham Curlew, whom he knew quite well, and permission to spend an evening in the Rectory. Curlew didn't like the idea of anyone staying the night, but Gordon didn't want to do that anyway; no one had ever heard or seen anything after ten-thirty. He asked me if I'd go with him. Patsy wouldn't – she thought it was all too adolescent and stupid.

'Of course I will,' I said. 'As long as you'll agree to our taking some sort of heating arrangement with us and brandy in case of need.'

By then it was the beginning of October and the evenings were turning cool. The day on which we decided to have our vigil happened also to be the one on which Stephen Galton and his wife moved out of Charlie Lawrence's cottage and left Shawley for good. According to the *Shawley Post*, he had got a living in Manchester. Mrs Grainger had gone back to her own home in London from where she had written an article about the Rectory for *Psychic News*.

Patsy shrieked with laughter to see the two of us setting

26

forth with our oil-stove, a dozen candles, two torches, and half a bottle of Courvoisier. She did well to laugh, her amusement wasn't misplaced. We crossed the lane and opened the Rectory gate and went up the gravel drive on which those spirit wheels had so often been heard to crunch. It was seven o'clock in the evening and still light. The day had been fine and the sky was red with the aftermath of a spectacular sunset.

I unlocked the front door and in we went.

The first thing I did was put a match to one of the candles because it wasn't at all light inside. We walked down the passage to the kitchens, I carrying the candle and Gordon shining one of the torches across the walls. The place was a mess. I suppose it hadn't had anything done to it, not even a cleaning, since the Loys moved out. It smelled damp and there was even fungus growing in patches on the kitchen walls. And it was extremely cold. There was a kind of deathly chill in the air, far more of a chill than one would have expected on a warm day in October. That kitchen had the feel you get when you open the door of a refrigerator that hasn't been kept too clean and is in need of defrosting.

We put our stuff down on a kitchen table someone had left behind and made our way up the back stairs. All the bedroom doors were open and we closed them. The upstairs had a neglected, dreary feel but it was less cold. We went down the main staircase, a rather fine curving affair with elegant banisters and carved newel posts, and entered the drawing-room. It was empty, palely lit by the evening light from two windows. On the mantelpiece was a glass jar with greenish water in it, a half-burnt candle in a saucer, and a screwed-up paper table napkin. We had decided not to remain in this room but to open the door and look in at ten-thirty; so accordingly we returned to the kitchen, fetched out candles and torches and brandy, and settled down in the morning-room, which was at the front of the house, on the other side of the front door.

Curlew had told Gordon there were a couple of deckchairs in this room. We found them resting against the wall and we put them up. We lit our oil-stove and a second candle, and we set one candle on the window-sill and one on the floor between us. It was still and silent and cold. The dark closed in fairly rapidly, the red fading from the sky, which became a deep hard blue, then indigo.

We sat and talked. It was about the haunting that we talked, collating the various pieces of evidence, assessing the times this or that was supposed to happen and making sure we both knew the sequence in which things happened. We were both wearing watches and I remember that we constantly checked the time. At half-past eight we again opened the drawing-room door and looked inside. The moon had come up and was shining through the windows as it had shone for Mrs Grainger.

Gordon went upstairs with a torch and checked that all the doors remained closed and then we both looked into the other large downstairs room, the dining-room, I suppose. Here a fanlight in one of the windows was open. That accounted for some of the feeling of cold and damp, Gordon said. The window must have been opened by some prospective buyer, viewing the place. We closed it and went back into the morning-room to wait.

The silence was absolute. We didn't talk any more. We waited, watching the candles and the glow of the stove, which had taken some of the chill from the air. Outside it was pitch-dark. The hands of our watches slowly approached nine.

At three minutes to nine we heard the noise.

Not wheels or doors closing or a tread on the stairs but a faint, dainty, pattering sound. It was very faint, it was distant, it was on the ground floor. It was as if made by something less

28

than human, lighter than that, tiptoeing. I had never thought
about this moment beyond telling myself that if anything did
happen, if there was a manifestation, it would be enormously
interesting. It had never occurred to me even once that I
should be so dreadfully, so hideously, afraid.

I didn't look at Gordon, I couldn't. I couldn't move either.
The pattering feet were less faint now, were coming closer. I
felt myself go white, the blood all drawn in from the surface of
my skin, as I was gripped by that awful primitive terror that
has nothing to do with reason or with knowing what you
believe in and what you don't.

Gordon got to his feet, and stood there looking at the door.
And then I couldn't stand it any more. I jumped up and threw
open the door, holding the candle aloft – and looked into a
pair of brilliant golden-green eyes, staring steadily back at me
about a foot from the ground.

'My God,' said Gordon. 'My God, it's the Lawrences' cat.
It must have got in through the window.'

He bent down and picked up the cat, a soft, stout, marma-
lade-coloured creature. I felt sick at the anti-climax. The time
was exactly nine o'clock. With the cat draped over his arm,
Gordon went back into the morning-room and I followed him.
We didn't sit down. We stood waiting for the wheels and the
closing of the doors.

Nothing happened.

I have no business to keep you in suspense any longer for
the fact is that after the business with the cat nothing
happened at all. At nine-fifteen we sat down in our deckchairs. The cat lay on the floor beside the oil-stove and went to
sleep. Twice we heard a car pass along Shawley Lane, a
remotely distant sound, but we heard nothing else.

'Feel like a spot of brandy?' said Gordon.

'Why not?' I said.

So we each had a nip of brandy and at ten we had another

29

look in the drawing-room. By then we were both feeling bored and quite sure that since nothing had happened at nine nothing would happen at ten-thirty either. Of course we stayed till ten-thirty and for half an hour after that, and then we decamped. We put the cat over the wall into the Lawrences' grounds and went back to Gordon's house where Patsy awaited us, smiling cynically.

I had had quite enough of the Rectory but that wasn't true of Gordon. He said it was well known that the phenomena didn't take place every night; we had simply struck an off-night, and he was going back on his own. He did too, half a dozen times between then and the 30th, even going so far as to have (rather unethically) a key cut from the one Curlew had lent him. Patsy would never go with him, though he tried hard to persuade her.

But in all those visits he never saw or heard anything. And the effect on him was to make him as great a sceptic as Patsy.

'I've a good mind to make an offer for the Rectory myself,' he said. 'It's a fine house and I've got quite attached to it.'

'You're not serious,' I said.

'I'm perfectly serious. I'll go to the auction with a view to buying if I can get Patsy to agree.'

But Patsy preferred her own house and, very reluctantly, Gordon had to give up the idea. The Rectory was sold for £62,000 to an American woman, a friend of Judy Lawrence. About a month after the sale the builders moved in. Eleanor used to get progress reports from Patsy, how they had rewired and treated the whole place for woodworm and painted and relaid floors. The central-heating engineers came too, much to Patsy's satisfaction.

We met Carol Marcus, the Rectory's new owner, when we were asked round to the Hall for drinks one Sunday morning. She was staying there with the Lawrences until such time as the improvements and decorations to the Rectory were complete. We were introduced by Judy to a very pretty, well-dressed woman in young middle age. I asked her when she expected to move in. April, she hoped, as soon as the builders had finished the two extra bathrooms. She had heard rumours that the Rectory was supposed to be haunted and these had amused her very much. A haunted house in the English countryside! It was too good to be true.

'It's all nonsense, you know,' said Gordon, who had joined us. 'It's all purely imaginary.' And he went on to tell her of his own experiences in the house during October – or his non-experiences, I should say.

'Well, for goodness' sake, I didn't *believe* it!' she said, and she laughed and went on to say how much she loved the house and wanted to make it a real home for her children to come to. She had three, she said, all in their teens, two boys away at school and a girl a bit older.

That was the only time I ever talked to her and I remember thinking she would be a welcome addition to the neighbourhood. A nice woman. Serene is the word that best described her. There was a man friend of hers there too. I didn't catch his surname but she called him Guy. He was staying at one of the local hotels, to be near her presumably.

'I should think those two would get married, wouldn't you?' said Eleanor on the way home. 'Judy told me she's waiting to get her divorce.'

Later that day I took Liam for a walk along Shawley Lane and when I came to the Rectory I found the gate open. So I walked up the gravel drive and looked through the drawing-room window at the new woodblock floor and ivory-painted walls and radiators. The place was swiftly being transformed. It was no longer sinister or grim. I walked round the back and peered in at the splendidly fitted kitchens, one a laundry now, and wondered what on earth had made sensible women like Mrs Buckland and Kate spread such vulgar tales and the

31

Galtons panic. What had come over them? I could only imagine that they felt a need to attract attention to themselves which they perhaps could do in no other way.

I whistled for Liam and strolled down to the gate and looked back at the Rectory. It stared back at me. Is it hindsight that makes me say this or did I really feel it then? I think I did feel it, that the house stared at me with a kind of steady insolence.

Carol Marcus moved in three weeks ago, on a sunny day in the middle of April. Two nights later, just before eleven, there came a sustained ringing at Gordon's front door as if someone were leaning on the bell. Gordon went to the door. Carol Marcus stood outside, absolutely calm but deathly white.

She said to him, 'May I use your phone, please? Mine isn't in yet and I have to call the police. I just shot my daughter.'

She took a step forward and crumpled in a heap on the threshold.

Gordon picked her up and carried her into the house and Patsy gave her brandy, and then he went across the road to the Rectory. There were lights on all over the house; the front door was open and light was streaming out on to the drive and the little Citroën Diane that was parked there.

He went into the house. The drawing-room door was open and he walked in there and saw a young girl lying on the carpet between the windows. She was dead. There was blood from a bullet wound on the front of her dress, and on a low round table lay the small automatic that Carol Marcus had used.

In the meantime Patsy had been the unwilling listener to a confession. Carol Marcus told her that the girl, who was nineteen, had unexpectedly driven down from London, arriving at the Rectory at nine o'clock. She had had a drink and something to eat and then said she had something to tell her mother, that was why she had come down. While in London she had been seeing a lot of the man called Guy and now they found that they were in love with each other. She knew it would hurt her mother, but she wanted to tell her at once, she wanted to be honest about it.

Carol Marcus told Patsy she felt nothing, no shock, no hatred or resentment, no jealousy. It was as if she were impelled by some external force to do what she did – take the gun she always kept with her from a drawer in the writing-desk and kill her daughter.

At this point Gordon came back and they phoned the police. Within a quarter of an hour the police were at the house. They arrested Carol Marcus and took her away and now she is on remand, awaiting trial on a charge of murder.

So what is the explanation of all this? Or does there, in fact, have to be an explanation? Eleanor and I were so shocked by what had happened, and awed too, that for a while we were somehow wary of talking about it even to each other. Then Eleanor said, 'It's as if all this time the coming event cast its shadow before it.'

I nodded, yet it didn't seem quite that to me. It was more that the Rectory was waiting for the right people to come along, the people who would *fit* its still unplayed scenario, the woman of forty, the daughter of nineteen, the lover. And only to those who approximated these characters could it show shadows and whispers of the drama; the closer the approximation, the clearer the sounds and signs.

The Loys were old and childless, so they saw nothing. Nor did Gordon and I – we were of the wrong sex. But the Bucklands, who had a daughter, heard and felt things, and so did Kate, though she was too old for the tragic leading role and her adolescent girl too young for victim. The Galtons had been nearly right – had Mrs Grainger once hoped the young Rector would marry her before he showed his preference for her daughter? – but the women had been a few years too senior for the parts. Even so, they had come closer to participation than those before them.

All this is very fanciful and I haven't mentioned a word of it to Gordon and Patsy. They wouldn't listen if I did. They persist in seeing the events of three weeks ago as no more than a sordid murder, a crime of jealousy committed by someone whose mind was disturbed.

But I haven't been able to keep from asking myself what would have happened if Gordon had bought the Rectory when he talked of doing so. Patsy will be forty this year. I don't think I've mentioned that she has a daughter by her first marriage who is away at university and going on nineteen now, a girl that they say is extravagantly fond of Gordon.

He is talking once more of buying, since Carol Marcus, whatever may become of her, will hardly keep the place now. The play is played out, but need that mean there will never be a repeat performance . . . ?

In the Confessional

Amelia B. Edwards

The things of which I write befell – let me see, some fifteen or eighteen years ago. I was not young then; I am not old now. Perhaps I was about thirty-two; but I do not know my age very exactly, and I cannot be certain to a year or two one way or the other.

My manner of life at that time was desultory and unsettled. I had a sorrow – no matter of what kind – and I took to rambling about Europe; not certainly in the hope of forgetting it, for I had no wish to forget, but because of the restlessness that made one place after another *triste* and intolerable to me.

It was change of place, however, and not excitement, that I sought. I kept almost entirely aloof from great cities, spas, and beaten tracks, and preferred for the most part to explore districts where travellers and foreigners rarely penetrated.

Such a district at that time was the Upper Rhine. I was traversing it that particular summer for the first time, and on foot; and I had set myself to trace the course of the river from its source in the great Rhine glacier to its fall at Schaffhausen. Having done this, however, I was unwilling to part company with the noble river; so I decided to follow it yet a few miles farther – perhaps as far as Mayence, but at all events as far as Basle.

And now began, if not the finest, certainly not the least charming part of my journey. Here, it is true, were neither

Alps, nor glaciers, nor ruined castles perched on inaccessible crags; but my way lay through a smiling country, studded with picturesque hamlets, and beside a bright river, hurrying along over swirling rapids, and under the dark arches of antique covered bridges, and between hillsides garlanded with vines.

It was towards the middle of a long day's walk among such scenes as these that I came to Rheinfelden, a small place on the left bank of the river, about fourteen miles above Basle.

As I came down the white road in the blinding sunshine, with the vines on either hand, I saw the town lying low on the opposite bank of the Rhine. It was an old walled town, enclosed on the land side and open to the river, the houses going sheer down to the water's edge, with flights of slimy steps worn smooth by the wash of the current, and over-hanging eaves, and little built-out rooms with penthouse roofs, supported from below by jutting piles black with age and tapestried with water-weeds. The stunted towers of a couple of churches stood up from amid the brown and tawny roofs within the walls.

Beyond the town, height above height, stretched a distance of wooded hills. The old covered bridge, divided by a bit of rocky island in the middle of the stream, led from bank to bank – from Germany to Switzerland. The town was in Switzerland; I, looking towards it from the road, stood on Baden territory; the river ran sparkling and foaming between.

I crossed, and found the place all alive in anticipation of a Kermess, or fair, that was to be held there the next day but one. The townsfolk were all out in the streets or standing about their doors; and there were carpenters hard at work knocking up rows of wooden stands and stalls the whole length of the principal thoroughfare. Shop-signs in open-work of wrought iron hung over the doors. A runlet of sparkling water babbled down a stone channel in the middle of the street. At almost every other house (to judge by the rows of tarnished watches hanging in the dingy parlour windows), there lived a watchmaker; and presently I came to a fountain – a regular Swiss fountain, spouting water from four ornamental pipes, and surmounted by the usual armed knight in old grey stone.

As I rambled on thus (looking for an inn, but seeing none), I suddenly found that I had reached the end of the street, and with it the limit of the town on this side. Before me rose a lofty, picturesque old gate-tower, with a tiled roof and a little window over the archway; and there was a peep of green grass and golden sunshine beyond. The town walls (sixty or seventy feet in height, and curiously roofed with a sort of projecting shed on the inner side) curved away to right and left, unchanged since the Middle Ages. A rude wain, laden with clover and drawn by mild-eyed, cream-coloured oxen, stood close by in the shade.

I passed out through the gloom of the archway into the sunny space beyond. The moat outside the walls was bridged over and filled in – a green ravine of grasses and wild-flowers. A stork had built its nest on the roof of the gate-tower. The cicadas shrilled in the grass. The shadows lay sleeping under the trees, and a family of cocks and hens went plodding inquisitively to and fro among the cabbages in the adjacent field. Just beyond the moat, with only this field between, stood a little solitary church – a church with a wooden porch, and a quaint, bright-red steeple, and a churchyard like a rose-garden, full of colour and perfume, and scattered over with iron crosses wreathed with immortelles.

The churchyard gate and the church door stood open. I went in. All was clean, and simple, and very poor. The walls were whitewashed; the floor was laid with red bricks; the roof raftered. A tiny confessional like a sentry-box stood in one corner; the font was covered with a lid like a wooden steeple;

and over the altar, upon which stood a pair of battered brass candlesticks and two vases of artificial flowers, hung a daub of the Holy Family, in oils.

All here was so cool, so quiet, that I sat down for a few moments and rested. Presently an old peasant woman trudged up the church-path with a basket of vegetables on her head. Having set this down in the porch, she came in, knelt before the altar, said her simple prayers, and went her way.

Was it not time for me also to go my way? I looked at my watch. It was past four o'clock, and I had not yet found a lodging for the night.

I got up, somewhat unwillingly; but, attracted by a tablet near the altar, crossed over to look at it before leaving the church. It was a very small slab, and bore a very brief German inscription to this effect:

To the Sacred Memory
OF
THE REVEREND PÈRE CHESSEZ,
For twenty years the beloved Pastor of this Parish.
Died April 16th, 1825. Aged 44.
HE LIVED A SAINT; HE DIED A MARTYR.

I read it over twice, wondering idly what story was wrapped up in the concluding line. Then, prompted by a childish curiosity, I went up to examine the confessional.

It was, as I have said, about the size of a sentry-box, and was painted to imitate old dark oak. On the one side was a narrow door with a black handle, on the other a little opening like a ticket-taker's window, closed on the inside by a faded green curtain.

I know not what foolish fancy possessed me, but, almost without considering what I was doing, I turned the handle and opened the door. Opened it – peeped in – found the priest sitting in his place – started back as if I had been shot – and stammered an unintelligible apology.

'I – I beg a thousand pardons,' I exclaimed. 'I had no idea – seeing the church empty – '

He was sitting with averted face, and clasped hands lying idly in his lap – a tall, gaunt man, dressed in a black soutane. When I paused, and not till then, he slowly, very slowly, turned his head, and looked me in the face.

The light inside the confessional was so dim that I could not see his features very plainly. I only observed that his eyes were large, and bright, and wild-looking, like the eyes of some fierce animal, and that his face, with the reflection of the green curtain upon it, looked lividly pale.

For a moment we remained thus, gazing at each other, as if fascinated. Then, finding that he made no reply, but only stared at me with those strange eyes, I stepped hastily back, shut the door without another word, and hurried out of the church.

I was very much disturbed by this little incident; more disturbed, in truth, than seemed reasonable, for my nerves for the moment were shaken. Never, I told myself, never while I lived could I forget that fixed attitude and stony face, or the glare of those terrible eyes. What was the man's history? Of what secret despair, of what life-long remorse, of what wild unsatisfied longings was he the victim? I felt I could not rest till I had learned something of his past life.

Full of these thoughts, I went on quickly into the town, half running across the field, and never looking back. Once past the gateway and inside the walls, I breathed more freely. The wain was still standing in the shade, but the oxen were gone now, and two men were busy forking out the clover into a little yard close by. Having enquired of one of these regarding an inn, and being directed to the Krone, 'over against the Frauenkirche', I made my way to the upper part of the town, and there, at one corner of a forlorn, weed-grown market-place, I found my hostelry.

The landlord, a sedate, bald man in spectacles, who, as I presently discovered, was not only an inn-keeper but a clockmaker, came out from an inner room to receive me. His wife, a plump, pleasant body, took my orders for dinner. His pretty daughter showed me to my room. It was a large, low, whitewashed room, with two lattice windows overlooking the market-place, two little beds, covered with puffy red eiderdowns at the farther end, and an army of clocks and ornamental timepieces arranged along every shelf, table, and chest of drawers in the room. Being left here to my meditations, I sat down and counted these companions of my solitude.

Taking little and big together, Dutch clocks, cuckoo clocks, *châlet* clocks, skeleton clocks, and *pendules* in ormolu, bronze, marble, ebony, and alabaster cases, there were exactly thirty-two. Twenty-eight were going merrily. As no two among them were of the same opinion as regarded the time, and as several struck the quarters as well as the hours, the consequence was that one or other gave tongue about every five minutes. Now, for a light and nervous sleeper such as I was at that time, here was a lively prospect for the night!

Going downstairs presently with the hope of getting my landlady to assign me a quieter room, I passed two eight-day clocks on the landing, and a third at the foot of the stairs. The public room was equally well-stocked. It literally bristled with clocks, one of which played a spasmodic version of 'Gentle Zitella' with variations every quarter of an hour. Here I found a little table prepared by the open window, and a dish of trout and a flask of country wine awaiting me. The pretty daughter waited upon me; her mother bustled to and fro with the dishes; the landlord stood by, and beamed upon me through his spectacles.

'The trout were caught this morning, about two miles from here,' he said, complacently.

'They are excellent,' I replied, filling him out a glass of wine, and helping myself to another. 'Your health, Herr Wirth.'

'Thanks, mein Herr – yours.'

Just at this moment two clocks struck at opposite ends of the room – one twelve, and the other seven. I ventured to suggest that mine host was tolerably well reminded of the flight of time; whereupon he explained that his work lay chiefly in the repairing and regulating line, and that at that precise moment he had no less than one hundred and eighteen clocks of various sorts and sizes on the premises.

'Perhaps the Herr Engländer is a light sleeper,' said his quick-witted wife, detecting my dismay. 'If so, we can get him a bedroom elsewhere. Not, perhaps, in the town, for I know no place where he would be as comfortable as with ourselves; but just outside the Friedrich's Thor, not five minutes' walk from our door.'

I accepted the offer gratefully.

'So long,' I said, 'as I ensure cleanliness and quiet, I do not care how homely my lodgings may be.'

'Ah, you'll have both, mein Herr, if you go where my wife is thinking of,' said the landlord. 'It is at the house of our pastor – the Père Chessez.'

'The Père Chessez!' I exclaimed. 'What, the pastor of the little church out yonder?'

'The same, mein Herr.'

'But – but surely the Père Chessez is dead! I saw a tablet to his memory in the chancel.'

'Nay, that was our pastor's elder brother,' replied the landlord, looking grave. 'He has been gone these thirty years and more. His was a tragical ending.'

But I was thinking too much of the younger brother just then to feel any curiosity about the elder; and I told myself that

I would put up with the companionship of any number of clocks, rather than sleep under the same roof with that terrible face and those unearthly eyes.

'I saw your pastor just now in the church,' I said, with apparent indifference. 'He is a singular-looking man.'

'He is too good for this world,' said the landlady.

'He is a saint upon earth!' added the pretty Fräulein.

'He is one of the best of men,' said, more soberly, the husband and father. 'I only wish he was less of a saint. He fasts, and prays, and works beyond his strength. A little more beef and a little less devotion would be all the better for him.'

'I should like to hear something more about the life of so good a man,' said I, having by this time come to the end of my simple dinner. 'Come, Herr Wirth, let us have a bottle of your best, and then sit down and tell me your pastor's history!'

The landlord sent his daughter for a bottle of the 'green seal', and, taking a chair, said:

'*Ach Himmel!* mein Herr, there is no history to tell. The good father has lived here all his life. He is one of us. His father, Johann Chessez, was a native of Rheinfelden and kept this very inn. He was a wealthy farmer and vine-grower. He had only those two sons – Nicholas, who took to the church and became pastor of Feldkirche; and this one, Matthias, who was intended to inherit the business; but who also entered religion after the death of his elder brother, and is now pastor of the same parish.'

'But why did he "enter religion"?' I asked. 'Was he in any way to blame for the accident (if it was an accident) that caused the death of his elder brother?'

'Ah Heavens no!' exclaimed the landlady, leaning on the back of her husband's chair. 'It was the shock – the shock that told so terribly upon his poor nerves! He was but a lad at that time, and as sensitive as a girl – but the Herr Engländer does not know the story. Go on, my husband.'

So the landlord, after a sip of the 'green seal', continued:

'At the time my wife alludes to, mein Herr, Johann Chessez was still living. Nicholas, the elder son, was in holy orders and established in the parish of Feldkirche, outside the walls; and Matthias, the younger, was a lad of about fourteen years old, and lived with his father. He was an amiable, good boy – pious and thoughtful – fonder of his books than of the business. The neighbour-folk used to say even then that Matthias was cut out for a priest, like his elder brother. As for Nicholas, he was neither more nor less than a saint. Well, mein Herr, at this time there lived on the other side of Rheinfelden, about a mile beyond the Basel Thor, a farmer named Caspar Rufenacht and his wife Margaret. Now Caspar Rufenacht was a jealous, quarrelsome fellow; and the Frau Margaret was pretty; and he led her a devil of a life. It was said that he used to beat her when he had been drinking, and that sometimes, when he went to fair or market, he would lock her up for the whole day in a room at the top of the house. Well, this poor, ill-used Frau Margaret – '

'Tut, tut, my man,' interrupted the landlady. 'The Frau Margaret was a light one!'

'Peace, wife! Shall we speak hard words of the dead? The Frau Margaret was young and pretty, and a flirt; and she had a bad husband, who left her too much alone.'

The landlady pursed up her lips and shook her head, as the best of women will do when the character of another woman is under discussion. The innkeeper went on.

'Well, mein Herr, to cut a long story short, after having been jealous first of one and then of another, Caspar Rufenacht became furious about a certain German, a Badener named Schmidt, living on the opposite bank of the Rhine. I remember the man quite well – a handsome, merry fellow, and no saint; just the sort to make mischief between man and wife. Well, Caspar Rufenacht swore a great oath

43

that, cost what it might, he would come at the truth about his wife and Schmidt; so he laid all manner of plots to surprise them – waylaid the Frau Margaret in her walks; followed her at a distance when she went to church; came home at unexpected hours; and played the spy as if he had been brought up to the trade. But his spying was all in vain. Either the Frau Margaret was too clever for him, or there was really nothing to discover; but still he was not satisfied. So he cast about for some way to attain his end, and, by the help of the Evil One, he found it.'

Here the innkeeper's wife and daughter, who had doubtless heard the story a hundred times over, drew near and listened breathlessly.

'What, think you,' continued the landlord, 'does this black-souled Caspar do? Does he punish the poor woman within an inch of her life, till she confesses? No. Does he charge Schmidt with having tempted her from her duty, and fight it out with him like a man? No. What else then? I will tell you. He waits till the vigil of St Margaret – her saint's day – when he knows the poor sinful soul is going to confession; and he marches straight to the house of the Père Chessez – the very house where our own Père Chessez is now living – and he finds the good priest at his devotions in his little study, and he says to him:

' "Father Chessez, my wife is coming to the church this afternoon to make her confession to you."

' "She is," replies the priest.

' "I want you to tell me all she tells you," says Caspar; "and I will wait here till you come back from the church, that I may hear it. Will you do so?"

' "Certainly not," replies the Père Chessez. "You must surely know, Caspar, that we priests are forbidden to reveal the secrets of the confessional."

' " That is nothing to me," says Caspar, with an oath. "I am

44

resolved to know whether my wife is guilty or innocent; and know it I will, by fair means or foul."

' "You shall never know it from me, Caspar," says the Père Chessez, very quietly.

' "Then, by Heavens!" says Caspar, "I'll learn it for myself." And with that he pulls out a heavy horse-pistol from his pocket, and with the butt end of it deals the Père Chessez a tremendous blow upon the head, and then another, and another, till the poor young man lay senseless at his feet. Then Caspar, thinking he had quite killed him, dressed himself in the priest's own soutane and hat; locked the door; put the key in his pocket; and stealing round the back way into the church, shut himself up in the confessional.'

'Then the priest died!' I exclaimed, remembering the epitaph upon the tablet.

'Ay, mein Herr – the Père Chessez died; but not before he had told the story of his assassination, and identified his murderer.'

'And Caspar Rufenacht, I hope, was hanged?'

'Wait a bit, mein Herr, we have not come to that yet. We left Caspar in the confessional, waiting for his wife.'

'And she came?'

'Yes, poor soul, she came.'

'And made her confession?'

'And made her confession, mein Herr.'

'What did she confess?'

The innkeeper shook his head.

'That no one ever knew, save the good God and her murderer.'

'Her murderer!' I exclaimed.

'Ay, just that. Whatever it was that she confessed, she paid for it with her life. He heard her out, at all events, without discovering himself, and let her go home believing that she had received absolution for her sins. Those who met her that afternoon said she seemed unusually bright and happy. As she passed through the town, she went into the shop in the Mongarten Strasse, and bought some ribbons. About half an hour later, my own father met her outside the Basel Thor, walking briskly homewards. He was the last who saw her alive.

'That evening (it was in October, and the days were short), some travellers coming that way into the town heard shrill cries, as of a woman screaming, in the direction of Caspar's farm. But the night was very dark, and the house lay back a little way from the road; so they told themselves it was only some drunken peasant quarrelling with his wife, and passed on. Next morning Caspar Rufenacht came to Rheinfelden, walked very quietly into the Polizei, and gave himself up to justice.

'"I have killed my wife," said he. "I have killed the Père Chessez. And I have committed sacrilege."

'And so, indeed, it was. As for the Frau Margaret, they found her body in an upper chamber, well-nigh hacked to pieces, and the hatchet with which the murder was committed lying beside her on the floor. He had pursued her, apparently, from room to room; for there were pools of blood and handfuls of long light hair, and marks of bloody hands along the walls, all the way from the kitchen to the spot where she lay dead.'

'And so he was hanged?' said I, coming back to my original question.

'Yes, yes,' replied the innkeeper and his womankind in chorus. 'He was hanged – of course he was hanged.'

'And it was the shock of this double tragedy that drove the younger Chessez into the church?'

'Just so, mein Herr.'

'Well, he carries it in his face. He looks like a most unhappy man.'

'Nay, he is not that, mein Herr!' exclaimed the landlady. 'He is melancholy, but not unhappy.'

46

'Well, then, austere.'

'Nor is he austere, except towards himself.'

'True, wife,' said the innkeeper; 'but, as I said, he carries that sort of thing too far. You understand, mein Herr,' he added, touching his forehead with his forefinger, 'the good pastor has let his mind dwell too much upon the past. He is nervous – too nervous, and too low.'

I saw it all now. That terrible light in his eyes was the light of insanity. That stony look in his face was the fixed, hopeless melancholy of a mind diseased.

'Does he know that he is mad?' I asked, as the landlord rose to go.

He shrugged his shoulders and looked doubtful.

'I have not said that the Père Chessez is *mad*, mein Herr,' he replied. 'He has strange fancies sometimes, and takes his fancies for facts – that is all. But I am quite sure that he does not believe himself to be less sane than his neighbours.'

So the innkeeper left me, and I (my head full of the story I had just heard) put on my hat, went out into the marketplace, asked my way to the Basel Thor, and set off to explore the scene of the Frau Margaret's murder.

I found it without difficulty – a long, low-fronted, beetle-browed farmhouse, lying back a meadow's length from the road. There were children playing upon the threshold, a flock of turkeys gobbling about the barn-door, and a big dog sleeping outside his kennel close by. The chimneys, too, were smoking merrily. Seeing these signs of life and cheerfulness, I abandoned all idea of asking to go over the house. I felt that I had no right to carry my morbid curiosity into this peaceful home; so I turned away, and retraced my steps towards Rheinfelden.

It was not yet seven, and the sun had still an hour's course to run. I re-entered the town, strolled back through the street, and presently came again to the Friedrich's Thor and the path leading to the church. An irresistible impulse seemed to drag me back to the place.

Shudderingly, and with a sort of dread that was half-longing, I pushed open the churchyard gate and went in. The doors were closed; a goat was browsing among the graves; and the rushing of the Rhine, some three hundred yards away, was distinctly audible in the silence. I looked round for the priest's house – the scene of the first murder; but from this side, at all events, no house was visible. Going round, however, to the back of the church, I saw a gate, a box-bordered path, and, peeping through some trees, a chimney and the roof of a little brown-tiled house.

This, then, was the path along which Caspar Rufenacht, with the priest's blood upon his hands and the priest's gown upon his shoulders, had taken his guilty way to the confessional! How quiet it all looked in the golden evening light! How like the church-path of an English parsonage!

I wished I could have seen something more of the house than that bit of roof and that one chimney. There must, I told myself, be some other entrance – some way round by the road! Musing and lingering thus, I was startled by a quiet voice close against my shoulder, saying:

'A pleasant evening, mein Herr!'

I turned, and found the priest at my elbow. He had come noiselessly across the grass, and was standing between me and the sunset, like a shadow.

'I – I beg your pardon,' I stammered, moving away from the gate. 'I was looking – "

I stopped in some surprise, and indeed with some sense of relief, for it was not the same priest that I had seen in the morning. No two, indeed, could well be more unlike, for this man was small, white-haired, gentle-looking, with a soft, sad smile inexpressibly sweet and winning.

'You were looking at my arbutus?' he said.

I had scarcely observed the arbutus till now, but I bowed and said something to the effect that it was an unusually fine tree.

'Yes,' he replied; 'but I have a rhododendron round at the front that is still finer. Will you come in and see it?'

I said I should be pleased to do so. He led the way, and I followed.

'I hope you like this part of our Rhine-country?' he said, as we took the path through the shrubbery.

'I like it so well,' I replied, 'that if I were to live anywhere on the banks of the Rhine, I should certainly choose some spot on the Upper Rhine between Schaffhausen and Basle.'

'And you would be right,' he said.

'Nowhere is the river so beautiful. Nearer the glaciers it is milky and turbid – beyond Basle it soon becomes muddy. Here we have it blue as the sky – sparkling as champagne. Here is my rhododendron. It stands twelve feet high, and measures as many in diameter. I had more than two hundred blooms upon it last spring.'

When I had duly admired this giant shrub, he took me to a little arbour on a bit of steep green bank overlooking the river, where he invited me to sit down and rest. From here I could see the porch and part of the front of his little house; but it was all so closely planted round with trees and shrubs that no clear view of it seemed obtainable in any direction. Here we sat for some time chatting about the weather, the approaching vintage, and so forth, and watching the sunset. Then I rose to take my leave.

'I heard of you this evening at the Krone, mein Herr,' he said. 'You were out, or I should have called upon you. I am glad that chance has made us acquainted. Do you remain over tomorrow?'

'No; I must go on tomorrow to Basle,' I answered. And

49

then, hesitating a little, I added: 'You heard of me, also, I fear, in the church.'

'In the church?' he repeated.

'Seeing the door open, I went in – from curiosity – as a traveller; just to look round for a moment and rest.'

'Naturally.'

'I – I had no idea, however, that I was not alone there. I would not for the world have intruded –'

'I do not understand,' he said, seeing me hesitate. 'The church stands open all day long. It is free to everyone.'

'Ah! I see he has not told you!'

The priest smiled but looked puzzled.

'He? Whom do you mean?'

'The other priest, mon père – your colleague. I regret to have broken in upon his meditation; but I had been so long in the church, and it was all so still and quiet, that it never occurred to me that there might be someone in the confessional.'

The priest looked at me in a strange, startled way.

'In the confessional!' he repeated, with a catching of his breath. 'You saw someone – in the confessional?'

'I am ashamed to say that, having thoughtlessly opened the door –'

'You saw – what did you see?'

'A priest, mon père.'

'A priest! Can you describe him? Should you know him again? Was he pale, and tall, and gaunt, with long black hair?'

'The same, undoubtedly.'

'And his eyes – did you observe anything particular about his eyes?'

'Yes; they were large, wild-looking, dark eyes, with a look in them – a look I cannot describe.'

'A look of terror!' cried the pastor, now greatly agitated. 'A look of terror – of remorse – of despair!'

'Yes, it was a look that might mean all that,' I replied, my astonishment increasing at every word. 'You seem troubled. Who is he?'

But instead of answering my question, the pastor took off his hat, looked up with a radiant, awe-struck face, and said:

'All-merciful God, I thank Thee! I thank Thee that I am not mad, and that Thou hast sent this stranger to be my assurance and my comfort!'

Having said these words, he bowed his head, and his lips moved in silent prayer. When he looked up again, his eyes were full of tears.

'My son,' he said, laying his trembling hand upon my arm, 'I owe you an explanation; but I cannot give it to you now. It must wait till I can speak more calmly – till tomorrow, when I must see you again. It involves a terrible story – a story peculiarly painful to myself – enough now if I tell you that I have seen the Thing you describe – seen It many times; and yet, because It has been visible to my eyes alone, I have doubted the evidence of my senses. The good people here believe that much sorrow and meditation have touched my brain. I have half believed it myself till now. But you – you have proved to me that I am the victim of no illusion.'

'But in Heaven's name,' I exclaimed, 'what do you suppose I saw in the confessional?'

'You saw the likeness of one who, guilty also of a double murder, committed the deadly sin of sacrilege in that very spot, more than thirty years ago,' replied the Père Chessez, solemnly.

'Caspar Rufenacht!'

'Ah! you have heard the story? Then I am spared the pain of telling it to you. That is well.'

I bent my head in silence. We walked together without another word to the wicket, and thence round to the church-yard gate. It was now twilight, and the first stars were out.

'Good-night, my son,' said the pastor, giving me his hand. 'Peace be with you.'

As he spoke the words, his grasp tightened – his eyes dilated – his whole countenance became rigid.

'Look!' he whispered. 'Look where it goes!'

I followed the direction of his eyes, and there, with a freezing horror which I have no words to describe, I saw – distinctly saw through the deepening gloom – a tall, dark figure in a priest's soutane and broad-brimmed hat, moving slowly across the path leading from the parsonage to the church. For a moment it seemed to pause – then passed on to the deeper shade, and disappeared.

'You saw it?' said the pastor.

'Yes – plainly.'

He drew a deep breath; crossed himself devoutly; and leaned upon the gate, as if exhausted.

'This is the third time I have seen it this year,' he said. 'Again I thank God for the certainty that I see a visible thing, and that His great gift of reason is mine unimpaired. But I would that He were graciously pleased to release me from the sight – the horror of it is sometimes more than I know how to bear. Good-night.'

With this he again touched my hand; and so, seeing that he wished to be alone, I silently left him. At the Friedrich's Thor I turned and looked back. He was still standing by the church-yard gate, just visible through the gloom of the fast deepening twilight.

I never saw the Père Chessez again. Save his own old servant, I was the last who spoke with him in this world. He died that night – died in his bed, where he was found next morning with his hands crossed upon his breast, and with a placid smile upon his lips, as if he had fallen asleep in the act of prayer.

As the news spread from house to house, the whole town

rang with lamentations. The church-bells tolled; the carpenters left their work in the streets; the children, dismissed from school, went home weeping.

''Twill be the saddest Kermess in Rheinfelden tomorrow, mein Herr!' said my good host of the Krone, as I shook hands with him at parting. 'We have lost the best of pastors and of friends. He was a saint. If you had come but one day later, you would not have seen him!'

And with this he brushed his sleeve across his eyes, and turned away.

Every shutter was up, every blind down, every door closed, as I passed along the Friedrich's Strasse about midday on my way to Basle; and the few townsfolk I met looked grave and downcast. Then I crossed the bridge and, having shown my passport to the German sentry on the Baden side, I took one long, last farewell look at the little walled town as it lay sleeping in the sunshine by the river – knowing that I should see it no more.

The Lady of Rosemount

Sir Thomas Graham Jackson

'And so, Charlton, you're going to spend part of the Long at Rosemount Abbey. I envy you. It's an awfully jolly old place, and you'll have a really good time.'

'Yes,' said Charlton, 'I am looking forward to it immensely. I have never seen it; you know it has only lately come to my uncle and they only moved into it last Christmas. I forgot that you knew it and had been there.'

'Oh! I don't know it very well,' said Edwards: 'I spent a few days there a year or two ago with the last owner. It will suit you down to the ground, for you are mad about old abbeys and ruins, and you'll find enough there to satisfy the whole Society of Antiquaries as well as yourself. When do you go?'

'Very soon. I must be at home for a week or so after we go down, and then I think my uncle will expect me at Rosemount. What are you going to do?'

'Well! I hardly know. Nothing very exciting. Perhaps take a short run abroad a little later. But I shall have to read part of the Long, for I am in for Greats next term. By the way, it is just possible I may be somewhere in your direction, for I have friends near Rosemount who want me to spend part of the vac. down there.'

'All right,' said Charlton, 'don't forget to come over and see me. I hope I may still be there. Meanwhile, *au revoir*, old man, and good luck to you.'

Charlton remained some time at his window looking on the quad of his college. Term at Oxford was just over and the men were rapidly going down. Hansoms were waiting at the gate, scouts and messengers were clattering down the staircases with portmanteaux and other paraphernalia proper to youth, and piling them on the cabs, friends were shaking hands, and bidding goodbye. In a few hours the college would be empty, and solitude would descend upon it for four months, broken only by occasional visitors, native or transatlantic. The flight of the men would be followed by that of the Dons to all parts of Europe or beyond, the hive would be deserted, and the porter would reign supreme over a vast solitude, monarch of all he surveyed.

Charlton was not due to go down till the next morning. He dined in the junior common-room with three or four other men, the sole survivors of the crowd, and then retired to his rooms to finish his packing. That done, he sat on the window-seat looking into the quad. It was a brilliant night; the moonshine slept on the grass, and silvered the grey walls and mullioned windows opposite, while the chapel and hall were plunged in impenetrable shadow. Everything was as still as death; no sound from the outer world penetrated the enclosure, and for the busy hive of men within, there was now the silence of a desert. There is perhaps no place where silence and solitude can be more sensibly felt than the interior of an Oxford college in vacation time, and there was something in the scene that appealed to the temperament of the young man who regarded it.

Henry Charlton was an only child. His father had died when he was a lad, and his mother, broken down by grief, had forsworn society and lived a very retired life in the country. At Winchester and Oxford he naturally mixed with others and made acquaintances, but his home life was somewhat sombre and his society restricted. He grew up a self-contained,

reserved lad, with few friendships, though those he formed
were sincere and his attachments were strong. His temperament – poetical and tinged with melancholy – naturally
inclined to romance, and from his early youth he delighted
in antiquarian pursuits, heraldic lore, and legend. At school
and college he revelled in the ancient architecture by which he
was surrounded. His tastes even carried him further, into the
region of psychical research, and the dubious revelations of
spiritualism; though a certain wholesome vein of scepticism
saved him from plunging deeply into those mazes, whether of
truth or imposture. As he sat at his window, the familiar scene
put on an air of romance. The silence sank into his soul; the
windows where a friendly light was wont to shine through red
curtains, inviting a visit, were now blind and dark; mystery
enveloped the well-known walls; they seemed a place for the
dead, no longer a habitation for living men, of whom he might
be the last survivor. At last, rising from his seat, and half
laughing at his own romantic fancies, Henry Charlton went to
bed.

A few weeks later he descended from the train at the little
country station of Brickhill, in Northamptonshire, and while
the porter was collecting his traps on a hand-barrow, he
looked out for the carriage that was to meet him.

'Hallo! Harry, here you are,' said a voice behind him, and
turning round he was warmly greeted by his cousin, Charley
Wilmot. A car was waiting, into which he and his belongings
were packed, and in five minutes they were off, bowling along
one of the wide Northamptonshire roads, with a generous
expanse of greensward on each side between the hedges, and
the hedgerow timber. The country was new to Henry Charlton, and he looked about him with interest. The estate of
Rosemount had lately come unexpectedly by the death of a
distant relation of his uncle, Sir Thomas Wilmot, and the
family had hardly had time yet to settle down in their new

home. His cousin Charley was full of the novelty of the situation, and the charms of the Abbey.

'I can tell you, it's a rattling old place,' said he, 'full of odd holes and corners, and there are the ruins of the church with all sorts of old things to be seen; but you'll have lots of time to look about and see it all, and here we are, and there's my dad waiting to welcome you at the hall-door.'

They had turned in at a lodge-gate, and passed up an avenue at the end of which Henry could see a hoary pile of stone gables, mullioned windows, massive chimneys, and a wide-arched portal, hospitably open, where Sir Thomas stood to welcome his nephew.

Some years had passed since Henry had seen his relatives, and he was glad to be with them again. A houseful of lively cousins rather younger than himself, had in former days afforded a welcome change from his own rather melancholy home, and he looked forward with pleasure to renewing the intimacy. His young cousin Charley was just at the end of his time at Eton, and was to go to university in October. The girls, Kate and Cissy, had shot up since he used to play with them in the nursery, and were now too old to be kissed. His uncle and aunt were as kind as ever, and after he had answered their enquiries about his mother, and given an account of his uneventful journey down, the whole party adjourned to the garden where tea awaited them under the trees, and then Henry for the first time saw something of the Abbey of Rosemount.

This ancient foundation, of Sanctus Egidius in Monte Rosarum, had been a Benedictine house, dating from the twelfth century, which at the Dissolution was granted to a royal favourite, who partly dismantled and partly converted it into a residence for himself. His descendants in the time of James I had pulled down a great part of the conventual buildings and substituted for the inconvenient cells of the

57

monks a more comfortable structure in the style of that day. Many fragments of the Abbey, however, were incorporated into the later house. The refectory of the monks was kept, and formed the great hall of the mansion with its vaulted roof and traceried windows, in which there even remained some of the old storied glass. The Abbot's kitchen still furnished Sir Thomas's hospitable board, and among the offices and elsewhere were embedded parts of the domestic buildings. North of the refectory, according to the usual Benedictine plan, had been the cloister and beyond that the church, which lay at a slightly lower level, the lie of the ground inclining that way from the summit of the Mount of Roses on which the habitable part of the convent had been built. Of the cloister enough remained, though much broken and dilapidated, to show what it had been, but the greater part of the church was destroyed for the sake of its materials when the Jacobean house was built. A considerable part of the nave, however, was still standing, part of it even with its vaulted roof intact, and of the rest, enough of the lower part of the walls was left to show that the church had been of a fair size, though not on the scale of the larger establishments.

Henry Charlton, with the greedy eye of the born antiquary, took in the general scheme of the Abbey with his tea and buttered toast under the shade of the elms that bounded the lawn on that side of the house. But he had to control his impatience to visit the ruins, for after tea his cousins insisted on a game of tennis, which lasted till it was time to dress for dinner, and after dinner it was too late and too dark for exploration.

They dined in the great hall, once the monks' refectory, but not too large for modern comfort, the Abbey having been one of the smaller houses of the Order, and the number of the brotherhood limited. Henry was enchanted and could not restrain the expression of his enthusiasm.

'Ah!' said his aunt, 'I remember your mother told me you were crazy about architecture and antiquities. Well, you'll have your fill of them here. For my part, I often sigh for a little more modern convenience.'

'But my dear aunt,' said Henry, 'there is so much to make up for little inconveniences in living in this lovely old place that they might be forgotten.'

'Why, what do you know about housekeeping?' said his aunt. 'I should like you to hear Mrs Baldwin, the housekeeper, on the subject. How she toils up one staircase only to have to go down another. The house, she says, is made up of stairs that are not wanted, and crooked passages that might have been straight, and it took the maids a fortnight to learn their way to the food-store.'

'It's of no use, mother,' said Charley, 'you'll never convince him. He would like to have those old monks back again, and to be one of them himself with a greasy cowl on his head and sandals on his naked feet, and nothing to eat but herbs washed down with water.'

'No, no!' said Henry, laughing, 'I don't want them back, for I like my present company too well. But I confess I like to call up in imagination the men who built and lived in these old walls. I believe I shall dream of them tonight.'

'Well, Harry,' said his uncle, 'you may dream of them as much as you please, so long as you don't bring them back to turn us out. And you shall have every opportunity, for you are to sleep in a bit of the old convent that the abbey builders of the modern house spared; and who knows but that the ghost of its former occupant may not take you at your word and come back to revisit his old quarters.'

Harry laughed as they rose from table, and said he trusted his visitor would not treat him as an intruder.

The long summer day had enabled them to finish dinner by daylight, and there was still light enough for the old painted glass to be seen. It was very fragmentary, and not one of the pictures was perfect. In one of the lights they could make out part of a female figure richly dressed; she had been holding something that was broken away, and beside her was the lower half of an unmistakable demon, with hairy legs and cloven hoof. The legend below ran thus, the last word being imperfect:

QVALITER DIABOLVS TENTAVIT COMITISSAM ALI...

The next light was still more imperfect, but there was part of the same female figure in violent action, with the fragment of a legend:

HIC COMITISSA TENTATA A DI...

Other parts evidently of the same story remained in the next window, but they were too fragmentary to be understood. In one light was a piece of a monk's figure and part of a legend:

HIC FRATER PAVLVS DAT COMI...

The last of all was tolerably perfect. It represented a female robed in black, and holding in her hand a little model of a church. She was on her knees prostrate before the Pope, who was seated and extended his hand in the act of benediction. The legend below said:

HIC COMITISSA A PAPA ABSOLVTA EST

Henry was much interested and wanted to know the story of the sinful Countess; but none of the party could tell him, and indeed, none of them had till then paid much attention to the glass. Sir Thomas had once made a slight attempt to trace the identity of the Countess, but with little success, and had soon given up the search.

'There is an antiquarian problem for you to solve, Harry,' said he, 'but I don't know where you should look for the solution. The annals of Rosemount are very imperfect. In those within my reach I could find nothing bearing on the subject.'

'I am afraid, sir,' said Harry, 'if you failed I am not likely to succeed, for I am only a very humble antiquary, and should not know where to begin. It seems to me, however, that the story must have had something to do with the history of the Abbey, and that its fortunes were connected with the wicked Countess, or the monks would not have put her story in their windows.'

'Well, then, there you have a clue to follow up,' said his uncle, 'and now let us join the ladies.'

The room where Henry Charlton was to sleep was on the ground floor in one corner of the house, and looked out upon the cloister and the ruined abbey-church. It was, as his uncle had said, a relic of the domestic part of the Abbey, and when he had parted with his cousin Charley, who guided him thither, he looked round the apartment with the keenest interest. It was a fair-sized room, low-pitched, with a ceiling of massive black timbers, plastered between the joists. The wall was so thick that there was room for a little seat in the window recess on each side, which was reached by a step, for the window-sill was rather high above the floor. Opposite the window yawned a wide fireplace with dogs for wood-logs, and a heap of wood ashes lying on the hearth. The walls were panelled with oak up to the ceiling, and the floor, where not covered with rugs, was of the same material polished brightly. But for the toilet appliances of modern civilization the room was unaltered from the time when the last brother of the convent left it, never to return. Henry tried to picture to himself his predecessor in the apartment; he imagined him sitting at the table, reading or writing, or on his knees in prayer; on his simple shelf would have been his few books and manuscripts, borrowed from the convent library, to which he had to return them when they met in chapter once a year, under severe penalty in case of loss or damage. As he lay on his bed Henry tried to imagine what his own thoughts would have been had he himself been that ghostly personage five centuries ago; he fancied himself in the choir of the great church; he heard the sonorous Gregorian chanting by a score of deep manly voices, ringing in the vaulted roof, and echoing through the aisles; he saw the embroidered vestments, the lights that shone clearer and brighter as the shades of evening wrapped arcade and triforium in gloom and mystery, and turned to blackness the storied windows that lately gleamed with the hues of the sapphire, the ruby and the emerald. Pleased with these fancies he lay awake till the clock struck twelve and then insensibly the vision faded and he fell asleep.

His sleep was not untroubled. Several times he half awoke, only to drop off again and resume the threat of a tiresome dream that puzzled and worried him but led to no conclusion. When morning came, he awoke in earnest, and tried to piece together the fragments he could remember, but made little of them. He seemed to have seen the monk sitting at the table as he had pictured him in imagination the evening before. The monk was not reading but turning over some little bottles which he took from a leathern case, and he seemed to be waiting for someone or something. Then Henry in his dream fancied that someone did come and something did happen, but what it was he could not remember, and of the visitor he could recall nothing, except that he felt there was a personality present, but not so as to be seen and recognized; more an impression than a fact. He could remember, however, a hand stretched out towards the seated figure and the objects he was handling. More than this he could not distinctly recall, but the same figures recurred each time he fell asleep with slightly varied attitude, though with no greater distinctness. For the monk he could account by the thoughts that had been in his mind the night before, but for the incident in his dream, if so vague a matter could be called an incident, he could trace no suggestion in his own mind.

The bright summer morning and the merry party at breakfast soon drove the memory of the dream out of his head. After breakfast there were the horses and dogs to be seen, and the garden to be visited, and it was not till the afternoon that his cousins let him satisfy his longing to visit the ruins of the church and cloister. There they all went in a body. The cloister lawn was mown smoothly and well tended, and here and there barely rising above the greensward were the stones that marked the resting places of the brotherhood. Part of the cloister retained its traceried windows and vaulted roof, and on the walls were inscribed the names of abbots and monks whose bones lay beneath the pavement. At the end of the western walk a finely sculptured door led into the nave of the church, the oldest part of the building, built when the ruder Norman work was just melting into greater refinement. Henry was in raptures, and vowed that neither Fountains nor Rievaulx could show anything more perfect. The girls were delighted to find their favourite parts of the building appreciated, and led him from point to point, determined that he should miss nothing.

'And now,' said Cissy, 'you have to see the best bit of all, hasn't he, Kate? We don't show it to everybody for fear strangers might do mischief.'

So saying she pushed open a door in the side wall and led them into a chantry chapel built out between two of the great buttresses of the nave aisle. It was indeed a gem of architecture of the purest fourteenth-century Gothic and Henry stood entranced before its loveliness. The delicate traceries on wall and roof were carved with the finish of ivory, and though somewhat stained by weather, for the windows had lost their glass, had kept all their sharp precision. Part of the outer wall had given way, weeds and ivy had invaded and partly covered the floor, and a thick mass of vegetation was piled up under the windows against the masonry.

'What a pity to let this lovely place get into such a mess,' said Henry. 'I have never seen anything more beautiful.'

'Well,' said Charley, 'it wouldn't take long to clear all this rubbish away. Suppose we set to work and do it?'

So while the girls sat and looked on, the two men fetched some garden tools, and cut, hacked and pulled up the weeds and ivy and brambles, which they threw out by the breach in the wall, and soon made a partial clearance. Henry had begun on the mass that stood breast-high next the window, when a sudden exclamation made the others look at him. He was peering down into the mass of vegetation, of which he had removed the top layer, with an expression of amazement that drew the others to his side. Looking up at them out of the mass of ivy was a face, the face of a beautiful woman, her hair disposed in graceful masses, and bound by a slender coronet. It was evident that under the pile of vegetation was a tomb with an effigy that had long been hidden, and the very existence of which had been forgotten. When the rest of the vegetation had been cleared away there appeared an altar tomb on the top of which lay the alabaster figure of a woman. The sides bore escutcheons of heraldry and had evidently once been coloured. The figure was exquisitely modelled, the work of no mean sculptor; the hands were crossed on the breast, and the drapery magnificently composed. But with the head of the figure the artist had surpassed himself. It was a triumph of sculpture. The features were of perfect beauty, regular and classical, but there was something about it that went beyond beauty, something akin to life, something that seemed to respond to the gaze of the observer, and to attract him unconsciously whether he would or not. The group of discoverers hung over it in a sort of fascination for some minutes saying nothing. At last Kate, the elder girl, drew back with a slight shiver, and said,

'Oh! What is it, what is the matter with me, I feel as if there was something wrong; it is too beautiful; I don't like it; come away, Cissy,' and she drew her sister out of the chapel, in a sort of tremor.

Charley followed them, and Henry was left alone with his gaze still fixed on the lovely face. As he looked he seemed to read fresh meaning in the cold alabaster features. The mouth, though perfectly composed in rest, appeared to express a certain covert satire: the eyes were represented as open, and they seemed to regard him with a sort of amused curiosity. There was a kind of diablerie about the whole figure. It was a long time before he could remove his eyes from the face that seemed to understand and return his gaze, and it was not without a wrench that at last he turned away. The features of the image seemed to be burned into his brain, and to remain fixed there indelibly, whether pleasurably or not he could not decide, for mixed with a strange attraction and even fascination he was conscious of an undercurrent of terror, and even of aversion, as from something unclean. As he moved away, his eye caught an inscription in Gothic lettering round the edge of the slab on which the figure lay.

HIC JACET ALIANORA COMITISSA PECCATRIX
QVÆ OBIT AÑO DÑI MCCCL CVIVS ANIMÆ
MISEREATVR DEVS.

He copied the epitaph in his notebook, remarking that it differed from the usual formula, and then closing the door of the chantry he followed his cousins back to the house.

* * *

'Well, here you are at last,' said Lady Wilmot, as Charley and his sisters emerged on the lawn. 'What a time you have been in the ruins, and the tea is getting cold. And what have you done with Harry?'

'Oh, mother,' cried Cissy, 'we have had such an adventure. You know that little chantry chapel we are so fond of; well, we thought it wanted tidying up, and so we cleared away the weeds and rubbish, and what do you think we found? Why, the most lovely statue you ever saw, and we left Harry looking at it as if he had fallen in love with it and could not tear himself away.'

'By Jove!' said Charley, 'just like old Pygmalion, who fell in love with a statue and got Venus to bring it to life for him.'

'Don't talk so, Charley,' said Kate, 'I am sure I don't want this stone lady to come to life. There is something uncanny about her, I can't describe what, but I was very glad to get away from her.'

'Yes, mother,' said Cissy, 'Kate was quite frightened of the stone lady and dragged me away, just as I was longing to look at her, for you never saw anything so lovely in your life.'

'But there is one thing I noticed, father,' said Charley, 'that I think wants looking to. I noticed a bad crack in that fine vault over the chantry which looks dangerous, and I think Parsons should be sent to have a look at it.'

'Thank you, Charley,' said Sir Thomas, 'I should be sorry if anything happened to that part of the building, for archæologists tell me it's the most perfect thing of its kind in England. Parsons is busy on other matters for the next few days, but I will have it seen to next week. By the way, we shall have another visitor tonight. You remember Harry's college friend, Mr Edwards; I heard he was staying at the Johnstons and so I asked him to come here for a few days while Harry is with us, and here I think he comes across the lawn.'

Edwards had some previous acquaintance with the

Wilmots, and was soon set down to tea with the rest, and engaged for lawn tennis afterwards, a game in which he had earned a great reputation.

Harry Charlton did not appear till the party were assembled in the drawing-room before dinner. On leaving the Abbey he was possessed by a disinclination for the lively society on the lawn. His nerves were in a strange flutter; he felt as if something unusual was impending, as if he had passed a barrier and shut the gate behind him, and had entered on a new life where strange experiences awaited him. He could not account for it. He tried to dismiss the finding of the statue as a mere antiquarian discovery, interesting both in history and in art; but it would not do. That face, with its enigmatical expression, haunted him, and would not be dismissed. He felt that this was not the end of the adventure; that in some mysterious way the dead woman of five centuries back had touched his life, and that more would come of it. To that something more he looked forward with the same indefinable mixture of attraction and repulsion which he had felt in the chapel while gazing at those pure alabaster features. He must be alone. He could not at present come back to the converse of ordinary life, and he set off on a swinging walk through field and woodland to try and steady his nerves, so as to meet his friends in the evening with composure. A good ten-mile stretch did something to restore him to his usual spirits. He was pleased to find his friend Edwards, of whose coming he had not been told, and when he took his place at the dinner table next to his aunt there was nothing unusual in his manner.

The conversation during dinner naturally turned on the discovery that had been made in the Abbey that afternoon. It was singular that so remarkable a work of art should have been forgotten, and been overlooked by the Northampton-shire Archæological Society, which had so many enthusiastic antiquaries in its ranks. There had been meetings of the society in the ruins, papers about them had been read and published, plans had been made and illustrations drawn of various parts of the building, including the chantry itself, but there was no mention or indication given of the monument either in the text or in the plates. Strange that no one should ever have thought of looking into that tangle of brambles by which it was concealed, till that very day.

'I must go first thing tomorrow,' said Sir Thomas, 'to see your wonderful discovery. The next thing will be to find out who this pretty lady was.'

'That I think I can tell you, sir,' said Henry, who now spoke for almost the first time, 'and I think it helps to solve the mystery of the sinful Countess in the painted windows opposite, which puzzled us last night.'

All eyes were turned to the fragments of painted glass in the hall windows, as Henry continued.

'You see in the first window the devil is tempting the Countess ALI –, the rest of her name being lost. Well, on the tomb is an epitaph, which gives the missing part. She is the Countess Alianora; no further title is given. But whoever she was, the lady whose tomb we found is the same no doubt as the lady whose adventures were depicted in the windows.'

'Now I know,' broke in Kate, 'why I was frightened in the chapel. She was a wicked woman, and something told me so, and made me want to go away from her.'

'Well,' said Lady Wilmot, 'let us hope she mended her ways and ended her life well. You see, she went to Rome and was absolved by the Pope.'

'Yes, but I bet she did not get absolution for nothing,' said Charley. 'Just look at her in the last picture and you will see she has a church in her hand. Depend on it, she got her wicked deeds pardoned in return for her gifts to Rosemount Abbey; and I daresay she rebuilt a great part of it and among the rest her own chantry.'

'Charley,' said Edwards, 'you ought to be a lawyer; you make out such a good case for the prosecution.'

'At all events,' said Sir Thomas, 'Charley gives us a good lead for our research. I will look out the old deeds and try to find what connection, if any, there was between Rosemount Abbey and a Countess Alianora of some place unknown.'

The rest of the evening passed in the usual way. A few friends from neighbouring houses joined the party; there was a little impromptu dancing, and it was near midnight by the time they retired to rest. Henry had enjoyed himself like the rest, and forgot the adventure of the afternoon till he found himself once more alone in the monastic cell, looking out on the ruined Abbey. The recollection of his dream of the night before then for the first time recurred to him; he wondered whether it had any connection with his later experience in the chantry, but he could trace none whatever. The dream seemed merely one of those fanciful imaginings with which we are all familiar, devoid of any further meaning.

He was not, however, destined to repose quietly. This time his dream showed him the same monk, he recognized him by his coarse features and shaggy brows, but he was in the nave of a church, and in the massive round pillars and severe architecture of the arches and triforium, Henry knew the nave of Rosemount Abbey, not as now, in ruins, but vaulted and entire. It was nearly dark, and the choir behind the pulpitum was wrapped in gloom, in the midst of which twinkled a few lights before the high altar and the various saintly shrines. The monk held something small in his hand, and was evidently, as on the night before, waiting for somebody or something. At last Henry was aware that somebody had indeed come. A shadowy figure draped in black moved swiftly out from behind a pillar and approached the monk. What the figure was he tried in vain to discover. All he could see was that just as had happened on the night before, a hand was stretched out and took something from the monk, which it promptly hid in the drapery with which the figure was covered. The hand, however, was more clearly seen this time. It was a woman's hand, white and delicate, and a jewel sparkled on her finger. The scene caused Henry a dull terror, as of some unknown calamity, or as of some crime that he had witnessed, and he woke with a start and found himself in a cold sweat.

He got up and paced his apartment to and fro, and then looked out of the window. It was brilliant moonlight, throwing strong shadows of the broken walls across the quiet cloister garth where the monks of old lay quietly sleeping till the last dread summons should awake them. The light fell full on the ancient nave walls

> Where buttress and buttress alternately
> Seemed framed of ebon and ivory

and the light touched with the magic of mystery the delicate traceries of the chantry where lay the Countess Alianora. Her face flashed upon his memory, with its enigmatical expression, half attracting, half repelling, and an irresistible desire impelled him to see her again. His window was open and the ground only a few feet below. He dressed himself hastily, and clambered out. Everything was still; all nature seemed asleep, not a breath of wind moved the trees or stirred the grass as he slowly passed along the cloister: his mind was in a strange state of nervous excitement; he was almost in a trance as he advanced into the nave where the shadows of column and arch fell black on the broken pavement. He paused a moment at the gate which led into the chantry, and then entered as if in a dream, for everything seemed to him unreal, and he himself a mere phantom. At last he stood beside the tomb and looked down on the lovely countenance which had bewitched him in the afternoon. The moonlight fell upon it, investing it with an unearthly mystery and charm. Its beauty was indescribable: never had he conceived anything so lovely. The strange semi-satirical expression of which he had been conscious in the afternoon had disappeared; nothing could be read in the features but sweetness and allurement. A passionate impulse seized him, and he bent down and kissed her on the lips. Was it fancy or was it real, that soft lips of warm life seemed to meet his own? He knew not: a delirious ecstasy transported him, the scene faded before his eyes and he sank on the floor in a swoon.

How long he lay he never knew. When he came to himself the moon had set, and he was in darkness. An indefinable terror seized him. He struggled to his feet, burst out of the Abbey, fled to his rooms, scrambling in through the window, and threw himself panting on his bed.

Henry Charlton was the last to appear next morning at the breakfast-table. He was pale and out of spirits, and roused himself with difficulty to take part in the discussion as to what was to be done that day. After breakfast he pleaded a head-ache, and retired with a book to the library, while the others betook themselves to various amusements or employments. The girls were in the garden where they found old Donald the gardener, whose life had been spent at Rosemount, and in whose eyes the garden was as much his as his master's, and perhaps more so.

'Yes, missy,' he was saying, 'the weeds do grow terrible this fine weather, and as you was saying it is time we cleaned up a bit in the old Abbey. But I see the young gentlemen has been doing a bit theirselves, chucking all them briars and rubbish out on the grass just as I had mown and tidied it.'

'Why Donald,' said Cissy, 'you ought to have thanked them, for the chapel was in an awful mess, and they have saved you some trouble.'

'Well, miss, I suppose they pleased theirselves, but that's not where I should have meddled, no, no!' and so saying he moved away.

'But why not there,' said Kate, 'why not there of all places?'

'Oh! I say nothing about it,' said Donald. 'Only folk do say that there's them there as don't like to be disturbed.'

'Indeed; what do they say in the village about it?'

'Oh! ay! I say nothing. I don't meddle with things above me. And I shan't tell ye any more, miss, it's not good for young women to know.'

'But do you know, Donald,' said Cissy, 'what we found there?'

'What did you find, miss? Not her? Oh, Lord! She was found once before, and no good come of it. There, don't ask me any more about it. It's not good for young women to know.' So saying Donald wheeled his barrow away into another part of the garden.

'Father,' said Kate, to Sir Thomas who now came up. 'Donald knows all about the tomb and the statue, and he won't tell us anything, except that the people think it unlucky to meddle with it. Have you ever heard of any superstition about it?'

'Nothing at all,' said he. 'I have just been down to look at your discovery. The statue is a wonderful piece of work. I have never seen anything finer either here or in Italy. But the chapel is in a bad way and part of the roof threatens to fall. I have just sent word to Parsons to come tomorrow morning and attend to it.'

They were joined presently by Edwards and Charley, and the day passed pleasantly enough, with the usual amusements of a country house in holiday time. Henry did not take much part with them. He was abstracted and inattentive, and altogether out of spirits. He had but a confused idea of what had happened the previous night, but there seemed still to linger on his lips that mystic, perhaps unhallowed kiss, and there still floated before his eyes the mocking enigma of that lovely countenance. He dreaded the approach of night, not knowing what it might bring, and did his best to divert his mind to other things, but without much success.

His friend Edwards was much concerned at the change in his behaviour, and asked Charley whether Henry had been upset in any way during his visit. He was assured that till yesterday afternoon Henry had been as happy and companionable as possible, and that it was only that morning that the change had come over him.

'But I can tell you one thing,' said Charley, 'I believe he was out of his room last night, for the flowerbeds show footmarks, and the creepers are torn outside his window, showing someone had been getting in and out, and there certainly has been no burglary in the house. Do you know whether he walks in his sleep?'

'I have never heard that he does,' said Edwards. 'We can't very well ask him whether anything is wrong, for he does not seem to invite enquiry, and has rather avoided us all day. But if it is a case of sleepwalking we might perhaps keep a look-out tonight to prevent his coming to mischief.'

'All right,' said Charley. 'My room is over his and looks out the same way. I'll try and keep awake till midnight, and will call you if I see anything of him.'

'That's well,' said Edwards, 'but we must be careful and not be seen, for it is dangerous to wake a somnambulist I believe.'

And so they departed to their several chambers.

The first part of the night passed peacefully enough with Henry. He had no dreams to trouble him, but towards midnight he began to turn uneasily in his bed, and to be oppressed by an uneasy feeling that he was not alone. He awoke to find the moon shining as brilliantly as on the

73

previous night, and bringing into view every detail of the ancient buildings opposite. A dull sense of some sinister influence weighed upon him: someone was with him whom he could not see, whispering in his ear, '*You are mine, you are mine.*' He could see no form, but to his mental vision was clearly visible the countenance of the figure in the chapel, now with the satirical, mocking expression more fully shown, and he felt himself drawn on he knew not whither. Again the mocking lips seemed to say, '*You are mine, you are mine.*' Half unconsciously he rose from his bed, and advanced towards the window. A faintly visible form seemed to move before him, he saw the features of the countess more plainly, and without knowing how he got there he found himself outside the room in the cloister garth, and entering the shade of the cloister. Something impalpable glided on before him, turning on him the face that attracted him though it mocked him, and which he could not but follow, though with an increasing feeling of terror and dislike. Still on his ear fell the words '*You are mine, you are mine*', and he was helpless to resist the spell that drew him on and on farther into the gloom of the ruined nave. And now the shape gathered consistency and he seemed to see the Countess Alianora standing facing him. On her features the same mocking smile, on her finger the jewel of his dream. '*You are mine,*' she seemed to say, '*mine, mine, you sealed it with a kiss*', and she outstretched her arms; but as she stood before him in her marvellous and unearthly beauty, a change came over her; her face sank into ghastly furrows, her limbs shrivelled, and as she advanced upon him, a mass of loathly corruption, and stretched out her horrible arms to embrace him, he uttered a dreadful scream as of a soul in torture, and sank fainting on the ground.

'Edwards, Edwards, come quick,' cried Charley, beating at his door. 'Harry is out of his room, and there is something with him, I don't know what it is, but hurry up or some mischief may happen.'

His friend was ready in a moment, and the two crept cautiously downstairs, and as the readiest way, not to disturb the household, got out into the cloister through the window of Harry's room. They noticed on the way that his bed had been slept in, and was tossed about in disorder. They took the way out of the cloister by which Charley had seen Harry go, and had just reached the door that led into the nave when his unearthly scream of terror fell on their ears. They rushed into the church, crying, 'Harry, Harry, here we are, what is it, where are you?' and having no reply they searched as well as they could in the moonlight. They found him at last, stretched on the ground at the entrance to the fatal chantry chapel. At first they thought he was dead, but his pulse beat faintly, and they carried him out, still insensible, into the outer air. He showed some signs of life before long, but remained unconscious. The house was aroused and he was put to bed, and messengers were sent for the doctor. As they watched by his bedside, a thundering crash startled them; looking out of the window they saw a cloud of dust where the chantry had been, and next morning it was seen that the roof had fallen in, and destroyed it.

Harry Charlton lay many weeks with a brain fever. From his cries and ravings something was gathered of the horrors of that fatal night, but he would never be induced to tell the whole story after he recovered.

The fallen ruin was removed, and Sir Thomas hoped that the beautiful statue might have escaped. But strange to say, though every fragment of masonry was carefully examined and accounted for, no trace could be found of any alabaster figure nor of the tomb of the Comitissa Alianora.

Father Macclesfield's Tale

R. H. Benson

Monsignor Maxwell announced next day at dinner that he had already arranged for the evening's entertainment. A priest, whose acquaintance he had made on the Palatine, was leaving for England the next morning; and it was our only chance therefore of hearing his story. That he had a story had come to the Canon's knowledge in the course of a conversation on the previous afternoon.

'He told me the outline of it,' he said. 'I think it very remarkable. But I had a great deal of difficulty in persuading him to repeat it to the company this evening. But he promised at last. I trust, gentlemen, you do not think I have presumed in begging him to do so.'

Father Macclesfield arrived at supper.

He was a little unimposing dry man, with a hooked nose, and grey hair. He was rather silent at supper; but there was no trace of shyness in his manner as he took his seat upstairs, and without glancing round once, began in an even and dispassionate voice:

'I once knew a Catholic girl that married an old Protestant three times her own age. I entreated her not to do so; but it was useless. And when the disillusionment came she used to write to me piteous letters, telling me that her husband had in reality no religion at all. He was a convinced infidel; and

76

scouted even the idea of the soul's immortality.

'After two years of married life the old man died. He was about sixty years old; but very hale and hearty till the end.

'Well, when he took to his bed, the wife sent for me; and I had half-a-dozen interviews with him; but it was useless. He told me plainly that he wanted to believe – in fact he said that the thought of annihilation was intolerable to him. If he had had a child he would not have hated death so much; if his flesh and blood in any manner survived him, he could have fancied that he had a sort of vicarious life left; but as it was there was no kith or kin of his alive; and he could not bear that.'

Father Macclesfield sniffed cynically, and folded his hands.

'I may say that his death-bed was extremely unpleasant. He was a coarse old fellow, with plenty of strength in him; and he used to make remarks about the churchyard – and – and in fact the worms, that used to send his poor child of a wife half fainting out of the room. He had lived an immoral life too, I gathered.

'Just at the last, it was – well – disgusting. He had no consideration (God knows why she married him!). The agony was a very long one; he caught at the curtains round the bed; calling out; and all his words were about death, and the dark. It seemed to me that he caught hold of the curtains as if to hold himself into this world. And at the very end he raised himself clean up in bed, and stared horribly out of the window that was open just opposite.

'I must tell you that straight away beneath the window lay a long walk, between sheets of dead leaves with laurels on either side, and the branches meeting overhead, so that it was very dark there even in summer; and at the end of the walk away from the house was the churchyard gate.'

Father Macclesfield paused and blew his nose. Then he went on still without looking at us.

'Well the old man died; and he was carried along this laurel path, and buried.

77

'His wife was in such a state that I simply dared not go away. She was frightened to death; and, indeed, the whole affair of her husband's dying was horrible. But she would not leave the house. She had a fancy that it would be cruel to him. She used to go down twice a day to pray at the grave; but she never went along the laurel walk. She would go round by the garden and in at a lower gate, and come back the same way, or by the upper garden.

'This went on for three or four days. The man had died on a Saturday, and was buried on Monday; it was in July; and he had died about eight o'clock.

'I made up my mind to go on the Saturday after the funeral. My curate had managed along very well for a few days; but I did not like to leave him for a second Sunday.

'Then on the Friday at lunch – her sister had come down, by the way, and was still in the house – on the Friday the widow said something about never daring to sleep in the room where the old man had died. I told her it was nonsense, and so on; but you must remember she was in a dreadful state of nerves, and she persisted. So I said I would sleep in the room myself. I had no patience with such ideas then.

'Of course she said all sorts of things, but I had my way; and my things were moved in on Friday evening.

'I went to my new room about a quarter before eight to put on my cassock for dinner. The room was very much as it had been – rather dark because of the trees at the end of the walk outside. There was the four-poster there with the damask curtains; the table and chairs, the cupboard where his clothes were kept, and so on.

'When I had put my cassock on, I went to the window to look out. To right and left were the gardens, with the sunlight just off them, but still very bright and gay, with the geraniums, and exactly opposite was the laurel walk, like a long green shady tunnel, dividing the upper and lower lawns.

'I could see straight down it to the churchyard gate, which was about a hundred yards away, I suppose. There were limes overhead, and laurels, as I said, on each side.

'Well – I saw someone coming up the walk; but it seemed to me at first that he was drunk. He staggered several times as I watched; I suppose he would be fifty yards away – and once I saw him catch hold of one of the trees and cling against it as if he were afraid of falling. Then he left it, and came on again slowly, going from side to side, with his hands out. He seemed desperately keen to get to the house.

'I could see his dress; and it astonished me that a man dressed so should be drunk; for he was quite plainly a gentleman. He wore a white top hat, and a grey cut-away coat, and grey trousers, and I could make out his white spats.

'Then it struck me he might be ill; and I looked harder than ever, wondering whether I ought to go down.

'When he was about twenty yards away he lifted his face; and, it struck me as very odd, but it seemed to me he was extraordinarily like the old man we had buried on Monday; but it was darkish where he was, and the next moment he dropped his face, threw up his hands and fell flat on his back.

'Well of course I was startled at that, and I leaned out of the window and called out something. He was moving his hands I could see, as if he were in convulsions; and I could hear the dry leaves rustling.

'Well, then I turned and ran out and downstairs.'

Father Macclesfield stopped a moment.

'Gentlemen,' he said abruptly, 'when I got there, there was not a sign of the old man. I could see that the leaves had been disturbed, but that was all.'

There was an odd silence in the room as he paused; but before any of us had time to speak he went on.

'Of course I did not say a word of what I had seen. We dined as usual; I smoked for an hour or so by myself after prayers;

and then I went up to bed. I cannot say I was perfectly comfortable, for I was not; but neither was I frightened.

'When I got to my room I lit all my candles, and then went to a big cupboard I had noticed, and pulled out some of the drawers. In the bottom of the third drawer I found a grey cutaway coat and grey trousers; I found several pairs of white spats in the top drawer; and a white hat on the shelf above. That is the first incident.'

'Did you sleep there, Father?' said a voice softly.

'I did,' said the priest; 'there was no reason why I should not. I did not fall asleep for two or three hours; but I was not disturbed in any way; and came to breakfast as usual.

'Well, I thought about it all a bit; and finally I sent a wire to my curate telling him I was detained. I did not like to leave the house just then.'

Father Macclesfield settled himself again in his chair and went on, in the same dry uninterested voice.

'On Sunday we drove over to the Catholic church, six miles off, and I said Mass. Nothing more happened till the Monday evening.

'That evening I went to the window again about a quarter before eight, as I had done both on the Saturday and Sunday. Everything was perfectly quiet, till I heard the churchyard gate unlatch; and I saw a man come through.

'But I saw almost at once that it was not the same man I had seen before; it looked to me like a keeper, for he had a gun across his arm; then I saw him hold the gate open an instant, and a dog came through and began to trot up the path towards the house with his master following.

'When the dog was about fifty yards away he stopped dead, and pointed.

'I saw the keeper throw his gun forward and come up softly; and as he came the dog began to slink backwards. I watched very closely, clean forgetting why I was there; and the next

80

instant something – it was too shadowy under the trees to see exactly what it was – but something about the size of a hare burst out of the laurels and made straight up the path, dodging from side to side, but coming like the wind.

'The beast could not have been more than twenty yards from me, when the keeper fired, and the creature went over and over in the dry leaves, and lay struggling and screaming. It was horrible! But what astonished me was that the dog did not come up. I heard the keeper snap out something, and then I saw the dog making off down the avenue in the direction of the churchyard as hard as he could go.

'The keeper was running now towards me; but the screaming of the hare, or of whatever it was, had stopped; and I was astonished to see the man come right up to where the beast was struggling and kicking, and then stop as if he was puzzled.

'I leaned out of the window and called to him.

' "Right in front of you, man," I said. "For God's sake kill the brute."

'He looked up at me, and then down again.

' "Where is it, sir?" he said. "I can't see it anywhere."

'And there lay the beast clear before him all the while, not a yard away, still kicking.

'Well, I went out of the room and downstairs and out to the avenue.

'The man was standing there still, looking terribly puzzled, but the hare was gone. There was not a sign of it. Only the leaves were disturbed, and the wet earth showed beneath.

'The keeper said that it had been a great hare; he could have sworn to it; and that he had orders to kill all hares and rabbits in the garden enclosure. Then he looked rather odd.

' "Did you see it plainly, sir?" he asked.

'I told him, not very plainly; but I thought it a hare too.

' "Yes, sir," he said, "it was a hare, sure enough; but do you

81

know, sir, I thought it to be a kind of silver grey with white feet. I never saw one like that before!"

'The odd thing was that not a dog would come near, his own dog was gone; but I fetched the yard dog – a retriever – out of his kennel in the kitchen yard; and if ever I saw a frightened dog it was this one. When we dragged him up at last, all whining and pulling back, he began to snap at us so fiercely that we let go, and he went back like the wind to his kennel. It was the same with the terrier.

'Well, the bell had gone, and I had to go in and explain why I was late; but I didn't say anything about the colour of the hare. That was the second incident.'

Father Macclesfield stopped again, smiling reminiscently to himself. I was very much impressed by his quiet air and composure. I think it helped his story a good deal.

Again, before we had time to comment or question, he went on.

'The third incident was so slight that I should not have mentioned it, or thought anything of it, if it had not been for the others; but it seemed to me there was a kind of diminishing gradation of energy, which explained. Well, now you shall hear.

'On the other nights of that week I was at my window again; but nothing happened till the Friday. I had arranged to go for certain next day; the widow was much better and more reasonable, and even talked of going abroad herself in the following week.

'On that Friday evening I dressed a little earlier, and went down to the avenue this time, instead of staying at my window, at about twenty minutes to eight.

'It was rather a depressing evening, without a breath of wind; and it was darker than it had been for some days.

'I walked slowly down the avenue to the gate and back again; and, I suppose it was fancy, but I felt more uncomfortable than I had felt at all up to then. I was rather relieved to see the widow come out of the house and stand looking down the avenue. I came out myself then and went towards her. She started rather when she saw me and then smiled.

'"I thought it was someone else," she said. "Father, I have made up my mind to go. I shall go to town tomorrow, and start on Monday. My sister will come with me."

'I congratulated her; and then we turned and began to walk back to the lime avenue. She stopped at the entrance and seemed unwilling to come any further.

'"Come down to the end," I said, "and back again. There will be time before dinner."

'She said nothing; but came back with me; and we went straight down to the gate and then turned to come back.

'I don't think either of us spoke a word; I was very uncomfortable indeed by now; and yet I had to go on.

'We were half-way back I suppose when I heard a sound like a gate rattling; and I whisked round in an instant, expecting to see someone at the gate. But there was no one.

'Then there came a rustling overhead in the leaves; it had been dead still before. Then I don't know why, but I took my friend suddenly by the arm and drew her to one side out of the path, so that we stood on the right hand, not a foot from the laurels.

'She said nothing, and I said nothing; but I think we were both looking this way and that, as if we expected to see something.

'The breeze died, and then sprang up again; but it was only a breath. I could hear the living leaves rustling overhead, and the dead leaves underfoot; and it was blowing gently from the churchyard.

'Then I saw a thing that one often sees; but I could not take my eyes off it, nor could she. It was a little column of leaves, twisting and turning and dropping and picking up again in the

83

wind, coming slowly up the path. It was a capricious sort of draught, for the little scurry of leaves went this way and that, to and fro across the path. It came up to us, and I could feel the breeze on my hands and face. One leaf struck me softly on the cheek, and I can only say that I shuddered as if it had been a toad. Then it passed on.

'You understand, gentlemen, it was pretty dark; but it seemed to me that the breeze died and the column of leaves – it was no more than a little twist of them – sank down at the end of the avenue.

'We stood there perfectly still for a moment or two; and when I turned, she was staring straight at me, but neither of us said one word.

'We did not go up the avenue to the house. We pushed our way through the laurels, and came back by the upper garden.

'Nothing else happened; and the next morning we all went off by the eleven o'clock train.

'That is all, gentlemen.'

The Abbey of Clunedale

Dr Nathan Drake

The last rays of the setting sun yet lingered on the mountains which surrounded the district of——; when Edward de Courtenay, after two fatiguing campaigns on the plains of Flanders, in one of which the gallant Sidney fell, re-entered his native village towards the end of August, 1587. He had lost his father a few months before his departure for the Continent, a loss which had occasioned him the most severe affliction, and had induced him thus early in life to seek, amid the din of arms, and the splendour of military parade, a pause from painful recollection. Time, however, though it had mitigated the first poignant emotions of grief, had not subdued the tender feelings of regret and sorrow, and the well-known objects of his early childhood and his opening youth, associated as they were with the salutary precepts and fond affection of the best of parents, awakened in his mind a train of melancholy yet soothing thoughts, as with slow and pausing steps he moved along the venerable avenue of trees, which led to his paternal mansion. Twilight had by this time wrapt every object in a veil of pleasing obscurity; all was hushed in the softest repose, and the massiness of the foliage under which he passed, and the magnitude and solitary grandeur of his Gothic halls impressed the imagination of Edward with deep sensations of solemnity and awe. Two grey-headed servants, who had lived for near half a century in the family, received their young master at the gate, and whilst the tears trickled down their withered cheeks, expressed with artless simplicity their joy, and blessed the return of the son of their ancient benefactor.

After some affectionate enquiries concerning the neighbouring villagers, and the families of these old men, Edward expressed his intention of walking to the Abbey of Clunedale, which lay about a mile distant from the house; his filial affection, the pensive retrospect of events endeared to memory, the sweetness and tranquillity of the evening, and that enthusiasm so congenial to the best emotions of the heart, gave birth to the wish of lingering a few moments over the turf which covered the remains of his beloved parent. Scarce, however, had he intimated this resolution, when the ghastly paleness which overspread the countenances of his domestics, and the dismay that sat upon their features, assured him that something extraordinary was connected with the determination he had adopted, and, upon enquiry, his terrified servants informed him, though with some confusion and reluctance, that, for some months past, they and the country round had been alarmed by strange sights and noises at the Abbey, and that no one durst approach the place after sunset. Edward, smiling at the superstitious fears of his attendants, which he attributed solely to their ignorance and their love for the marvellous, assured them he entertained no apprehensions for the event, and that he hoped shortly to convince them that their alarm was altogether unfounded. Saying this, he turned into the great avenue, and striking off to the left, soon reached the river, on whose winding banks a pathway led to the Abbey.

This venerable structure had been surrendered to the rapacity of Henry the Eighth in 1540, and having been partly unroofed during the same year, had experienced a rapid decay. It continued, however, along with the sacred ground adjoining to it, to be a depository of the dead, and part of the family of

86

the Courtenays had for some centuries reposed in vaults built on the outside of the great west entrance of the church. In a spot adjacent to this ancient cemetery lay also the remains of the father of Edward, and hither filial piety was now conducting the young warrior as the gathering shades of evening dropped their deep grey tints on all around.

The solemn stillness of the air, the tremulous and uncertain light through which every object appeared, the soothing murmur of the water, whose distant track could be discovered only by the white vapour which hovered on its surface, together with the sedate and sweeping movement of the melancholy owl as it sailed slowly and conspicuously down the valley, had all a natural tendency to induce a state of mind more than usually susceptible of awful impressions. Over Edward, predisposed to serious reflection by the sacred purport of his visit, they exerted a powerful dominion, and he entered the precincts of the Abbey in deep meditation on the possibility of the reappearance of the departed.

The view of the Abbey, too, dismantled and falling fast to decay, presented an image of departed greatness admirably calculated to awaken recollections of the mutability and transient nature of all human possessions. Its fine Gothic windows and arches streaming with ivy, were only just perceptible through the dusk, as Edward reached the consecrated ground; where, kneeling down at the tomb of his father, he remained for some time absorbed in the tender indulgence of sorrow. Having closed, however, his pious petitions for the soul of the deceased, he was rising from the hallowed mould, and about to retrace his pathway homewards, when a dim light glimmering from amidst the ruins arrested his attention. Greatly astonished at a phenomenon so singular, and suddenly calling to remembrance the ghastly appearance and fearful reports made by his servants, he stood for some moments riveted to the spot, with his eyes fixed on the light, which still continued to gleam steadily though faintly from the same quarter. Determined, however, to ascertain from what cause it proceeded, and almost ashamed of the childish apprehensions he had betrayed, he cautiously, and without making the least noise, approached the west entrance of the church; here the light, however, appeared to issue from the choir, which being at a considerable distance, and towards the other end of the building, he glided along its exterior, and passing the refectory and chapter-house, re-entered the church by the south portal near the choir. With footsteps light as air he moved along the damp and mouldering pavement, whilst pale rays gleaming from afar faintly glanced on the shafts of some pillars seen in distant perspective down the great aisle. Having now entered the choir, he could distinctly perceive the place whence the light proceeded, and, on approaching still nearer, dimly distinguished a human form kneeling opposite to it. Not an accent, however, reached his ear, and, except the rustling noise occasioned by the flight of some night-birds along remote parts of the ruin, a deep and awful silence prevailed.

The curiosity of Courtenay being now strongly excited, though mingled with some degree of apprehension and wonder, he determined to ascertain, if possible, who the stranger was, and from what motives he visited, at so unusual an hour, a place so solitary and deserted; passing therefore noiseless along one of the side aisles separated from the choir by a kind of elegant latticework, he at length stood parallel with the spot where the figure was situated, and had a perfect side view of the object of his search. It appeared to be a middle-aged man, who was kneeling on a white-marble slab, near the great altar, and before a small niche in the screen which divides the choir from the east end of the church; in the niche were placed a lamp and a crucifix; he had round him a coarse black garment bound with a leathern girdle, but no covering on his head; and, as the light gleamed upon his features, Edward was shocked at the despair that seemed fixed in their expression: his hands were clasped together, his eyes turned towards heaven, and heavy and convulsive sighs at intervals escaped from his bosom, whilst the breeze of night, lifting at times his disordered hair, added peculiar wildness to a countenance which, though elegantly moulded, was of ghastly paleness, and had a sternness and severity in its aspect, and every now and then displayed such an acute sense of conscious guilt, as chilled the beholder, and almost suppressed the rising emotions of pity. Edward, who had impatiently witnessed this extraordinary scene, was about to address the unhappy man, when groans as from a spirit in torture, and which seemed to rend the very bosom from which they issued, prevented his intention, and he beheld the miserable stranger prostrate in agony on the marble. In a few minutes, however, he arose, and drawing from beneath his garment an unsheathed sword, held it stretched in his hands towards heaven, whilst his countenance assumed still deeper marks of horror, and his eyes glared with the lightning of frenzy. At this instant, when, apprehensive for the event, Edward deemed it highly necessary to interfere, and was stepping forward with that view, his purpose was suddenly arrested by the sound of distant music, which stealing along the remote parts of the Abbey in notes that breathed a soothing and delicious harmony, seemed the work of enchantment, or to arise from the viewless harps of spirits of the blest. Over the agitated soul of the stranger it appeared to diffuse the balm of peace; his features became less rigid and stern, his eyes assumed a milder expression, he crossed his arms in meek submission on his bosom, and as the tones, now swelling with the richest melody of heaven, now tremulously dying away in accents of the most ravishing sweetness, approached still nearer, the tears started in his eyes, and coursing down his cheeks bathed the deadly instrument yet gleaming in his grasp;

this, however, with a heavy sigh he now placed in the niche, and bowing gently forward seemed to pray devoutly: the convulsions which had shaken his frame ceased; tranquillity sat upon his brow, whilst, in strains that melted into holy rapture every harsh emotion, the same celestial music still passed along the air, and filled the compass of the Abbey.

Courtenay, whose every faculty had been nearly absorbed through the influence of this unseen minstrelsy, had yet witnessed, with sincere pleasure, the favourable change in the mind and countenance of the stranger, who still knelt before the lamp, by whose pale light he beheld a perfect resignation tranquillize those features which a few minutes before had been distorted by the struggles of remorse; for such had been the soothing and salutary effects of harmony in allaying the perturbations of a wounded and self-accusing spirit, that hope now cheered the bosom so recently the mansion of despair.

Whilst Edward, in sacred regard to the noblest feelings of humanity, forbore to interrupt the progress of emotions so friendly to virtue and contrition, the music, which had gradually, and with many a dying close, breathed fainter and fainter on the ear, now, in tones that whispered peace and mercy, and which sounded sweet as the accents of departed saints, melted into air, and deep silence again pervaded the Abbey. This, however, continued not long, for in a few moments was heard the echo of light footsteps, and presently Courtenay, by the glimmering of the lamp, indistinctly beheld some object which, gliding rapidly up the choir, moved towards the spot where the stranger was yet kneeling. His astonishment was increased when, on its approaching nearer, he could perceive the form of a young and elegant woman. She was clothed perfectly in white, except where the vest was bound by a black zone, and over her shoulders flowed negligently a profusion of light brown hair.

A smile of the most winning sweetness played upon her features, though the dewy lustre of her eyes, and the tears that lingered on her cheek, revealed the struggles of the heart. The stranger, who had risen at her approach, embraced her with the most affectionate emotion; they were both silent, however, and both now kneeling on the marble slab employed some time in prayer. Nothing ever appeared to Courtenay more interesting than the countenance of this beautiful young woman, thus lighted up by all the sensibility of acute feeling; her eyes bathed in tears, and lifted towards heaven, beamed forth an expression truly angelic, whilst the exquisite delicacy of her complexion and features, over which the pensive graces had diffused their most fascinating charms, together with the simplicity and energy of her devotion as with clasped hands and trembling lips she implored the assistance of the Divine Spirit, formed a picture worthy of the canvas of Raphael.

Edward now saw before him the cause of those rumours and fears which had been circulated with so much industry in the neighbourhood, for, since the appearance of this amiable young woman, he had been perfectly convinced that the music to which he had lately listened with so much rapture, had its origin with her. In a still night these sounds might be heard to some distance, and, together with the glimmering of the light, would occasion no small alarm to the peasant who should happen at that time to be passing near the Abbey, and whose apprehensions, thus excited, might easily create some imaginary being, the offspring of innocence and terror; or perhaps some pilgrim, more daring than the rest, had penetrated the interior of the ruin, and had probably beheld one of the very striking figures now present to his eyes. This, without further enquiry, he had deemed, what indeed would, at first, be the surmise of any spectator, some vision of another world, and had thus strengthened the superstition of the country, and protected the seclusion of the strangers.

As these reflections were passing through his mind, the interesting objects which had given them birth had risen from their kneeling posture, and after interchanging looks of mingled gratitude and delight, were arm in arm retiring from the sacred marble, when Edward, whose eagerness to discover the motives of the elder stranger's conduct had been greatly augmented since the appearance of his fair companion, determined, if possible, to trace them to the place of their abode. Entering the choir, therefore, by one of the lateral doors, he followed them with slow and silent footsteps, preserving such a distance as, he thought, might prevent the lamp from revealing his person. He had pursued them in this manner unobserved through the choir, but upon their suddenly turning at an acute angle to enter the cloisters, the light streaming faintly on his figure discovered him to the younger stranger, who, uttering a loud shriek, leaned trembling on the arm of her friend.

Courtenay now immediately rushing forward endeavoured to allay their apprehensions, by informing them of his name and place of residence, and the motives which had, at this time of night, led him to visit the Abbey: he told them that, filial piety having drawn him to the tomb of his father, he had very unexpectedly perceived a light in the interior of the building; which strongly exciting his curiosity, and corroborating the reports of the country, he had endeavoured to ascertain its cause, and in so doing had discovered the attitude and employment of the elder stranger, who, together with his fair attendant, rather increasing than mitigating his astonishment, he had attempted, by following them at a distance, to ascertain their abode, it being his intention at some future period to solicit an explanation of what he had now witnessed.

Whilst Edward was yet speaking, a ghastly paleness overspread the countenance of the elder stranger; it was momentary, however; for, soon resuming his tranquillity, he addressed Courtenay in a low but firm tone of voice.

'I am sorry, sir,' said he, 'to have occasioned, by my partial residence here, so much apprehension among the inhabitants of your village; but as I have reasons for wishing concealment, at least for a time, I have thought it necessary, though acquainted with their fears, not to undeceive them. But with you I know already I can have no motives for disguise; for, though from great change of feature, brought on by deep sorrow, and great change of apparel, I have hitherto escaped your recognition, you will find by-and-by that we were formerly better acquainted. In the mean time I will conduct you to the spot we inhabit, where, should you wish for an explanation of the extraordinary scenes you have been a spectator of this night, the recital, though it will cost me many struggles, shall be given you, and I do this, strange as it may now sound to you, actuated by the recollection of past friendship.'

Having said thus, he and his beautiful partner, who had listened with almost as much surprise as Edward to an address so unexpected, moved slowly on, and Courtenay, occupied in fruitless conjecture, followed in silence.

They passed along a large portion of the cloisters, whose perspective, as seen by the dreary light of the lamp, had a singularly aweful effect, and then, ascending some steps, entered what is termed the Dormitory, and which was carried over this part of the Abbey to a considerable distance. Here, in two small chambers, where the roof remained sufficiently entire, were a couple of beds, and a small quantity of neat furniture, and here the stranger, pausing, invited Edward to enter.

'These rooms,' observed he, 'are my occasional habitation for at least twice-a-week during the night: but before I commence the melancholy narrative of my crimes and sufferings, I will endeavour to recall your recollection to your companion-in-arms upon the Continent; for this purpose I will retire for a few minutes and put on the dress I usually come hither in, the habit you now see upon me being merely assumed after reaching this place as best suited to the situation of my mind, to the penitence and humiliation that await me here.'

His tone of speaking, as he thus addressed Courtenay, was perceivably altered, being much more open and full than before, and brought to Edward's ear a voice he had been accustomed to, though he could not at the moment appropriate it to any individual of his acquaintance. During his absence, his amiable companion, who had not perfectly recovered from the alarm into which she had been thrown by Courtenay's intrusion, sat silent and reserved, until Edward, observing some manuscript-music in the room, ventured to enquire if the exquisite performance he had listened to with so much delight in the Abbey had not originated with her. A deep sigh at this question escaped her bosom, and her eyes filled with tears, whilst in tremulous accents she replied, that, owing to the great relief and support her brother experienced from music, she always accompanied him to this place, and that it was a source of the purest happiness to her to be thus able, through the medium of her harp and voice, to alleviate and soothe his sorrows. For this purpose the instrument was left at the Abbey, and was placed in that part of the ruin where its tones were best heard and produced the most pleasing effect. At this instant the door opening, the stranger entered clothed in a mourning military undress, and bearing a taper in his hand; he placed himself, the light gleaming steadily on his countenance, opposite Courtenay, who involuntarily stared at his appearance.

'Do you not remember,' he exclaimed, 'the officer who was wounded by your side at the battle of Zutphen?'

'My God!' cried Edward, 'can it be Clifford?'

'The same, my friend, the same,' he replied; 'though action has anticipated on his features the characters of age. You behold, Courtenay, the most unfortunate, the most miserable of men – but let me not pain my sweet Caroline by the recital of facts which have already wounded almost to dissolution her tender heart – we will walk, my friend, into the Abbey; its aweful gloom will better suit the dreadful tale I have to unfold.'

Saying this, and promising his sister to return in a few minutes, they descended into the cloisters, and thence through the choir into the body of the church.

The tranquillity of the night, and the light and refreshing breeze that yet lingered amid the ruin, and swept through its long withdrawing aisles, were unavailing to mitigate the agitation of Clifford, as with trembling footsteps he passed along the choir.

'O, my friend,' he exclaimed, 'the spirits of those I have injured hover near us! Beneath that marble slab, my Courtenay, on which you saw me kneel with so much horror and remorse, repose the reliques of a beloved wife, of the most amiable of her sex, and who owes her death (God of mercy register not the deed!) to the wild suggestion of my jealous frenzy.'

Whilst thus speaking, they hurried rapidly forwards towards the western part of the Abbey; and here Clifford, resuming more composure, proceeded in his narrative.

'You may probably recollect about a twelvemonth ago my obtaining leave of the Earl of Leicester to visit England; I came, my friend, upon a fatal errand. I had learnt, through the medium of an officious relation, that my wife, my beloved Matilda, of whose affection and accomplishments you have frequently heard me speak with rapture, had attached herself to a young man who had visited in the neighbourhood of my estate at C——n, but that she had lately removed for the summer months to a small house and farm I possess within a mile or two of this Abbey, and that here likewise she continued to receive the attentions of the young stranger. Fired by representations such as these, and racked with cureless jealousy, I returned to England in disguise, and found the report of my relation the theme of common conversation in the county. It was on the evening of a fine summer's day that I reached the hamlet of G——, and with a trembling hand and palpitating heart knocked at my own door. The servant informed me that Matilda had walked towards the Abbey. I immediately took the same route: the sun had set; and the grey tinting of evening had wrapt every object in uniform repose; the moon, however, was rising, and in a short time silvered parts of the ruin and its neighbouring trees. I placed myself in the shadow of one of the buttresses, and had not waited long ere Matilda, my beautiful Matilda, appeared, leaning on the arm of the stranger. You may conceive the extreme agitation of my soul at a spectacle like this; unhappily, revenge was, at the instant, the predominating emotion, and rushing forward with my sword, I called upon the villain, as I then thought him, to defend himself. Shocked by the suddenness of the attack, and the wild impetuosity of my manner, Matilda fell insensible on the earth, and only recovered recollection at the moment when my sword had pierced the bosom of the stranger, through whose guard I had broken in the first fury of the assault. With shrieks of agony and despair she sprang towards the murdered youth, and falling on his body exclaimed, "My brother, my dear, dear brother!"

'Had all nature fallen in dissolution around me, my astonishment and horror could not have been greater than what I felt from these words. The very marrow froze in my bones, and I stood fixed to the ground an image of despair and guilt. Meantime the life-blood of the unhappy Walsingham ebbed fast away, and he expired at my feet, and in the arms of his beloved sister, who, at this event, perhaps fortunately for us both, relapsed into a state of insensibility. My own emotions, on recovering from the stupor into which I had been thrown, were those I believe of frenzy, nor can I now dwell upon them with safety, nor without a partial dereliction of intellect. Suffice it to say, that I had sufficient presence of mind left to apply for assistance at the nearest cottage, and that the hapless victims of my folly were at length conveyed to the habitation of Matilda. Another dreadful scene awaited her, the recognition of her husband as the murderer of her brother – this, through the attention of my friends, for I myself was incapable of acting with rationality, was for some time postponed; it came at length, however, through the agonies of my remorse and contrition, to her knowledge, and two months have scarce elapsed since I placed her by the side of her poor brother, who, at the fatal moment of our rencounter, had not been many months returned from the Indies, and was in person a perfect stranger to your friend. Beneath that marble slab they rest, my Courtenay, and ere this, I believe, and through the medium of my own lawless hand, I should have partaken of their grave, had not my beloved sister, my amiable and gentle Caroline, stepped in, like an angel, between her brother and destruction.

'Singular as it may appear, the greatest satisfaction I now receive, is from frequent visits to the tomb of Matilda and her brother; there, over the reliques of those I have injured, to implore the mercy of an offended Deity; such, however, are the agonies I suffer from the recollection of my crime, that even this resource would be denied me were it not for the intervention of the powers of music; partial I have ever been to this enchanting art, and I am indebted to it for the mitigation and repression of feelings that would otherwise exhaust my shattered frame. You have witnessed the severe struggles of

97

remorse which at times agitate this afflicted heart, you have likewise seen the soothing and salutary effects of harmony. My Caroline's voice and harp have thus repeatedly lulled to repose the fever of a wounded spirit, the workings nearly of despair. A state of mind friendly to devotion, and no longer at war with itself, is usually the effect of her sweet and pathetic strains; it is then I think myself forgiven; it is then I seem to hear the gentle accents of my Matilda in concert with the heavenly tones; they whisper of eternal peace, and sensations of unutterable pleasure steal through every nerve.

'When such is the result, when peace and piety are the offspring of the act, you will not wonder at my visits to this melancholy ruin; soon as the shades of evening have spread their friendly covert, twice-a-week we hasten hither from our cottage; a scene, similar to what you have been a spectator of tonight, takes place, and we retire to rest in the little rooms which we have rendered habitable in the Dormitory. In the morning very early we quit the house of penitence and prayer; and such is the dread which the occasional glimmering of lights and the sounds of distant music have given birth to in the country, that none but our servant, who is faithful to the secret, dare approach near the place; we have consequently hitherto, save by yourself, remained undiscovered, and even unsuspected.

'Such, my friend, is the history of my crimes and sufferings, and such the causes of the phenomena you have beheld tonight – but see, Courtenay, my lovely Caroline, she to whom under heaven I am indebted for any portion of tranquillity I yet enjoy, is approaching to meet us. I can discern her by the whiteness of her robes gliding down yon distant aisle.'

Caroline had become apprehensive for her brother, and had stolen from the Dormitory with the view of checking a conversation which she was afraid would prove too affecting for his spirits. Edward beheld her, as she drew near, rather as a being from the regions of the blest, the messenger of peace and virtue, than as partaking of the frailties of humanity. If the beauties of her person had before interested him in her favour, her conduct towards the unhappy Clifford had given him the fullest conviction of the purity and goodness of her heart, of the strength and energy of her mind; and from this moment he determined, if possible, to secure an interest in a bosom so fraught with all that could exalt and decorate the lot of life.

He was now compelled, however, though greatly reluctant, to take leave of his friends for the night, and hasten to remove the extreme alarm into which his servants had been thrown by his unexpected detention. They had approached, as near as their fears would permit them, to the Abbey, for to enter its precincts was a deed they thought too daring for man, and had there exerted all their strength, though in vain, in repeatedly calling him by his name. It was therefore with a joy little short of madness they again beheld their master, who, as soon as these symptoms of rapture had subsided, had great difficulty in repressing their curiosity, which was on full stretch for information from another world.

It may here perhaps be necessary to add, that time, and the soothing attentions of his beloved sister, restored at length to perfect peace, and to the almost certain hope of pardon from the Deity, the hitherto agitated mind of Clifford. – I can also add, that time saw the union of Caroline and Edward, and that with them, at the hospitable mansion of the Courtenays, Clifford passed the remainder of his days.

Man-Size in Marble

Edith Nesbit

Although every word of this story is as true as despair, I do not expect people to believe it. Nowadays a 'rational explanation' is required before belief is possible. Let me, then, at once offer the 'rational explanation' which finds most favour among those who have heard the tale of my life's tragedy. It is held that we were 'under a delusion', Laura and I, on that 31st of October; and that this supposition places the whole matter on a satisfactory and believable basis. The reader can judge, when he, too, has heard my story, how far this is an 'explanation', and in what sense it is 'rational'. There were three who took part in this: Laura and I and another man. The other man still lives, and can speak to the truth of the least credible part of my story.

I never in my life knew what it was to have as much money as I required to supply the most ordinary needs – good colours, books, and cab-fares – and when we were married we knew quite well that we should only be able to live at all by 'strict punctuality and attention to business'. I used to paint in those days, and Laura used to write, and we felt sure we could keep the pot at least simmering. Living in town was out of the question, so we went to look for a cottage in the country, which should be at once sanitary and picturesque. So rarely do these two qualities meet in one cottage that our search was for some time quite fruitless. But when we got away from friends and house-agents, on our honeymoon, our wits grew clear again, and we knew a pretty cottage when at last we saw one.

It was at Brenzett – a little village set on a hill over against the southern marshes. We had gone there, from the seaside village where we were staying, to see the church, and two fields from the church we found this cottage. It stood quite by itself, about two miles from the village. It was a long, low building, with rooms sticking out in unexpected places. There was a bit of stonework – ivy-covered and moss-grown, just two old rooms, all that was left of a big house that had once stood there – and round this stonework the house had grown up. Stripped of its roses and jasmine it would have been hideous. As it stood it was charming, and after a brief examination we took it. It was absurdly cheap. There was a jolly old-fashioned garden, with grass paths, and no end of hollyhocks and sunflowers and big lilies. From the window you could see the marsh-pastures, and beyond them the blue, thin line of the sea.

We got a tall old peasant woman to do for us. Her face and figure were good, though her cooking was of the homeliest; but she understood all about gardening, and told us all the old names of the coppices and cornfields, and the stories of the smugglers and highwaymen, and, better still, of the 'things that walked', and of the 'sights' which met one in lonely glens of a starlight night. We soon came to leave all the domestic business to Mrs Dorman, and to use her legends in little magazine stories which brought in the jingling guinea.

We had three months of married happiness, and did not have a single quarrel. One October evening I had been down to smoke a pipe with the doctor – our only neighbour – a pleasant young Irishman. Laura had stayed at home to finish a comic sketch. I left her laughing over her own jokes, and came in to find her a crumpled heap of pale muslin, weeping on the window seat.

'Good heavens, my darling, what's the matter?' I cried, taking her in my arms. 'What is the matter? Do speak.'

'It's Mrs Dorman,' she sobbed.

'What has she done?' I enquired, immensely relieved.

'She says she must go before the end of the month, and she says her niece is ill; she's gone down to see her now, but I don't believe that's the reason, because her niece is always ill. I believe someone has been setting her against us. Her manner was so queer –'

'Never mind, Pussy,' I said; 'whatever you do, don't cry, or I shall have to cry too to keep you in countenance, and then you'll never respect your man again.'

'But you see,' she went on, 'it is really serious, because these village people are so sheepy, and if one won't do a thing you may be quite sure none of the others will. And I shall have to cook the dinners and wash up the hateful greasy plates; and you'll have to carry cans of water about and clean the boots and knives – and we shall never have any time for work or earn any money or anything.'

I represented to her that even if we had to perform these duties the day would still present some margin for other toils and recreations. But she refused to see the matter in any but the greyest light.

'I'll speak to Mrs Dorman when she comes back, and see if I can't come to terms with her,' I said. 'Perhaps she wants a rise. It will be all right. Let's walk up to the church.'

The church was a large and lonely one, and we loved to go there, especially upon bright nights. The path skirted a wood, cut through it once, and ran along the crest of the hill through two meadows, and round the churchyard wall, over which the old yews loomed in black masses of shadow.

This path, which was partly paved, was called 'the bier-walk', for it had long been the way by which the corpses had been carried to burial. The churchyard was richly treed, and was shaded by great elms which stood just outside and stretched their majestic arms in benediction over the happy dead. A large, low porch let one into the building by a Norman doorway and a heavy oak door studded with iron. Inside, the arches rose into darkness, and between them the reticulated windows, which stood out white in the moonlight. In the chancel, the windows were of rich glass, which showed in faint light their noble colouring, and made the black oak of the choir pews hardly more solid than the shadows. But on each side of the altar lay a grey marble figure of a knight in full plate armour lying upon a low slab, with hands held up in everlasting prayer, and these figures, oddly enough, were always to be seen if there was any glimmer of light in the church. Their names were lost, but the peasants told of them that they had been fierce and wicked men, marauders by land and sea, who had been the scourge of their time, and had been guilty of deeds so foul that the house they had lived in – the big house, by the way, that had stood on the site of our cottage – had been stricken by lightning and the vengeance of Heaven. But for all that, the gold of their heirs had bought them a place in the church. Looking at the bad, hard faces reproduced in the marble, this story was easily believed.

The church looked at its best and weirdest on that night, for the shadows of the yew trees fell through the windows upon the floor of the nave and touched the pillars with tattered shade. We sat down together without speaking, and watched the solemn beauty of the old church with some of the awe which inspired its early builders. We walked to the chancel and looked at the sleeping warriors. Then we rested some time on the stone seat in the porch, looking out over the stretch of quiet moonlit meadows, feeling in every fibre of our being the peace of the night and of our happy love; and came away at last with a sense that even scrubbing and black-leading were but small troubles at their worst.

Mrs Dorman had come back from the village, and I at once invited her to a *tête-à-tête*.

'Now, Mrs Dorman,' I said, when I had got her into my painting-room, 'what's all this about your not staying with us?'

'I should be glad to get away, sir, before the end of the month,' she answered, with her usual placid dignity.

'Have you any fault to find, Mrs Dorman?'

'None at all, sir: you and your lady have always been most kind, I'm sure –'

'Well, what is it? Are your wages not high enough?'

'No, sir, I gets quite enough.'

'Then why not stay?'

'I'd rather not' – with some hesitation – 'my niece is ill.'

'But your niece has been ill ever since we came. Can't you stay for another month?'

'No, sir, I'm bound to go by Thursday.'

And this was Monday!

'Well, I must say, I think you might have let us know before. There's no time now to get anyone else, and your mistress is not fit to do heavy housework. Can't you stay till next week?'

'I might be able to come back next week.'

'But why must you go this week?' I persisted. 'Come out with it.'

Mrs Dorman drew the little shawl, which she always wore, tightly across her bosom, as though she were cold. Then she said, with a sort of effort:

'They say, sir, as this was a big house in Catholic times, and there was a many deeds done here.'

The nature of the 'deeds' might be vaguely inferred from the inflection of Mrs Dorman's voice – which was enough to make one's blood run cold. I was glad that Laura was not in the room. She was always nervous, as highly strung natures are, and I felt that these tales about our house, told by this old peasant woman, with her impressive manner and contagious credulity, might have made our home less dear to my wife.

'Tell me all about it, Mrs Dorman,' I said; 'you needn't mind about telling me. I'm not like the young people who make fun of such things.'

Which was partly true.

'Well, sir' – she sank her voice – 'you may have seen in the church, beside the altar, two shapes.'

'You mean the effigies of the knights in armour,' I said cheerfully.

'I mean them two bodies, drawed out man-size in marble,' she returned, and I had to admit that her description was a thousand times more graphic than mine, to say nothing of a certain weird force and uncanniness about the phrase 'drawed out man-size in marble'.

'They do say, as on All Saints' Eve them two bodies sits up on their slabs, and gets off of them, and then walks down the aisle *in their marble*' – (another good phrase, Mrs Dorman) – 'and as the church clock strikes eleven they walks out of the church door, and over the graves, and along the bier-walk, and if it's a wet night there's the marks of their feet in the morning.'

'And where do they go?' I asked, rather fascinated.

'They comes back here to their home, sir, and if anyone meets them –'

'Well, what then?' I asked.

But no – not another word could I get from her, save that her niece was ill and she must go.

'Whatever you do, sir, lock the door early on All Saints' Eve, and make the cross-sign over the doorstep and on the windows.'

'But has anyone ever seen these things?' I persisted. 'Who was here last year?'

'No one, sir; the lady as owned the house only stayed here in summer, and she always went to London a full month afore *the* night. And I'm sorry to inconvenience you and your lady, but my niece is ill and I must go Thursday.'

I could have shaken her for her absurd reiteration of that obvious fiction, after she had told me her real reasons.

I did not tell Laura the legend of the shapes that 'walked in their marble', partly because a legend concerning our house might perhaps trouble my wife, and partly, I think, from some more occult reason. This was not quite the same to me as any other story, and I did not want to talk about it till the day was over. I had very soon ceased to think of the legend, however. I was painting a portrait of Laura, against the lattice window, and I could not think of much else. I had got a splendid background of yellow and grey sunset, and was working away with enthusiasm at her face. On Thursday, Mrs Dorman went. She relented, at parting, so far as to say:

'Don't you put yourself about too much, ma'am, and if there's any little thing I can do next week I'm sure I shan't mind.'

Thursday passed off pretty well. Friday came. It is about what happened on that Friday that this is written.

I got up early, I remember, and lighted the kitchen fire, and had just achieved a smoky success when my little wife came running down as sunny and sweet as the clear October morning itself. We prepared breakfast together, and found it very good fun. The housework was soon done, and when brushes and brooms and pails were quiet again the house was still indeed. It is wonderful what a difference one makes in a house. We really missed Mrs Dorman, quite apart from considerations concerning pots and pans. We spent the day in dusting our books and putting them straight, and dined on cold steak and coffee. Laura was, if possible, brighter and gayer and sweeter than usual, and I began to think that a little domestic toil was really good for her. We had never been so merry since we were married, and the walk we had that afternoon was, I think, the happiest time of all my life. When we had watched the deep scarlet clouds slowly pale into leaden grey against a pale green sky and saw the white mists curl up along the hedgerows in the distant marsh we came back to the house hand in hand.

'You are sad, my darling,' I said, half-jestingly, as we sat down together in our little parlour. I expected a disclaimer, for my own silence had been the silence of complete happiness. To my surprise she said:

'Yes, I think I am sad, or, rather, I am uneasy. I don't think I'm very well. I have shivered three or four times since we came in; and it is not cold, is it?'

'No,' I said, and hoped it was not a chill caught from the treacherous mists that roll up from the marshes in the dying night. No – she said, she did not think so. Then, after a silence, she spoke suddenly:

'Do you ever have presentiments of evil?'

'No,' I said, smiling, 'and I shouldn't believe in them if I had.'

'I do,' she went on, 'the night before my father died I knew it, though he was right away in the North of Scotland.' I did not answer in words.

She sat looking at the fire for some time in silence, gently stroking my hand. At last she sprang up, came behind me, and, drawing my head back, kissed me.

'There, it's over now,' she said. 'What a baby I am! Come, light the candles, and we'll have some of these new Rubinstein duets.'

And we spent a happy hour or two at the piano.

At about half-past ten I began to long for the good-night pipe, but Laura looked so white that I felt it would be brutal of me to fill our sitting-room with the fumes of strong cavendish.

'I'll take my pipe outside,' I said.

'Let me come, too.'

'No, sweetheart, not tonight; you're much too tired. I shan't be long. Get to bed, or I shall have an invalid to nurse tomorrow as well as the boots to clean.'

I kissed her and was turning to go when she flung her arms round my neck and held me as if she would never let me go again. I stroked her hair.

'Come, Pussy, you're over-tired. The housework has been too much for you.'

She loosened her clasp a little and drew a deep breath.

'No. We've been very happy today, Jack, haven't we? Don't stay out too long.'

'I won't, my dearie.'

I strolled out of the front door, leaving it unlatched. What a night it was! The jagged masses of heavy dark cloud were rolling at intervals from horizon to horizon, and thin white wreaths covered the stars. Through all the rush of the cloud river the moon swam, breasting the waves and disappearing again in the darkness.

I walked up and down, drinking in the beauty of the quiet earth and the changing sky. The night was absolutely silent. Nothing seemed to be abroad. There was no scurrying of rabbits, or twitter of the half-asleep birds. And though the clouds went sailing across the sky, the wind that drove them never came low enough to rustle the dead leaves in the woodland paths. Across the meadows I could see the church tower standing out black and grey against the sky. I walked there thinking over our three months of happiness.

I heard a bell-beat from the church. Eleven already! I turned to go in, but the night held me. I could not go back into our warm rooms yet. I would go up to the church.

I looked in at the low window as I went by. Laura was half lying on her chair in front of the fire. I could not see her face, only her little head showed dark against the pale blue wall. She was quite still. Asleep, no doubt.

I walked slowly along the edge of the wood. A sound broke the stillness of the night, it was a rustling in the wood. I stopped and listened. The sound stopped too. I went on, and now distinctly heard another step than mine answer mine like an echo. It was a poacher or a wood-stealer, most likely, for these were not unknown in our Arcadian neighbourhood. But, whoever it was, he was a fool not to step more lightly. I turned into the wood and now the footstep seemed to come from the path I had just left. It must be an echo, I thought. The wood looked perfect in the moonlight. The large dying ferns and the brushwood showed where through thinning foliage the pale light came down. The tree trunks stood up like Gothic columns all around me. They reminded me of the church, and I turned into the bier-walk, and passed through the corpse-gate between the graves to the low porch.

I paused for a moment on the stone seat where Laura and I had watched the fading landscape. Then I noticed that the door of the church was open, and I blamed myself for having left it unlatched the other night. We were the only people who ever cared to come to the church except on Sundays, and I was vexed to think that through our carelessness the damp autumn airs had had a chance of getting in and injuring the old fabric. I went in. It will seem strange, perhaps, that I should have gone half-way up the aisle before I remembered – with a sudden chill, followed by a sudden rush of self-contempt – that this was the very day and hour when, according to tradition, the 'shapes drawed out man-size in marble' began to walk.

Having thus remembered the legend, and remembered it with a shiver, of which I was ashamed, I could not do otherwise than walk up towards the altar, just to look at the figures – as I said to myself; really what I wanted was to assure myself, first, that I did not believe the legend, and secondly, that it was not true. I was rather glad that I had come. I thought now I could tell Mrs Dorman how vain her fancies were, and how peacefully the marble figures slept on through the ghastly hour. With my hands in my pockets I passed up the aisle. In the grey dim light the eastern end of the church looked larger than usual, and the arches above the two tombs looked larger too. The moon came out and showed me the reason. I stopped short, my heart gave a leap that nearly choked me, and then sank sickeningly.

The 'bodies drawed out man-size' *were gone*! and their marble slabs lay wide and bare in the vague moonlight that slanted through the east window.

Were they really gone, or was I mad? Clenching my nerves, I stooped and passed my hand over the smooth slabs and felt their flat unbroken surface. Had someone taken the things away? Was it some vile practical joke? I would make sure, anyway. In an instant I had made a torch of newspaper, which happened to be in my pocket, and, lighting it, held it high above my head. Its yellow glare illumined the dark arches and those slabs. The figures *were* gone. And I was alone in the church; or was I alone?

And then a horror seized me, a horror indefinable and indescribable – an overwhelming certainty of supreme and accomplished calamity. I flung down the torch and tore along the aisle and out through the porch, biting my lips as I ran to keep myself from shrieking aloud. Oh, was I mad – or what was this that possessed me? I leaped the churchyard wall and took the straight cut across the fields, led by the light from our windows. Just as I got over the first stile a dark figure seemed to spring out of the ground. Mad still with that certainty of misfortune, I made for the thing that stood in my path, shouting, 'Get out of the way, can't you!'

But my push met with a more vigorous resistance than I had expected. My arms were caught just above the elbow and held as in a vice, and the raw-boned Irish doctor actually shook me.

110

'Let me go, you fool,' I gasped. 'The marble figures have gone from the church; I tell you they've gone.'

He broke into a ringing laugh. 'I'll have to give you a draught tomorrow, I see. Ye've bin smoking too much and listening to old wives' tales.'

'I tell you, I've seen the bare slabs.'

'Well, come back with me. I'm going up to old Palmer's – his daughter's ill; we'll look in at the church and let me see the bare slabs.'

'You go, if you like,' I said, a little less frantic for his laughter; 'I'm going home to my wife.'

'Rubbish, man,' said he; 'd'ye think I'll permit of that? Are ye to go saying all yer life that ye've seen solid marble endowed with vitality, and me to go all me life saying ye were a coward? No, sir – ye shan't do ut.'

The night air – a human voice – and I think also the physical contact with this six feet of solid common sense, brought me back to my ordinary self, and the word 'coward' was a mental shower-bath.

'Come on, then.' I said sullenly; 'perhaps you're right.'

He still held my arm tightly. We got over the stile and back to the church. All was still as death. The place smelt very damp and earthly. We walked up the aisle. I am not ashamed to confess that I shut my eyes: I knew the figures would not be there. I heard Kelly strike a match.

'Here they are, ye see, right enough; ye've been dreaming or drinking, asking yer pardon for the imputation.'

I opened my eyes. By Kelly's expiring vesta I saw two shapes lying 'in their marble' on their slabs. I drew a deep breath.

'I'm awfully indebted to you,' I said. 'It must have been some trick of light, or I have been working rather hard, perhaps that's it. I was quite convinced they were gone.'

'I'm aware of that,' he answered rather grimly; 'ye'll have to be careful of that brain of yours, my friend, I assure ye.'

He was leaning over and looking at the right-hand figure, whose stony face was the most villainous and deadly in expression.

'By Jove,' he said, 'something has been afoot here – this hand is broken.'

And so it was. I was certain that it had been perfect the last time Laura and I had been there.

'Perhaps someone has *tried* to remove them,' said the young doctor.

'Come along,' I said, 'or my wife will be getting anxious. You'll come in and have a drop of whisky and drink confusion to ghosts and better sense to me.'

'I ought to go up to Palmer's, but it's so late now I'd best leave it till the morning,' he replied.

I think he fancied I needed him more than did Palmer's girl, so, discussing how such an illusion could have been possible, and deducing from this experience large generalities concerning ghostly apparitions, we walked up to our cottage. We saw, as we walked up the garden path, that bright light streamed out of the front door, and presently saw that the parlour door was open, too. Had she gone out?

'Come in,' I said, and Dr Kelly followed me into the parlour. It was all ablaze with candles, not only the wax ones, but at least a dozen guttering, glaring tallow dips, stuck in vases and ornaments in unlikely places. Light, I knew, was Laura's remedy for nervousness. Poor child! Why had I left her? Brute that I was.

We glanced round the room, and at first we did not see her. The window was open, and the draught set all the candles flaring one way. Her chair was empty and her handkerchief and book lay on the floor. I turned to the window. There, in the recess of the window, I saw her. Oh, my child, my love, had she gone to that window to watch for me? And what had come into the room behind her? To what had she turned with that

112

look of frantic fear and horror? Oh, my little one, had she
thought that it was I whose step she heard, and turned to meet
– what?

She had fallen back across a table in the window, and her
body lay half on it, and half on the window-seat, and her head
hung down over the table, the brown hair loosened and fallen
to the carpet. Her lips were drawn back, and her eyes wide
open. They saw nothing now. What had they seen last?

The doctor moved towards her, but I pushed him aside and
sprang to her; caught her in my arms and cried:

'It's all right, Laura! I've got you safe, wifie.'

She fell into my arms in a heap. I clasped her and kissed her,
and called her by pet names, but I think I knew all the time
that she was dead. Her hands were tightly clenched. In one of
them she held something fast. When I was quite sure that she
was dead, and that nothing mattered at all any more, I let him
open her hand to see what she held.

It was a grey marble finger.

The Devil's Wager

W. M. Thackeray

It was the hour of the night when there be none stirring save churchyard ghosts – when all doors are closed except the gates of graves, and all eyes shut but the eyes of wicked men.

When there is no sound on the earth except the ticking of the grasshopper, or the croaking of obscene frogs in the pool.

And no light except that of the blinking stars, and the wicked and devilish wills-o'-the-wisp, as they gambol among the marshes, and lead good men astray.

When there is nothing moving in heaven except the owl, as he flappeth along lazily; or the magician, as he rideth on his infernal broomstick, whistling through the air like the arrows of a Yorkshire archer.

It was at this hour (namely, at twelve o'clock of the night) that two things went winging through the black clouds, and holding converse with each other.

Now the first was Mercurius, the messenger, not of gods (as the heathens feigned), but of demons; and the second, with whom he held company, was the soul of Sir Roger de Rollo, the brave knight. Sir Roger was Count of Chauchigny, in Champagne; Seigneur of Santerre, Villacerf and *autre lieux*. But the great die as well as the humble; and nothing remained of brave Roger now, but his coffin and his deathless soul.

And Mercurius, in order to keep fast the soul, his companion, had bound him round the neck with his tail; which, when

114

the soul was stubborn, he would draw so tight as to strangle him well-nigh, sticking into him the barbed point thereof; whereat the poor soul, Sir Rollo, would groan and roar lustily.

Now they two had come together from the gates of purgatory, being bound to these regions of fire and flame where poor sinners fry and roast *in saecula saeculorum*.

'It is hard,' said the poor Sir Rollo, as they went gliding through the clouds, 'that I should thus be condemned for ever, and all for want of a single ave.'

'How, Sir Soul?' said the demon. 'You were on earth so wicked, that not one, or a million of aves, could suffice to keep from hell-flame a creature like thee; but cheer up and be merry; thou wilt be but a subject of our lord the Devil, as am I; and, perhaps, thou wilt be advanced to posts of honour, as am I also': and to show his authority, he lashed with his tail the ribs of the wretched Rollo.

'Nevertheless, sinner as I am, one more ave would have saved me; for my sister, who was Abbess of St Mary of Chauchigny, did so prevail, by her prayer and good works, for my lost and wretched soul, that every day I felt the pains of purgatory decrease; the pitchforks which, on my first entry, had never ceased to vex and torment my poor carcass, were now not applied above once a week; the roasting had ceased, the boiling had discontinued; only a certain warmth was kept up, to remind me of my situation.'

'A gentle stew,' said the demon.

'Yea, truly, I was but in a stew, and all from the effects of the prayers of my blessed sister. But yesterday, he who watched me in purgatory told me, that yet another prayer from my sister, and my bonds should be unloosed, and I, who am now a devil, should have been a blessed angel.'

'And the other ave?' said the demon.

'She died, sir – my sister died – death choked her in the middle of the prayer.' And hereat the wretched spirit began to weep and whine piteously; his salt tears falling over his beard, and scalding the tail of Mercurius the devil.

'It is, in truth, a hard case,' said the demon; 'but I know of no remedy save patience, and for that you will have an excellent opportunity in your lodgings below.'

'But I have relations,' said the Earl; 'my kinsman Randal, who has inherited my lands, will he not say a prayer for his uncle?'

'Thou didst hate and oppress him when living.'

'It is true; but an ave is not much; his sister, my niece, Matilda –'

'You shut her in a convent, and hanged her lover.'

'Had I not reason? besides, has she not others?'

'A dozen, without a doubt.'

'And my brother, the prior?'

'A liege subject of my lord the Devil: he never opens his mouth, except to utter an oath, or to swallow a cup of wine.'

'And yet, if but one of these would but say an ave for me, I should be saved.'

'Aves with them are *rarae* aves,' replied Mercurius, wagging his tail right waggishly; 'and, what is more, I will lay thee any wager that no one of these will say a prayer to save thee.'

'I would wager willingly,' responded he of Chauchigny; 'but what has a poor soul like me to stake?'

'Every evening, after the day's roasting, my lord Satan giveth a cup of cold water to his servants; I will bet thee thy water for a year, that none of the three will pray for thee.'

'Done!' said Rollo.

'Done!' said the demon; 'and here, if I mistake not, is thy castle of Chauchigny.'

Indeed, it was true. The soul, on looking down, perceived the tall towers, the courts, the stables, and the fair gardens of the castle. Although it was past midnight, there was a blaze of light in the banqueting-hall, and a lamp burning in the open window of the Lady Matilda.

'With whom shall we begin?' said the demon: 'with the baron or the lady?'

'With the lady, if you will.'

'Be it so; her window is open, let us enter.'

So they descended, and entered silently into Matilda's chamber.

The young lady's eyes were fixed so intently on a little clock, that it was no wonder that she did not perceive the entrance of her two visitors. Her fair cheek rested in her white arm, and her white arm on the cushion of a great chair in which she sat, pleasantly supported by sweet thoughts and swansdown; a lute was at her side, and a book of prayers lay under the table (for piety is always modest). Like the amorous Alexander, she sighed and looked (at the clock) – and sighed for ten minutes or more, when she softly breathed the word 'Edward!'

At this the soul of the Baron was wroth. 'The jade is at her old pranks,' said he to the devil; and then addressing Matilda: 'I pray thee, sweet niece, turn thy thoughts for a moment from that villainous page, Edward, and give them to thine affectionate uncle.'

When she heard the voice, and saw the awful apparition of her uncle (for a year's sojourn in purgatory had not increased the comeliness of his appearance), she started, screeched, and of course fainted.

But the devil Mercurius soon restored her to herself. 'What's o'clock?' said she, as soon as she had recovered from her fit: 'is he come?'

'Not thy lover, Maude, but thine uncle – that is, his soul. For the love of heaven, listen to me: I have been frying in purgatory for a year past, and should have been in heaven but for the want of a single ave.'

'I will say it for thee tomorrow, uncle.'

'Tonight, or never.'

'Well, tonight be it': and she requested the devil Mercurius
to give her the prayer-book from under the table; but he had
no sooner touched the holy book than he dropped it with a
shriek and a yell. It was hotter, he said, than his master Sir
Lucifer's own particular pitchfork. And the lady was forced to
begin her ave without the aid of her missal.

At the commencement of her devotions the demon retired,
and carried with him the anxious soul of poor Sir Roger de
Rollo.

The lady knelt down – she sighed deeply; she looked again
at the clock, and began –

'*Ave Maria.*'

When a lute was heard under the window, and a sweet voice
singing –

'Hark!' said Matilda.

> Now the toils of day are over,
>   And the sun hath sunk to rest,
> Seeking, like a fiery lover,
>   The bosom of the blushing west –
>
> The faithful night keeps watch and ward,
>   Raising the moon, her silver shield,
> And summoning the stars to guard
>   The slumbers of my fair Mathilde!

'For mercy's sake!' said Sir Rollo, 'the ave first, and next the
song.'

So Matilda again dutifully betook her to her devotions, and
began –

'*Ave Maria gratia plena!*' but the music began again, and the
prayer ceased of course.

The faithful night! Now all things lie
   Hid by her mantle dark and dim,
In pious hope I hither hie,
   And humbly chant mine ev'ning hymn.

Thou art my prayer, my saint, my shrine!
   (For never holy pilgrim kneel'd,
Or wept at feet more pure than mine),
   My virgin love, my sweet Mathilde!

'Virgin love!' said the Baron. 'Upon my soul, this is too bad!' and he thought of the lady's lover whom he had caused to be hanged.

But *she* only thought of him who stood singing at her window.

'Niece Matilda!' cried Sir Roger, agonizedly, 'wilt thou listen to the lies of an impudent page, whilst thine uncle is waiting but a dozen words to make him happy?'

At this Matilda grew angry: 'Edward is neither impudent nor a liar, Sir Uncle, and I will listen to the end of the song.'

'Come away,' said Mercurius; 'he hath yet got wield, field, sealed, congealed, and a dozen other rhymes beside; and after the song will come the supper.'

So the poor soul was obliged to go; while the lady listened, and the page sung away till morning.

'My virtues have been my ruin,' said poor Sir Rollo, as he and Mercurius slunk silently out of the window. 'Had I hanged that knave Edward, as I did the page his predecessor, my niece would have sung mine ave, and I should have been by this time an angel in heaven.'

'He is reserved for wiser purposes,' responded the devil: 'he will assassinate your successor, the lady Mathilde's brother; and, in consequence, will be hanged. In the love of the lady he will be succeeded by a gardener, who will be replaced by a monk, who will give way to an ostler, who will be deposed by a Jew pedlar, who shall, finally, yield to a noble earl, the future husband of the fair Mathilde. So that, you see, instead of having one poor soul a-frying, we may now look forward to a goodly harvest for our lord the Devil.'

The soul of the Baron began to think that his companion knew too much for one who would make fair bets; but there was no help for it; he would not, and he could not cry off: and he prayed inwardly that the brother might be found more pious than the sister.

But there seemed little chance of this. As they crossed the court, lackeys, with smoking dishes and full jugs, passed and repassed continually, although it was long past midnight. On entering the hall, they found Sir Randal at the head of a vast table, surrounded by a fiercer and more motley collection of individuals than had congregated there even in the time of Sir Rollo. The lord of the castle had signified that 'it was his royal pleasure to be drunk', and the gentlemen of his train had obsequiously followed their master. Mercurius was delighted with the scene, and relaxed his usually rigid countenance into a bland and benevolent smile, which became him wonderfully.

The entrance of Sir Roger, who had been dead about a year, and a person with hoofs, horns and a tail, rather disturbed the hilarity of the company. Sir Randal dropped his cup of wine; and Father Peter, the confessor, incontinently paused in the midst of a profane song, with which he was amusing the society.

'Holy Mother!' cried he, 'it is Sir Roger.'

'Alive!' screamed Sir Randal.

'No, my lord,' Mercurius said; 'Sir Roger is dead, but cometh on a matter of business; and I have the honour to act as his counsellor and attendant.'

'Nephew,' said Sir Roger, 'the demon saith justly; I am come on a trifling affair, in which thy service is essential.'

'I will do anything, uncle, in my power.'

'Thou canst give me life, if thou wilt?' But Sir Randal looked very blank at this proposition. 'I mean life spiritual, Randal,' said Sir Roger; and thereupon he explained to him the nature of the wager.

Whilst he was telling his story, his companion Mercurius was playing all sorts of antics in the hall; and, by his wit and fun, became so popular with this godless crew, that they lost all the fear which his first appearance had given them. The friar was wonderfully taken with him, and used his utmost eloquence and endeavours to convert the devil; the knights stopped drinking to listen to the argument; the men-at-arms forbore brawling; and the wicked little pages crowded round the two strange disputants, to hear their edifying discourse. The ghostly man, however, had little chance in the controversy, and certainly little learning to carry it on. Sir Randal interrupted him.

'Father Peter,' said he, 'our kinsman is condemned for ever, for want of a single ave: wilt thou say it for him?'

'Willingly, my lord,' said the monk, 'with my book'; and accordingly he produced his missal to read, without which aid it appeared that the holy father could not manage the desired prayer. But the crafty Mercurius had, by his devilish art, inserted a song in the place of the ave, so that Father Peter, instead of chanting a hymn, sang the following irreverent ditty:

> Some love the matin-chimes, which tell
>   The hour of prayer to sinner:
> But better far's the midday bell,
>   Which speaks the hour of dinner;
> For when I see a smoking fish,
>   Or capon drowned in gravy,

Or noble haunch on silver dish,
　Full glad I sing mine ave.

My pulpit is an ale-house bench,
　Whereon I sit so jolly;
A smiling rosy country wench
　My saint and patron holy.
I kiss her cheek so red and sleek,
　I press her ringlets wavy.
And in her willing ear I speak
　A most religious ave.

And if I'm blind, yet heaven is kind,
　And holy saints forgiving;
For sure he leads a right good life
　Who thus admires good living.
Above they say, our flesh is air,
　Our blood celestial ichor:
Oh, grant! mid all the changes there,
　They may not change our liquor!

And with this pious wish the holy confessor tumbled
under the table in an agony of devout drunkenness; whilst
the knights, the men-at-arms, and the wicked little pages,
rang out the last verse with a most melodious and emphatic
glee.

'I am sorry, fair uncle,' hiccuped Sir Randal, 'that, in the
matter of the ave, we could not oblige thee in a more orthodox
manner; but the holy father has failed, and there is not another
man in the hall who hath an idea of a prayer.'

'It is my own fault,' said Sir Rollo; 'for I hanged the last
confessor.' And he wished his nephew a surly good-night, as
he prepared to quit the room.

'*Au revoir*, gentlemen,' said the devil Mercurius; and once more fixed his tail round the neck of his disappointed companion.

The spirit of poor Rollo was sadly cast down; the devil, on the contrary, was in high good humour. He wagged his tail with the most satisfied air in the world, and cut a hundred jokes at the expense of his poor associate. On they sped, cleaving swiftly through the cold night winds, frightening the birds that were roosting in the woods, and the owls that were watching in the towers.

In the twinkling of an eye, as it is known, devils can fly hundreds of miles: so that almost the same beat of the clock which left those two in Champagne found them hovering over Paris. They dropped into the court of the Lazarist Convent, and winded their way, through passage and cloister, until they reached the door of the prior's cell.

Now the prior, Rollo's brother, was a wicked and malignant sorcerer; his time was spent in conjuring devils and doing wicked deeds, instead of fasting, scourging, and singing holy psalms: this Mercurius knew; and he, therefore, was fully at ease as to the final result of his wager with poor Sir Roger.

'You seem to be well acquainted with the road,' said the knight.

'I have reason,' answered Mercurius, 'having, for a long period, had the acquaintance of his reverence, your brother; but you have little chance with him.'

'And why?' said Sir Rollo.

'He is under a bond to my master, never to say a prayer, or else his soul and his body are forfeited at once.'

'Why, thou false and traitorous devil!' said the enraged knight;—'and thou knewest this when we made our wager?'

'Undoubtedly: do you suppose I would have done so had there been any chance of losing?'

And with this they arrived at Father Ignatius's door.

'Thy cursed presence threw a spell on my niece, and stopped

the tongue of my nephew's chaplain; I do believe that had I seen either of them alone, my wager had been won.'

'Certainly; therefore, I took good care to go with thee; however, thou mayest see the prior alone, if thou wilt; and lo! his door is open. I will stand without for five minutes when it will be time to commence our journey.'

It was the poor Baron's last chance: and he entered his brother's room more for the five minutes' respite than from any hope of success.

Father Ignatius, the prior, was absorbed in magic calculations: he stood in the middle of a circle of skulls, with no garment except his long white beard, which reached to his knees; he was waving a silver rod, and muttering imprecations in some horrible tongue.

But Sir Rollo came forward and interrupted his incantation. 'I am,' said he, 'the shade of thy brother Roger de Rollo; and have come, from pure brotherly love, to warn thee of thy fate.'

'Whence camest thou?'

'From the abode of the blessed in Paradise,' replied Sir Roger, who was inspired with a sudden thought; 'it was but five minutes ago that the Patron Saint of thy church told me of thy danger, and of thy wicked compact with the fiend. "Go," said he, "to thy miserable brother, and tell him there is but one way by which he may escape from paying the awful forfeit of his bond."'

'And how may that be?' said the prior; 'the false fiend hath deceived me; I have given him my soul, but have received no worldly benefit in return. Brother! dear brother! how may I escape?'

'I will tell thee. As soon as I heard the voice of blessed St Mary Lazarus' (the worthy Earl had, at a pinch, coined the name of a saint), 'I left the clouds, where, with other angels, I was seated, and sped hither to save thee. "Thy brother," said the Saint, "hath but one day more to live, when he will become for all eternity the subject of Satan; if he would escape, he must boldly break his bond, by saying an ave."''

'It is the express condition of the agreement,' said the unhappy monk, 'I must say no prayer, or that instant I become Satan's, body and soul.'

'It is the express condition of the Saint,' answered Roger, fiercely; 'pray, brother, pray, or thou art lost for ever.'

So the foolish monk knelt down, and devoutly sung out an ave. 'Amen!' said Sir Roger, devoutly.

'Amen!' said Mercurius, as, suddenly, coming behind, he seized Ignatius by his long beard, and flew up with him to the top of the church-steeple.

The monk roard, and screamed, and swore against his brother; but it was of no avail: Sir Roger smiled kindly on him, and said, 'Do not fret, brother; it must have come to this in a year or two.'

And he flew alongside of Mercurius to the steeple-top; *but this time the devil had not his tail round his neck.* 'I will let thee off thy bet,' said he to the demon; for he could afford, now, to be generous.

'I believe, my lord,' said the demon, politely, 'that our ways separate here.' Sir Roger sailed gaily upwards: while Mercurius having bound the miserable monk faster than ever, he sunk downwards to earth, and perhaps lower. Ignatius was heard roaring and screaming as the devil dashed him against the iron spikes and buttresses of the church.

The Case of the
Reverend Mr Toomey

'S. B. T.'

The time has come when the truth of this matter should be set on record.

I was six-and-twenty, sparkling with diplomas, full of science, when I joined my father in the Tyneside village of Cloughshaw; and the step to a partnership in the family practice was a crowning glory.

At Oxford I had found peace from the turmoil of an adolescent conscience under the direction of a Jesuit father. Later on, it is true, things went badly with me – to wit, when I came up to London and began to attend lectures at a famous medical school. It was not long before little matters which had been the subject of blushing confidences beneath the pale gleam of the half-seen ivory Christ furnished matter for ribald conversation in an atmosphere of tobacco and alcohol; and by the time the Royal College of Surgeons had gained in me an efficient member, the Catholic Church had practically lost a son.

Spring was melting into summer when I took possession of the rooms set apart for me in the wide rambling house that was my father's: earth was habited in new green; Easter smiled behind the tragedy of Holy Week.

On Good Friday morning I rode down the home side of the valley, across the wide, shallow river, and, bending to the left half-way up the opposite hill, followed the windings of a shady road as far as the park gates of Ridstowe Castle, a country house, the property of an ancient family by tradition faithful to the Old Religion. Upon the farther side of the house stands the Presbytery, where the family chaplain resides; his house-keeper it was whom my father had placed upon my list.

I committed my horse to a groom, for I had a purpose of assisting at the offices of the day, and walked the remaining hundred yards along a lane that shone with last night's downpour, past the prim little Presbytery standing four-square upon its margin, to the Catholic chapel.

This chapel is built in a parallelogram of stone fencing, end-long to the lane, which bends sharply to the left; and is backed by an amphitheatre of green hills. One of them carries a faint scar, the work of pious feet, bearing to the right over its brow. But for a stone cross surmounting its western gable, the building might be a barn for its simplicity, if you should fail to note at the farther or eastward end the little rusty bell swinging in a crutch of masonry.

One side of this, I remember, was prolonged with an iron funnel, whence a thread of blue smoke went slenderly up.

The inside, as I found upon opening the door, matched well with this exterior. From the left, immediately within, came the warm gleam of candles, reflected from poor red hangings about the little temporary altar where, since the Mass of the day before, the sepulchred Sacrament had reposed. Rough benches accommodated a scanty congregation of simple folk, grey-headed many of them, tanned and whole-some, a few damsels of some pretension to gentility, a sprinkling of bright-eyed children. The high altar of rough sandstone faced me, stripped and cold, with its candles yet unlit. The priest at the Gospel side in a low harsh voice was reciting the Passion according to St John, while the people stood patiently and reverently, some telling their beads, some reading an English version of the narrative, some vaguely immersed in contemplation; the children striving for the most part with miniature jests to relieve the tedium of an unintelligible rite. I watched the officiant. A huge bulk of a red-haired, bull-throated personage, he stood there at the simple altar, his back from half to three-quarters towards me, leaning slightly forward over the missal, reading away for his life. His stature and vast proportions seemed to dwarf his environment, the oblong of his black chasuble to be but a patch upon the whiteness of the broad-stretched alb. Having finished the Passion, he turned and received his biretta from the server. I composed myself to an air of respectful attention.

It was not long, nor was it difficult to understand, the discourse that was roared from the altar-steps in tones of a trombone inflated with a zeal that is not according to knowledge: an orthodox exposition of the doctrine of Sacrifice; its terms crude, the application narrow. The gnawing of an empty stomach perhaps suggested to the preacher that much was yet to do before it might receive the solacement it craved, and he drew with welcome precipitancy to a close.

Meanwhile I had had time and a fair opportunity more exactly to observe him. At the base of a brow that retreated swiftly aloft bushy red tufts shadowed the caves in which smouldered two lacklustre eyes of indeterminate colour; a fat snub nose, with round distended nostrils, was mounted above an upper lip of portentous length; the mouth was wide and loose, the teeth jagged and discoloured; the chin and lower jaw were those of a prize-fighter. The accent which differentiated his speech I conjectured to be the strange resultant of Irish home influences modified by years spent at the Scots College under Italian professors, and subsequent residence in the North of England.

The ceremonies of the Mass of the Presanctified were resumed. Three audible grunts accompanied the triple genuflection with which the officiant in his stockinged feet led the way to pay reverence to the Crucifix lying cushioned before the Communion-rail. His offering for the Holy Places he deposited wrapped modestly in paper; and presently after, a little procession wended to the altar of repose.

I had never seen the ritual of the Church carried out with this extreme simplicity – the barest rubrical necessities, and no note of music to disguise the shuffling of heavy boots. Four grey-headed yeomen carried the simple canopy, whose bells tinkled warning of the priest's return bearing the Holy of Holies in a little fragrant cloud.

So strangely are common things transfigured by the touch of the great Mother Church. This dowdy little act of faith, by its very squalor of circumstance, moved me as nothing had had the power since the Pope's Mass, years before, and the silver trumpets. The rough features of the attendants were rigid with devout recollection; the priest's massive face was composed to a grave aspect of conscious responsibility, and his eyes were reverently fastened upon the swathed burden of the sepulchred Sacrament. A beam from a southern window lit up his cropped hair to a shining aureola.

Outside the chapel, while the people trailed heavily up the track to the top of the hill and disappeared one by one, I awaited his coming; and the last was hardly out of sight when, with a light coat drawn over his soutane, he issued. On seeing me he stretched out at once a cordial hand.

'I bid you welcome, sir,' he cried in his composite brogue. 'You'll be, I doubt not, Dr Moyes, the younger of the name. Your respectable father gave me to understand that your advent was expected, and that you were of the Household of the Faith.'

'On Tuesday I arrived,' I answered. 'A most interesting little church you have here, and a charming corner of the world this, to live in. The building, snug between the hills, has a romantic air; hidden away, one might guess, from persecution in the good old times of prescription and the penal laws. Eighteenth century?'

'Bedad, sir, and you've mistaken entirely, though I don't say but it may have the air. Thirty years is the outside of its age; built by the gentleman who owns yon house and supports the mission. A great gentleman in London, but we see nothing of him here. He is proud of the church.'

'Why, as to its architectural pretensions –'

'Architecture! He boasts that it is the cheapest church in the land.'

'Ah, in that case it may be that he has foundation.'

'More than the building has, you'll agree, if you observed the walls. But you'll come into my house and let me offer you a little refreshment?'

We were at the door, and I followed him in. The room (he named it parlour) was such as I had expected to find it – poor, not with the clean, wholesome nakedness of St Francis' bride, but with the tawdriness of early-Victorian frippery. Set along two adjacent sides were half a dozen horsehair-covered chairs; a third wall was skirted by a sofa of uninviting exterior, from the vantage-ground of whose shining convexities a lace antimacassar perplexed the eye and set the teeth on edge. The centre of the scheme was a round mahogany table draped with a distressing entanglement of black ivy-leaves upon a scarlet ground. A gilt-framed mirror was based upon the mantel; below, an arrested rapid of coloured paper cloaked the empty grate.

'And there's my housekeeper, good woman: you'll be combining professional with religious duties, sir. I'll be right glad you should see her: I have faith in young men; for your science is not like mine, which can tell you little more than it could in the days of St Thomas Aquinas: and it's enough too, and be damned to it – we'll know the rest in good time. But

130

this good woman of mine, Dr Moyes,' he resumed anxiously, 'you'll do your best for her, sir? She's not as young as she was. She must be kept going – kept on, and on; be kept going, you understand, because I can't do without her – can't do without her.'

The speech ended with a silly quaver, and I stared at him. The bully host was eclipsed, and what emotion had wrought the change I could not understand; but, to my thinking, the man seemed afraid.

A lad brought in coffee and a light breakfast. After supplying me, he filled a vast beaker for himself and consumed it greedily, with infinite hoisting of eyebrow tufts and protrusion of heavy lips, with much puffing, and with noisy inarticulate expressions of satisfaction. He drank a second, and a third, sent the coffee-pot out to be refilled, and began upon the modest collation permitted in addition to the solitary full meal of a fast-day.

'It's a sore trial to a man of my physique, Dr Moyes, is the law of fasting. I am grievously tempted whiles to seek dispensation, but there's that in me likes ill to be beaten.' I expressed sympathy. 'And now,' he continued, 'perhaps you would like to meet Mrs Nolan – that keeps my house?'

The housekeeper I found to be a tall, dark Irishwoman, some fifty years of age, becomingly habited with strict regard to neatness in a dark gown set closely upon a spare figure, which apparently had yielded nothing of its spring and vigour to advancing years. Her iron-grey hair, parted in the mathematical middle, and drawn symmetrically to right and left over her ears, was surmounted by a decent cap. She was said to be suffering from an aneurism, and my brief examination tended to confirm the theory. It was further evident that her nerves were in a strained, overwrought condition. There was an appearance of tension about the pallid face; her eyes were stretched to a weary watchfulness; the white lips were sucked in at the corners, as if to constrain them to immobility; her emaciated body leaned forward as if awaiting the signal of an invisible starter. The woman's manner was full of suppressions, of suspicions, of delayed hopes, of anticipated causes of terror.

When I questioned her as to her state of health her manner evinced indifference; it was that of one who is forced by a tactless companion to pursue a tasteless talk. I had even to reassure myself by a direct question whether there were anyone else in need of my services. Her sharp features became more pinched, her deep-set grey eyes lightened at me. Satisfied by her glance, she resumed her former demeanour as swiftly as on the instant she had left it, and lapsed into her previous condition of preoccupied civility. Having seen me at church –

'A Catholic?' she asked, with some animation.

'Of sorts.'

'Well, there is, maybe, hope for us yet,' she said, only half aloud; 'but I am getting an old woman.'

I took no pains to understand this comment on my answer; not every riddle is worth the reding.

'And what,' enquired her master upon my return to the parlour, 'might you think of her state of health?'

'I am but young to the trade, yet I cannot suffer your Reverence to rifle me of an opinion at such short notice.'

'That's well said – I will not press you. She is sixty, and I am forty; which, think you, has the better life?'

I smiled; it seemed a sufficient answer. His face clouded.

'There are other housekeepers,' I hinted.

'Who was denying it?' he cried roughly. 'And other priests, aye, and other doctors too; and what then?'

The tone of this reply reduced me to silence, and shortly after I took my leave.

The study into which on the occasion of my next visit he profusely welcomed me was a shade less dazzling than the parlour. On the shelves were ranged the standard books of theology, among them Gury's *Casus Conscientiæ*, St Alphonsus' *Homo Apostolicus*, a copy of the *Summa*, Lingard's *History of England* in eight volumes, and the three spare tomes of a Mechlin Breviary. A large writing-table, supporting a crucifix and an image of Our Lady, and faced by a swivel chair, strove to suggest literary habits.

Upon the table, under the sheet of a local newspaper, peeped the shining segment of an iron ring.

My host followed me fussily, and gesticulated me into an easy chair. Seated, I found myself opposite the window, with the profile of the hearth and the length of the writing-table intervening. He turned to the latter to draw the swivel-chair nearer to me; there was an unevenness in his movements, and when his face came again into view it was dusky and the deep-set little eyes glanced towards me apprehensively. I averted mine, sweeping the table as I turned to the view from the window; the steel was hidden.

I made a remark about the fishing-tackle, of which there was plenty. His face smoothed.

'You'll be a sportsman, sir?'

'I am no fisherman, father.'

'You like a more vigorous sport. You're a strong man, Dr Moyes: a fine pair of shoulders you have on you, and your horse has need to be up to a heavy weight.'

'Twelve-stone-seven I rowed in the trials – for the University eight, you know – but I am in no sort of condition now.'

He fixed his eyes upon me watchfully.

'I am a strong man myself,' he said. 'Have you an arm to beat that?' And to my surprise he began to divest himself of his cassock and to roll up his shirt-sleeve. The childish display was accompanied by nothing of boastfulness; rather, as he gazed at the knotted muscles, his face clouded with profound dejection. In compliance with his request I exposed my arm for comparison. He paid me a compliment, and concluded, with a sigh, 'You're little more than a child to me.' It was the truth.

I paid a visit to Mrs Nolan in her room. Hers was a case for which a doctor could do little; and after giving her some general advice I returned to the study. The priest was sitting in a brooding attitude before the paper Niagara, and seemed hardly aware of my entrance. The woman came in behind me.

'Just to bid your Reverence good-day.' And I offered a hand.

He hardly touched it, and turning to the housekeeper said in a husky voice, 'The lamp!'

The woman smothered an ejaculation, and her face was white as a leper's while she hurriedly guided me to the door.

Before I had descended the three little white steps it was abruptly closed.

This was the Tuesday in Easter week. On Wednesday I heard that Father Toomey's housekeeper was dead.

I waited a day, and received no summons. On Thursday I determined to call.

The man himself came to the door. He looked flabby and frightened. His eyes were red, his great cheeks hung down, his shoulders were bowed; shame and defiance were mingled in his bearing.

'I saw who it was,' he said; 'and though I did not send for you, you are welcome. There is a woman here who has done what was necessary, but there must be a certificate. This way – follow me.'

He led upstairs to a darkened room, where the scent of flowers was heavy in the air, with the effluvia of burning wax. Six yellow flames stooped towards the open door.

The face was bare, and almost seemed that of a young woman. A holy-water stoup with an aspersory stood at the feet.

'I will send the woman up to you,' he said, 'in case you think it necessary to make any examination.'

When I descended, I believed myself justified in certifying that the woman died from the rupture of an aneurism.

Downstairs in the study the priest was sitting doubled up in his armchair, and his face wore a grey look of despair which, while it moved pity, kindled once again my curiosity as to the true relations of these persons; for that they were merely those of master and servant I could not pretend to believe. It was no business of mine – and yet, who could say?

'A great loss to you, Father Toomey. I condole with you very sincerely, believe me.' And I took his hand, which was limp and cold.

'You would say so,' he replied, 'if you knew all. Did you ever lose a mother?' he asked, looking up.

'My mother is living.'

'Mine is dead; you have just seen all that is left of her. But what is that – a mother? Most men live to see their mothers die; it is the order of Nature. But not while they have need of them – my God! – need of them. You wonder,' he went on, constraining his tone, 'how you came to find her here in the character of a housekeeper?'

'Tell me nothing more than you are disposed to say: I ask for no confidences.'

'Oh, it was simple: just a mother's pride – an Irish mother's pride – that has a son a priest. I must have a servant, and she must be there to see the glory – rest her soul! – that is how it began. And then – then, sir, came the need!'

'The need?'

'The need.' He steadied his gaze upon me as he spoke, leaning forward with his elbow on his knee and his great chin resting on the palm of his hand.

'It is not difficult to conceive that the loss of your mother's presence will be a bitter grief to you,' I began.

He laughed in my face, and the sound was not a merry one.

'My dear young man, we are two professional consolers; and we know too well the tricks of the trade to derive consolation from them. Also, allow me to say, you clean mistake the situation. If she that's gone had been related to me in any other degree of consanguinity, or in none, I'd be in just the same quandary. I will be frank with you, and you shall give me your professional word to observe my confidence; at present I can see but one way out of it – and that goes straight to Hell.'

I looked at him, and he meant it.

'Father Toomey,' I said, after a moment's reflection, 'you have given me a confidence which I would gladly have been dispensed from receiving – enough to make me very anxious about you, while it leaves me perfectly impotent to aid. I can imagine no motive for your saying so much unless a fancy that I may be able to help you; and that I will do very readily if you will show me how. But you must be good enough to tell me more. I am still too much in the dark to pretend to be of the slightest assistance. If you are willing to give me your full confidence I am ready to guard it.'

During this long exhortation he had grown distracted. I waited for an answer, but none came. Then rising abruptly, and stretching out his hand as I was preparing to leave him: 'The funeral,' he said, 'will be on Friday. Goodbye.'

'Come and see me on Friday,' he cried, as I mounted.

I nodded a promise.

Mr Toomey celebrated the Requiem Mass on the Friday with about as much show of emotion as if the intention were one of a batch. He aspersed the corpse with an air of conscious efficiency; and when it had been lowered into the grave, turned his back at once, doffed the sacred vestments, and returned to the house ravening. I found him swilling coffee at a vast rate.

His mood seemed uncommunicative, but I waited on. The man's affairs were nothing to me: the less I knew of them, perhaps, the better; yet if he had need of my assistance, either as a doctor or as a fellow-creature, he should have his opportunity. Half an hour of his futile chatter wearied me; I remembered that there were patients, and rose to go.

'Goodbye, sir, and God bless you! It was a kind attention on your part to assist at the Mass today. And as to the matter I spoke to you about when last you were here – well, you'll please to forget it. I was not, perhaps, altogether myself at the time, and since then I have seen reason to believe that the affair is settled. The good woman that's gone, I have little doubt, has attained to her reward; she was a saint; and I know I can depend upon her making good use of her opportunities.'

He watched me away, with a confident smile upon his wide face.

For a fortnight I saw nothing of him. I had no professional call to his house, and the man himself, with his abrupt changes from morbid dread to a chuckling security – from what? – did not please me. There was something inhuman about him.

Then, on Thursday of the third week, as I was on the point to set out for my afternoon round, a telegram: 'At once; come without delay. – Toomey.'

Nothing less than a case of extreme necessity could excuse its peremptory tone. His confidence in heavenly intercession appeared to be intermittent.

'How is Father Toomey?' I asked of the lad who opened the door.

'Father Toomey is quite well,' he answered, 'thank you, sir.'

'The devil he is!' I thought; 'and that is a piece of impertinence on his part anyway, unless the new housekeeper is the patient.'

'Who is ill?' I asked.

'Nobody,' he replied.

'Is Father Toomey in?'

'He is in, sir: will you step forward?'

I stepped forward, opened the door of the study, and, without waiting to be announced, walked in.

'What brings you?' he asked, looking at me dully.

I showed him the telegram. 'You sent it?' I enquired.

'Aye, I sent it, and it's that has been troubling me – whether I had or no. I had an impression, but they are treacherous things.'

'Telegrams?'

'Impressions.'

'And now, perhaps, you will tell me what it is you want?'

'Want! Help it is I want, and shielding, and constraining, maybe; and strengthening to strive against it, and hope to win through with it, and a stout heart to give me courage; and where shall I look for them? I know of none for certain in the width and length of the land who can help me through. There was one: she is gone.'

'Let me, at least –'

'You must not interrupt me,' he hurried on, with an impetuous gesture. 'I have chosen to place confidence in you, and you must not fail me. You have a strong head and strong arms, if the call comes, and, I do believe, a strong heart; and it's of that above all there is need; for you must help me alone, and you must keep my secret. I am a priest, mind you; I love my office; I will live and die in the service of the altar.'

'My dear Father Toomey, I protest I have not the ghost of an idea what you are driving at, or what it is you want me to do; but it shall be done if it lies reasonably within my power.'

'Will you spend this night here?'

'You are very kind.'

'You will perhaps not say that tomorrow. I ask you as a favour; I beg you not to say no.'

'I will spend the night here.'

'Thank you – thank God! There is a saint above, and I do think there is no need, but I dare not watch by myself.' He turned his eyes upon me.

'You'll stay now?' he asked.

'I have patients.'

'Tomorrow for them?'

'Today.'

'What time will you be back?'

'Seven your dinner-hour?'

'It shall be. You'll not be late?'

'You may depend on me.'

We sat silent after dinner, smoking, thinking. I had learned the ugly story; the origin of his sufferings (but I am not to write his confession), the various forms of the recurrent horror, through which the mother had devoted herself to his service, his hopes for the future. And particularly he had shown me his spirits swinging between exultation and despair for the event of that cardinal night.

The long hand hid the short at the apex of the dial, the hammer rang upon the silver gong.

'The new day!' he cried. ' 'Tis good to have a friend at Court.'

My heart went forth to the man, and I stretched out my hand. There was no response. I looked. His face had fallen; the ray of exultation had deserted it, its ruddiness was fled, its lines gone smooth, its character all changed.

His voice when he spoke was another voice, thin and piping; I could scarcely realize that it came from the same throat. And he seemed to strive with a recalcitrant tongue; as a man strives in a dream to make his speech articulate, he babbled awhile

139

before the vagrant syllables cohered into words – into a phrase:

'Mother – the lamp – is going down!'

His eyes were directed, not to the globe which lighted the room, but towards a spot on the wall to one side of it. They were silly and unfocussed, like machines out of gear, and the voice was the voice of a frightened child. The man's whole frame, too, had lost its tenseness and vigour, and had gone slack, like his face. His arms hung limply over the sides of the chair, the veins at the back of them all swollen. His knees leaned foolishly against each other, the feet apart; his tufted red eyebrows, raised ridiculously, showed the little doting eyes too large. I knew that his hope had failed him, that it rested with me to save the man from the dangers to which, while the trial should endure, he would be exposed. For years his mother's magnetic presence had been his safeguard, so that the means of forcible restraint, the chance glimpse of which some time before had surprised me, had been unnecessary. But tonight he was in strange hands, and when I looked at the herculean form opposed to me, and remembered that within a certain space it might be as animated by a wild beast – when I remembered that by my promise I was bound to worry through the trial alone, without aid from any other creature – I confess that my heart sank.

The further events of this night, as I am about to record them, I have no theory to explain. A theologian would be ready enough with his solution; but I am a man of science, and shall content myself with writing down the things I saw and heard.

Presently the clouded eyes cleared, the loose mouth took shape, the dangling knock-kneed form was braced, and the person who sat there spoke.

The voice was the voice of a stranger – different from the childish falsetto which had whined of the failing light, quite another than the brassy roar in which the priest was accustomed to speak. This voice was round and full, and rich with musical modulations. The Reverend Mr Toomey talked habitually with an accent of blended provincialism; grammatically indeed, but with the pedantic syntax of a man whose ears had first been opened amongst the illiterate. The Voice spoke a language of noble literary form, articulated with a due consciousness of syllabic force and the distinction of vowel sounds. And the matter of the discourse offered a still more striking contrast. But my wits are too dull, my pen too clumsy to record the words that streamed from those gross lips during the hours of that wonderful night.

It was the speech of one to whom the events of the twilight past, to others matter of difficult conjecture, were of secure knowledge – the recurrence of ice-ages the incidents of a circling year. The secrets that scientists are feeling after he betrayed, as if by inadvertence, and apologized. History was unfolded, as by photographs thrown three hundred a minute onto a screen; the astonished hearer saw the world's events happen; smelt carnage, tasted blood; the music of pæans, the chuckle of successful diplomacy, sounded in his ears.

With fiery, luminous phrase he painted wonders of other worlds, as might have done a tout for some celestial Cook; every word convincing as a bullet, phrases that made the mind blink as at the bright shining of new horizons.

All literature was open, from the *Vedas* to the last sonnet of the last new minor poet. The speaker knew all philosophies with the intimacy of one who has watched (as one might watch under a microscope the activities of an anthill) great minds at work.

Hour after hour the wondrous golden speech flowed on, and held me hypnotized.

It was five o'clock, and the light of the young day crept through crevices in the shutters. There was a pause. Then the mouth

141

opened again, and this time the Voice sang. At first a barbarous recitative, the long passages of monotone relieved by rare and vague inflections; the words articulate but unintelligible, and that not with the unintelligibility of a contemporary foreign speech, but with the doubtfulness of semi-bestial sounds indicative of simple emotions. The tone became purer, the intervals more justly defined; the scales were unfamiliar, but the melodies expressed the emotions of civilized life; and from the deepest recesses of my memory blurred reminiscences of the Greek classics came flitting forth in response. Great songs, caught from the dying breath of defunct races and vanished societies, hymned the elemental forces, Nature's springs.

Beneath the vaulting of a mediæval choir black-robed Benedictines chanted the great pæan of the Veiled Presence, *Lauda Sion Salvatorem*, and candles were red through incense fog. A puff of ribald parody extinguished them.

A certain fugue of Bach's in A, not printed in the ordinary collections, is familiar to me. That fugue the singer sang, all the twining phrases of it, in four distinct voices from his one mouth. While he sang I watched him, and this is what I am prepared to attest: that during the whole of that weird performance Mr Toomey's chest was *still*.

Of the paroxysm which he had warned me was customarily the last phase of the seizure, I had seen no sign. The means of restraint were to my hand, but I let the moment pass. A full chord from the one mouth, and then, in the pause of half a bar, the change came. The eyes became suffused and glared shiftily upon my face, the red shock of hair bristled erect, the yellow teeth were bare of the quivering updrawn lip, and with a snarl the Beast was upon me.

The blow with which I met the oncoming hardly checked it. The face where I had struck showed a hollow, but the creature's course was not stayed, nor did the burning eyes so much as blink; only the assailant modified his manner of

142

attack. The hands, which had been stretched towards my neck, seized upon my left arm, which had struck, and, while the creature's head was recklessly exposed to my right hand, the fangs crunched through the flesh of my left forearm and gnawed the bones.

The agony of this bestial attack multiplied my force. By a supreme effort I threw the grunting devil to the floor. He dragged me with him by his teeth still grimly fleshed, while with my free hand I strove to clutch his windpipe. In vain I stiffened my fingers upon the great throat; there was no sign of congestion about the face, the eyes burned with the same fire of undistracted cruelty, the heavy jawbone ground upon the lacerated limb as we rolled over and over in the stale light of the smoking lamp.

Upon our death-grapple broke in the tinkle of the bell from the little church, the first stroke of the morning Angelus. The Beast's teeth relaxed, and I fell round onto my back, lost for the moment to consciousness. The last strokes were still sounding when I recovered my senses and sprang up.

There upon the carpet lay the body of the Beast. From the widespread nostrils issued no breath; the eyes were open and glassy. I laid my hand upon the region of the heart; there was not the faintest flutter.

And the corpse of the man with whom not a hundred seconds before I had been at death-grips was stone cold. My fist had dented – not bruised – the face. That is, the man had been dead for hours.

But upon the fallen jaw my blood *was wet*.

The Story of the Unknown Church

William Morris

I was the master-mason of a church that was built more than
six hundred years ago; it is now two hundred years since that
church vanished from the face of the earth; it was destroyed
utterly – no fragment of it was left; not even the great pillars
that bore up the tower at the cross, where the choir used to join
the nave. No one knows now even where it stood, only in this
very autumn-tide, if you knew the place, you would see the
heaps made by the earth-covered ruins heaving the yellow
corn into glorious waves, so that the place where my church
used to be is as beautiful now as when it stood in all its
splendour. I do not remember very much about the land where
my church was; I have quite forgotten the name of it, but I
know it was very beautiful, and even now, while I am thinking
of it, comes a flood of old memories, and I almost seem to see
it again – that old beautiful land! only dimly do I see it in
spring and summer and winter, but I see it in autumn-tide
clearly now; yes, clearer, clearer, oh! so bright and glorious!
yet it was beautiful too in spring, when the brown earth began
to grow green: beautiful in summer, when the blue sky looked
so much bluer, if you could hem a piece of it in between the
new white carving; beautiful in the solemn starry nights, so
solemn that it almost reached agony – the awe and joy one had
in their great beauty. But of all these beautiful times I
remember the whole only of autumn-tide; the others come

in bits to me; I can think only of parts of them, but all of autumn; and of all days and nights in autumn I remember one more particularly. That autumn day the church was nearly finished, and the monks, for whom we were building the church, and the people, who lived in the town hard by, crowded round us oftentimes to watch us carving.

Now the great church, and the buildings of the Abbey where the monks lived, were about three miles from the town, and the town stood on a hill overlooking the rich autumn country: it was girt about with great walls that had overhanging battlements, and towers at certain places all along the walls, and often we could see from the churchyard or the Abbey garden the flash of helmets and spears, and the dim shadowy waving of banners, as the knights and lords and men-at-arms passed to and fro along the battlements; and we could see too in the town the three spires of the three churches; and the spire of the Cathedral, which was the tallest of the three, was gilt all over with gold, and always at night-time a great lamp shone from it that hung in the spire midway between the roof of the church and the cross at the top of the spire. The Abbey where we built the church was not girt by stone walls, but by a circle of poplar trees, and whenever a wind passed over them, were it ever so little a breath, it set them all a-ripple; and when the wind was high they bowed and swayed very low, and the wind, as it lifted the leaves and showed their silvery white sides, or as again in the lulls of it, it let them drop, kept on changing the trees from green to white, and white to green; moreover, through the boughs and trunks of the poplars, we caught glimpses of the great golden corn sea; waving, waving, waving for leagues and leagues; and among the corn grew burning scarlet poppies and blue cornflowers; and the corn-flowers were so blue that they gleamed, and seemed to burn with a steady light, as they grew beside the poppies among the gold of the wheat. Through the corn sea ran a blue river, and

always green meadows and lines of tall poplars followed its
windings. The old church had been burned, and that was the
reason why the monks caused me to build the new one; the
buildings of the Abbey were built at the same time as the
burned-down church, more than a hundred years before I was
born, and they were on the north side of the church, and joined
to it by a cloister of round arches, and in the midst of the
cloister was a lawn, and in the midst of that lawn a fountain of
marble, carved round about with flowers and strange beasts;
and at the edge of the lawn, near the round arches, were a great
many sunflowers that were all in blossom on that autumn day;
and up many of the pillars of the cloister crept passion-flowers
and roses. Then farther from the church, and past the cloister
and its buildings, were many detached buildings, and a great
garden round them, all within the circle of the poplar trees; in
the garden were trellises covered over with roses and con-
volvulus and the great-leaved fiery nasturtium; and specially
all along by the poplar trees were there trellises, but on these
grew nothing but deep crimson roses; the hollyhocks too were
all out in blossom at that time, great spires of pink, and
orange, and red, and white, with their soft downy leaves. I said
that nothing grew on the trellises by the poplars but crimson
roses, but I was not quite right, for in many places the wild
flowers had crept into the garden from without; lush green
briony, with green-white blossoms that grows so fast, one
could almost think that we see it grow, and deadly nightshade,
La bella donna. Oh! so beautiful; red berry, and purple,
yellow-spiked flower, and deadly, cruel-looking, dark green
leaf, all growing together in the glorious days of early autumn.
And in the midst of the great garden was a conduit, with its
sides carved with histories from the Bible, and there was on it
too, as on the fountain in the cloister, much carving of flowers
and strange beasts. Now the church itself was surrounded on
every side but the north by the cemetery, and there were many

graves there, both of monks and of laymen, and often the friends of those, whose bodies lay there, had planted flowers about the graves of those they loved. I remember one such particularly, for at the head of it was a cross of carved wood, and at the foot of it, facing the cross, three tall sunflowers; then in the midst of the cemetery was a cross of stone, carved on one side with the Crucifixion of our Lord Jesus Christ, and on the other with Our Lady holding the Divine Child. So that day that I specially remember in autumn-tide, when the church was nearly finished, I was carving in the central porch of the west front (for I carved all those bas-reliefs in the west front with my own hand); beneath me my sister Margaret was carving at the flower-work, and the little quatrefoils that carry the sign of the zodiac and emblems of the months; now my sister Margaret was rather more than twenty years old at that time, and she was very beautiful, with dark brown hair and deep calm violet eyes. I had lived with her all my life, lived with her almost alone latterly, for our father and mother died when she was quite young, and I loved her very much, though I was not thinking of her just then, as she stood beneath me carving. Now the central porch was carved with a bas-relief of the Last Judgment and it was divided into three parts by horizontal bands of deep flower-work. In the lowest division, just over the doors, was carved The Rising of the Dead; above were angels blowing long trumpets, and Michael the Archangel weighing the souls, and the blessed led into heaven by angels, and the lost into hell by the devil; and in the topmost division was the Judge of the world.

All the figures in the porch were finished except one, and I remember when I woke that morning my exultation at the thought of my church being so nearly finished. I remember, too, how a kind of misgiving mingled with the exultation, which, try all I could, I was unable to shake off; I thought then it was a rebuke for my pride; well, perhaps it was. The figure I had to carve was Abraham, sitting with a blossoming tree on each side of him, holding in his two hands the corners of his great robe, so that it made a mighty fold, wherein, with their hands crossed over their breasts, were the souls of the faithful, of whom he was called Father: I stood on the scaffolding for some time, while Margaret's chisel worked on bravely down below. I took mine in my hand, and stood so, listening to the noise of the masons inside, and two monks of the Abbey came and stood below me, and a knight, holding his little daughter by the hand, who every now and then looked up at him, and asked him strange questions. I did not think of these long, but began to think of Abraham, yet I could not think of him sitting there, quiet and solemn, while the Judgment-Trumpet was being blown; I rather thought of him as he looked when he chased those kings so far; riding far ahead of any of his company, with his mailhood off his head, and lying in grim folds down his back, with the strong west wind blowing his wild black hair far out behind him, with the wind rippling the long scarlet pennon of his lance; riding there amid the rocks and the sands alone; with the last gleam of the armour of the beaten kings disappearing behind the winding of the pass; with his company a long, long way behind, quite out of sight, though their trumpets sounded faintly among the clefts of the rocks; and so I thought I saw him, till on his fierce chase he leapt, horse and man, into a deep river, quiet, swift, and smooth; and there was something in the moving of the water-lilies as the breast of the horse swept them aside, that suddenly took away the thought of Abraham and brought a strange dream of lands I had never seen; and the first was of a place where I was quite alone, standing by the side of a river, and there was the sound of singing a very long way off, but no living thing of any kind could be seen, and the land was quite flat, quite without hills, and quite without trees too, and the river wound very much, making all kinds of quaint curves, and on the side where I stood there grew nothing but long grass, but on the other side grew, quite on to the horizon, a great sea of red corn-poppies, only paths of white lilies wound all among them, with here and there a great golden sunflower. So I looked down at the river by my feet, and saw how blue it was, and how, as the stream went swiftly by, it swayed to and fro the long green weeds, and I stood and looked at the river for long, till at last I felt someone touch me on the shoulder, and, looking round, I saw standing by me my friend Amyot, whom I love better than anyone else in the world, but I thought in my dream that I was frightened when I saw him, for his face had changed so, it was so bright and almost transparent, and his eyes gleamed and shone as I had never seen them do before. Oh! he was so wondrously beautiful, so fearfully beautiful! and as I looked at him the distant music swelled, and seemed to come close up to me, and then swept by us, and fainted away, at last died off entirely; and then I felt sick at heart, and faint, and parched, and I stooped to drink of the water of the river, and as soon as the water touched my lips, lo! the river vanished, and the flat country with its poppies and lilies, and I dreamed that I was in a boat by myself again, floating in an almost land-locked bay of the northern sea, under a cliff of dark basalt. I was lying on my back in the boat, looking up at the intensely blue sky, and a long low swell from the outer sea lifted the boat up and let it fall again and carried it gradually nearer and nearer towards the dark cliff; and as I moved on, I saw at last, on the top of the cliff, a castle, with many towers, and on the highest tower of the castle there was a great white banner floating, with a red chevron on it, and three golden stars on the chevron; presently I saw too on one of the towers, growing in a cranny of the worn stones, a great bunch of golden and blood-red wallflowers, and I watched the wallflowers and banner for long; when suddenly I heard a trumpet blow from the castle, and saw a rush of armed men on to the battlements, and there was a fierce fight, till at last it was ended, and one went to the banner and pulled it down and cast it over the cliff into the sea, and it came down in long sweeps, with the wind making little ripples in it – slowly, slowly it came, till at last it fell over me and covered me from my feet till over my breast, and I let it stay there and looked again at the castle, and then I saw that there was an amber-coloured banner floating over the castle in place of the red chevron, and it was much larger than the other: also now, a man stood on the battlements, looking towards me; he had a tilting helmet on, with the visor down, and an amber-coloured surcoat over his armour; his right hand was ungauntleted, and he held it high above his head, and in his hand was the bunch of wallflowers that I had seen growing on the wall; and his hand was white and small, like a woman's, for in my dream I could see even very far-off things much clearer than we see real material things on the earth: presently he threw the wallflowers over the cliff, and they fell in the boat just behind my head, and then I saw, looking down from the battlements of the castle, Amyot. He looked down towards me very sorrowfully, I thought, but, even as in the other dream, said nothing; so I thought in my dream that I wept for very pity, and for love of him, for he looked as a man just risen from a long illness, and who will carry till he dies a dull pain about with him. He was very thin, and his long black hair drooped all about his face as he leaned over the battlements looking at me; he was quite pale, and his cheeks were hollow, but his eyes large, and soft, and sad. So I reached out my arms to him, and suddenly I was walking with him in a lovely garden, and we said nothing, for the music which I had heard at first was sounding close to us now, and there were many birds in the boughs of the trees; oh, such birds! gold and ruby and emerald, but they sung not at all, but were quite silent, as though they too were listening to the music. Now all this time

Amyot and I had been looking at each other, but just then I turned my head away from him, and as soon as I did so, the music ended with a long wail, and when I turned again Amyot was gone; then I felt even more sad and sick at heart than I had been before when I was by the river, and I leaned against a tree, and put my hands before my eyes. When I looked again the garden was gone, and I knew not where I was, and presently all my dreams were gone. The chips were flying bravely from the stone under my chisel at last, and all my thoughts now were in my carving, when I heard my name, 'Walter', called, and when I looked down I saw one standing below me, whom I had seen in my dreams just before – Amyot. I had no hopes of seeing him for a long time, perhaps I might never see him again, I thought, for he was away (as I thought) fighting in the holy wars, and it made me almost beside myself to see him standing close by me in the flesh. I got down from my scaffolding as soon as I could, and all thoughts else were soon drowned in the joy of having him by me; Margaret, too, how glad she must have been, for she had been betrothed to him for some time before he went to the wars and he had been five years away; five years! and how we had thought of him through those many weary days! how often his face had come before me! his brave, honest face, the most beautiful among all the faces of men and women I have ever seen. Yes, I remember how five years ago I held his hand as we came together out of the cathedral of that great, far-off city, whose name I forget now; and then I remember the stamping of the horses' feet; I remember how his hand left mine at last, and then, someone looking back at me earnestly as they all rode on together – looking back, with his hand on the saddle behind him, while the trumpets sang in long solemn peals as they all rode on together, with the glimmer of arms and the fluttering of banners, and the clinking of the rings of the mail, that sounded like the falling of many drops of water into the deep, still waters of some pool that the rocks nearly meet over; and the gleam and flash of the swords, and the glimmer of the lance-heads and the flutter of the rippled banners, that streamed out from them, swept past me and were gone, and they seemed like a pageant in a dream, whose meaning we know not; and those sounds too, the trumpets, and the clink of the mail, and the thunder of the horse-hoofs, they seemed dream-like too – and it was all like a dream that he should leave me, for we had said that we should always be together; but he went away, and now he is come back again.

We were by his bedside, Margaret and I; I stood and leaned over him, and my hair fell sideways over my face and touched his face; Margaret kneeled beside me, quivering in every limb, not with pain, I think, but rather shaken by a passion of earnest prayer. After some time (I know not how long) I looked up from his face to the window underneath which he lay. I do not know what time of the day it was, but I know that it was a glorious autumn day, a day soft with melting, golden haze: a vine and a rose grew together, and trailed half across the window, so that I could not see much of the beautiful blue sky, and nothing of town or country beyond; the vine leaves were touched with red here and there, and three overblown roses, light pink roses, hung amongst them. I remember dwelling on the strange lines the autumn had made in red on one of the gold-green vine leaves, and watching one leaf of one of the overblown roses, expecting it to fall every minute; but as I gazed, and felt disappointed that the rose leaf had not fallen yet, I felt my pain suddenly shoot through me, and I remembered what I had lost; and then came bitter, bitter dreams – dreams which had once made me happy – dreams of the things I had hoped would be, of the things that would never be now; they came between the fair vine leaves and rose blossoms and that which lay before the window; they came as before, perfect in colour and form, sweet sounds and shapes.

But now in every one was something unutterably miserable; they would not go away, they put out the steady glow of the golden haze, the sweet light of the sun through the vine leaves, the soft leaning of the full-blown roses. I wandered in them for a long time; at last I felt a hand put me aside gently, for I was standing at the head of – of the bed; then someone kissed my forehead, and words were spoken – I know not what words. The bitter dreams left me for the bitter reality at last; for I had found him that morning lying dead, only the morning after I had seen him when he had come back from his long absence – I had found him lying dead, with his hands crossed downwards, with his eyes closed, as though the angels had done that for him; and now when I looked at him he still lay there, and Margaret knelt by him with her face touching his; she was not quivering now, her lips moved not at all as they had done just before; and so, suddenly those words came to my mind which she had spoken when she kissed me, and which at the time I had only heard with my outward hearing, for she had said, 'Walter, farewell, and Christ keep you; but for me, I must be with him, for so I promised him last night that I would never leave him any more, and God will let me go.' And verily Margaret and Amyot did go, and left me very lonely and sad.

It was just beneath the westernmost arch of the nave, there I carved their tomb: I was a long time carving it; I did not think I should be so long at first, and I said, 'I shall die when I have finished carving it', thinking that would be a very short time. But so it happened after I had carved those two whom I loved, lying with clasped hands like husband and wife above their tomb, that I could not yet leave carving it; and so that I might be near them I became a monk, and used to sit in the choir and sing, thinking of the time when we should be all together again. And as I had time I used to go to the westernmost arch of the nave and work at the tomb that was there under the great, sweeping arch; and in process of time I raised a marble canopy that reached quite up to the top of the arch, and I painted it too as fair as I could, and carved it all about with many flowers and histories, and in them I carved the faces of those I had known on earth (for I was not as one on earth now, but seemed quite away out of the world). And as I carved sometimes the monks and other people too would come and gaze, and watch how the flowers grew; and sometimes too as they gazed, they would weep for pity, knowing how all had been. So my life passed, and I lived in that abbey for twenty years after he died, till one morning, quite early, when they came into the church for matins, they found me lying dead, with my chisel in my hand, underneath the last lily of the tomb.

The Beckoning Monk

Christopher Park

I watched, bewitched, as the huge black-and-white swallowtail hovered over my sun-bronzed arm and then settled on the back of my hand. The sensation was curious – almost like someone placing a piece of fairy furniture, a chair or a small occasional table, on my skin. I remembered my father saying once that butterflies were the souls of the dead. He would open a drawer or enter a dusty old shed and be surprised when a pair of white or multicoloured wings flitted past him and then, inevitably, would come the news a day or two later that another ageing relative had died at that very moment when the insect had appeared.

And now he was dead too and here was this monstrous soul flexing its huge wings on my hand, oblivious of my nakedness in the heat, intent only on feeding around the fennel fronds that grow next to Theo's cottage in the olive grove that straddles this sun-parched rocky mountain in the southern Mediterranean.

If God was going to be anywhere, I'd calculated, Crete would be as good a place as any to start looking. It was here, after all, that Zeus had been born and was buried, and at this time of year a closer approximation to paradise I could not envisage. In the wake of my calamitous short marriage and the destruction of my house in Hampshire I'd somehow been granted a boon. With the collapse of everything which I'd formerly held dear I'd somehow felt liberated. And the income from both the insurance on Beauchamp Place and compensation from the courts for my wife's infidelity, combined with the generous annuity from my father's estate and the gift of an open-ended round-the-world ticket from my elder brother, meant that I was a man in his mid-forties considerably eased of financial burden for the rest of his life.

However, inner comfort was a different matter. The problem was that, after meeting up with one of my ex-wife's relatives who had once been a priest, my outlook had changed somewhat. His views had admittedly been far from orthodox, some might even have called them heretical, but their curious mixture of off-beat theology and what appeared to be sound philosophy had somehow struck a note in my mind at a time when the stresses which surrounded me had begun to take on a sinister aspect which had given me cause for concern for my sanity. I had thus decided to enter on a quest, a pilgrimage if you like, which had a bizarre, devotional aspect and yet which was also, in a sense, a genuine urge to try and pin down something about the ideas of spirits, souls and so forth which had set me thinking. Hence, as if on cue, the butterfly. What I had not expected to encounter, however, were ghosts.

At school a group of my classmates and I had formed ourselves into a pseudo-religious society called the Apostles. There were, naturally enough, twelve of us, only it wasn't God whom we worshipped but the associated palindrome: DOG. My ex-wife and all her family had been simply potty about cats but I, along with my erstwhile schoolfellows, had been a dyed-in-the-fur dog-lover since I had been in short trousers. I had thus decided to avail myself of my brother's travel offer and combine my long-projected pilgrimage in search of inner revelation with an international tour of the world visiting my far-flung comrades-in-arms, all eleven of whom had at the tender age of eight pledged to become lifelong dog-owners once they had left home, and the more unusual the hound the better. My days as Judas – being the only disciple who, at my wife's insistence, had owned cats instead of dogs – were now over. And thus now, I hoped, I would be welcomed back into the fold. In consequence, letters had been written, warm invitations had indeed been received in reply and the appropriate international flight details had been booked. Crete was to be my first port of call . . .

Theo was out when I'd arrived that May morning and had left me a note with the key under a flowerpot saying that he'd had to take some German tourists on a trek round the White Mountains and that he'd be back at dusk. If Ray turned up, would I please feed him, otherwise I was to feel free to wander about, swim in the rockpool at the bottom of the hill, etc. However, he warned me not to try to get into the chapel-like building as it was rather unsafe structurally and anyway was locked because there had been some trouble in the neighbourhood recently with thieves coming from outside the area to steal sacred artefacts. Looking around, there had been no immediate sign of Ray, who I gathered from Theo's doodle-caricature next to the animal's name was the dog. However, there was something about the drawing I couldn't quite fathom. It showed a dog's head all right, but coming out of his mouth was a cartoon bubble containing a four-letter word beginning with a B followed by three asterisks. A simple enough riddle – childish even – but what was the point of it?

The reference to the chapel also confused me somewhat as there seemed to be two, not one, places of worship in the area. A tiny, curiously un-Greek-style – one might almost say, Norman – building could be seen jutting out of the olive grove further up the mountain. A brief survey seemed to indicate that this could only be reached via a treacherous-looking crumbly rock path with very little cover against the midday heat. However, in addition, according to a sign in Greek to the right of Theo's cottage, there was nearby an ancient hermitage. At first this didn't appear to point anywhere, but after some aimless wandering I discovered the remains of an ancient stone cross standing in front of a small hole about two feet in diameter in the side of the hill. Outside the entrance were a number of thin candles and a box of matches. I struck one and peered in but it looked very dark and the long narrow passage reminded me of nothing so much as a rabbit-warren. There was also a curious smell. My innate claustrophobia made me shudder and my discomfort was further increased when I became convinced that I could hear something rustling about inside.

Moving swiftly away, I had then wandered across to an opening in the olive grove, discovered a truly wonderful-looking rockpool surrounded by bougainvillaea and oleander bushes, and clambered the 50 or so feet down to it. The water was as clear as crystal, about 10 feet deep in the centre and deliciously inviting. I stripped off my remaining clothes and plunged in. Resurfacing I then paddled about for a while, watching as garishly coloured dragonflies dodged above my head. Then I turned over and floated, face-down, observing the fish, eels, and flora iridescent beneath me. Sated at last I hauled myself up on to a rock, dried off leisurely in the sun and then picked my way back up to the clearing near the cottage. Here I covered myself liberally with tanning-oil and collapsed, naked, on a pile of my clothes in the sweltering heat. Some time later the gradual awareness that I was starting to burn, combined with the loud and insistent throbbing of the cicadas, awoke me just in time to feel the fairy footsteps of the swallowtail on my right hand ...

The next moment this rural idyll was shattered as a huge dog bounded into view, dislodged the butterfly in the blink of an eye and pursued it down the olive grove. Shocked, I stood up and reached for my clothes. I had just managed to put on my underwear when the dog returned heading straight for me at great speed and with an uncompromising look in its eye.

Somehow remembering my Homer, I had the presence of mind to sit down on the ground as Odysseus had done when confronted by wild dogs on his return to Greece. The ruse worked, thank heavens. The hound, recognizing the convention among its kind for submission, circled me for a few minutes. Then, looking over my right shoulder towards the cottage, it sat down itself and began wagging its tail. Then an extraordinary thing happened; its mouth opened and shut and it started to talk!

'Hi, you must be Toby,' the creature began in a guttural Irish voice. 'I'm Ray,' and he held up a paw.

I shook the proffered foot in amazement and stammered foolishly, 'How do you do, Ray.'

Too dumbfounded to say any more and oblivious of my surroundings, I listened as the dog went on.

'You know why I'm called Ray, Toby?' he asked. I shook my head. 'Well, perhaps you'd better ask Theo here . . .'

There was a crunch of gravel beside me and I looked up to see a short, gaunt and very tanned-looking man wearing an old, loose-fitting, blue silk shirt, a pair of baggy, dark blue cotton trousers and leather toe-sandals.

'Well, I'll be . . .' I began and then, as he continued speaking in the same lilting tones, I detected the ruse.

'The reason I'm called Ray,' said the voice, 'is because it is short for Panta Korey, and Theo is a great fan of the ancient Greek philosopher, Heraclitus, who held that things are not always what they seem. "All is in a state of flux" is one of his sayings, or in Greek *panta korey*. And not only that, but he is a bloody good ventriloquist too!'

I laughed, stood up and shook hands with my old school-friend who looked immensely lean and fit compared to my baggy half-naked figure. We exchanged pleasantries for a few minutes and then Theo suggested we go back into the cottage for a drink. On the way I remarked on his monk-like tonsure and wondered if he had taken up holy orders.

He laughed. 'Oh no, that's another illusion, I'm afraid. It's just my bald patch. I'm not quite sure why it grows in such an odd way but there it is. And Ray, whom you've just met, is also remarkable in that he can't bark – he was born dumb. It is thus easy for me to project my voice into his every time he opens his mouth in greeting.'

We wandered back up the path and into the shade. Theo reached into a cupboard and fetched out some Greek Gold beer – it was either that or Dutch Amstel brewed in Athens, he said, as he couldn't stand *ouzo* or *raki* – and he apologized for the fact that it wasn't cold as there was no electricity in the cottage.

'But what about the radio over in the corner?' I asked, having spotted a magnificent old 1930s bakelite Echo receiver above the sink when I'd first arrived. 'Or is it a wireless?'

'Oh yes, that's a classic,' he remarked. 'Why don't you turn it on?' I crossed the room and reached up to turn the switch. It made some crackling noises as I tried to tune it in and then went quiet. I continued turning the knob for a few seconds as Theo went on, 'The only trouble is that it only seems to receive old-fashioned radio programmes.'

At that a rather nasal upper-class voice emitted from the machine: 'Jairmany calling, Jairmany calling.' I was stunned to hear Lord Haw-Haw's familiar wartime catchphrase and swivelled round to look at Theo who had begun laughing. Of course, he had been throwing his voice again!

'*Panta korey*, my friend.'

As we took our bottles and sat down to drink at the kitchen

table, he explained how he had for a while earned a modest part-time living in the bars of northern Crete, making suitcases appear to talk and the like. He had even had a proper dummy made up. At this point he went into the main bedroom and came back with a large cardboard box from which he produced a lanky, articulated, long-haired toy figure clad only in a loin cloth and a purple cloak, and with stigmata on its feet and hands, a wound in its chest and a crown of thorns.

'Meet Joshua,' he announced with a flourish. He then brought the dummy to life with an appalling Jewish/Irish accent and a classic deadpan delivery worthy of the best stand-up comedians. Amongst the jokes was one about the disciples asking him to prove he's the Messiah by walking on water.

'I sank, of course,' the dummy said. 'And so I turned to Simon and I told him: "Hey Simon. What do you expect with these two great holes in my feet?!"'

After a number of gags in similar vein I asked him why he was called Joshua.

'Well, that was Jesus's original name, you see, in Hebrew. Jesus was just the Latinized version. They were under Roman rule at the time don't forget. I expect his Mum and mates called him Josh for short. And as he's the dummy in my vent. performance I suppose that that, literally, makes me "the voice of God" – which is what I called the act at first. Unfortunately, if you'll forgive the pun, all this joshing of Jesus got me into a bit of trouble with the local authorities once they got wind of it. At first I was mostly entertaining young north European package holidaymakers, who aren't particularly religious. But then word got around and so I changed him into the Pope.' Theo leaned over and produced a white overall and skullcap from the box and started holding the dummy's hand up in a mock blessing.

'But surely that's almost as bad?' I asked.

'Well, as it turned out, yes it was,' he continued. 'The Protestant German and British tourists took it all OK and I'd assumed that as the Greek Orthodox Church had broken away from the Roman Catholics in the Middle Ages they'd also come to dislike the Pope. But it wasn't as simple as that, and anyway, my critics argued, wasn't I still taking the Lord's name in vain? Satire is a house built on shaky foundations.' He paused. 'You see that?'

He pointed to an extraordinary framed caricature on the wall of a hideous creature playing what seemed to be a set of bagpipes with a tonsured human head as its bellows.

'That's a sixteenth-century German Roman Catholic caricature of the devil playing Martin Luther's head – the devil is playing his tune, as it were. So that's what I went for in the end . . .' He reached into the box again, produced a new head and a brown habit with a hood and arranged on his lap the legs of what could now be seen to be a medieval monk – apparently somewhat the worse for drink judging by his red cheeks and befuddled expression – and able to give a long sly wink with either eye.

'Not Luther but a monk. Monks and nuns have always been pretty fair game and this one is based on one of the monks who used to live in that hole known as the Hermitage down the hill. When I'm not doing walking tours for English-speaking visitors, or when the weather's bad – especially in the winter – I still manage to make a few bob in local bars by dressing up in the same clerical garb myself and dangling this chap on my knee with his "gottle of egglesiastical geer".'

The following day was another scorcher but thunder threatened according to the weather forecast. As there was no electricity in the old stone cottage – it was in fact a converted olive-workers' hut – we had walked down into the village in the broad moonlight when it had got dark and had had supper and a few drinks there before retiring for the night, being guided safely home by the remarkably reliable Ray the dog.

In the course of the evening Theo had filled me in on his career since leaving school: university, exhibition work, a dull job in a library then shoestring-budget travel, ending up here where the cost of living was remarkably low. And because he apparently also had some 'psychological disability', known only to himself and a slightly corrupt doctor friend, he was able to draw welfare payments from Britain to fund his existence in Crete. The tour-guide work and the occasional ventriloquist jobs were, of course, cash in hand and so – unless someone blew the whistle on him – would not affect his entitlement to UK benefit.

I asked him what had drawn him to Crete and this particular place in the White Mountains and in response he said that he too had at one time reached a point where he had somehow felt a need for some kind of religion or at least spiritual fulfilment and had had a flash of enlightenment when visiting an old girlfriend here many years ago when he was on his travels. The woman had been living in a cave with a group of hippies, which was a common enough sight in this part of the world in the 1970s, and he had been deeply affected by the area. The tranquillity, the vision of so many stars in the pitch-black night sky, the clear blue sea lapping on the beaches below, the bougainvillaea and oleander all around – somehow something felt right here.

And the stone cottage . . . ? Well, it had been very cheap to rent as it had no electricity and only cold water, and it was also totally isolated. One additional reason for this abandonment by the locals was because they believed the place to be haunted and wouldn't go near it at night.

The original occupant of the Hermitage, it appeared, was one St Alexander Stylites, who earned his sobriquet by being a follower of the fifth-century hermit St Simeon Stylites of Syria who had spent thirty years seated on a stone pillar 60 feet high. The stylites were named after the Greek word for pillar which is *stulos*. Alexander, however, had two pillars – one inside the cave formed out of an enormous stalagmite, the other outside in the upper olive grove, on the site of which now stands the Norman-style chapel.

In fact, as Theo pointed out, it was not really a church at all but a small Benedictine monastery which had been built in the Norman manner to honour Alexander and had been occupied for some twenty years by his only two followers – comprising the entire Alexandrian order. These two medieval monks were called Nikos and Andros and the story goes that one moonless night, on the eve of St Alexander's officially designated saint's day, Andros had been caught by his fellow monk in an indelicate act with a local shepherdess. Incensed by this double sacrilege by a supposed celibate, a heated argument had begun between the two holy men. The row had continued well into the night and, aided by the potent Benedictine-like liqueur which the couple distilled in the cave, eventually had become very heated indeed. The upshot was that the younger man had pushed Nikos down a nearby gully and killed him outright that pitch-black night.

Now, legend has it that every year on the eve of St Alexander, the ghost of the drunken Andros, condemned for eternity to owning up to his crime, can be seen beckoning passers-by to look into the gully into which he pushed his former comrade. He is known locally as the Beckoning Monk. However, the gully in question is so precipitous that many inquisitive travellers, thinking they have come across a real person, have followed the inviting hand-signals of the fiendish ghoul and plunged to their deaths.

As it happened, St Alexander's Eve would be the following day and I was intrigued enough by the story to ask Theo to show me round the tiny monastery and the adjoining Hermitage. By my good fortune he had little tour work to do that day so, accompanied by Ray, we began the difficult trek up the hill towards the building above the cottage.

The sun was blazing down when we set off, and giant black bees the size of small mice hummed over our heads as we walked beneath the grapevine-covered trellis outside the cottage. Having burnt my neck the previous day, I draped an old sweatshirt over my shoulders and on my head wore a crumpled panama Theo had given me. He, of course, despite his bald patch, needed no protection against the heat as he had become hardened to it over the years. He also walked at an incredible pace while I stumbled along behind, pausing every few minutes to wipe the sweat from my brow.

About half-way to the church, while I was resting under an olive tree, another swallowtail butterfly flitted past and I mentioned to Theo about my father's theory of souls.

'That's interesting,' he replied, 'because it ties in a bit with a local tradition concerning the Death's-Head Moth. Apparently, if you see one of those a terrible accident will occur near that spot within twenty-four hours.'

Ray the dog kept ahead of us during our journey and at the top he bark-mimed his silent greeting and wagged his tail as we toiled the last few paces.

'Good boy, Ray,' Theo said as he patted his head, then turned to me. 'Another thing I forgot to mention is that I am a sort of unofficial custodian for the monastery and the Hermitage cave. The government allow me a small percentage of the olives and olive oil from the trees around here, as well as oranges, lemons and various other fruit and vegetables grown on the estate, in return for keeping an eye on the place. I've got a key to the church and Ray here tends to sleep during the day in the cool shade of the tunnel entrance to the cave – a bit like Cerberus guarding the gates to Hades in Greek mythology.'

'Ah, that explains the rustling sounds I heard inside the Hermitage when I first arrived,' I said.

Theo took out the key from his pocket and was just about to put it in the lock when he changed his mind. 'Oh, before we go in, I'd like to show you the gully which the drunken Andros pushed Nikos into – it's just around the back here.'

We followed a little track to the right of the church, past some simple stained-glass windows covered with iron bars on the outside, towards the apse at the rear before entering a little copse. Green lizards darted under stones out of our way and as I watched a huge cricket leapt and glided right in front of us and then suddenly, with no warning at all, the path simply disappeared. I looked on in amazement as the cricket, wings extended, sailed over a sheer rockface and floated down what must have been a 200-foot drop to what I immediately recognized as the idyllic rockpool I had bathed in earlier.

Just in time, Theo grabbed my arm and managed to prevent me from toppling over the edge.

'So there you are,' he said. 'The very spot, tradition has it, where Nikos met his end. Of course there wouldn't have been water at the bottom then. That's only filled up because the stream has been diverted recently to help with irrigating the olive groves. So I expect bits of his bleached bones can still be found at the bottom of the pond.'

I shuddered at the thought that only yesterday I had been splashing around in what I thought to be the most beautiful, innocent pool in paradise, when in fact it had once been the scene of a gruesome murder and I had been swimming amongst the mangled remains of a dead monk – things are not as they seem indeed! I turned away from the edge and urged Theo back to the church.

Inside, the stained-glass window shed bars of red, blue and green light across a large, sparsely furnished room that contained a long refectory table, two beds, a covered washstand, a lectern for reading Scripture excerpts, and a small stone altar. As we approached the altar I could see that upon its surface stood a large crucifix made out of a crystal cross and a silver Jesus. On either side of this were gold candlesticks and an ornate chalice which had a silver lining and was encrusted on the outside with a number of precious gems.

Theo turned to me. 'So now you see why we have to lock the place up. According to the police in neighbouring districts who have had their churches robbed recently, this particular thief, or gang of thieves, only usually operates – naturally enough – on moonless nights. He or they had a go at our little monastery last month but, by chance, I'd fallen asleep up here after having a bit too much to drink, and Ray – who would normally have been down with me in the cottage – saw them off. However, I'm pretty sure they'll have another go tonight so I'm taking the loot from here and the Hermitage down the hill to the cottage just to be on the safe side. Here, give me a hand.'

With that he went into an alcove and fetched a holdall which we then filled with the valuables. After we had packed them all he went back into the alcove and unlocked a tiny cupboard out of which he produced a large bottle of green liquid.

'We might as well take this with us too,' he said with a conspiratorial wink. 'It's some of the hooch those old Benedictine monks used to make – or a pretty close imitation of it. After Nikos's death Andros took to the booze more and more and, increasingly befuddled, used to get some of the local people to help him make the stuff. It's him I model my ventriloquist act on. The original still is in the Hermitage. As a result, the recipe got out and when he died – his bones are under the altar there – the locals continued to make it. However, as an offering to the monks' memory, as well as to the church and St Alexander Stylites, they donate one of these 2-litre flagons to the monastery on the anniversary of the saint's day and take away the empty one. They know I drink it – it's part of their gift to me as custodian. But as it happens I've been off the booze for a bit – doctor's orders. He gave me some pills for a while which I wasn't allowed to mix with alcohol. Until last month, that was. Which probably accounts for why I got so drunk and fell asleep the night the thieves came round – I must have been out of practice. The good side, though, is that there is still about half a litre left and it's got to be finished up before tomorrow when they come to take the bottle away!'

This cheered me up immensely and I offered to carry the flagon down the hill myself – just for safekeeping, of course. Unscrewing the top, I took a whiff and was hit in the face by the powerful aroma, which made my eyes stream. As we turned to leave the church I went up to the hand-basin and, on a whim, lifted off the wooden lid. To my surprise I discovered inside a large dead moth lying on its back. Theo came up behind me and turned the insect over. We looked at each other with apprehension when we both recognized the distinct and unmistakable skull-shaped motif on its back signifying the Death's-Head Moth.

Nervously I put the lid back on the stone bowl and suggested to Theo that perhaps because it was dead it didn't have the same significance. Theo smiled uncertainly.

'Yes, you're probably right. Anyway, it's just an old wives' tale. Come on, let's get moving.'

When we got to the bottom of the hill again, Theo nipped inside the cottage and locked the valuables away before re-emerging wearing a pair of old trainers.

I remarked on these: 'Why the change of shoes?'

'Well, you'll see – it gets pretty slippery underfoot in the cave. My leather sandals have no real grip on the soles, but you'll be all right with those old daps of yours.' He used what I had assumed was just a West Country term for plimsolls but evidently it had crept over to Ireland as well.

It wasn't far to the Hermitage. Ray raced on ahead into the tunnel as we picked up some candles and lit one each before bending down and crawling into the narrow passageway. The strange heavy odour I'd noticed when I arrived the previous day assaulted my nostrils once more but this time I recognized it as the smell of the monks' home-brewed liqueur. Indeed, as we scrambled the last few yards into the main cave and were able to stand upright and light some of the larger candles which had been placed around the walls we could make out, on our right, the original old still itself – now mostly rusted away but none the less identifiable. However, as my eyes got used to the dim light and Theo lit ever more candles I began to look above my head and was amazed.

The Hermitage was a truly massive cavity in solid limestone. The ceiling was as high as many cathedrals I have visited and hanging from its dripping surface were row after row of fantastically shaped stalactites. Beneath them, the corresponding stalagmites had mostly been levelled to make room for a row of stone seats. For it appeared, as Theo explained, that in ancient times, locals would come and hold services in here to venerate St Alexander.

'And here,' Theo continued, walking further back into the long nave of the Hermitage with a candle above his head, 'is where the great saint himself used to sit.'

He pointed upwards and I followed his finger. Before me was the most massive natural pillar I have ever seen. It must have extended upwards for some 40 feet and seemed to have a flat top. All the sides were covered in ancient Greek and Minoan-style decorations as well as Christian motifs, which led me to believe that perhaps the cave pre-dated Christianity as a place of worship. Theo agreed that this was probably true.

'But how on earth did he get up there?' I asked, as there

seemed to be no visible means of access. 'Did he lasso the top
and climb up on a rope?'

'Ah, there's the trick, you see – *panta korey* yet again. And I
see that in fact the eponymous Ray is himself already one *step*
ahead of us, as it were.'

We walked around the back of the column and could then
see that a steep diagonal path had been cut into the side of the
cave and ran up towards the roof. We gingerly climbed up to
the top, where Ray was waiting and looking across at the pillar
– which we could now see did indeed have a flattened top. I
could also now make out a rope bridge suspended from a row
of small stalactites which ran across the roof at roughly 3-foot
intervals before joining the central pillar some 15 feet from
where we stood at the top of the path.

Theo took my candle and motioned for me to cross over. I
looked apprehensively down at the 40-foot drop on to bare
wet rock.

'Oh, don't worry, it's all right – you don't think this is the
original rope bridge, do you? That would have crumbled away
centuries ago! No, this is one the authorities had put up last
year. You see, they are slowly trying to turn all these sites into
tourist attractions. But this one isn't quite ready for public
access yet.'

With that I slowly walked across the bridge and, my heart
in my mouth, eventually reached the centre. Then, to my
horror, Theo blew out his candles and put them in his pockets
to free his hands, leaving us in almost complete blackness as
he crossed over himself. I was terrified and sat down immediately, hoping I would not topple over the edge of the
small platform, which couldn't have been more than 6 feet
across at the most. Theo called for me to hold out my hand so
that he wouldn't knock me over as he stepped on to the
platform and then lit the candles again. I could see from the
light that Ray had had more sense than even to attempt to

walk over the bridge and was lying down at the top of the path opposite.

I now looked over the edge, very carefully, and could see the little altar with its simple silver cross and silver candlesticks at the bottom of the pillar and the rows of stone seats ranged in front of it by the tunnel entrance. Feeling a bit dizzy I then looked up towards the ceiling and noticed that the stalactite immediately above had been smoothed off to give us – and St Alexander – headspace but that the adjoining one, in the row which extended across the top of the cave in the same line as those which suspended the bridge, had sheared off.

I pointed this out to Theo.

'Oh that,' he said. 'Yes, I meant to tell you about that when we were discussing the monks. You see, that is how the sinner Andros finally met his come-uppance. A year or two after his murder of Nikos he was kneeling before the altar in his daily devotions when that particular pinnacle of rock broke away from the roof and plummeted downwards and crushed him flat, killing him instantly. The altar you now see replaced a much earlier one, which was a foot or two closer to the pillar and is in fact made out of the remains of the stalactite, smoothed flat on the top. The few bones they were able to salvage from the mess were moved up to the altar in the monastery and the rest, undoubtedly, are still embedded in solid limestone in the floor of the cave.'

I shuddered as Theo continued.

'In fact, the ghost of Andros is supposed to walk from the Hermitage here, where he died himself, to the gully up above by the church where he killed Nikos. And anyone fool enough to be inside this cave at night on St Alexander's Eve is likely to witness the full horror of Andros's death, it is said. But again that's only local legend . . .'

I suddenly began to feel queasy and, with Theo's help, we rapidly recrossed the bridge, descended the path and, after collecting the few sacred valuables in the cave for safekeeping, followed the faithful Ray out of the cold and damp cave and into the bright sunshine once more.

Back in the house over a lunch of bread, *feta* cheese and *retsina*, Theo explained his plan for trying to catch the thieves – or at least to frighten them away from the area once and for all.

'So I reckon that if the thieves know that there are valuables in the Hermitage and the monastery then they probably also know about the legend of the Beckoning Monk and the fact that the ghost is supposed to walk on the moonless night before St Alexander's Day. But, thieves being what they are, they will either not be superstitious at all or their greed will conquer their fears. Added to which, if they are not from Crete itself, they will probably fall back on the old saying that "All Cretans are liars".'

'But isn't that a famous paradox?' I interrupted.

'No,' Theo continued with a grin. 'Only if the speaker is a Cretan. Then, of course, it follows that what he is saying is false and hence some Cretans are not liars... But anyway, back to the plot. My plan is to dress up in my ventriloquist monk's gear and walk up from the Hermitage to the monastery at midnight tonight on St Alexander's Eve and scare the living daylights out of them.'

'But what if they attack you?'

'Well, in the event that they are not frightened by my ghostly hooded figure beckoning them, they most probably will be by a savage dog which shouts imprecations at them in a human voice!' At this he patted Ray who was lying under the table panting from the heat.

It seemed a good enough plan in the circumstances and, after clearing away the dishes, we went to our separate rooms, lay across our beds under tent-like mosquito nets and settled down to our siestas.

Not being used to sleeping in the middle of the day it took me a long time to drift off, but after reading some more about the wisdom of Heraclitus in a book called *The Presocratic Philosophers* in Theo's extensive library which surrounded me, I began dozing fitfully and then fell into a deep dreamless sleep. Indeed, the combined effects of the *retsina*, the heat and the physical exhaustion from all the climbing we had done must have been considerable as when I awoke it was already getting dark.

Getting up, I dressed and opened the glass door into the main living area to find Theo gone and a note saying that he had walked into the village for some provisions for a special supper and would be back at about six. Almost at that very moment I heard a sound outside the cottage and looked through the open window. A lean, youngish man was running away from the house down the olive grove and then a few seconds later I could see Ray thundering off behind him. The next sound was of a motorcycle starting up on the main track and speeding off down the hill. As Ray returned so did Theo, heavily laden with groceries.

'Damn, he got away,' said Theo. 'I bet that was our thief, giving the place the once-over, just to make sure of the layout before raiding us tonight. It's lucky he didn't get inside the cottage or we would have lost the treasures after all – you must have frightened him off. I expect he thought there was no one here having seen me and Ray go down the hill a little while ago and thus, not realizing I had a visitor, had assumed it was safe.'

Pleased that I had been some help I gave Theo a hand with the groceries and together we prepared a veritable banquet of vegetarian and small meat and fish dishes, together with local bread, cheese, beer and wine and finishing off with the wonderful Cretan concoction of yogurt and fruit with honey. The 'Feast of St Alexander', Theo called it, and we certainly did the ancient hermit proud on the eve of his special day. After the preparation we both in turn took candles round to the shower at the back of the building and bathed – the water was freezing but when your body is pouring out sweat in buckets nothing could possibly be more refreshing. Later, appropriately washed and dressed for the occasion, we sat down on the verandah to eat.

It was a long, drawn-out meal – a proper Greek *meze* – and we talked of old friends, dogs, women, the pursuit of happiness, Heraclitus and things not being as they seem. We filled and refilled our glasses, banging their bases on the table and clinking them together in the traditional manner and saying '*ya mas*' in a bizarre series of toasts that ranged from the Queen and Ray to mosquitoes and the Beckoning Ghost himself. One by one the bottles of alcohol all miraculously 'evaporated' – 'It must be the heat,' I laughed – until there were none left. And then Theo raised a finger and disappeared into the dark interior of the cottage, returning triumphantly a few moments later and presenting, with a flourish and a huge grin, the monstrous flagon of green Benedictine hooch.

How long we sat there drinking this potent brew, telling increasingly ludicrous stories that seemed to reach no obvious conclusion against the background chatter of cicadas and crickets, I can't recall. However, judging from the chimes of the clock tower in the village below it must certainly have been near midnight when Ray's ears pricked up and a sound like the breaking of twigs underfoot was heard in the olive grove. Theo straightened up immediately and threw on his monk's outfit which he had placed nearby for this purpose. Then, having no need of candles as his knowledge of the area was so good, he headed off into the night. As he reached the edge of our circle of light he turned and, putting his finger to his lips to maintain my silence, signed for me to wait there and guard base. Ray followed him into the darkness at a tense crouch, his eyes keen and his nose twitching.

A few minutes passed, and as nothing seemed to be happening I poured myself another glass of Benedictine. By now the flagon was nearly empty and after all the beer and wine I confess my mind was starting to reel somewhat. It was also uncomfortably humid, a thunderstorm still threatened and a heavy mist seemed to permeate the trees around the cottage.

It was about five minutes later that I thought I saw a faint glimmer of light around the area of the Hermitage but then it disappeared. The village clock then began to chime the last hour of the day. Almost as the last bell faded there was a terrible scream and then all went quiet. I called out Theo's name to see if he was all right and peered out into the darkness. There was nothing to see. Concerned in case something had happened to my friend, I picked up a few candles and put on my shoes ready to move at a moment's notice if required.

My mind was put at ease when a few moments later, again just beyond the cottage's circle of light, I could make out Theo's hooded figure in the mist beckoning me to follow him and once more putting his finger to his mouth for me to keep quiet. There was no sign of Ray but I assumed he had gone on ahead.

Lighting one of my candles, I headed off in the direction Theo had taken, which seemed to be up the steep rise towards the old monastery. After a few false starts bumping into trees, I eventually found the path and tried to keep up with the hooded figure in front of me but only proceeded at a snail's pace. Pausing for a moment I looked back down the hill and could now see a flickering light again near the Hermitage. I was about to continue my climb after Theo when I heard a shout in his voice coming from below. Mystified, but assuming he was playing his ventriloquist's games again, I began climbing up the path once more. The next thing I knew was that something rushed past me at great speed up the path and knocked the candle out of my hand, extinguishing it instantly.

Terrified, I fumbled around for my matches in case whatever had struck me should return. Resting against a tree trunk, I was just about to strike a light with trembling hands when all at once the Thing was upon me.

I was knocked to the ground by the sudden impact of its weight. As I lashed out at it I had a horrific sensation that claws, not hands, touched my skin. There was also a sickly, snapping sound like the jaws of a bleached skull rapidly opening and shutting, opening and shutting, and then the smell – the damp, foul breath that I couldn't avoid inhaling as it was so close to my face – which seemed to come from hell itself. I wrestled with the creature's sinewy arms that appeared to be covered in wiry hair and then, fearing that I was not fighting a human thief but the grisly murdering monk himself returned from the dead, I began to despair of my life. I cried out in the direction of the monastery for Theo to help, but it only came out as one of those strangled cries one utters in nightmares, and I knew I was doomed.

Then suddenly a flickering light appeared on the path below us and I could make out Theo's worried face holding a candle. As if confronted by God himself, in an instant my attacker fell back and I stood up to gain my bearings. Lighting a candle myself now as Theo approached, divested of his monkly attire, I looked around me but could find no trace of my assailant.

'Where did he – It? – go?' I asked tremulously as Theo came up, followed by Ray.

'He ran up towards the monastery,' Theo replied in a low voice, 'and I am afraid that Ray must have mistaken you for our thief. It's very lucky I wasn't far behind and could hear you calling my name – are you all right?'

I was dumbfounded and breathed a huge sigh of relief. Of

course, it had been the dog! I'd got so drunk I'd even started to believe the story of the ghoulish monk myself! When I explained my fears to Theo he smiled briefly then signalled for me to keep my voice down and together we quickly climbed in silence the final stretch of path towards the church.

When we were only yards from the top we were both rooted to the spot by a blood-curdling wail and then, a few seconds later, a tremendous splash.

'The monk,' I gibbered. 'This time it really is the Horror.'

'No, no, calm down,' said Theo. 'It's the thief. He must have lost his footing and fallen over the ravine into the river. Quick, follow me – there's a short cut to the bottom down this goat track.'

Still shaking, I hurried as fast as I could down the pre-cipitous hillside but was unable to keep up with Theo and the dog. By the time I reached the rockpool everything appeared to be under control. The thief, a surly-looking type, probably from North Africa rather than Greece, stood dripping wet but otherwise miraculously intact physically after his fall into the water. His mental state was another matter. Neither Theo nor I could make out what he was saying in his curious accent but he kept pointing up to the monastery and the Hermitage with genuine fear in his eyes and held his arms out to us in supplication to fellow human beings.

Theo, however, suspecting a trick, slipped into the sha-dows, put on his monk's habit and started to throw his voice. The man's eyes bulged as the talking dog threatened even worse horrors if he didn't come quietly. Suddenly, looking at us as if we were not alive but shades of the night, the man became as meek as a lamb and we led him back through the valley to the outskirts of the village.

Reaching the house of the butcher, a mountain of a man with a huge, black beard and arms like small tree trunks, we phoned the local police and handed over the miscreant to his care while we returned to check what, if anything, had been stolen.

As an afterthought, as we turned to leave, Theo gestured to Ray to stay and keep guard over the thief as well while we returned to the cottage. He didn't look too happy at the prospect at first but apparently the dog knew the butcher well, as he was always giving him scraps of leftover meat, and he obeyed in due course. However, to maintain the mystery of the talking dog for the superstitious young thief, Theo turned back at the door and projected a final monologue into the dog's opening and shutting jaws.

'So, you'd leave me here with this filthy robber, would you? Well, just for that I'll never talk again!' And thereafter no sound emitted from his mouth. The butcher, who knew about Theo's ventriloquist act and Ray's inability to bark, smiled secretly, but the thief was completely taken in. He took off the crucifix on a chain around his neck and began to pray.

The next morning we both awoke with severe hangovers and, in my case at least, a large number of mosquito bites in the most unlikely places from wandering about near the rockpool after dark. The weather didn't help either as there was a leaden sky and the humidity was intense. Ray greeted me with a breathy lick and brought back memories of my terrifying encounter of the previous night – that dog really did have a personal hygiene problem!

Theo went out while I performed my ablutions and later returned to brew up some coffee on a Calor gas stove. We took this out on to the verandah and sipped it while we tried to piece together the final events of the early hours of St Alexander's Eve...

After returning from the butcher's house to the cottage, I had been instructed to check the treasures in the cupboard while Theo started to wander down to the Hermitage.

However, before I could do so Theo returned, saying that it was too dark to do the job properly now and anyway it had been a tiring night – better to wait until the morning. (It was this check that Theo had just performed while I was washing – nothing seemed to be missing.) At about this point the previous night Ray had turned up carrying a note attached to his collar and written by the local police chief. It basically thanked us and the dog for all our help and would we be so kind as to come down to the police station whenever was convenient to fill out the appropriate forms and to prefer any charges against our North African friend who had been safely locked up. Also, and this was rather curious, there had been an additional request:

> ... I would also be grateful, Theo, if you could sub-
> stantiate or otherwise the miscreant's allegation that a
> murder was committed in the vicinity of your cottage this
> evening. He names you as the perpetrator of this deed
> and claims that you then tried 'to kill him by throwing
> him over the cliff into the rockpool and were in league
> with the Hounds of Hell'. The offender seems to be
> somewhat unbalanced, eyes rolling and so forth, and
> is probably raving and just trying to distract the forces of
> the law from his guilt as a thief. That he is a stealer of
> religious artefacts is known to us as, by coincidence, we
> had recently found evidence of his crimes in a cave which
> also contained his motorbike. As a result we are pretty
> suspicious of anything he might say. However, I would
> appreciate it if you could shed any light on these allega-
> tions. Many thanks.
>
> Sergeant Manolis

At the time, we'd both been dead tired and, in my case at least, still pretty drunk. So we had basically concurred with

Manolis's deductions that the man was either simply lying to distract the attention of the authorities or had been so affected by his terrible fall and the confrontation with Ray, the apparently talking dog, that his mind had become unhinged. In short, we had laughed it off and gone wearily to bed, glad that we had caught a criminal.

However, as we sat there the following morning sipping coffee, Theo unfolded the sheet again in preparation for making an official reply and read it out aloud. When he reached the bit in the note about the murder allegations he suddenly paused and looked at me in a curious way. He raised his finger. 'I wonder...'

But I was already ahead of him. 'You don't seriously think that the thief had actually witnessed the impaling of the monk Andros in the Hermitage?'

'What do you think?' he replied, and he wasn't joking.

As the implications of this began to sink in, I asked Theo what he had discovered down at the Hermitage when he'd first heard the noise the previous evening.

'Well, the first thing that I noticed as I strolled through the olive grove in the dark was the flickering of a candle in front of me. Then it seemed to disappear. Now this could of course have meant that it had blown out, or he'd dropped it or ... that he'd gone inside the tunnel to the cave.'

'Then there was the scream,' I interrupted. 'And it certainly wasn't the sort of cry you'd make if you'd burnt yourself on a candle – it was horrible. I could hear the village clock striking the hour only shortly before. And then you came back to the cottage and told me to follow you up the hill and I dropped my candle and...'

'Wait a minute,' said Theo, putting his hand on my arm. 'What do you mean? I never came back to the cottage. The next time I saw you was on the path just after Ray had jumped on you thinking you were the thief.'

180

I took another sip of coffee. 'No, no, Theo, you came back to the cottage wearing your monk's gear – without Ray – and I followed you up the hill. Then someone knocked the candle out of my hand which I suppose now must have been the thief running past me up the hill to the monastery. And only *then* did I do my "wrestling the ghost" act. God! How stupid I feel about that now, but it was certainly pretty scary at the time, and I hope I didn't hurt the dear old dog.' I leant down and stroked Ray's head.

Theo put his cup down and suddenly looked ashen-faced. He looked straight at me.

'But don't you see, Toby, old friend, it *couldn't* have been me at the house then, as I was running after the thief from *below* the cottage. When you were fighting off your imaginary assailant you must have noticed that when I arrived I was coming *up* the hill, not down it.'

'Ye-es...' I agreed reluctantly, and then must have looked puzzled, as he then continued:

'And I wasn't wearing my monk's habit by then. It had been far too hot and cumbersome when I began to chase after the thief so I had taken it off after I had encountered him on the path as I was going down, racing – as we now suppose – away from the horrors of the Hermitage. *I wasn't wearing the hooded costume, Toby ...*'

A horrible silence then ensued as we both realized the ghastly truth. I must really have seen the Beckoning Monk, en route from the Hermitage and the scene of his own death to the clifftop where he had murdered his colleague – the legendary ghost really had walked on St Alexander's Eve!

I still couldn't register what I was hearing.

'But it *was* you, Theo. You even put your finger to your mouth to keep quiet the way you'd done earlier. And ... and you were standing in the mist just outside the circle of light ... It was you, Theo. Come on, you're winding me up. There are no such things as ghosts ... Theo? – *For God's sake, man!*'

My memories suddenly became ever more frightening as Theo's voice broke in to try and comfort me.

'Hey, relax, my friend, it's all over. And anyway you should thank your lucky stars that good old Ray here knocked you down and someone else – the thief – accidentally followed the ghost up the hill. Though, as it happens, in this case it was presumably both to get away from the sight in the Hermitage and to try and steal the treasures in the monastery rather than following his beckoning finger.'

'Why, what's so good about being knocked over by a dog that scared me half to death?' I asked.

'But don't you see? It was a true Act of Dog, as it were. Otherwise it might have been *you* who would have ended up in the rockpool, not our North African friend. And don't forget, he was a lot fitter and leaner than you. If you had fallen 200 feet you might not have come out of it so well.'

Theo's supposed words of comfort had quite the opposite effect on me. I could have died last night, I now realized. I had seen a genuine ghost and really could have died. I stared around the beautiful countryside about the cottage in disbelief. The happy drone of the giant black bees, the scent of oleander, the olive grove, the crickets and cicadas – I might never have witnessed beauty again. And all this, instead of being a welcoming change in my humdrum life, would in retrospect have been seen as the opening chapter of the nightmare story of my death. Nothing, indeed, is quite what it seems.

Then, as if drawn by some strange magnetic force, my gaze drifted towards the fennel patch once more. And there, flitting innocently in this apparent paradise, were a pair of delightful swallowtail butterflies, hovering and darting in a ritual that dates from the beginning of time. I watched as they fluttered ever upwards towards the grapevines on the trellis and across towards the window of my room. There was a twitch in the corner of the glass as they flew past and one of those long-legged Cretan spiders moved out from the shadows. Caught in its web was a Death's-Head Moth.

The first drops of rain from the thunderstorm that had threatened for days then began to fall. Within seconds all hell let loose.

Thurnley Abbey

Perceval Landon

Three years ago I was on my way out to the East, and as an extra day in London was of some importance, I took the Friday evening mail-train to Brindisi instead of the usual Thursday morning Marseilles express. Many people shrink from the long forty-eight-hour train journey through Europe, and the subsequent rush across the Mediterranean on the nineteen-knot *Isis* or *Osiris*; but there is really very little discomfort on either the train or the mail-boat, and unless there is actually nothing for me to do, I always like to save the extra day and a half in London before I say goodbye to her for one of my longer tramps. This time – it was early, I remember, in the shipping season, probably about the beginning of September – there were few passengers, and I had a compartment in the P. & O. Indian express to myself all the way from Calais. All Sunday I watched the blue waves dimpling the Adriatic, and the pale rosemary along the cuttings; the plain white towns, with their flat roofs and their bold *duomos*, and the grey-green gnarled olive orchards of Apulia. The journey was just like any other. We ate in the dining-car as often and as long as we decently could. We slept after luncheon; we dawdled the afternoon away with yellow-backed novels; sometimes we exchanged platitudes in the smoking-room, and it was there that I met Alastair Colvin.

Colvin was a man of middle height, with a resolute, well-cut jaw; his hair was turning grey; his moustache was sun-whitened, otherwise he was clean-shaven – obviously a gentleman, and obviously also a preoccupied man. He had no great wit. When spoken to, he made the usual remarks in the right way, and I dare say he refrained from banalities only because he spoke less than the rest of us; most of the time he buried himself in the Wagon-lit Company's timetable, but seemed unable to concentrate his attention on any one page of it. He found that I had been over the Siberian railway, and for a quarter of an hour he discussed it with me. Then he lost interest in it, and rose to go to his compartment. But he came back again very soon, and seemed glad to pick up the conversation again.

Of course this did not seem to me to be of any importance. Most travellers by train become a trifle infirm of purpose after thirty-six hours' rattling. But Colvin's restless way I noticed in somewhat marked contrast with the man's personal importance and dignity; especially ill suited was it to his finely made large hand with strong, broad, regular nails and its few lines. As I looked at his hand I noticed a long, deep, and recent scar of ragged shape. However, it is absurd to pretend that I thought anything was unusual. I went off at five o'clock on Sunday afternoon to sleep away the hour or two that had still to be got through before we arrived at Brindisi.

Once there, we few passengers transhipped our hand baggage, verified our berths – there were only a score of us in all – and then, after an aimless ramble of half an hour in Brindisi, we returned to dinner at the Hôtel International, not wholly surprised that the town had been the death of Virgil. If I remember rightly, there is a gaily painted hall at the International – I do not wish to advertise anything, but there is no other place in Brindisi at which to await the coming of the mails – and after dinner I was looking with awe at a trellis overgrown with blue vines, when Colvin moved across the room to my table. He picked up *Il Secolo*, but almost immediately gave up the pretence of reading it. He turned squarely to me and said:

'Would you do me a favour?'

One doesn't do favours to stray acquaintances on Continental expresses without knowing something more of them than I knew of Colvin. But I smiled in a noncommittal way, and asked him what he wanted. I wasn't wrong in part of my estimate of him; he said bluntly:

'Will you let me sleep in your cabin on the *Osiris*?' And he coloured a little as he said it.

Now, there is nothing more tiresome than having to put up with a stable-companion at sea, and I asked him rather pointedly:

'Surely there is room for all of us?' I thought that perhaps he had been partnered off with some mangy Levantine, and wanted to escape from him at all hazards.

Colvin, still somewhat confused, said: 'Yes; I am in a cabin by myself. But you would do me the greatest favour if you would allow me to share yours.'

This was all very well, but, besides the fact that I always sleep better when alone, there had been some recent thefts on board English liners, and I hesitated, frank and honest and self-conscious as Colvin was. Just then the mail-train came in with a clatter and a rush of escaping steam, and I asked him to see me again about it on the boat when we started. He answered me curtly – I suppose he saw the mistrust in my manner – 'I am a member of White's.' I smiled to myself as he said it, but I remembered in a moment that the man – if he were really what he claimed to be, and I make no doubt that he was – must have been sorely put to it before he urged the fact as a guarantee of his respectability to a total stranger at a Brindisi hotel.

That evening, as we cleared the red and green harbour-lights of Brindisi, Colvin explained. This is his story in his own words.

'When I was travelling in India some years ago, I made the acquaintance of a youngish man in the Woods and Forests. We camped out together for a week, and I found him a pleasant companion. John Broughton was a light-hearted soul when off duty, but a steady and capable man in any of the small emergencies that continually arise in that department. He was liked and trusted by the natives, and though a trifle over-pleased with himself when he escaped to civilization at Simla or Calcutta, Broughton's future was well assured in Government service, when a fair-sized estate was unexpectedly left to him, and he joyfully shook the dust of the Indian plains from his feet and returned to England. For five years he drifted about London. I saw him now and then. We dined together about every eighteen months, and I could trace pretty exactly the gradual sickening of Broughton with a merely idle life. He then set out on a couple of long voyages, returned as restless as before, and at last told me that he had decided to marry and settle down at his place, Thurnley Abbey, which had long been empty. He spoke about looking after the property and standing for his constituency in the usual way. Vivien Wilde, his fiancée, had, I suppose, begun to take him in hand. She was a pretty girl with a deal of fair hair and rather an exclusive manner; deeply religious in a narrow school, she was still kindly and high-spirited, and I thought that Broughton was in luck. He was quite happy and full of information about his future.

'Among other things, I asked him about Thurnley Abbey. He confessed that he hardly knew the place. The last tenant, a man called Clarke, had lived in one wing for fifteen years and seen no one. He had been a miser and a hermit. It was the rarest thing for a light to be seen at the Abbey after dark. Only the barest necessities of life were ordered, and the tenant himself received them at the side-door. His one half-caste manservant, after a month's stay in the house, had abruptly left without warning, and had returned to the Southern States. One thing Broughton complained bitterly about: Clarke had wilfully spread the rumour among the villagers that the Abbey was haunted, and had even condescended to play childish tricks with spirit-lamps and salt in order to scare trespassers away at night. He had been detected in the act of this tomfoolery, but the story spread, and no one, said Broughton, would venture near the house except in broad daylight. The hauntedness of Thurnley Abbey was now, he said with a grin, part of the gospel of the countryside, but he and his young wife were going to change all that. Would I propose myself any time I liked? I, of course, said I would, and equally, of course, intended to do nothing of the sort without a definite invitation.

'The house was put in thorough repair, though not a stick of the old furniture and tapestry were removed. Floors and ceilings were relaid: the roof was made watertight again, and the dust of half a century was scoured out. He showed me some photographs of the place. It was called an Abbey, though as a matter of fact it had been only the infirmary of the long-vanished Abbey of Closter some five miles away. The larger part of this building remained as it had been in pre-Reformation days, but a wing had been added in Jacobean times, and that part of the house had been kept in something like repair by Mr Clarke. He had in both the ground and first floors set a heavy timber door, strongly barred with iron, in the passage between the earlier and the Jacobean parts of the house, and had entirely neglected the former. So there had been a good deal of work to be done.

'Broughton, whom I saw in London two or three times about this period, made a deal of fun over the positive refusal of the workmen to remain after sundown. Even after electric light had been put into every room, nothing would induce them to remain, though, as Broughton observed, electric light was death on ghosts. The legend of the Abbey's ghosts had gone far and wide, and the men would take no risks. They went home in batches of five and six, and even during the daylight hours there was an inordinate amount of talking between one and another, if either happened to be out of sight of his companion. On the whole, though nothing of any sort or kind had been conjured up even by their heated imaginations during their five months' work upon the Abbey, the belief in the ghosts was rather strengthened than otherwise in Thurnley because of the men's confessed nervousness, and local tradition declared itself in favour of the ghost of an immured nun.

' "Good old nun!" said Broughton.

'I asked him whether in general he believed in the possibility of ghosts, and, rather to my surprise, he said that he couldn't say he entirely disbelieved in them. A man in India had told him one morning in camp that he believed that his mother was dead in England, as her vision had come to his tent the night before. He had not been alarmed, but had said nothing, and the figure vanished again. As a matter of fact, the next possible *dak-walla* brought on a telegram announcing the mother's death. "There the thing was," said Broughton. But at Thurnley he was practical enough. He roundly cursed the idiotic selfishness of Clarke, whose silly antics had caused all the inconvenience. At the same time, he couldn't refuse to sympathize to some extent with the ignorant workmen. "My own idea," said he, "is that if a ghost ever does come in one's way, one ought to speak to it."

'I agreed. Little as I knew of the ghost world and its conventions, I had always remembered that a spook was in honour bound to wait to be spoken to. It didn't seem much to do, and I felt that the sound of one's own voice would at any rate reassure oneself as to one's wakefulness. But there are few ghosts outside Europe – few, that is, that a white man can see – and I had never been troubled with any. However, as I have said, I told Broughton that I agreed.

'So the wedding took place, and I went to it in a tall hat which I bought for the occasion, and the new Mrs Broughton smiled very nicely at me afterwards. As it had to happen, I took the Orient Express that evening and was not in England again for nearly six months. Just before I came back I got a letter from Broughton. He asked if I could see him in London or come to Thurnley, as he thought I should be better able to help him than anyone else he knew. His wife sent a nice message to me at the end, so I was reassured about at least one thing. I wrote from Budapest that I would come and see him at Thurnley two days after my arrival in London, and as I sauntered out of the Pannonia into the Kerepesi Utcza to post my letters, I wondered of what earthly service I could be to Broughton. I had been out with him after tiger on foot, and I could imagine few men better able at a pinch to manage their own business. However, I had nothing to do, so after dealing with some small accumulations of business during my absence, I packed a kit-bag and departed to Euston.

'I was met by Broughton's great limousine at Thurnley Road station, and after a drive of nearly seven miles we echoed through the sleepy streets of Thurnley village, into which the main gates of the park thrust themselves, splendid with pillars and spreadeagles and tom-cats rampant atop of them. I never was a herald, but I know that the Broughtons have the right to supporters – Heaven knows why! From the gates a quadruple avenue of beech-trees led inwards for a quarter of a mile. Beneath them a neat strip of fine turf edged the road and ran back until the poison of the dead beech-leaves killed it under the trees. There were many wheel-tracks on the road, and a comfortable little pony trap jogged past me laden with a country parson and his wife and daughter. Evidently there was some garden party going on at the Abbey. The road dropped away to the right at the end of the avenue, and I could see the Abbey across a wide pasturage and a broad lawn thickly dotted with guests.

'The end of the building was plain. It must have been almost mercilessly austere when it was first built, but time had crumbled the edges and toned the stone down to an orange-lichened grey wherever it showed behind its curtain of magnolia, jasmine, and ivy. Further on was the three-storeyed Jacobean house, tall and handsome. There had not been the slightest attempt to adapt the one to the other, but the kindly ivy had glossed over the touching-point. There was a tall flèche in the middle of the building, surmounting a small bell-tower. Behind the house there rose the mountainous verdure of Spanish chestnuts all the way up the hill.

'Broughton had seen me coming from afar, and walked across from his other guests to welcome me before turning me over to the butler's care. This man was sandy-haired and rather inclined to be talkative. He could, however, answer hardly any questions about the house; he had, he said, only been there three weeks. Mindful of what Broughton had told me, I made no enquiries about ghosts, though the room into which I was shown might have justified anything. It was a very large low room with oak beams projecting from the white ceiling. Every inch of the walls, including the doors, was covered with tapestry, and a remarkably fine Italian four-poster bedstead, heavily draped, added to the darkness and dignity of the place. All the furniture was old, well made, and dark. Underfoot there was a plain green pile carpet, the only new thing about the room except the electric light fittings and the jugs and basins. Even the looking-glass on the dressing-table was an old pyramidal Venetian glass set in a heavy repoussé frame of tarnished silver.

'After a few minutes' cleaning up, I went downstairs and out upon the lawn, where I greeted my hostess. The people gathered there were of the usual country type, all anxious to be pleased and roundly curious as to the new master of the Abbey. Rather to my surprise, and quite to my pleasure, I rediscovered Glenham, whom I had known well in the old days in Barotseland: he lived quite close, as, he remarked with a grin, I ought to have known. "But," he added, "I don't live in a place like this." He swept his hand to the long, low lines of the Abbey in obvious admiration, and then, to my intense interest, muttered beneath his breath, "Thank God!" He saw that I had overheard him, and turning to me said decidedly, "Yes, 'thank God' I said, and I meant it. I wouldn't live at the Abbey for all Broughton's money."

' "But surely," I demurred, "you know that old Clarke was discovered in the very act of setting light to his bug-a-boos?"

'Glenham shrugged his shoulders. "Yes, I know about that. But there is something wrong with the place still. All I can say is that Broughton is a different man since he has lived here. I don't believe that he will remain much longer. But – you're staying here? – well, you'll hear about it tonight. There's a big dinner, I understand." The conversation turned off to old reminiscences, and Glenham soon after had to go.

'Before I went to dress that evening I had twenty minutes' talk with Broughton in his library. There was no doubt that the man was altered, gravely altered. He was nervous and fidgety, and I found him looking at me only when my eye was off him. I naturally asked him what he wanted of me. I told him I would do anything I could, but that I couldn't conceive what he lacked that I could provide. He said with a lustreless smile that there was, however, something, and that he would tell me the following morning. It struck me that he was somehow ashamed of himself, and perhaps ashamed of the part he was asking me to play. However, I dismissed the subject from my mind and went up to dress in my palatial room. As I shut the door a draught blew out the Queen of Sheba from the wall, and I noticed that the tapestries were not fastened to the wall at the bottom. I have always held very practical views about spooks, and it has often seemed to me that the slow waving in firelight of loose tapestry upon a wall would account for ninety-nine per cent of the stories one hears. Certainly the dignified undulation of this lady with her attendants and huntsmen – one of whom was untidily cutting the throat of a fallow deer upon the very steps on which King Solomon, a grey-faced Flemish nobleman with the order of the Golden Fleece, awaited his fair visitor – gave colour to my hypothesis.

'Nothing much happened at dinner. The people were very much like those of the garden party. A young woman next to me seemed anxious to know what was being read in London. As she was far more familiar than I with the most recent magazines and literary supplements, I found salvation in being myself instructed in the tendencies of modern fiction. All true art, she said, was shot through and through with melancholy. How vulgar were the attempts at wit that marked so many modern books! From the beginning of literature it had always been tragedy that embodied the highest attainment of every age. To call such works morbid merely begged the question. No thoughtful man – she looked sternly at me through the steel rim of her glasses – could fail to agree with me. Of course, as one would, I immediately and properly said that I slept with Pett Ridge and Jacobs under my pillow at night, and that if *Jorrocks* weren't quite so large and cornery, I would add him to the company. She hadn't read any of them, so I was saved – for a time. But I remember grimly that she said that the dearest wish of her life was to be in some awful and soul-freezing situation of horror, and I remember that she dealt hardly with the hero of Nat Paynter's vampire story, between nibbles at her brown-bread ice. She was a cheerless soul, and I couldn't help thinking that if there were many such in the neighbourhood, it was not surprising that old Glenham had been stuffed with some nonsense or other about the Abbey. Yet nothing could well have been less creepy than the glitter of silver and glass, and the subdued lights and cackle of conversation all round the dinner-table.

'After the ladies had gone, I found myself talking to the rural dean. He was a thin, earnest man, who at once turned the conversation to old Clarke's buffooneries. But, he said, Mr Broughton had introduced such a new and cheerful spirit, not only into the Abbey, but, he might say, into the whole neighbourhood, that he had great hopes that the ignorant superstitions of the past were henceforth destined to oblivion. Thereupon his other neighbour, a portly gentleman of independent means and position, audibly remarked "Amen", which damped the rural dean, and we talked of partridges past, partridges present, and pheasants to come. At the other end of the table Broughton sat with a couple of his friends, red-faced hunting men. Once I noticed that they were discussing me, but I paid no attention to it at the time. I remembered it a few hours later.

'By eleven all the guests were gone, and Broughton, his wife, and I were alone together under the fine plaster ceiling of the Jacobean drawing-room. Mrs Broughton talked about one or two of the neighbours, and then, with a smile, said that she knew I would excuse her, shook hands with me, and went off to bed. I am not very good at analysing things, but I felt that she talked a little uncomfortably and with a suspicion of effort, smiled rather conventionally, and was obviously glad to go. These things seem trifling enough to repeat, but I had throughout the faint feeling that everything was not square.

Under the circumstances, this was enough to set me wondering what on earth the service could be that I was to render – wondering also whether the whole business were not some ill-advised jest in order to make me come down from London for a mere shooting-party.

'Broughton said little after she had gone. But he was evidently labouring to bring the conversation round to the so-called haunting of the Abbey. As soon as I saw this, of course, I asked him directly about it. He then seemed at once to lose interest in the matter. There was no doubt about it: Broughton was somehow a changed man, and to my mind he had changed in no way for the better. Mrs Broughton seemed no sufficient cause. He was clearly very fond of her, and she of him. I reminded him that he was going to tell me what I could do for him in the morning, pleaded my journey, lighted a candle, and went upstairs with him. At the end of the passage leading into the old house he grinned weakly and said, "Mind, if you see a ghost, do talk to it; you said you would." At the door of his dressing-room he paused once more. "I'm here," he called out, "if you should want anything. Good night," and he shut his door.

'I went along the passage to my room, undressed, switched on a lamp beside my bed, read a few pages of *The Jungle Book*, and then, more than ready for sleep, turned the light off and went fast asleep.

'Three hours later I woke up. There was not a breath of wind outside. There was not even a flicker of light from the fireplace. As I lay there, an ash tinkled slightly as it cooled, but there was hardly a gleam of the dullest red in the grate. An owl cried among the silent Spanish chestnuts on the slope outside. I idly reviewed the events of the day, hoping that I should fall off to sleep again before I reached dinner. But at the end I seemed as wakeful as ever. There was no help for it. I must

195

read my *Jungle Book* again till I felt ready to go off, so I fumbled for the pear at the end of the cord that hung down inside the bed, and I switched on the bedside lamp. The sudden glory dazzled me for a moment. I felt under my pillow for my book with half-shut eyes. Then, growing used to the light, I happened to look down to the foot of my bed.

'I can never tell you really what happened then. Nothing I could ever confess in the most abject words could even faintly picture to you what I felt. I know that my heart stopped dead, and my throat shut automatically. In one instinctive movement I crouched back up against the head-boards of the bed, staring at the horror. The movement set my heart going again, and the sweat dripped from every pore. I am not a particularly religious man, but I had always believed that God would never allow any supernatural appearance to present itself to man in such a guise and in such circumstances that harm, either bodily or mental, could result to him. I can only tell you that at that moment both my life and my reason rocked unsteadily on their seats.'

The other *Osiris* passengers had gone to bed. Only he and I remained leaning over the starboard railing, which rattled uneasily now and then under the fierce vibration of the over-engined mail-boat. Far over, there were the lights of a few fishing-smacks riding out the night, and a great rush of white combing and seething water fell out and away from us over-side.

At last Colvin went on:

'Leaning over the foot of my bed, looking at me, was a figure swathed in a rotten and tattered veiling. This shroud passed over the head, but left both eyes and the right side of the face bare. It then followed the line of the arm down to where the hand grasped the bed-end. The face was not entirely that of a skull, though the eyes and the flesh of the face were

196

totally gone. There was a thin, dry skin drawn tightly over the features, and there was some skin left on the hand. One wisp of hair crossed the forehead. It was perfectly still. I looked at it, and it looked at me, and my brains turned dry and hot in my head. I had still got the pear of the electric lamp in my hand, and I played idly with it; only I dared not turn the light out again. I shut my eyes, only to open them in a hideous terror the same second. The thing had not moved. My heart was thumping, and the sweat cooled me as it evaporated. Another cinder tinkled in the grate, and a panel creaked in the wall.

'My reason failed me. For twenty minutes, or twenty seconds, I was able to think of nothing else but this awful figure, till there came, hurtling through the empty channels of my senses, the remembrance that Broughton and his friends had discussed me furtively at dinner. The dim possibility of its being a hoax stole gratefully into my unhappy mind, and once there, one's pluck came creeping back along a thousand tiny veins. My first sensation was one of blind unreasoning thankfulness that my brain was going to stand the trial. I am not a timid man, but the best of us needs some human handle to steady him in time of extremity, and in this faint but growing hope that after all it might be only a brutal hoax, I found the fulcrum that I needed. At last I moved.

'How I managed to do it I cannot tell you, but with one spring towards the foot of the bed I got within arm's-length and struck out one fearful blow with my fist at the thing. It crumpled under it, and my hand was cut to the bone. With a sickening revulsion after my terror, I dropped half-fainting across the end of the bed. So it was merely a foul trick after all. No doubt the trick had been played many a time before: no doubt Broughton and his friends had had some large bet among themselves as to what I should do when I discovered the gruesome thing. From my state of abject terror I found myself transported into an insensate anger. I shouted curses upon Broughton. I dived rather than climbed over the bed-end on to the sofa. I tore at the robed skeleton – how well the whole thing had been carried out, I thought – I broke the skull against the floor, and stamped upon its dry bones. I flung the head away under the bed, and rent the brittle bones of the trunk in pieces. I snapped the thin thigh-bones across my knee, and flung them in different directions. The shin-bones I set against a stool and broke with my heel. I raged like a Berserker against the loathly thing, and stripped the ribs from the backbone and slung the breastbone against the cupboard. My fury increased as the work of destruction went on. I tore the frail rotten veil into twenty pieces, and the dust went up over everything, over the clean blotting-paper and the silver inkstand. At last my work was done. There was but a raffle of broken bones and strips of parchment and crumbling wool. Then, picking up a piece of the skull – it was the cheek and temple bone of the right side, I remember – I opened the door and went down the passage to Broughton's dressing-room. I remember still how my sweat-dripping pyjamas clung to me as I walked. At the door I kicked and entered.

'Broughton was in bed. He had already turned the light on and seemed shrunken and horrified. For a moment he could hardly pull himself together. Then I spoke. I don't know what I said. Only I know that from a heart full and over-full with hatred and contempt, spurred on by shame of my own recent cowardice, I let my tongue run on. He answered nothing. I was amazed at my own fluency. My hair still clung lankily to my wet temples, my hand was bleeding profusely, and I must have looked a strange sight. Broughton huddled himself up at the head of the bed just as I had. Still he made no answer, no defence. He seemed preoccupied with something besides my reproaches, and once or twice moistened his lips with his tongue. But he could say nothing though he moved his hands now and then, just as a baby who cannot speak moves its hands.

'At last the door into Mrs Broughton's room opened and she came in, white and terrified. "What is it? What is it? Oh, in God's name! what is it?" she cried again and again, and then she went up to her husband and sat on the bed in her night-dress, and the two faced me. I told her what the matter was. I spared her husband not a word for her presence there. Yet he seemed hardly to understand. I told the pair that I had spoiled their cowardly joke for them. Broughton looked up.

' "I have smashed the foul thing into a hundred pieces," I said. Broughton licked his lips again and his mouth worked. "By God!" I shouted, "it would serve you right if I thrashed you within an inch of your life. I will take care that not a decent man or woman of my acquaintance ever speaks to you again. And there," I added, throwing the broken piece of the skull upon the floor beside his bed, "there is a souvenir for you, of your damned work tonight!"

'Broughton saw the bone, and in a moment it was his turn to frighten me. He squealed like a hare caught in a trap. He screamed and screamed till Mrs Broughton, almost as bewildered as myself, held on to him and coaxed him like a child to be quiet. But Broughton – and as he moved I thought that ten minutes ago I perhaps looked as terribly ill as he did – thrust her from him, and scrambled out of the bed on to the floor, and still screaming put out his hand to the bone. It had blood on it from my hand. He paid no attention to me whatever. In truth I said nothing. This was a new turn indeed to the horrors of the evening. He rose from the floor with the bone in his hand and stood silent. He seemed to be listening. "Time, time, perhaps," he muttered, and almost at the same moment fell at full length on the carpet, cutting his head against the fender. The bone flew from his hand and came to rest near the door. I picked Broughton up, haggard and broken, with blood over his face. He whispered hoarsely and quickly, "Listen, listen!" We listened.

199

'After ten seconds' utter quiet, I seemed to hear something. I could not be sure, but at last there was no doubt. There was a quiet sound as of one moving along the passage. Little regular steps came towards us over the hard oak flooring. Broughton moved to where his wife sat, white and speechless, on the bed, and pressed her face into his shoulder.

'Then, the last thing that I could see as he turned the light out, he fell forward with his own head pressed into the pillow of the bed. Something in their company, something in their cowardice, helped me, and I faced the open doorway of the room, which was outlined fairly clearly against the dimly lighted passage. I put out one hand and touched Mrs Broughton's shoulder in the darkness. But at the last moment I too failed. I sank on my knees and put my face in the bed. Only we all heard. The footsteps came to the door, and there they stopped. The piece of bone was lying a yard inside the door. There was a rustle of moving stuff, and the thing was in the room. Mrs Broughton was silent: I could hear Broughton's voice praying, muffled in the pillow. I was cursing my own cowardice. Then the steps moved out again on the oak boards of the passage, and I heard the sounds dying away. In a flash of remorse I went to the door and looked out. At the end of the corridor I thought I saw something that moved away. A moment later the passage was empty. I stood with my forehead against the jamb of the door almost physically sick.

' "You can turn the light on," I said, and there was an answering flare. There was no bone at my feet. Mrs Broughton had fainted. Broughton was almost useless, and it took me ten minutes to bring her to. Broughton only said one thing worth remembering. For the most part, he went on muttering prayers. But I was glad afterwards to recollect that he had said that thing. He said in a colourless voice, half as a question, half as a reproach, "You didn't speak to her."

'We spent the remainder of the night together. Mrs

Broughton actually fell off into a kind of sleep before dawn, but she suffered so horribly in her dreams that I shook her into consciousness again. Never was dawn so long in coming. Three or four times Broughton spoke to himself. Mrs Broughton would then just tighten her hold on his arm, but she could say nothing. As for me, I can honestly say that I grew worse as the hours passed and the light strengthened. The two violent reactions had battered down on my steadiness of view, and I felt that the foundations of my life had been built upon sand. I said nothing, and after binding up my hand with a towel, I did not move. It was better so. They helped me and I helped them, and we all three knew that our reason had gone very near to ruin that night. At last, when the light came in pretty strongly, and the birds outside were chattering and singing, we felt that we must do something. Yet we never moved. You might have thought that we should particularly dislike being found as we were by the servants; yet nothing of that kind mattered a straw, and an overpowering listlessness bound us as we sat, until Chapman, Broughton's man, actually knocked and opened the door. None of us moved. Broughton, speaking hardly and stiffly, said, "Chapman, you can come back in five minutes." Chapman was a discreet man, but it would have made no difference to us if he had carried his news to the "room" at once.

'We looked at each other and I said I must go back. I meant to wait outside till Chapman returned. I simply dared not re-enter my bedroom alone. Broughton roused himself and said that he would come with me. Mrs Broughton agreed to remain in her own room for five minutes if the blinds were drawn up and all the doors left open.

'So Broughton and I, leaning stiffly one against the other, went down to my room. By the morning light that filtered past the blinds we could see our way, and I released the blinds. There was nothing wrong in the room from end to end, except

201

smears of my own blood on the end of the bed, on the sofa, and on the carpet where I had torn the thing to pieces.'

Colvin had finished his story. There was nothing to say. Seven bells stuttered out from the fo'c'sle, and the answering cry wailed through the darkness. I took him downstairs.

'Of course I am much better now, but it is a kindness of you to let me sleep in your cabin.'

Gray Dolphin

Rev. R. H. Barham

'He won't – won't he? Then bring me my boots!' said the Baron.

Consternation was at its height in the castle of Shurland – a caitiff had dared to disobey the Baron! and – the Baron had called for his boots!

A thunderbolt in the great hall had been a *bagatelle* to it.

A few days before, a notable miracle had been wrought in the neighbourhood; and in those times miracles were not so common as they are now; no royal balloons, no steam, no railroads – while the few Saints who took the trouble to walk with their heads under their arms, or to pull the Devil by the nose – scarcely appeared above once in a century; so the affair made the greater sensation.

The clock had done striking twelve, and the Clerk of Chatham was untrussing his points preparatory to seeking his truckle-bed; a half-emptied tankard of mild ale stood at his elbow, the roasted crab yet floating on its surface. Midnight had surprised the worthy functionary while occupied in discussing it, and with his task yet unaccomplished. He meditated a mighty draft; one hand was fumbling with his tags, while the other was extended in the act of grasping the jorum, when a knock on the portal, solemn and sonorous, arrested his fingers. It was repeated thrice ere Emmanuel Saddleton had presence of mind sufficient to enquire who sought admission at that untimeous hour.

'Open! open! good Clerk of St Bridget's,' said a female voice, small, yet distinct and sweet – an excellent thing in woman.

The Clerk arose, crossed to the doorway, and undid the latchet.

On the threshold stood a lady of surpassing beauty: her robes were rich, and large, and full; and a diadem sparkling with gems that shed a halo around, crowned her brow: she beckoned the Clerk as he stood in astonishment before her.

'Emmanuel!' said the Lady; and her tones sounded like those of a silver flute. 'Emmanuel Saddleton, truss up your points, and follow me!'

The worthy Clerk stared aghast at the vision; the purple robe, the cymar, the coronet – above all, the smile; no, there was no mistaking her: it was the blessed St Bridget herself!

And what could have brought the sainted lady out of her warm shrine at such a time of night? and on such a night? for it was as dark as pitch, and, metaphorically speaking, 'rained cats and dogs'.

Emmanuel could not speak, so he looked the question.

'No matter for that,' said the Saint, answering to his thought. 'No matter for that, Emmanuel Saddleton; only follow me, and you'll see!'

The Clerk turned a wistful eye at the corner cupboard.

'Oh! never mind the lantern, Emmanuel: you'll not want it, but you may bring a mattock and a shovel.' As he spoke, the beautiful apparition held up her delicate hand. From the tip of each of her long taper fingers issued a lambent flame of such surpassing brilliancy as would have plunged a whole gas company into despair – it was a 'Hand of Glory', such a one as tradition tells us yet burns in Rochester Castle every St Mark's Eve. Many are the daring individuals who have watched in Gundulph's Tower, hoping to find it, and the treasure it guards – but none of them ever did.

'This way, Emmanuel!' and a flame of peculiar radiance

streamed from her little finger as it pointed to the pathway leading to the churchyard.

Saddleton shouldered his tools, and followed in silence.

The cemetery of St Bridget's was some half-mile distant from the Clerk's domicile, and adjoined a chapel dedicated to that illustrious lady, who, after leading but a so-so life, had died in the odour of sanctity. Emmanuel Saddleton was fat and scant of breath, the mattock was heavy, and the Saint walked too fast for him: he paused to take second wind at the end of the first furlong.

'Emmanuel,' said the holy lady good-humouredly, for she heard him puffing; 'rest awhile, Emmanuel, and I'll tell you what I want with you.'

Her auditor wiped his brow with the back of his hand, and looked all attention and obedience.

'Emmanuel,' continued she, 'what did you and Father Fothergill, and the rest of you, mean yesterday by burying that drowned man so close to me? He died in mortal sin, Emmanuel; no shrift, no unction, no absolution; why, he might as well have been excommunicated. He plagues me with his grinning, and I can't have any peace in my shrine. You must howk him up again, Emmanuel!'

'To be sure, madam – my lady – that is, your holiness,' stammered Saddleton, trembling at the thought of the task assigned him. 'To be sure, your ladyship; only – that is –'

'Emmanuel,' said the Saint, 'you'll do my bidding; or it would be better you had!' and her eye changed from a dove's eye to that of a hawk, and a flash came from it as bright as the one from her little finger. The Clerk shook in his shoes; and, again dashing the cold perspiration from his brow, followed the footsteps of his mysterious guide.

The next morning all Chatham was in an uproar. The Clerk of St Bridget's had found himself at home at day-break,

seated in his own armchair, the fire out, and – the tankard of
ale out too! Who had drunk it? – where had he been? – how
had he got home? – all was mystery! – he remembered 'a mass
of things but nothing distinctly'; all was fog and fantasy.
What he could clearly recollect was, that he had dug up the
Grinning Sailor, and that the Saint had helped to throw him
into the river again. All was thenceforth wonderment and
devotion. Masses were sung, tapers were kindled, bells were
tolled; the monks of St Romuald had a solemn procession,
the abbot at their head, the sacristan at their tail, and the holy
breeches of St Thomas à Becket in the centre; Father
Fothergill brewed a XXX puncheon of holy water. The
Rood of Gillingham was deserted; the chapel of Rainham
forsaken; everyone who had a soul to be saved, flocked with
his offering to St Bridget's shrine, and Emmanuel Saddleton
gathered more fees from the promiscuous piety of that one
week than he had pocketed during the twelve preceding
months.

Meanwhile the corpse of the ejected reprobate oscillated like
a pendulum between Sheerness and Gillingham Reach. Now
borne by the Medway into the Western Swale, now carried by
the refluent tide back to the vicinity of its old quarters – it
seemed as though the River-god and Neptune were amusing
themselves with a game of subaqueous battledore, and had
chosen this unfortunate carcass as a marine shuttlecock. For
some time the alternation was kept up with great spirit, till
Boreas, interfering in the shape of a stiffish 'Nor'-wester',
drifted the bone (and flesh) of contention ashore on the
Shurland domain, where it lay in all the majesty of mud. It
was soon discovered by the retainers, and dragged from its
oozy bed, grinning worse than ever. Tidings of the godsend
were of course carried instantly to the castle, for the Baron was
a very great man; and if a dun cow had flown across his
property unannounced by the warder, the Baron would have

kicked him, the said warder, from the topmost battlement into the bottommost ditch – a descent of peril, and one which 'Ludwig the Leaper', or the illustrious Trenck himself, might well have shrunk from encountering.

'An't please your lordship –' said Peter Periwinkle.

'No, villain! it does not please me!' roared the Baron.

His lordship was deeply engaged with a peck of Faversham oysters – he doted on shellfish, hated interruption at meals, and had not yet despatched more than twenty dozen of the 'natives'.

'There's a body, my lord, washed ashore in the lower creek,' said the seneschal.

The Baron was going to throw the shells at his head; but paused in the act, and said with much dignity –

'Turn out the fellow's pockets!'

But the defunct had before been subjected to the double scrutiny of Father Fothergill and the Clerk of St Bridget's. It was ill gleaning after such hands; there was not a single maravedi.

We have already said that Sir Robert de Shurland, Lord of the Isle of Sheppey, and of many a fair manor on the mainland, was a man of worship. He had rights of freewarren, saccage and sockage, cuisage and jambage, fosse and fork, infang theofe and outfang theofe; and all waifs and strays belonged to him in fee simple.

'Turn out his pockets!' said the knight.

'An't please you, my lord, I must say as how they was turned-out afore, and the devil a rap's left.'

'Then bury the blackguard!'

'Please your lordship, he has been buried once.'

'Then bury him again, and be –!' The Baron bestowed a benediction.

The seneschal bowed low as he left the room, and the Baron went on with his oysters.

Scarcely ten dozen more had vanished when Periwinkle reappeared.

'An't please you, my lord, Father Fothergill says as how that it's the Grinning Sailor, and he won't bury him anyhow.'

'Oh! he won't – won't he?' said the Baron. Can it be wondered at that he called for his boots?

Sir Robert de Shurland, Lord of Shurland and Minster, Baron of Sheppey *in comitatu* Kent, was, as has been before hinted, a very great man. He was also a very little man; that is, he was relatively great, and relatively little – or physically little, and metaphorically great – like Sir Sidney Smith and the late Mr Buonaparte. To the frame of a dwarf he united the soul of a giant, and the valour of a gamecock. Then, for so small a man, his strength was prodigious; his fist would fell an ox, and his kick! – oh! his kick was tremendous, and when he had his boots on, would – to use an expression of his own, which he had picked up in the holy wars – would 'send a man from Jericho to June'. He was bull-necked and bandy-legged; his chest was broad and deep, his head large and uncommonly thick, his eyes a little bloodshot, and his nose *retroussé* with a remarkable red tip. Strictly speaking, the Baron could not be called handsome; but his *tout ensemble* was singularly impressive: and when he called for his boots, everybody trembled and dreaded the worst.

'Periwinkle,' said the Baron, as he encased his better leg, 'let the grave be twenty feet deep!'

'Your lordship's command is law.'

'And, Periwinkle' – Sir Robert stamped his left heel into its receptacle –'and, Periwinkle, see that it be wide enough to hold not exceeding two!'

'Ye-ye-yes, my lord.'

'And, Periwinkle – tell Father Fothergill I would fain speak with his Reverence.'

'Ye-ye-yes, my lord.'

The Baron's beard was peaked; and his moustaches, stiff and stumpy, projected horizontally like those of a Tom Cat; he twirled the one, he stroked the other, he drew the buckle of his surcingle a thought tighter, and strode down the great staircase three steps at a stride.

The vassals were assembled in the great hall of Shurland Castle; every cheek was pale, every tongue was mute: expectation and perplexity were visible on every brow. What would his lordship do? Were the recusant anybody else, gyves to the heels and hemp to the throat were but too good for him: but it was Father Fothergill who had said 'I won't'; and though the Baron was a very great man, the Pope was a greater, and the Pope was Father Fothergill's great friend – some people said he was his uncle.

Father Fothergill was busy in the refectory trying conclusions with a venison pasty, when he received the summons of his patron to attend him in the chapel cemetery. Of course he lost no time in obeying it, for obedience was the general rule in Shurland Castle. If anybody ever said, 'I won't', it was the exception; and, like all other exceptions, only proved the rule the stronger. The Father was a friar of the Augustine persuasion; a brotherhood which, having been planted in Kent soil some few centuries earlier, had taken very kindly to the soil, and overspread the county much as hops did some few centuries later. He was plump and portly, a little thickwinded, especially after dinner, stood five feet four in his sandals, and weighed hard upon eighteen stone. He was, moreover, a personage of singular piety; and the iron girdle, which, he said, he wore under his cassock to mortify withal, might have been well mistaken for the tyre of a cartwheel. When he arrived, Sir Robert was pacing up and down by the side of a newly opened grave.

'*Benedicite!* fair son!' (the Baron was as brown as a cigar).

'*Benedicite!*' said the Chaplain.

The Baron was too angry to stand upon compliment.

'Bury me that grinning caitiff there!' quoth he, pointing to the defunct.

'It may not be, fair son,' said the friar; 'he hath perished without absolution.'

'Bury the body!' roared Sir Robert.

'Water and earth alike reject him,' returned the Chaplain; 'holy St Bridget herself –'

'Bridget me no Bridgets! – do me thine office quickly, Sir Shaveling! or, by the Piper that played before Moses –' The oath was a fearful one; and whenever the Baron swore to do mischief, he was never known to perjure himself. He was playing with the hilt of his sword. 'Do me thine office, I say. Give him his passport to heaven.'

'He is already gone to hell!' stammered the Friar.

'Then do you go after him!' thundered the Lord of Shurland.

His sword half leaped from its scabbard. No! – the trenchant blade, that had cut Suleiman Ben Malek Ben Buckskin from helmet to chine, disdained to daub itself with the cerebellum of a miserable monk; it leaped back again; and as the Chaplain, scared at its flash, turned him in terror, the Baron gave him a kick! – one kick! – it was but one! – but such a one! Despite its obesity, up flew his holy body in an angle of forty-five degrees; then having reached its highest point of elevation, sunk headlong into the open grave that yawned to receive it. If the reverend gentleman had possessed such a thing as a neck, he had infallibly broken it! as he did not, he only dislocated his vertebrae – but that did quite as well. He was as dead as ditch-water!

'In with the other rascal!' said the Baron – and he was obeyed; for there he stood in his boots. Mattock and shovel made short work of it; 20 feet of superincumbent mould pressed down alike the saint and the sinner. 'Now sing a requiem who list!' said the Baron, and his lordship went back to his oysters.

The vassals at Castle Shurland were astounded, or, as the Seneschal Hugh better expressed it, 'perfectly conglomerated', by this event. What! murder a monk in the odour of sanctity – and on consecrated ground too! They trembled for the health of the Baron's soul. To the unsophisticated many it seemed that matters could not have been much worse had he shot a bishop's coachhorse – all looked for some signal judgment. The melancholy catastrophe of their neighbours at Canterbury was yet rife in their memories: not two centuries had elapsed since those miserable sinners had cut off the tail of the blessed Sir Thomas's mule. The tail of the mule, it was well known, had been forthwith affixed to that of the Mayor; and rumour said it had since been hereditary in the corporation. The least that could be expected was, that Sir Robert should have a friar tacked on to his for the term of his natural life! Some bolder spirits there were, 'tis true, who viewed the matter in various lights, according to their different temperaments and dispositions; for perfect unanimity existed not even in the good old times. The verderer, roistering Hob Roebuck, swore roundly, ' 'Twere as good a deed as eat to kick down the chapel as well as the monk.' Hob had stood there in a white sheet for kissing Giles Miller's daughter. On the other hand, Simpkin Agnew, the bell-ringer, doubted if the devil's cellar, which runs under the bottomless abyss, were quite deep enough for the delinquent, and speculated on the probability of a hole being dug in it for his especial accommodation. The philosophers and economists thought, with Saunders M'Bullock, the Baron's bagpiper, that a 'feckless monk more or less was nae great subject for a clamjamphry', especially as 'the supply considerably exceeded the demand'; while Malthouse, the tapster, was arguing to Dame Martin that a murder now and then was a seasonable check to population, without which the Isle of

Sheppey would in time be devoured, like a mouldy cheese, by inhabitants of its own producing. Meanwhile, the Baron ate his oysters and thought no more of the matter.

But this tranquillity of his lordship was not to last. A couple of Saints had been seriously offended; and we have all of us read at school that celestial minds are by no means insensible to the provocations of anger. There were those who expected that St Bridget would come in person, and have the friar up again, as she did the sailor: but perhaps her ladyship did not care to trust herself within the walls of Shurland Castle. To say the truth, it was scarcely a decent house for a female saint to be seen in. The Baron's gallantries, since he became a widower, had been but too notorious; and her own reputation was a little blown upon in the earlier days of her earthly pilgrimage: then things were so apt to be misrepresented – in short, she would leave the whole affair to St Austin, who, being a gentleman, could interfere with propriety, avenge her affront as well as his own, and leave no loop-hole for scandal. St Austin himself seems to have had his scruples, though of their precise nature it would be difficult to determine, for it were idle to suppose him at all afraid of the Baron's boots. Be this as it may, the mode which he adopted was at once prudent and efficacious. As an ecclesiastic, he could not well call the Baron out – had his boots been out of the question; so he resolved to have recourse to the law. Instead of Shurland Castle, therefore, he repaired forthwith to his own magnificent monastery, situate just without the walls of Canterbury, and presented himself in a vision to its abbot. No one who has ever visited that ancient city can fail to recollect the splendid gateway which terminates the vista of St Paul's Street, and stands there yet in all its pristine beauty. The tiny train of miniature artillery which now adorns its battlements is, it is true, an ornament of a later date; and is said to have been added some centuries after by a learned but jealous proprietor, for the purpose of shooting any wiser man than himself, who might chance to come that way. Tradition is silent as to any discharge having taken place, nor can the oldest inhabitant of modern days recollect any such occurrence. Here it was, in a handsome chamber, immediately over the lofty archway, that the Superior of the monastery lay buried in a brief slumber, snatched from his accustomed vigils. His mitre – for he was a mitred Abbot, and had a seat in parliament – rested on a table beside him; near it stood a silver flagon of Gascony wine, ready, no doubt, for the pious uses of the morrow. Fasting and watching had made him more than usually somnolent, than which nothing could have been better for the purpose of the Saint, who now appeared to him radiant in all the colours of the rainbow.

'Anselm!' said the beatific vision. 'Anselm! are you not a pretty fellow to lie snoring there when your brethren are being knocked at head, and Mother Church herself is menaced? – It is a sin and a shame, Anselm!'

'What's the matter? – Who are you?' cried the Abbot, rubbing his eyes, which the celestial splendour of his visitor had set a-winking. 'Ave Maria. St Austin himself! Speak, *Beatissime!* what would you with the humblest of your votaries?'

'Anselm!' said the Saint, 'a brother of our order whose soul Heaven assoilzie! hath been foully murdered. He hath been ignominiously kicked to the death, Anselm; and there he lieth cheek-by-jowl with a wretched carcass, which our Sister Bridget has turned out of her cemetery for unseemly grinning. Arouse thee, Anselm!'

'Ay, so please you, *Sanctissime!*' said the Abbot. 'I will order forthwith that thirty masses be said, thirty *Paters*, and thirty *Aves.*'

'Thirty fools' heads!' interrupted his patron, who was a little peppery.

'I will send for bell, book, and candle –'

'Send for an inkhorn, Anselm. Write me now a letter to his Holiness the Pope in good round terms, and another to the Coroner, and another to the Sheriff, and seize me the never-enough-to-be-anathematized villain who hath done this deed! Hang him as high as Haman, Anselm! – up with him! – down with his dwelling-place, root and branch, hearth-stone and roof-tree – down with it all, and sow the site with salt and sawdust!'

St Austin, it will be perceived, was a radical reformer.

'Marry will I,' quoth the Abbot, warming with the Saint's eloquence; 'ay, marry will I, and that *instanter*. But there is one thing you have forgotten, most Beatified – the name of the culprit.'

'Robert de Shurland!'

'The Lord of Sheppey! Bless me!' said the Abbot, crossing himself; 'won't that be rather inconvenient? Sir Robert is a bold baron, and a powerful; blows will come and go, and crowns will be cracked, and –'

'What is that to you, since yours will not be of the number?'

'Very true, *Beatissime!* – I will don me with speed, and do your bidding.'

'Do so, Anselm! – fail not to hang the Baron, burn his castle, confiscate his estate, and buy me two large wax candles for my own particular shrine out of your share of the property.'

With this solemn injunction the vision began to fade.

'One thing more!' cried the Abbot, grasping his rosary.

'What is that?' asked the Saint.

'*O Beate Augustine, ora pro nobis!*'

'Of course I shall,' said St Austin. '*Pax vobiscum!*' – and Abbot Anselm was left alone.

Within an hour all Canterbury was in commotion. A friar had been murdered – two friars – ten – twenty; a whole convent had been assaulted, sacked, burned – all the monks had been killed, and all the nuns had been kissed! Murder! fire! sacrilege! Never was city in such an uproar. From St George's Gate to St Dunstan's suburb, from the Donjon to the borough of Staplegate, it was noise and hubbub. 'Where was it?' – 'When was it?' – 'How was it?' The Mayor caught up his chain, the Aldermen donned their furred gowns, the Town Clerk put on his spectacles. 'Who was he?' – 'What was he?' – 'Where was he?' – 'He should be hanged – he should be burned – he should be broiled – he should be fried – he should be scraped to death with red-hot oyster shells!' – 'Who was he?' – 'What was his name?'

The Abbot's Apparitor drew forth his roll and read aloud: 'Sir Robert de Shurland, Knight banneret, Baron of Shurland and Minster, and Lord of Sheppey.'

The Mayor put his chain in his pocket, the Aldermen took off their gowns, the Town Clerk put his pen behind his ear. It was a county business altogether: the Sheriff had better call out the *posse comitatus*.

While saints and sinners were thus leaguing against him, the Baron de Shurland was quietly eating his breakfast. He had passed a tranquil night, undisturbed by dreams of cowl or capuchin; nor was his appetite more affected than his conscience. On the contrary, he sat rather longer over his meal than usual: luncheon-time came, and he was ready as ever for his oysters; but scarcely had Dame Martin opened his first half-dozen when the warder's horn was heard from the barbican.

'Who the devil's that?' said Sir Robert. 'I'm not at home, Periwinkle. I hate to be disturbed at meals, and I won't be at home to anybody.'

'An't please your lordship,' answered the Seneschal, 'Paul Prior hath given notice that there is a body –'

'Another body!' roared the Baron. 'Am I to be everlastingly

215

plagued with bodies? No time allowed me to swallow a morsel. Throw it into the moat!'

'So please you, my lord, it is a body of horse – and – and Paul says there is a still larger body of foot behind it; and he thinks, my lord – that is, he does not know, but he thinks – and we all think, my lord, that they are coming to – to besiege the castle!'

'Besiege the castle! Who? What? What for?'

'Paul says, my lord, that he can see the banner of St Austin, and the bleeding heart of Hamo de Crevecœur, the Abbot's chief vassal; and there is John de Northwood, the sheriff, with his red cross engrailed; and Hever, and Leybourne, and Heaven knows how many more; and they are all coming on as fast as ever they can.'

'Periwinkle,' said the Baron, 'up with the drawbridge: down with the portcullis; bring me a cup of canary, and my nightcap. I won't be bothered with them. I shall go to bed.'

'To bed, my lord?' cried Periwinkle, with a look that seemed to say, 'He's crazy!'

At this moment the shrill tones of a trumpet were heard to sound thrice from the champaign. It was the signal for parley: the Baron changed his mind; instead of going to bed, he went to the ramparts.

'Well, rapscallions! and what now?' said the Baron.

A herald, two pursuivants and a trumpeter occupied the foreground of the scene; behind them, some three hundred paces off, upon a rising ground, was drawn up in battle-array the main body of the ecclesiastical forces.

'Hear you, Robert de Shurland, Knight, Baron of Shurland and Minster, and Lord of Sheppey, and know all men, by these presents, that I do hereby attach you, the said Robert, of murder and sacrilege, now, or of late, done and committed by you, the said Robert, contrary to the peace of our Sovereign Lord the King, his crown and dignity: and I do hereby require and charge you, the said Robert, to forthwith surrender and give up your own proper person, together with the castle of Shurland aforesaid, in order that the same may be duly dealt with according to law. And here standeth John de Northwood, Esquire, good man and true, sheriff of this his Majesty's most loyal county of Kent, to enforce the same, if need be, with his *posse comitatus* – '

'His what?' said the Baron.

'His *posse comitatus*, and – '

'Go to Bath!' said the Baron.

A defiance so contemptuous roused the ire of the adverse commanders. A volley of missiles rattled about the Baron's ears. Nightcaps avail little against contusions. He left the walls and retired to the great hall.

'Let them pelt away,' quoth the Baron: 'there are no windows to break, and they can't get in.' So he took his afternoon nap, and the siege went on.

Towards evening his lordship awoke, and grew tired of the din. Guy Pearson, too, had got a black eye from a brickbat, and the assailants were clambering over the outer wall. So the Baron called for his Sunday hauberk of Milan steel, and his great two-handed sword with the terrible name – it was the fashion in feudal times to give names to swords: King Arthur's was christened Excalibur; the Baron called his Tickletoby, and whenever he took it in hand it was no joke.

'Up with the portcullis! down with the bridge!' said Sir Robert; and out he sallied, followed by the *élite* of his retainers. Then there was a pretty-to-do. Heads flew one way – arms and legs another; round went Tickletoby; and, wherever it alighted, down came horse and man: the Baron excelled himself that day. All that he had done in Palestine faded in the comparison; he had fought for fun there, but now it was for life and lands. Away went John de Northwood; away went William of Hever, and Roger of Leybourne. Hamo

217

de Crevecœur, with the church vassals and the banner of St Austin, had been gone some time. The siege was raised, and the Lord of Sheppey was left alone in his glory.

But, brave as the Baron undoubtedly was, and total as had been the defeat of his enemies, it cannot be supposed that *La Stoccata* would be allowed to carry it away thus. It has before been hinted that Abbot Anselm had written to the Pope, and Boniface the Eighth piqued himself on his punctuality as a correspondent in all matters connected with Church discipline. He sent back an answer by return of post; and by it all Christian people were strictly enjoined to aid in exterminating the offender, on pain of the greater excommunication in this world, and a million of years of purgatory in the next. But then, again, Boniface the Eighth was rather at a discount in England just then. He had affronted Longshanks, as the royal lieges had nicknamed their monarch; and Longshanks had been rather sharp upon the clergy in consequence. If the Baron de Shurland could but get the King's pardon for what, in his cooler moments, he admitted to be a peccadillo, he might sniff at the Pope and bid him 'do his devilmost'.

Fortune, who, as the poet says, delights to favour the bold, stood his friend on this occasion. Edward had been for some time collecting a large force on the coast of Kent, to carry on his French wars for the recovery of Guienne; he was expected shortly to review it in person; but, then, the troops lay principally in cantonments about the mouth of the Thames, and his Majesty was to come down by water. What was to be done? – the royal barge was in sight, and John de Northwood and Hamo de Crevecœur had broken up all the boats to boil their camp-kettles. A truly great mind is never without resources.

'Bring me my boots!' said the Baron.

They brought him his boots, and his dapple-gray steed along with them. Such a courser! all blood and bone, short-backed, broad-chested, and – but that he was a little ewe-necked – faultless in form and figure. The Baron sprang upon his back, and dashed at once into the river.

The barge which carried Edward Longshanks and his fortunes had by this time nearly reached the Nore; the stream was broad and the current strong, but Sir Robert and his steed were almost as broad, and a great deal stronger. After breasting the tide gallantly for a couple of miles, the knight was near enough to hail the steersman.

'What have we got here?' said the King. 'It's a mermaid,' said one. 'It's a grampus,' said another. 'It's the devil,' said a third. But they were all wrong; it was only Robert de Shurland. 'Grammercy,' said the King, 'that fellow was never born to be drowned!'

It has been said before that the Baron had fought in the Holy Wars; in fact, he had accompanied Longshanks, when only heir-apparent, in his expedition twenty-five years before, although his name is unaccountably omitted by Sir Harris Nicolas in his list of crusaders. He had been present at Acre when Amirand of Joppa stabbed the prince with a poisoned dagger, and had lent Princess Eleanor his own toothbrush after she had sucked out the venom from the wound. He had slain certain Saracens, contented himself with his own plunder, and never dunned the commissariat for arrears of pay. Of course he ranked high in Edward's good graces, and had received the honour of knighthood at his hands on the field of battle.

In one so circumstanced it cannot be supposed that such a trifle as the killing of a frowsy friar would be much resented, even had he not taken so bold a measure to obtain his pardon. His petition was granted, of course, as soon as asked; and so it would have been had the indictment drawn up by the Canterbury town-clerk, viz., 'That he, the said Robert de Shurland, etc., had then and there, with several, to wit, one thousand, pairs of boots, given sundry, to wit, two thousand kicks, and therewith and thereby killed divers, to wit, ten thousand, Austin Friars,' been true to the letter.

Thrice did the gallant gray circumnavigate the barge, while Robert de Winchelsey, the chancellor and archbishop to boot, was making out, albeit with great reluctance, the royal pardon. The interval was sufficiently long to enable his Majesty, who, gracious as he was, had always an eye to business, just to hint that the gratitude he felt towards the Baron was not unmixed with a lively sense of services to come; and that, if life were now spared him, common decency must oblige him to make himself useful. Before the archbishop, who had scalded his fingers with the wax in affixing the great seal, had time to take them out of his mouth, all was settled, and the Baron de Shurland had pledged himself to be forthwith in readiness, *cum suis*, to accompany his liege lord to Guienne.

With the royal pardon secured in his vest, boldly did his lordship turn again to the shore; and as boldly did his courser oppose his breadth of chest to the stream. It was a work of no common difficulty or danger; a steed of less 'mettle and bone' had long since sunk in the effort; as it was, the Baron's boots were full of water, and Gray Dolphin's chamfrain more than once dipped beneath the wave. The convulsive snorts of the noble animal showed his distress; each instant they became more loud and frequent; when his hoof touched the strand, and 'the horse and his rider' stood once again in safety on the shore.

Rapidly dismounting, the Baron was loosening the girths of his demi-pique, to give the panting animal breath, when he was aware of as ugly an old woman as he had ever clapped eyes upon, peeping at him under the horse's belly.

'Make much of your steed, Robert Shurland! Make much of your steed!' cried the hag, shaking at him her long and bony finger. 'Groom to the hide, and corn to the manger! He has saved your life, Robert Shurland, for the nonce; but he shall yet be the means of your losing it for all that!'

The Baron stared: 'What's that you say, you old faggot?' He ran round by his horse's tail; the woman was gone!

The Baron paused; his great soul was not to be shaken by trifles; he looked around him, and solemnly ejaculated the word 'Humbug!' then, slinging the bridle across his arm, walked slowly on in the direction of the castle.

The appearance, and still more, the disappearance of the crone, had, however, made an impression; every step he took he became more thoughtful. ''Twould be deuced provoking, though, if he *should* break my neck after all.' He turned and gazed at Dolphin with the scrutinizing eye of a veterinary surgeon. 'I'll be shot if he is not groggy!' said the Baron.

With his lordship, like another great commander, 'Once to be in doubt, was once to be resolved': it would never do to go to the wars on a rickety prad. He dropped the rein, drew forth Tickletoby, and, as the enfranchised Dolphin, good easy horse, stretched out his ewe-neck to the herbage, struck off his head at a single blow. 'There, you lying old beldame!' said the Baron; 'now take him away to the knacker's.'

Three years were come and gone. King Edward's French wars were over; both parties, having fought till they came to a standstill, shook hands, and the quarrel, as usual, was patched up by a royal marriage. This happy event gave his Majesty leisure to turn his attention to Scotland, where things, through the intervention of William Wallace, were looking rather queerish. As his reconciliation with Philip now allowed of his fighting the Scotch in peace and quietness, the monarch lost no time in marching his long legs across the border, and the short ones of the Baron followed him, of course. At Falkirk, Tickletoby was in great request; and in the year following, we find a contemporary poet hinting at his master's prowess under the walls of Caerlaverock:

> Ovec eus fu achiminez
> Li beau Robert de Shurland
> Ki kant seoit sur le cheval
> Ne sembloit home ke someille.

A quatrain which Mr Simpkinson translates,

> With them was marching
> The good Robert de Shurland,
> Who, when seated on horseback,
> Does not resemble a man asleep!

So thoroughly awake, indeed, does he seem to have proved himself, that the bard subsequently exclaims in an ecstasy of admiration,

> Si je estoie une pucelette
> Je li donrie ceur et cors
> Tant est de lu bons li recors.

> If I were a young maiden,
> I would give my heart and person,
> So great is his fame!

Fortunately the poet was a tough old monk of Exeter; since such a present to a nobleman, now in his grand climacteric, would hardly have been worth the carriage. With the reduction of this stronghold of the Maxwells seem to have concluded the Baron's military services; as on the very first day of the fourteenth century we find him once more landed on his native shore, and marching, with such of his retainers as the wars had left him, towards the hospital shelter of Shurland Castle. It was then, upon that very beach, some hundred yards distant from high-water mark, that his eye fell upon something like an ugly old woman in a red cloak. She was seated on what seemed to be a large stone, in an interesting attitude, with her elbows resting upon her knees, and her chin upon her thumbs. The Baron started: the remembrance of his interview with a similar personage in the same place, some three years since, flashed upon his recollection. He rushed towards the spot, but the form was gone – nothing remained but the seat it had appeared to occupy. This, on examination, turned out to be no stone, but the whitened skull of a dead horse! A tender remembrance of the deceased Gray Dolphin shot a momentary pang into the Baron's bosom; he drew the back of his hand across his face; the thought of the hag's prediction in an instant rose, and banished all softer emotions. In utter contempt of his own weakness, yet with a tremor that deprived his redoubtable kick of half its wonted force, he spurned the relic with his foot. One word alone issued from his lips, elucidatory of what was passing in his mind – it long remained imprinted on the memory of his faithful followers – that word was 'Gammon!' The skull bounded across the beach till it reached the very margin of the stream – one instant more and it would be engulfed for ever. At that moment a loud 'Ha! ha! ha!' was distinctly heard by the whole train to issue from its bleached and toothless jaws: it sank beneath the flood in a horse-laugh.

Meanwhile Sir Robert de Shurland felt an odd sort of sensation in his right foot. His boots had suffered in the wars. Great pains had been taken for their preservation. They had been 'soled' and 'heeled' more than once – had they been 'goloshed' their owner might have defied Fate! Well has it been said that 'there is no such thing as a trifle'. A nobleman's life depended upon a question of ninepence.

The Baron marched on; the uneasiness in his foot increased.

He plucked off his boot – a horse's tooth was sticking in his great toe!

The result may be anticipated. Lame as he was, his lordship, with characteristic decision, would hobble on to Shurland; his walk increased the inflammation; a flagon of *aqua vitæ* did not mend matters. He was in a high fever; he took to his bed. Next morning the toe presented the appearance of a Bedfordshire carrot; by dinner-time it had deepened to beetroot; and when Bargrave, the leech, at last sliced it off, the gangrene was too confirmed to admit of remedy. Dame Martin thought it high time to send for Miss Margaret, who, ever since her mother's death, had been living with her maternal aunt, the abbess, in the Ursuline convent at Greenwich. The young lady came, and with her came one Master Ingoldsby, her cousin-german by the mother's side; but the Baron was too far gone in the dead-thraw to recognize either. He died as he lived, unconquered and unconquerable. His last words were – 'Tell the old hag she may go to –' Whither remains a secret. He expired without fully articulating the place of her destination.

But who and what *was* the crone who prophesied the catastrophe? Ay, 'that is the mystery of this wonderful history'. Some say it was Dame Fothergill, the late confessor's mamma; others, St Bridget herself; others thought it was nobody at all, but only a phantom conjured up by conscience. As we do not know, we decline giving an opinion.

And what became of the Clerk of Chatham? Mr Simpkinson avers that he lived to a good old age, and was at last hanged by Jack Cade, with his inkhorn about his neck, for 'setting boys copies'. In support of this he adduces his name 'Emmanuel', and refers to the historian Shakespeare. Mr Peters, on the contrary, considers this to be what he calls one of Mr Simpkinson's 'Anacreonisms', inasmuch as, at the introduction of Mr Cade's reform measure, the Clerk, if alive, would have been hard upon two hundred years old. The probability is that the unfortunate alluded to was his great-grandson.

Margaret Shurland in due course became Margaret Ingoldsby: her portrait still hangs in the gallery at Tappington. The features are handsome, but shrewish, betraying, as it were, a touch of the old Baron's temperament; but we never could learn that she actually kicked her husband. She brought him a very pretty fortune in chains, owches, and Saracen ear-rings; the barony, being a male fief, reverted to the Crown.

In the abbey-church at Minster may yet be seen the tomb of a recumbent warrior, clad in the chain-mail of the thirteenth century. His hands are clasped in prayer; his legs, crossed in that position so prized by Templars in ancient, and tailors in modern days, bespeak him a soldier of the faith in Palestine. Close behind his dexter calf lies sculptured in bold relief a horse's head: and a respectable elderly lady, as she shows the monument, fails not to read her auditors a fine moral lesson on the sin of ingratitude, or to claim a sympathizing tear to the memory of poor 'Gray Dolphin'!

The Monk of Horror

or

The Conclave of Corpses

Anonymous

Some three hundred years since, when the convent of Kreutz-berg was in its glory, one of the monks who dwelt therein, wishing to ascertain something of the hereafter of those whose bodies lay all undecayed in the cemetery, visited it alone in the dead of night for the purpose of prosecuting his enquiries on that fearful subject. As he opened the trap-door of the vault a light burst from below; but deeming it to be only the lamp of the sacristan, the monk drew back and awaited his departure concealed behind the high altar. The sacristan emerged not, however, from the opening; and the monk, tired of waiting, approached, and finally descended the rugged steps which led into the dreary depths. No sooner had he set foot on the lower-most stair, than the well-known scene underwent a complete transformation in his eyes. He had long been accustomed to visit the vault, and whenever the sacristan went thither, he was almost sure to be with him. He therefore knew every part of it as well as he did the interior of his own narrow cell, and the arrangement of its contents was perfectly familiar to his eyes. What, then, was his horror to perceive that this arrangement, which even but that morning had come under his observation as usual, was altogether altered, and a new and wonderful one

226

substituted in its stead.

A dim lurid light pervaded the desolate abode of darkness, and it just sufficed to give to his view a sight of the most singular description.

On each side of him the dead but imperishable bodies of the long-buried brothers of the convent sat erect in their lidless coffins, their cold, starry eyes glaring at him with lifeless rigidity, their withered fingers locked together on their breasts, their stiffened limbs motionless and still. It was a sight to petrify the stoutest heart; and the monk's quailed before it, though he was a philosopher, and a sceptic to boot. At the upper end of the vault, at a rude table formed of a decayed coffin, or something which once served the same purpose, sat three monks. They were the oldest corpses in the charnel-house, for the inquisitive brother knew their faces well; and the cadaverous hue of their cheeks seemed still more cadaverous in the dim light shed upon them, while their hollow eyes gave forth what looked to him like flashes of flame. A large book lay open before one of them, and the others bent over the rotten table as if in intense pain, or in deep and fixed attention. No word was said; no sound was heard; the vault was as silent as the grave, its awful tenants still as statues.

Fain would the curious monk have receded from this horrible place, fain would he have retraced his steps and sought again his cell, fain would he have shut his eyes to the fearful scene; but he could not stir from the spot, he felt rooted there; and though he once succeeded in turning his eyes to the entrance of the vault, to his infinite surprise and dismay he could not discover where it lay, nor perceive any possible means of exit. He stood thus for some time. At length the aged monk at the table beckoned him to advance. With slow tottering steps he made his way to the group, and at length stood in front of the table, while the other monks raised their heads and glanced at him with fixed, lifeless looks that froze

227

the current of his blood. He knew not what to do; his senses were fast forsaking him; Heaven seemed to have deserted him for his incredulity. In this moment of doubt and fear he bethought him of a prayer, and as he proceeded he felt himself becoming possessed of a confidence he had before unknown. He looked on the book before him. It was a large volume, bound in black, and clasped with bands of gold, with fastenings of the same metal. It was inscribed at the top of each page.

'*Liber Obedientiæ.*'

He could read no further. He then looked, first in the eyes of him before whom it lay open, and then in those of his fellows. He finally glanced around the vault on the corpses who filled every visible coffin in its dark and spacious womb. Speech came to him, and resolution to use it. He addressed himself to the awful beings in whose presence he stood, in the words of one having authority with them.

'*Pax vobis,*' twas thus he spake – 'Peace be to ye.'

'*Hic nulla pax,*' replied an aged monk, in a hollow, tremulous tone, baring his breast the while – 'Here is no peace.'

He pointed to his bosom as he spoke, and the monk, casting his eye upon it, beheld his heart within surrounded by living fire, which seemed to feed on it but not consume it. He turned away in affright, but ceased not to prosecute his enquiries.

'*Pax vobis, in nomine Domini,*' he spake again – 'Peace be to ye, in the name of the Lord.'

'*Hic non pax,*' the hollow and heart-rending tones of the ancient monk who sat at the right of the table were heard to answer.

On glancing at the bared bosom of this hapless being also the same sight was exhibited – the heart surrounded by a devouring flame, but still remaining fresh and unconsumed under its operation. Once more the monk turned away and addressed the aged man in the centre.

'*Pax vobis, in nomine Domini,*' he proceeded.

At these words, the being to whom they were addressed raised his head, put forward his hand, and closing the book with a loud clap, said –

'Speak on. It is yours to ask, and mine to answer.'

The monk felt reassured, and his courage rose with the occasion.

'Who are ye?' he enquired; 'who may ye be?'

'We know not!' was the answer, 'alas! we know not!'

'We know not, we know not!' echoed in melancholy tones the denizens of the vault.

'What do ye here?' pursued the querist.

'We await the last day, the day of the last judgment! Alas for us! woe! woe!'

'Woe! woe!' resounded on all sides.

The monk was appalled, but still he proceeded.

'What did ye to deserve such doom as this? What may your crime be that deserves such dole and sorrow?'

As he asked the question the earth shook under him, and a crowd of skeletons uprose from a range of graves which yawned suddenly at his feet.

'These are our victims,' answered the old monk. 'They suffered at our hands. We suffer now, while they are at peace; and we shall suffer.'

'For how long?' asked the monk.

'For ever and ever!' was the answer.

'For ever and ever, for ever and ever!' died along the vault.

'May God have mercy on us!' was all the monk could exclaim.

The skeletons vanished, the graves closing over them. The aged men disappeared from his view, the bodies fell back in their coffins, the light fled, and the den of death was once more enveloped in its usual darkness.

On the monk's revival he found himself lying at the foot of

the altar. The grey dawn of a spring morning was visible, and he was fain to retire to his cell as secretly as he could, for fear he should be discovered.

From thenceforth he eschewed vain philosophy, says the legend, and, devoting his time to the pursuit of true knowledge, and the extension of the power, greatness, and glory of the Church, died in the odour of sanctity, and was buried in that holy vault, where his body is still visible.

Resurgam

Rina Ramsay

I

The London parson had taken a night off to run down and preach for Stackhouse.

He liked the change. It was like dipping into another world to slip out of his own restless parish into the utterly different atmosphere of this quiet country town. It had struck him most in the pulpit, when the lights went up on the sleepy congregation and he gave out a concluding hymn. How alike they were, all one pattern, all known to each other, all leading the same staid, ordinary lives. What a blessed tonic, his brief sojourn in this placid community.

He puffed out his chest, drinking in the soft night air that was so good to swallow. He was a big man and burly, and the narrow pavement would hardly hold the three of them abreast, so he was walking between the other two down the middle of the darkened street. They passed various worshippers in the glimmer – families, friends, and sweethearts – all of them pausing to say good-night. Such a peaceable little town and so friendly! It struck him again as comical that it should have been Stackhouse and not himself who had had a nervous breakdown last summer.

He burst out chuckling, and then, on the point of sharing his amusement at such an anomaly, was discreet. Those highly strung

231

individuals were so touchy. And Stackhouse did not seem in the humour for chaffing. His mouth was set in an odd line of strained endurance and he hardly spoke. His long, lean, ascetic figure had something monkish about it as he stalked along in his cassock. His eyes were staring into the gloom ahead.

Mrs Stackhouse, on the other side, was making up for her husband's silence. Robinson had had no idea she was such a chattering woman. It began to annoy him. It seemed to him that there was a suggestion of hysteria in her incessant prattle.

Near the vicarage gate they overtook a woman of the charwoman class, and the vicar's wife hailed her with the usual salutation and asked why Bessy had missed Sunday-school. The woman unlatched the gate for them. She had a small child with her, and spoke for its benefit in a mincing tone.

'Bessy's bin a very bad girl, ma'am. She's been telling lies.'

'Oh, dear!' said Mrs Stackhouse, properly scandalized.

'Yes, ma'am; the young monkey! She *will* have it her lady, as used to, sat with her on Sunday night.'

'Oh!' said Mrs Stackhouse again, but swiftly. 'Nonsense, nonsense!'

She whisked through the gate, which clanged after them, leaving the woman outside with the infant, unadmonished, hanging to her skirt with a finger in its mouth. In the light of the hall lamp she glanced furtively at her husband.

'My dear boy!' she said, hurriedly, almost wildly, 'a child of four –!'

Stackhouse dropped his eyes from hers, and lifted his hand with a curious gesture as if he were wiping the sweat from his brow.

Inside the house Mrs Stackhouse fled to the kitchen to hurry that uncomfortable meal called supper, and the two men waited a minute or two by the study fire.

'Awfully good of you to come down, Robinson,' said the vicar. He spoke in a strained voice; there was something in it that sounded like expectation, like some faint hope; but the Londoner, for all his alertness, had not the clue. He noticed, however, that his host's knuckles gleamed white as he gripped hard on the edge of the chimney-piece. These long, weedy men had no stamina, physical or nervous. It must have been his temperament, certainly not his surroundings, that had made Stackhouse go to pieces.

'Good of you to ask me,' he said, politely. 'I love this quiet place. Such a contrast to my parish! You should see us up there, how crowded, quarrelling and fighting. I'm afraid that sea voyage didn't set you up altogether?'

'I thought it had, though,' said Stackhouse, abruptly. 'When I came back –'

He shut his mouth suddenly in the middle of the sentence, but looked hard at his fellow-priest. In his look was wistfulness and an imminent despair.

'I'd like to ask you something,' he said, 'but – I dare not.' He let go the chimney-piece and led the way into the dining-room, where Mrs Stackhouse was calling them. She was too anxiously hospitable for comfort, bouncing up and down behind her coffee-pot, fussing about the food, and rattling on feverishly; but keeping, the visitor could see, a distracted eye on her husband. There was not much coherence in her prattle, and sometimes she lost the thread of it and looked for a minute helpless. Only at such disconcerting moments could the Londoner, coming to the rescue, get a word in.

Why would the woman insist on talking, and what was she afraid of? Some outbreak of nerves on the part of the silent man? Was it pure hysteria on her part, or was she trying to cover some private fear?

He seized the first opportunity to take his share in the conversation, mildly humorous, but conscious all the while of the peculiar strain in the atmosphere. And then, incidentally, he remembered something.

'By the way,' he said, 'you lucky people, you know all your congregation. Who is the lady who sat in the side aisle alone in the seat next the pillar? A singularly interesting face –'

Mrs Stackhouse started violently.

'Wh – what was she like?' she asked.

'Rather eager and sad,' said Robinson, reflecting, 'but quite a girl. She had a pointed chin, and dark hair, I think, and large, dark eyes – penetrating eyes; and she wore some kind of glittering jewel hung round her neck. It was her troubled expression that struck me first –'

He broke off astonished. For Stackhouse had stood up and was staring at him, gripping the table, leaning over. His look was half incredulous, half unspeakable relief.

'Then,' he said, in a choked voice, 'you, too, saw her. Thank Heaven! I am not mad.'

Mrs Stackhouse hid her face suddenly in her hands and burst into an uncontrollable fit of crying.

The visitor looked from one to the other in real alarm. He could see nothing in his harmless remark to affect them so deeply, or to relax, as it seemed, an intolerable strain.

'I'm afraid –' he began.

Mrs Stackhouse sat up and smiled.

'But we are so thankful to you,' she said, still sobbing. 'Oh, you can't imagine what a relief it is! You're an independent witness – unprejudiced – and you saw her. Oh, you don't know what it means to us. We were both so terrified that his mind was going –'

'Still,' said the Londoner, puzzled, 'I can't see how my mentioning that young lady –'

She interrupted him. Something like awe hushed her excited voice.

'The girl you saw in church,' she said, 'died last year.'

'Impossible!' said Robinson.

Stackhouse – who was with difficulty controlling a nervous

tremor that shook him from head to foot, but whose voice was steady – moved to the door.

'Let us go back to the study,' he said, 'and talk it over.'

His whole manner was changed as he stood on the hearthrug looking down on his guest and his wife. He had lost the pathetic hesitation that Robinson had noticed in him that night, and recovered something of his old bearing of priestly pomp.

'Most of us believe in the unseen,' he pronounced; 'but to find what belongs to the other world made visible – brought so close – is a dreadful shock. My wife thought it must be an hallucination; she thought I was going mad – and I, too, grew horribly afraid. You see, I had had that nervous breakdown before, and the doctors sent me away for six months. It looked as if the prescription had failed. We thought that my break-down must have been the warning of a mental collapse. We – I can't tell you, Robinson, what we suffered. And yet I saw that poor girl, night after night, so plainly –'

'She was *such* a nice girl!' broke in Mrs Stackhouse, in her gasping treble; 'and such a help in the parish. We liked her so much. And, of course, we were getting no letters – the doctors had forbidden it; we had heard nothing whatever till we came home and they told us she had committed suicide soon after we went away. I thought the shock of it had been too much for George. No wonder – such a *good* girl, Mr Robinson. She – she used to sit in that seat with the schoolchildren to keep them quiet. No one could have *dreamt* she could do anything so wicked –'

'Do you mean,' said Robinson, bluntly, 'that I saw a ghost?'

Stackhouse bent his head. His wife shivered suddenly as if she had not till then fully realized what it meant. Her mind had been so possessed by fear for the sanity of her husband; her relief had been too intense.

'I – suppose so,' she said, in an awe-stricken whisper.

There followed a short pause; no sound but the fire crackling and the night wind sighing a little outside the room. Mrs

Stackhouse drew in nearer the fender as if she were very cold, and made a little gasp in her throat. The Londoner, looking from one to the other with his kindly, humorous glance, began to talk common sense.

'Of course it's a mistake,' he said. 'The girl I saw in church tonight was real. It can only be some chance likeness – perhaps a relation – '

Stackhouse shook his head.

'No,' he said. 'There's no one like her. Poor girl, poor girl; her spirit cannot rest. God forgive me, there must have been something deadly wrong in my teaching, since it could not keep her from such a dreadful act. Is it strange that she looks reproachful?'

'But haven't you made enquiries?'

'We have not dared to speak of it to a soul!' cried Mrs Stackhouse. 'They would all have believed – as I did – that George was going mad. Oh, can't you see the horrible difficulty? And then – '

'I am not going to have my church made a public show for the rabble,' said Stackhouse, violently. 'I won't have that desecration! Can't you see them crowding here in their thousands, staring, scoffing, profaning a holy place? The newspapers would seize on the tale in a moment! For Heaven's sake, man, hold your tongue.'

He stopped, and again that nervous tremor took him.

'Do you mind telling me the circumstances? Who was this girl?' said the Londoner, curious, but stoutly incredulous. 'It certainly wasn't the face of a suicide that I saw – '

'No. It's incomprehensible,' said Stackhouse, trying to recover a sort of calm. 'She was the last person in the world, you would have said. How little we creatures know! She lived with her uncle, a solicitor here, and kept house for him. The uncle is my churchwarden. She was going out shortly to India to be married. There was nothing to worry her.'

'Poor little Kitty!' said Mrs Stackhouse, in a sobbing breath. 'If only we had been there –'

'Yes, she might have confided in us,' said Stackhouse. 'But the priest I left in charge here was a young man, lately ordained; shy, and not observant. And nobody had noticed anything strange about her. Only her uncle said at the inquest that he was afraid she had been a little scared at the idea of her approaching marriage. She had lived in this place all her life, and it was a wrench to leave it; and she had not seen the man for five years. He was afraid she must have been brooding in secret and dreading the journey; and he blamed himself for thinking it only natural a girl should be flustered at the prospect of such a tremendous step. Poor man, he must have been terribly distressed. One of the jury told me that if they could have found any possible excuse they would have brought it in misadventure, if only to spare his feelings –'

'But she went down to the chemist herself and bought the stuff,' broke in Mrs Stackhouse. 'She told them she wanted it for an old dog that had been run over; she signed the poison book and asked him particularly if it would be painless. Of course, knowing her as he did, he never dreamt –'

'And the dog?' said Robinson.

'There was no dog,' said Stackhouse. 'No one in the house had heard of it. She locked her door as usual at night – she had done it ever since an alarm of burglars in the house years ago; and when they got frightened in the morning and burst it in she was found dead in bed. She had drunk the poison in the lemonade she took up with her every night.'

'And they buried her with a mutilated service!' said Mrs Stackhouse, shuddering.

'Poor girl!' said Stackhouse, and turned away his head.

The London parson broke the distressing silence.

'A very sad case,' he said; 'but aren't you letting it overcome your judgement? Why in this case beyond all others should her unhappy spirit be allowed to haunt the church? I dare say it is just what a miserable soul would wish, sorrowful, self-tormenting – if uncontrolled. But I see no reason why it should be permitted. And assuming it could be, I'm curious to know why she should appear to you and not to her own relation. *He* would have spoken of it, wouldn't he, if she had?'

'Poor man!' said Mrs Stackhouse, with an hysterical laugh that she was unable to check; 'he would have raised the whole neighbourhood.'

'Probably,' said Stackhouse, the grave line of his mouth relaxing, 'but he shut up his house and went away; the loneliness was too much for him. And I hear that on his travels he seems to have come across a sensible woman who took him and married him. Some middle-aged person like himself, who had no ties and was feeling lonely. It's the best that could happen.'

'The blinds were up as I passed the house yesterday,' said Mrs Stackhouse.

'Heavens, Robinson, what's to be done?' burst out Stackhouse. 'Look at us, talking coolly in the face of this horror! I can't stand the thing much longer. Think of it, man! Week after week, there she sits, with her eyes fixed on me –'

'Oh, George, George!' said his wife, shuddering.

Robinson was sorry for them both. Evidently both of them were neurotic, and the tragic circumstance they related had affected them; their highly strung temperaments, acting on each other, had worked them up to a really dangerous pitch. And Stackhouse hadn't enough to do. Perhaps it was worse for him to rust in this quiet parish than to wear himself out with work. The doctors had sent him on a sea voyage, had they? Months of idleness and too much introspection. Fools!

'Look here,' he said, 'you go up and take over my job for a bit, and I'll stop down here and discover something. You'll be giddy at first, but the organization's good, and I've got a regular martinet of a curate. He'll manage you and see you don't kill yourself. And I think Mrs Stackhouse will find my house quite comfortable for a bachelor's. *I* want a holiday badly – and you'll soon shake off this obsession of yours in a London slum.'

Mrs Stackhouse looked up eagerly at her husband. Relief at the great suggestion shone in her eyes.

'It would be cowardly to do that,' said Stackhouse, irresolutely. 'I should feel as if I had deserted a poor soul that needs my help.'

'You're not fit to help anyone in the present state of your nerves,' said his fellow-parson, and clinched the argument like a Jesuit. 'How do you know she wants your help more than mine? Didn't I see her too?'

II

The October sun shone aslant the quiet street as the Rev. Mr Robinson marched along it to call on his – or, rather, on Stackhouse's truant churchwarden, Mr Parker. He had a straw hat on and swung his stick.

Personally, he was hugely enjoying his interval of peace, and he had in his pocket a letter from his head curate extolling Stackhouse, who was working like a demon, and looked less ill. It only remained for Robinson to clear up the ghost worry in unmistakable fashion, which ought not to be too hard. He smiled. Odd tricks one's imagination played sometimes! Recollecting Stackhouse's unbalanced asseveration, he had himself experienced a slight thrill as he peered down the glimmering aisle on the following Sunday evening, and saw the same face that had impressed him before, the same dark eyes riveted on him. His robust intellect, that admitted all things to be possible, but few of them expedient, had been a little staggered by the sad intensity – imagination again – of her look. But a very commonplace incident had rescued him from any foolishness; just a little nodding child that had snuggled up against her as she gathered it in her arm.

He told himself that what he had to do was simply to make a few discreet enquiries and get acquainted with the disturbing young woman. He had spoken to the clerk after service, but that ancient worthy had not noticed who was sitting by the pillar; his sight, he explained, was not so good as it might be, with that chancy gas. Happen it was some stranger; folk was a bit shy of sitting that side because of the children fidgeting, and them boys – you couldn't keep them boys quiet! Happen it was a teacher?

Clearly there was no disquieting rumour current, no local gossip; there seemed to be no foundation for any supernatural hypothesis but the overwrought condition of the parson's nerves.

Robinson reached his destination, and pushed open the iron gate. Mr Parker was out, but Mrs Parker was at home, and the caller was marched into the drawing-room.

This was a mixture of ancient middle-class superstition and modern ease. It amused Robinson to compare the two, and even to track the ancestral album to its lurking-place behind a potted palm. While he waited he undid the stiff clasp and turned over the pages. Pity that people had given up that instructive custom of pillorying different generations for the good of posterity! It was an interesting study to look back and mark how family traits persisted, how they cropped up on occasion as ineradicable as weeds. He went through the book with the keen eye of an anthropologist. There was something elusive, something distantly familiar running through the whole collection. He must have met a member of that family at one time without knowing it. On the very last page he saw her; a photograph of a girl.

Breaking in on his moment of stupefaction, Mrs Parker sailed into the room, having furbished herself for the occasion with fresh and violent scent on her handkerchief. A dashing female, with quantities of blazing yellow hair and round eyes that stared and challenged; a splendid presence, indeed, in this sober house. But not at all the expected type of a middle-aged comforter. Much more like a firework.

She excused her husband in a high London voice. He was obliged to be at his office. Everything was in a muddle owing to things being left so long to the clerks. It really was time they came back, though how she was to endure this place – ! Still, of course, with a motor – ! Dull, did he say? It was simply dreadful. She had always warned Jimmy that it would be too much for her, but he had persuaded her at last.

'How lucky for him!' said Robinson, politely. The lady agreed at once.

'Rather!' she said. 'Poor Jimmy! He must have proposed to me twenty times in the last two years!'

The accelerated clatter of a tea-tray approached. The bride was not going to allow her one visitor to escape her. She began moving things on the table.

'I have just been looking through that album,' said Robinson, turning it over as carelessly as he could. 'That is a striking photograph on the last page. I fancy I have seen the original.'

She uttered a little shriek and closed the book.

'Oh!' she said. 'Don't you know? It's Mr Parker's niece who committed suicide. A shocking thing, wasn't it? Haven't you heard about it? It was in all the papers!'

Eagerly she plunged into the story. His shocked countenance encouraged her to enlarge. He sat facing her across the gaudy little painted tea-cups ('a wedding present from one of my pals,' she remarked) that surrounded the heavy silver pot.

She poured out the whole history as Robinson had heard it from his fellow-parson, but with amplifications. He heard what a queer temper poor Kitty had, and what a drag on a girl it was to be tied by a long engagement. When a man she hadn't seen for years wrote suddenly wanting her to come out at once and be married, no wonder the poor girl was terrified. Men alter so. He might have taken to drinking, he might even have grown a beard! And she didn't dare to back out of it, because she was a religious girl, and she'd promised; and very likely he needed her bit of money. She wasn't dependent on her uncle – oh, dear, no! Why, that heavy old tea-pot that made your arm ache belonged to her share! And she'd never stirred an inch from home. If Jimmy had had a grain of sense he would have put his foot down and said if the man really wanted her he must come and fetch her. But he didn't think of it, and so – and so – Well, it must have sent her crazy. Look at her artfulness, making up that story about the dog, when she went out to buy the poison! Wasn't it awful how cunning a person could be, and yet not right in the head, of course!

Her ear-rings tinkled as she shook her head with an air of wisdom. Her eager relation was no more personal than that of anybody retailing the latest sensational case in the papers – except in so far as she possessed the distinction of inside knowledge. There was a certain pride in her glib recital. But she was utterly unaffected by any breath of superstition, any hint of the supernatural hovering.

'Did you know her well?' said Robinson, trying to shake off his strange feeling of mental numbness.

'Oh, my goodness, no!' she said. 'I never saw her. I didn't get engaged to Jimmy till it was all over, and he came up to town more dead than alive, poor fellow, and told me how his circumstances had changed; and I was so sorry for him I just got married to him at once and off we went to Monte Carlo.'

An incongruous picture presented itself to her listener's mind, the spectacle of this splendid person leading a dazed mourner by the scruff of his neck towards consolation. But the flicker of humour passed.

'I should like to meet your husband,' he said. She took, or mistook, him to be severe.

'I'm afraid we have both been naughty,' she said. 'I know we have never been to church, and Mr Parker's a churchwarden, too! I used always to call him "the churchwarden" when I wanted to tease him – and he used to get red and say it was a very important office. I must really apologize. And the cook says nobody will call on me till we've appeared at church. I'll *promise* to bring him next Sunday evening. The cook says it used to be his turn to take round the plate at night.'

Eagerly, but with condescension, she gave this undertaking to satisfy the conventions (the cook having omitted to point out the superior social stamp of Morning Service), and effusively she shook hands. Robinson got out of the house and into the empty street. His mind began to work slowly, in jerks, like a jarred machine.

It was the original of that dead girl's photograph he had seen.

Something remarkably like panic shook him. He drew his hand across his forehead and found that it was wet.

By an odd trick of memory his own involuntary gesture reminded him of Stackhouse, who had wiped the sweat from his brow like that when the charwoman complained that her little girl had been telling lies. The insignificant incident, printed unconditionally on his brain, came back to him now with an unearthly meaning. He remembered that baby face, wide-eyed, insistent, too young to explain, too little to understand. And he remembered a sleepy head supported safely within a protecting arm.

'Good Lord!' he said, and his ruddy face was pale.

III

It was a hot, full church, the atmosphere thick with the breath of humanity and the purring gas. Evening service was popular with the multitude, and a wet night had driven all and sundry who would have been taking walks in the lanes to the only alternative. They pushed in, furling their dripping umbrellas and stacking them in the porch, till there was scarcely an inch of room in the middle aisle. And as the organ ceased rumbling and the packed congregation prepared to shout out the opening hymn, a small rabbit-faced man came stealing up the nave.

In his wake, plumed and hatted and scented, advanced Mrs Parker, making her triumphal entry. Indisputably there was nobody in the church dressed like her. The man ushered her into her place, and took up his own, with a countenance of uneasy rapture, beside this tremendous fine bird he had somehow caged.

Robinson, at the reading-desk, shot one furtive glance at the side aisle and withdrew his eyes. He was conscious of a mixed sensation of relief and of disappointment. His timorous look had travelled along rows of blank, unimportant faces, and seen nothing to send a shock to his sober sense. The appearance, whatever under God's mysterious providence it might be, was not there. He took heart to rate himself inwardly for a pusillanimous yielding to superstition. Obstinately he refused to let his attention wander and pinned his eyes to his book.

The service wore on, chant and psalm, prayer and preaching. He found himself halting unaccountably in the pulpit; the terse, vigorous words he sought for became jumbled in his head. In his struggle to keep the thread of his discourse and be lucid he had to fight a growing horror of expectation, a kind of strange foreknowledge that pressed on him. His eyes searched the dim spaces while his tongue stumbled over platitudes. He tried vainly to pierce the veil of mystery that hung over the darkened church. It was not time yet.

And then the glimmering lights went up.

She was there, in her place by the pillar, with her tragic eyes raised to him and the jewel glittering on her breast. All the other faces around her seemed indistinct, as if she alone were real – and yet the seat had been packed with worshippers standing up finding the places for the concluding hymn. Straight and still she stood among them, and, filled with a sense of impending climax, Robinson found it impossible to turn from gazing and go down the pulpit stairs. He, too, waited, watching, holding his breath, while the organ struck up and the churchwardens began to take the collection under cover of a lusty, long-winded hymn.

All at once, without consciously looking in that direction, he became aware that Mr Parker's place was vacant. He saw the small, rabbit-faced man drawing himself up to be stiff and pompous, carrying out his duty. Row after row he collected gravely, passing down the nave and coming up the side aisle. With a shock that staggered him for a moment the watcher realized that it was Mr Parker's part to collect on that side of the church. Would nothing happen, or would he, too, be granted the power to see?

The people were swinging through the third verse to an undercurrent of tinkling pennies. Nearer and nearer the man approached. Mechanically the watcher in the pulpit counted. Three more rows – two more – he had nearly reached her, but had made no sign. One more row and then – *crash!* The plate of coins went spinning in all directions. The man lay still where he had dropped on his face.

He did not die immediately. The numbing paralysis took a little time to kill. But he lay like a trodden insect, muttering, muttering. Blank terror was fixed immutably on his face.

It was clear from his own words that he had murdered his niece, but even the doctors did not know how much was intelligent confession and how much the involuntary betrayal of a stricken brain automatically reeling off old thoughts and guarded secrets.

'She'll not have me, she'll not have me, she says I'm not rich enough –'

That was his continual refrain, the fixed idea that had obsessed him, and that found utterance now at intervals, breaking even through the more coherent statements that had been taken down.

'It was all Bill's fault. Why didn't he leave his money to me instead of the girl? If I had it now; if I had it –! That fool of a girl, she thinks of nothing but her lover –'

Only for a moment the muttering voice would pause. Robinson, watching beside him, would speak of the everlasting mercy.

'She'll not have me, she'll not have me; she says I'm not rich enough!' And then, in the monotonous babble that was like a recitation, 'I did it. Draw up the legal documents. Put it down. They called it suicide, that's why she can't forgive me. That's why she came. Look at her, reproaching me with her eyes! Oh, my God, Kitty, take your eyes off me –'

On it went, over and over.

'I sent her to get the poison. I told her the dog had been run over in the street. I said I had shut it in the coach-house and the only merciful thing was to put it out of its pain. I told her to hurry and not to say anything to the servants – they would come bothering round, and they would not understand it was kindness – And I took it from her and put it into her lemonade on the sideboard. It was so easy. Look at her, look at her, come back to curse me!'

It was not hard to reconstruct the whole sordid story of a weak man's infatuation and greed. It was also wiser, remembering Stackhouse and his horror of letting his church be profaned by a sightseeing crowd, to acquiesce in the public view that it was remorse that had brought on the stroke that killed Kitty's uncle. And so Robinson held his peace.

Green Tea

Sheridan Le Fanu

PROLOGUE

MARTIN HESSELIUS, THE GERMAN PHYSICIAN

Though carefully educated in medicine and surgery, I have never practised either. The study of each continues, nevertheless, to interest me profoundly. Neither idleness nor caprice caused my secession from the honourable calling which I had just entered. The cause was a very trifling scratch inflicted by a dissecting knife. This knife cost me the loss of two fingers, amputated promptly, and the more painful loss of my health, for I have never been quite well since, and have seldom been twelve months together in the same place.

In my wanderings I became acquainted with Dr Martin Hesselius, a wanderer like myself, like me a physician, and, like me, an enthusiast in his profession. Unlike me in this: that his wanderings were voluntary, and he a man, if not of fortune, as we estimate fortune in England, at least in what our forefathers used to term 'easy circumstances'. He was an old man when I first saw him; nearly five-and-thirty years my senior.

In Dr Martin Hesselius, I found my master. His knowledge was immense, his grasp of a case was an intuition. He was the very man to inspire a young enthusiast, like me, with awe and delight. My admiration has stood the test of time and survived the separation of death. I am sure it was well founded.

For nearly twenty years I acted as his medical secretary. His immense collection of papers he has left in my care, to be arranged, indexed, and bound. His treatment of some of these cases is curious. He writes in two distinct characters. He describes what he saw and heard as an intelligent layman might, and when in this style of narrative he had seen the patient either through his own hall door, to the light of day, or through the gates of darkness to the caverns of the dead, he returns upon the narrative, and in the terms of his art, and with all the force and originality of genius, proceeds to the work of analysis, diagnosis, and illustration.

Here and there a case strikes me as of a kind to amuse or horrify a lay reader with an interest quite different from the peculiar one which it may possess for an expert. With slight modifications, chiefly of language and, of course, a change of names, I copy the following. The narrator is Dr Martin Hesselius. I find it among the voluminous notes of cases which he made during a tour in England about sixty-four years ago.

It is related to a series of letters to his friend Professor Van Loo of Leyden. The professor was not a physician, but a chemist, and a man who read history and metaphysics and medicine, and had, in his day, written a play.

The narrative is, therefore, if somewhat less valuable as a medical record, necessarily written in a manner more likely to interest an unlearned reader.

These letters, from a memorandum attached, appear to have been returned on the death of the professor, in 1819, to Dr Hesselius. They are written, some in English, some in French, but the greater part in German. I am a faithful, though, I am conscious, by no means a graceful translator, and although here and there I omit some passages, and shorten others, and disguise names, I have interpolated nothing.

I

DR HESSELIUS RELATES HOW HE MET
THE REV. MR JENNINGS

The Rev. Mr Jennings is tall and thin. He is middle-aged, and dresses with a natty, old-fashioned, high-church precision. He is naturally a little stately, but not at all stiff. His features, without being handsome, are well formed, and their expression extremely kind, but also shy.

I met him one evening at Lady Mary Heyduke's. The modesty and benevolence of his countenance are extremely prepossessing.

We were but a small party, and he joined agreeably enough in the conversation. He seems to enjoy listening very much more than contributing to the talk; but what he says is always to the purpose and well said. He is a great favourite of Lady Mary's, who, it seems, consults him upon many things, and thinks him the most happy and blessed person on earth. Little knows she about him.

The Rev. Mr Jennings is a bachelor, and has, they say, sixty thousand pounds in the funds. He is a charitable man. He is most anxious to be actively employed in his sacred profession, and yet, though always tolerably well elsewhere, when he goes down to his vicarage in Warwickshire, to engage in the actual duties of his sacred calling, his health soon fails him, and in a very strange way. So says Lady Mary.

There is no doubt that Mr Jennings' health does break down in, generally, a sudden and mysterious way, sometimes in the very act of officiating in his old and pretty church at Kenlis. It may be his heart, it may be his brain. But so it has happened three or four times, or oftener, that after proceeding a certain way in the service, he has on a sudden stopped short, and after a silence, apparently quite unable to resume, he has fallen into solitary, inaudible prayer, his hands and eyes uplifted; and then, pale as death, and in the agitation of a strange shame and horror, descended trembling, and got into the vestry-room, leaving his congregation, without explanation, to themselves. This occurred when his curate was absent. When he goes down to Kenlis now, he always takes care to provide a clergyman to share his duty, and to supply his place on the instant should he become thus suddenly incapacitated.

When Mr Jennings breaks down quite, and beats a retreat from the vicarage, and returns to London, where, in a dark street off Piccadilly, he inhabits a very narrow house, Lady Mary says that he is always perfectly well. I have my own opinion about that. There are degrees, of course. We shall see.

Mr Jennings is a perfectly gentleman-like man. People, however, remark something odd. There is an impression a little ambiguous. One thing which certainly contributes to it, people I think don't remember; or, perhaps, distinctly remark. But I did, almost immediately. Mr Jennings has a way of looking sidelong upon the carpet, as if his eye followed the movements of something there. This, of course, is not always. It occurs only now and then. But often enough to give a certain oddity, as I have said, to his manner, and in this glance travelling along the floor there is something both shy and anxious.

A medical philosopher, as you are good enough to call me, elaborating theories by the aid of cases sought out by myself, and by him watched and scrutinized with more time at command, and consequently infinitely more minuteness than the ordinary practitioner can afford, falls insensibly into habits of observation, which accompany him everywhere, and are exercised, as some people would say, impertinently, upon every subject that presents itself with the least likelihood of rewarding enquiry.

There was a promise of this kind in the slight, timid, kindly, but reserved gentleman whom I met for the first time at this agreeable little evening gathering. I observed, of course, more than I here set down; but I reserve all that borders on the technical for a strictly scientific paper.

I may remark that when I speak of medical science I do so as I hope some day to see it more generally understood, in a much more comprehensive sense than its generally material treatment would warrant. I believe the entire natural world is but the ultimate expression of that spiritual world from which, and in which alone, it has its life. I believe that the essential man is a spirit, that the spirit is an organized substance, but as different in point of material from what we ordinarily understand by matter, as light or electricity is; that the material body is, in the most literal sense, a vesture, and death consequently no interruption of the living man's existence, but simply his extrication from the natural body – a process which commences at the moment of what we term death, and the completion of which, at furthest a few days later, is the resurrection 'in flower'.

The person who weighs the consequences of these positions will probably see their practical bearing upon medical science. This is, however, by no means the proper place for displaying the proofs and discussing the consequences of this too generally unrecognized state of facts.

In pursuance of my habit, I was covertly observing Mr Jennings, with all my caution – I think he perceived it – and I saw plainly that he was as cautiously observing me. Lady Mary happening to address me by my name as Dr Hesselius, I saw that he glanced at me more sharply, and then became thoughtful for a few minutes.

After this, as I conversed with a gentleman at the other end of the room, I saw him look at me more steadily, and with an interest which I thought I understood. I then saw him take an opportunity of chatting with Lady Mary, and was – as one always is – perfectly aware of being the subject of a distant enquiry and answer.

This tall clergyman approached me by and by; and in a little time we had got into conversation. When two people, who like reading, and know books and places, having travelled, wish to discourse, it is very strange if they can't find topics. It was no accident that brought him near me, and led him into conversation. He knew German, and had read my *Essays on Metaphysical Medicine*, which suggest more than they actually say.

This courteous gentleman, shy, plainly a man of thought and reading, who, moving and talking among us, was not altogether of us, and whom I already suspected of leading a life whose transactions and alarms were carefully concealed, with an impenetrable reserve, from not only the world, but his best beloved friends – was cautiously weighing in his own mind the idea of taking a certain step with regard to me.

I penetrated his thoughts without his being aware of it, and was careful to say nothing which could betray to his sensitive vigilance my suspicions respecting his position, or my surmises about his plans respecting myself.

We chatted upon indifferent subjects for a time, but at last he said:

'I was very much interested by some papers of yours, Dr Hesselius, upon what you term metaphysical medicine. I read them in German ten or twelve years ago. Have they been translated?'

'No, I'm sure they have not – I should have heard. They would have asked my leave, I think.'

'I asked the publishers here, a few months ago, to get the book for me in the original German; but they tell me it is out of print.'

'So it is, and has been for some years; but it flatters me as an author to find that you have not forgotten my little book, although,' I added, laughing, 'ten or twelve years is a considerable time to have managed without it; but I suppose you have been turning the subject over again in your mind, or something has happened lately to revive your interest in it.'

At this remark, accompanied by a glance of enquiry, a sudden embarrassment disturbed Mr Jennings, analogous to that which makes a young lady blush and look foolish. He dropped his eyes, and folded his hands together uneasily, and looked oddly, and, you would have said, guiltily, for a moment.

I helped him out of his awkwardness in the best way, by appearing not to observe it and, going straight on, I said: 'Those revivals of interest in a subject happen to me often; one book suggests another, and often sends me back on a wild-goose chase over an interval of twenty years. But, if you still care to possess a copy, I shall be only too happy to provide you; I have still got two or three by me – and if you allow me to present one I shall be very much honoured.'

'You are very good indeed,' he said, quite at his ease again in a moment. 'I almost despaired – I don't know how to thank you.'

'Pray, don't say a word; the thing is really so little worth that I am only ashamed of having offered it, and if you thank me any more I shall throw it into the fire in a fit of modesty.'

Mr Jennings laughed. He enquired where I was staying in London, and after a little more conversation on a variety of subjects he took his departure.

II

THE DOCTOR QUESTIONS LADY MARY, AND SHE ANSWERS

'I like your vicar so much, Lady Mary,' said I, as soon as he was gone. 'He has read, travelled, and thought, and having also suffered, he ought to be an accomplished companion.'

'So he is, and, better still, he is a really good man,' said she. 'His advice is invaluable about my schools, and all my little undertakings at Dawlbridge, and he's so painstaking, he takes so much trouble – you have no idea – wherever he thinks he can be of use; he's so good-natured and so sensible.'

'It is pleasant to hear so good an account of his neighbourly virtues. I can only testify to his being an agreeable and gentle companion, and, in addition to what you have told me, I think I can tell you two or three things about him,' said I.

'Really!'

'Yes, to begin with, he's unmarried.'

'Yes, that's right – go on.'

'He has been writing, that is he *was*, but for two or three years, perhaps, he has not gone on with his work, and the book was upon some rather abstract subject – perhaps theology.'

'Well, he was writing a book, as you say; I'm not quite sure what it was about, but only that it was nothing that I cared for; very likely you are right, and he certainly did stop – yes.'

'And although he only drank a little coffee here tonight, he likes tea, at least, did like it, extravagantly.'

'Yes, that's *quite* true.'

'He drank green tea, a good deal, didn't he?' I pursued.

'Well, that's very odd! Green tea was a subject on which we used almost to quarrel.'

'But he has quite given that up,' said I.

'So he has.'

'And now, one more fact. His mother or his father, did you know them?'

'Yes, both; his father is only ten years dead, and their place is near Dawlbridge. We knew them very well,' she answered.

'Well, either his mother or his father – I should rather think his father – saw a ghost,' said I.

'Well, you really are a conjurer, Dr Hesselius.'

'Conjurer or no, haven't I said right?' I answered merrily.

'You certainly have, and it *was* his father: he was a silent, whimsical man, and he used to bore my father about his dreams, and at last he told him a story about a ghost he had seen and talked with, and a very odd story it was. I remember it particularly, because I was so afraid of him. This story was long before he died – when I was quite a child – and his ways were so silent and moping, and he used to drop in sometimes, in the dusk, when I was alone in the drawing-room, and I used to fancy there were ghosts about him.'

I smiled and nodded.

'And now, having established my character as a conjurer, I think I must say good-night,' said I.

'But how *did* you find it out?'

'By the planets, of course, as the gipsies do,' I answered, and so, gaily, we said good-night.

Next morning I sent the little book he had been enquiring after, and a note to Mr Jennings, and, on returning later that evening, I found that he had called at my lodgings, and left his card. He asked whether I was at home, and asked at what hour he would be most likely to find me.

Does he intend opening his case, and consulting me 'professionally', as they say. I hope so. I have already conceived a theory about him. It is supported by Lady Mary's answers to my parting questions. I should like much to ascertain from his own lips. But what can I do, consistently with good breeding, to invite a confession? Nothing. I rather think he meditates one. At all events, my dear Van L., I shan't make myself difficult of access; I mean to return his visit tomorrow. It will be only civil in return for his politeness, to ask to see him. Perhaps something may come of it. Whether much, little, or nothing, my dear Van L., you shall hear.

III

DR HESSELIUS PICKS UP SOMETHING IN LATIN BOOKS

Well, I have called at Blank Street.

On enquiring at the door, the servant told me that Mr Jennings was engaged very particularly with a gentleman, a clergyman from Kenlis, his parish in the country. Intending to reserve my privilege, and to call again, I merely intimated that I should try another time, and had turned to go, when the servant begged my pardon, and asked me, looking at me a little more attentively than well-bred persons of his order usually do, whether I was Dr Hesselius; and on learning that I was, he said, 'Perhaps, then, sir, you would allow me to mention it to Mr Jennings, for I am sure he wishes to see you.'

The servant returned in a moment, with a message from Mr Jennings, asking me to go into his study, which was in effect his back drawing-room, promising to be with me in a very few minutes.

This was really a study – almost a library. The room was lofty, with two tall, slender windows, and rich, dark curtains. It was much larger than I had expected and stored with books on every side, from the floor to the ceiling. The upper carpet – for to my tread it felt that there were two or three – was a Turkey carpet. My steps fell noiselessly. The bookcases standing out, placed the windows, particularly narrow ones, in deep recesses. The effect of the room was, although extremely comfortable, and even luxurious, decidedly gloomy, and, aided by the silence, almost oppressive. Perhaps, however, I ought to have allowed something for association. My mind had connected peculiar ideas with Mr Jennings. I stepped into this perfectly silent room of a very silent house with a peculiar foreboding; and its darkness, and solemn clothing of books, for except where two narrow looking-glasses were set in the wall they were everywhere, helped this sombre feeling.

While awaiting Mr Jennings' arrival, I amused myself by looking into some of the books with which his shelves were laden. Not among these, but immediately under them, with their backs upward on the floor, I lighted upon a complete set

of Swedenborg's *Arcana Cælestia*, in the original Latin, a very
fine folio set, bound in the natty livery which theology affects,
pure vellum; namely, gold letters, and carmine edges. There
were paper markers in several of these volumes. I raised and
placed them, one after the other, upon the table, and, opening
where these papers were placed, I read, in the solemn Latin
phraseology, a series of sentences indicated by a pencilled line
at the margin. Of these I copy here a few, translating them into
English.

When man's interior sight is opened, which is that of his
spirit, then there appear the things of another life, which
cannot possibly be made visible to the bodily sight...

By the internal sight it has been granted me to see the
things that are in the other life, more clearly than I see
those that are in the world. From these considerations, it
is evident that external vision exists from interior vision,
and this from a vision still more interior, and so on...

There are with every man at least two evil spirits...

With wicked genii there is also a fluent speech, but
harsh and grating. There is also among them a speech
which is not fluent, wherein the dissent of the thoughts is
perceived as something secretly creeping along within it.

The evil spirits associated with man are, indeed, from
the hells, but when with man they are not then in hell, but
are taken out thence. The place where they then are, is in
the midst between heaven and hell, and is called the world
of spirits – when the evil spirits who are with man, are in
that world, they are not in any infernal torment, but in
every thought and affection of the man, and so, in all that
the man himself enjoys. But when they are remitted into
their hell, they return to their former state...

If evil spirits could perceive that they were associated
with man, and yet that they were spirits separate from

him and if they could flow into the things of his body, they would attempt by a thousand means to destroy him; for they hate man with a deadly hatred...

Knowing, therefore, that I was a man in the body, they were continually striving to destroy me, not as to the body only, but especially as to the soul; for to destroy any man or spirit is the very delight of the life of all who are in hell; but I have been continually protected by the Lord. Hence it appears how dangerous it is for man to be in a living consort with spirits, unless he be in the good of faith...

Nothing is more carefully guarded from the knowledge of associate spirits than their being thus conjoint with a man, for if they knew it they would speak to him, with the intention to destroy him...

The delight of hell is to do evil to man, and to hasten his eternal ruin.

A long note, written with a very sharp and fine pencil, in Mr Jennings' neat hand, at the foot of the page, caught my eye. Expecting his criticism upon the text, I read a word or two, and stopped, for it was something quite different, and began with these words, *Deus misereatur mei* – 'May God compassionate me.' Thus, warned of its private nature, I averted my eyes and shut the book, replacing all the volumes as I had found them, except one which interested me, and in which, as men studious and solitary in their habits will do, I grew so absorbed as to take no cognizance of the outer world, nor to remember where I was.

I was reading some pages which refer to 'representatives' and 'correspondents', in the technical language of Swedenborg, and had arrived at a passage, the substance of which is, that evil spirits, when seen by other eyes than those of their internal associates, present themselves, by 'correspondence' in the shape of the beast (*fera*) which represents their particular lust and life, in aspect direful and atrocious. This is a long passage, and particularizes a number of those bestial forms.

IV

FOUR EYES WERE READING THE PASSAGE

I was running the head of my pencil-case along the line as I read it, and something caused me to raise my eyes.

Directly before me was one of the mirrors I have mentioned, in which I saw reflected the tall shape of my friend, Mr Jennings, leaning over my shoulder, and reading the page at which I was busy, and with a face so dark and wild that I should hardly have known him.

I turned and rose. He stood erect, and with an effort laughed a little, saying:

'I came in and asked you how you did, but without succeeding in awaking you from your book; so I could not restrain my curiosity, and very impertinently, I'm afraid, peeped over your shoulder. This is not your first time of looking into those pages. You have looked into Swedenborg, no doubt, long ago?'

'Oh dear, yes! I owe Swedenborg a great deal; you will discover traces of him in the little book on metaphysical medicine, which you were so good as to remember.'

Although my friend affected a gaiety of manner, there was a slight flush on his face, and I could perceive that he was inwardly much perturbed.

'I'm scarcely yet qualified, I know so little of Swedenborg. I've only had them a fortnight,' he answered, 'and I think they are rather likely to make a solitary man nervous – that is, judging from the very little I have read – I didn't say that they have made me so,' he laughed; 'and I'm so very much obliged for the book. I hope you got my note?'

259

I made all proper acknowledgments and modest disclaimers.

'I never read a book that I go with so entirely as that of yours,' he continued. 'I saw at once there is more in it than is quite unfolded. Do you know Dr Harley?' he asked, rather abruptly.

(In passing, the editor remarks that the physician here named was one of the most eminent who had ever practised in England.)

I did, having had letters to him, and had experienced from him great courtesy and considerable assistance during my visit to England.

'I think that man one of the very greatest fools I ever met in my life,' said Mr Jennings.

This was the first time I had ever heard him say a sharp thing of anybody, and such a term applied to so high a name a little startled me.

'Really! and in what way?' I asked.

'In his profession,' he answered.

I smiled.

'I mean this,' he said; 'he seems to me, one half, blind – I mean one half of all he looks at is dark – preternaturally bright and vivid all the rest; and the worst of it is, it seems *wilful*. I can't get him – I mean he won't – I've had some experience of him as a physician, but I look on him as, in that sense, no better than a paralytic mind, an intellect half dead. I'll tell you – I know I shall some time – all about it,' he said, with a little agitation. 'You stay some months longer in England. If I should be out of town during your stay for a little time, would you allow me to trouble you with a letter?'

'I should be only too happy,' I assured him.

'Very good of you. I am so utterly dissatisfied with Harley.'

'A little leaning to the materialistic school,' I said.

'A *mere* materialist,' he corrected me; 'you can't think how that sort of thing worries one who knows better. You won't tell anyone – any of my friends you know – that I am hippish; now, for instance, no one knows – not even Lady Mary – that I have seen Dr Harley or any other doctor. So pray don't mention it; and, if I should have any threatening of an attack, you'll kindly let me write, or, should I be in town, have a little talk with you.'

I was full of conjecture, and unconsciously I found I had fixed my eyes gravely on him, for he lowered his for a moment, and he said:

'I see you think I might as well tell you now, or else you are forming a conjecture; but you may as well give it up. If you were guessing all the rest of your life, you will never hit on it.'

He shook his head smiling, and over that wintry sunshine a black cloud suddenly came down, and he drew his breath in, through his teeth as men do in pain.

'Sorry, of course, to learn that you apprehend occasion to consult any of us; but, command me when and how you like, and I need not assure you that your confidence is sacred.'

He then talked of quite other things, and in a comparatively cheerful way and after a little time I took my leave,

V

DR HESSELIUS IS SUMMONED TO RICHMOND

We parted cheerfully, but he was not cheerful, nor was I. There are certain expressions of that powerful organ of spirit – the human face – which, although I have seen them often, and possess a doctor's nerve, yet disturb me profoundly. One look of Mr Jennings haunted me. It had seized my imagination with so dismal a power that I changed my plans for the evening, and went to the opera, feeling that I wanted a change of ideas.

I heard nothing of or from him for two or three days, when

a note in his hand reached me. It was cheerful, and full of hope. He said that he had been for some little time so much better – quite well, in fact – that he was going to make a little experiment, and run down for a month or so to his parish, to try whether a little work might not quite set him up. There was in it a fervent religious expression of gratitude of this restoration, as he now almost hoped he might call it.

A day or two later I saw Lady Mary, who repeated what his note had announced, and told me that he was actually in Warwickshire, having resumed his clerical duties at Kenlis; and she added, 'I begin to think that he is really perfectly well, and that there never was anything the matter, more than nerves and fancy; we are all nervous, but I fancy there is nothing like a little hard work for that kind of weakness, and he has made up his mind to try it. I should not be surprised if he did not come back for a year.'

Notwithstanding all this confidence, only two days later I had this note, dated from his house off Piccadilly:

Dear Sir,
I have returned disappointed. If I should feel at all able to see you I shall write to ask you kindly to call. At present, I am too low, and, in fact, simply unable to say all I wish to say. Pray don't mention my name to my friends. I can see no one. By and by, please God, you shall hear from me. I mean to take a run into Shropshire, where some of my people are. God bless you! May we, on my return, meet more happily than I can now write.

About a week after this I saw Lady Mary at her own house, the last person, she said, left in town, and just on the wing for Brighton, for the London season was quite over. She told me that she had heard from Mr Jennings' niece, Martha, in Shropshire. There was nothing to be gathered from her letter, more than that he was low and nervous. In those words, of which healthy people think so lightly, what a world of suffering is sometimes hidden!

Nearly five weeks had passed without any further news of Mr Jennings. At the end of that time I received a note from him. He wrote:

I have been in the country, and have had change of air, change of scene, change of faces, change of everything and in everything – but myself. *I have made up my mind, so far as the most resolute creature on earth can do it, to tell my case fully to you. If your engagements will permit, pray come to me today, tomorrow, or the next day; but pray defer as little as possible. You know not how much I need help. I have a quiet house at Richmond, where I now am. Perhaps you can manage to come to dinner, or to luncheon, or even to tea. You shall have no trouble in finding me out. The servant at Blank Street, who takes this note, will have a carriage at your door at any hour you please; and I am always to be found. You will say that I ought not to be alone. I have tried everything. Come and see.*

I called up the servant, and decided on going out the same evening, which accordingly I did.

He would have been much better in a lodging-house, or hotel, I thought, as I drove up through a short, double row of sombre elms to a very old-fashioned brick house, darkened by the foliage of these trees, which overtopped and nearly surrounded it. It was a perverse choice, for nothing could be imagined more *triste* and silent. The house, I found, belonged to him. He had stayed for a day or two in town, and, finding it for some cause insupportable, had come out here, probably because being furnished and his own, he was relieved of the thought and delay of selection by coming here.

The sun had already set, and the red reflected light of the western sky illuminated the scene with the peculiar effect with which we are all familiar. The hall seemed very dark, but, getting to the back drawing-room, whose windows command the west, I was again in the same dusky light.

I sat down, looking out upon the richly wooded landscape that glowed in the grand and melancholy light which was every moment fading. The corners of the room were already dark; all was growing dim, and the gloom was insensibly toning my mind, already prepared for what was sinister. I was waiting alone for his arrival, which soon took place. The door communicating with the front room opened, and the tall figure of Mr Jennings, faintly seen in the ruddy twilight, came, with quiet, stealthy steps, into the room.

We shook hands, and, taking a chair to the window, where there was still light enough to enable us to see each other's faces, he sat down beside me, and, placing his hand upon my arm, with scarcely a word of preface began his narrative.

VI

HOW MR JENNINGS MET HIS COMPANION

The faint glow of the west, the pomp of the then lonely woods of Richmond, were before us, behind and about us the darkening room, and on the stony face of the sufferer – for the character of his face, though still gentle and sweet, was changed – rested that dim, odd glow which seems to descend and produce, where it touches, lights, sudden though faint, which are lost, almost without gradation, in darkness. The silence too was utter; not a distant wheel, nor bark, nor whistle from without; and within the depressing stillness of an invalid bachelor's house.

I guessed well the nature, though not even vaguely the

particulars, of the revelations I was about to receive from that fixed face of suffering that, so oddly flushed, stood out, like a portrait of Schalken's, before its background of darkness.

'It began,' he said, 'on the 15th of October, three years and eleven weeks ago, and two days – I keep very accurate count for every day is torment. If I leave anywhere a chasm in my narrative tell me.

'About four years ago I began a work which had cost me very much thought and reading. It was upon the religious metaphysics of the ancients.'

'I know,' said I, 'the actual religion of educated and thinking paganism, quite apart from symbolic worship? A wide and very interesting field.'

'Yes; but not good for the mind – the Christian mind, I mean. Paganism is all bound together in essential unity, and, with evil sympathy, their religion involves their art, and both their manners and the subject is a degrading fascination and the Nemesis sure. God forgive me!

'I wrote a great deal; I wrote late at night. I was always thinking on the subject, walking about, wherever I was, everywhere. It thoroughly infected me. You are to remember that all the material ideas connected with it were more or less of the beautiful, the subject itself delightfully interesting, and I, then, without a care.'

He sighed heavily.

'I believe that everyone who sets about writing in earnest does his work, as a friend of mine phrased it, *on* something – tea, or coffee, or tobacco. I suppose there is a material waste that must be hourly supplied in such occupations, or that we should grow too abstracted, and the mind, as it were, pass out of the body, unless it were reminded often of the connection by actual sensation. At all events, I felt the want, and I supplied it. Tea was my companion – at first the ordinary black tea, made in the usual way, not too strong; but I drank a good deal, and increased its strength as I went on. I never experienced an uncomfortable symptom from it. I began to take a little green tea. I found the effect pleasanter, it cleared and intensified the power of thought so. I had come to take it frequently, but not stronger than one might take it for pleasure. I wrote a great deal out here, it was so quiet, and in this room. I used to sit up very late, and it became a habit with me to sip my tea – green tea – every now and then as my work proceeded. I had a little kettle on my table that swung over a lamp, and made tea two or three times between eleven o'clock and two or three in the morning – my hours of going to bed. I used to go into town every day. I was not a monk, and although I spent an hour or two in a library, hunting up authorities and looking out lights upon my theme, I was in no morbid state as far as I can judge. I met my friends pretty much as usual and enjoyed their society, and, on the whole, existence had never been, I think, so pleasant before.

'I had met with a man who had some odd old books, German editions in medieval Latin, and I was only too happy to be permitted access to them. This obliging person's books were in the City, a very out-of-the-way part of it. I had rather out-stayed my intended hour, and, on coming out, seeing no cab near, I was tempted to get into the omnibus which used to drive past this house. It was darker than this by the time the bus had reached an old house, you may have remarked, with four poplars at each side of the door, and there the last passenger but myself got out. We drove along rather faster. It was twilight now. I leaned back in my corner next the door ruminating pleasantly.

'The interior of the omnibus was nearly dark. I had observed in the corner opposite to me at the other side, and at the end next the horses, two small circular reflections, as it seemed to me, of a reddish light. They were about two inches apart, and about the size of those small brass buttons that yachting men used to put upon their jackets. I began to speculate, as listless men will, upon this trifle, as it seemed. From what centre did that faint but deep red light come, and from what – glass beads, buttons, toy decorations – was it reflected? We were lumbering along gently, having nearly a mile still to go. I had not solved the puzzle, and it became in another minute more odd, for these two luminous points, with a sudden jerk, descended nearer the floor, keeping still their relative distance and horizontal position, and then, as suddenly, they rose to the level of the seat on which I was sitting and I saw them no more.

'My curiosity was now really excited, and, before I had time to think, I saw again these two dull lamps, again together, near the floor; again they disappeared, and again in their old corner I saw them.

'So, keeping my eyes upon them, I edged quietly up my own side, towards the end at which I still saw these tiny discs of red.

'There was very little light in the bus. It was nearly dark. I leaned forward to aid my endeavour to discover what these little circles really were. They shifted their position a little as I did so. I began now to perceive an outline of something black, and I soon saw, with tolerable directness, the outline of a small black monkey, pushing its face forward in mimicry to meet mine; those were its eyes, and I now dimly saw its teeth grinning at me.

'I drew back, not knowing whether it might not meditate a spring. I fancied that one of the passengers had forgot this ugly pet, and wishing to ascertain something of its temper, though not caring to trust my fingers to it, I poked my umbrella softly towards it. It remained immovable – up to it – *through* it. For through it, and back and forward it passed, without the slightest resistance.

'I can't, in the least, convey to you the kind of horror that I felt. When I had ascertained that the thing was an illusion, as

267

I then supposed, there came a misgiving about myself and a terror that fascinated me in impotence to remove my gaze from the eyes of the brute for some moments. As I looked, it made a little skip back, quite into the corner, and I, in a panic, found myself at the door, having put my head out, drawing deep breaths of the outer air, and staring at the lights and trees we were passing, too glad to reassure myself of reality.

'I stopped the bus and got out. I perceived the man look oddly at me as I paid him. I dare say there was something unusual in my looks and manner, for I had never felt so strangely before.

VII

THE JOURNEY: FIRST STAGE

'When the omnibus drove on, and I was alone upon the road, I looked carefully round to ascertain whether the monkey had followed me. To my indescribable relief I saw it nowhere: I can't describe easily what a shock I had received, and my sense of genuine gratitude on finding myself, as I supposed, quite rid of it.

'I had got out a little before we reached this house – two or three hundred steps. A brick wall runs along the footpath, and inside the wall is a hedge of yew, or some dark evergreen of that kind, and within that again the row of fine trees which you may have remarked as you came.

'This brick wall is about as high as my shoulder, and happening to raise my eyes I saw the monkey, with that stooping gait, on all fours, walking or creeping, close beside me on top of the wall. I stopped, looking at it with a feeling of loathing and horror. As I stopped so did it. It sat up on the wall with its long hands on its knees looking at me. There was not light enough to see it much more than in outline, nor was it dark enough to bring the peculiar light of its eyes into strong relief. I still saw, however, that red foggy light plainly enough. It did not show its teeth, nor exhibit any sign of irritation, but seemed jaded and sulky, and was observing me steadily.

'I drew back into the middle of the road. It was an unconscious recoil, and there I stood, still looking at it. It did not move.

'With an instinctive determination to try something – anything – I turned about and walked briskly towards town with askance look, all the time watching the movements of the beast. It crept swiftly along the wall, at exactly my pace.

'Where the wall ends, near the turn of the road, it came down, and with a wiry spring or two brought itself close to my feet, and continued to keep up with me, as I quickened my pace. It was at my left side, so close to my leg that I felt every moment as if I should tread upon it.

'The road was quite deserted and silent, and it was darker every moment. I stopped, dismayed and bewildered, turning, as I did so, the other way – I mean, towards this house, away from which I had been walking. When I stood still, the monkey drew back to a distance of, I suppose, about five or six yards, and remained stationary, watching me.

'I had been more agitated than I have said. I had read, of course, as everyone has, something about "spectral illusions", as you physicians term the phenomena of such cases. I considered my situation, and looked my misfortune in the face.

'These affections, I had read, are sometimes transitory and sometimes obstinate. I had read of cases in which the appearance, at first harmless, had, step by step, degenerated into something direful and insupportable, and ended by wearing its victim out. Still, as I stood there, but for my bestial companion, quite alone, I tried to comfort myself by repeating again and again the assurance "the thing is purely disease, a well-known physical affection, as distinctly as smallpox or neuralgia. Doctors are all agreed on that, philosophy demonstrates it. I must not be a fool. I've been sitting up too late, and I dare say my digestion is quite wrong, and, with God's help, I shall be all right, and this is but a symptom of nervous dyspepsia." Did I believe all this? Not one word of it, no more than any other miserable being ever did who is once seized and riveted in this satanic captivity. Against my convictions – I might say my knowledge – I was simply bullying myself into a false courage.

'I now walked homeward. I had only a few hundred yards to go. I had forced myself into a sort of resignation, but I had not got over the sickening shock and the flurry of the first certainty of my misfortune.

'I made up my mind to pass the night at home. The brute moved close beside me, and I fancied there was the sort of anxious drawing towards the house, which one sees in tired horses or dogs, sometimes as they come towards home.

'I was afraid to go into town. I was afraid of anyone seeing and recognizing me. I was conscious of an irrepressible agitation in my manner. Also I was afraid of any violent change in my habits, such as going to a place of amusement, or walking from home in order to fatigue myself. At the hall door it waited till I mounted the steps, and when the door was opened entered with me.

'I drank no tea that night. I got cigars and some brandy and water. My idea was that I should act upon my material system, and by living for a while in sensation apart from thought send myself forcibly, as it were, into a new groove. I came up here to this drawing-room. I sat just here. The monkey then got upon a small table that then stood *there*. It looked dazed and languid. An irrepressible uneasiness as to its movements kept my eyes always open upon it. Its eyes were half closed, but I could see them glow. It was looking steadily at me. In all situations, at all hours, it is awake and looking at me. That never changes.

'I shall not continue in detail my narrative of this particular night. I shall describe, rather, the phenomena of the first year, which never varied, essentially. I shall describe the monkey as it appeared in daylight. In the dark, as you shall presently hear, there are peculiarities. It is a small monkey, perfectly black. It had only one peculiarity – a character of malignity – unfathomable malignity. During the first year it looked sullen and sick. But this character of intense malice and vigilance was always underlying that surly languor. During all that time it acted as if on a plan of giving me as little trouble as was consistent with watching me. Its eyes were never off me. I have never lost sight of it, except in my sleep, light or dark, day or night, since it came here, excepting when it withdraws for some weeks at a time, unaccountably.

'In total dark it is visible as in daylight. I do not mean merely its eyes. It is *all* visible distinctly in a halo that resembles a glow of red embers, and which accompanies it in all its movements.

'When it leaves me for a time, it is always at night, in the dark, and in the same way. It grows at first uneasy, and then furious, and then advances towards me, grinning and shaking, its paws clenched, and, at the same time, there comes the appearance of fire in the grate. I never have any fire. I can't sleep in the room where there is any, and it draws nearer and nearer to the chimney, quivering, it seems, with rage, and when its fury rises to the highest pitch, it springs into the grate, and up the chimney, and I see it no more.

'When first this happened, I thought I was released. I was now a new man. A day passed – a night – and no return, and a blessed week – a week – another week. I was always on my knees, Dr Hesselius, always, thanking God and praying. A whole month passed of liberty, but on a sudden, it was with me again.'

VIII

THE SECOND STAGE

'It was with me, and the malice which before was torpid under a sullen exterior, was now active. It was perfectly unchanged in every other respect. This new energy was apparent in its activity and its looks, and soon in other ways.

'For a time, you will understand, the change was shown only in an increased vivacity, and an air of menace, as if it was always brooding over some atrocious plan. Its eyes, as before, were never off me.'

'Is it here now?' I asked.

'No,' he replied, 'it has been absent exactly a fortnight and a day – fifteen days. It has sometimes been away so long as nearly two months, once for three. Its absence always exceeds a fortnight, although it may be but by a single day. Fifteen days having past since I saw it last, it may return now at any moment.'

'Is its return,' I asked, 'accompanied by any peculiar manifestation?'

'Nothing – no,' he said. 'It is simply with me again. On lifting my eyes from a book, or turning my head, I see it, as usual, looking at me, and then it remains as before, for its appointed time. I have never told so much and so minutely before to anyone.'

I perceived that he was agitated, and looking like death, and he repeatedly applied his handkerchief to his forehead; I suggested that he might be tired, and told him that I would call, with pleasure, in the morning, but he said:

'No, if you don't mind hearing it all now. I have got so far, and I should prefer making one effort of it. When I spoke to Dr Harley I had nothing like so much to tell. You are a philosophic physician. You give spirit its proper rank. If this

272

thing is real – '

He paused, looking at me with agitated enquiry.

'We can discuss it by and by, and very fully. I will give you all I think,' I answered, after an interval.

'Well – very well. If it is anything real, I say, it is prevailing, little by little, and drawing me more interiorly into hell. Optic nerves, he talked of. Ah, well – there are other nerves of communication. May God Almighty help me! You shall hear.

'Its power of action, I tell you, had increased. Its malice became, in a way, aggressive. About two years ago, some questions that were impending between me and the bishop having been settled, I went down to my parish in Warwick-shire, anxious to find occupation in my profession. I was not prepared for what happened, although I have since thought I might have apprehended something like it. The reason of my saying so is this – '

He was beginning to speak with a great deal more effort and reluctance, and sighed often, and seemed at times nearly overcome. But at this time his manner was not agitated. It was more like that of a sinking patient, who has given himself up.

'Yes, but I will first tell you about Kenlis, my parish.

'It was with me when I left this place for Dawlbridge. It was my silent travelling companion, and it remained with me at the vicarage. When I entered on the discharge of my duties, another change took place. The thing exhibited an atrocious determination to thwart me. It was with me in the church – in the reading-desk – in the pulpit – within the communion rails. At last, it reached this extremity, that while I was reading to the congregation, it would spring upon the open book and squat there, so that I was unable to see the page. This happened more than once.

'I left Dawlbridge for a time. I placed myself in Dr Harley's hands. I did everything he told me. He gave my case a great

deal of thought. It interested him, I think. He seemed success-
ful. For nearly three months I was perfectly free from a return.
I began to think I was safe. With his full assent I returned to
Dawlbridge.

'I travelled in a chaise. I was in good spirits. I was more – I
was happy and grateful. I was returning, as I thought, delivered
from a dreadful hallucination, to the scene of duties which I
longed to enter upon. It was a beautiful, sunny evening,
everything looked serene and cheerful, and I was delighted, I
remember, looking out of the window to see the spire of my
church at Kenlis among the trees, at the point where one has the
earliest view of it. It is exactly where the little stream that
bounds the parish passes under the road by a culvert, and where
it emerges at the road-side, a stone with an old inscription is
placed. As we passed this point, I drew my head in and sat
down, and in the corner of the chaise was the monkey.

'For a moment I felt faint, and then quite wild with despair
and horror. I called to the driver, and got out, and sat down at
the road-side, and prayed to God silently for mercy. A
despairing resignation supervened. My companion was with
me as I re-entered the vicarage. The same persecution followed.
After a short struggle I submitted, and soon I left the place.

'I told you,' he said, 'that the beast has before this become in
certain ways aggressive. I will explain a little. It seemed to be
actuated by intense and increasing fury whenever I said my
prayers, or even meditated prayer. It amounted at last to a
dreadful interruption. You will ask how could a silent immaterial phantom effect that? It was thus, whenever I meditated praying; it was always before me, and nearer and nearer.

'It used to spring on a table, on the back of a chair, on the
chimney-piece, and slowly to swing itself from side to side,
looking at me all the time. There is in its motion an indefinable
power to dissipate thought, and to contract one's attention to
that monotony, till the ideas shrink, as it were, to a point, and

274

at last to nothing – and unless I had started up, and shook off the catalepsy, I have felt as if my mind were on the point of losing itself. There are other ways,' he sighed heavily; 'thus, for instance, while I pray with my eyes closed, it comes closer and closer, and I see it. I know it is not to be accounted for physically, but I do actually see it, though my lids are closed, and so it rocks my mind, as it were, and overpowers me, and I am obliged to rise from my knees. If you had ever yourself known this, you would be acquainted with desperation.'

IX

THE THIRD STAGE

'I see, Dr Hesselius, that you don't lose one word of my statement. I need not ask you to listen specially to what I am now going to tell you. They talk of the optic nerves, and of spectral illusions, as if the organ of sight was the only point assailable by the influences that have fastened upon me – I know better. For two years in my direful case that limitation prevailed. But as food is taken in softly at the lips, and then brought under the teeth; as the tip of the little finger caught in a mill crank will draw in the hand, and the arm, and the whole body, so the miserable mortal who has been once caught firmly by the end of the finest fibre of his nerve, is drawn in and in, by the enormous machinery of hell, until he is as I am. Yes, Doctor, as *I* am, for while I talk to you, and implore relief, I feel that my prayer is for the impossible, and my pleading with the inexorable.'

I endeavoured to calm his visibly increasing agitation, and told him that he must not despair.

While we talked the night had overtaken us. The filmy moonlight was wide over the scene which the window commanded, and I said:

'Perhaps you would prefer having candles. This light, you know, is odd. I should wish you, as much as possible, under your usual conditions while I make my diagnosis, shall I call it, otherwise I don't care.'

'All lights are the same to me,' he said: 'except when I read or write, I care not if night were perpetual. I am going to tell you what happened about a year ago. The thing began to speak to me.'

'Speak! How do you mean – speak as a man does, do you mean?'

'Yes; speak in words and consecutive sentences, with perfect coherence and articulation; but there is a peculiarity. It is not like the tone of a human voice. It is not by my ears it reaches me – it comes like a singing through my head.

'This faculty, the power of speaking to me, will be my undoing. It won't let me pray, it interrupts me with dreadful blasphemies. I dare not go on, I could not. Oh, Doctor, can the skill, and thought, and prayers of man avail me nothing?'

'You must promise me, my dear sir, not to trouble yourself with unnecessarily exciting thoughts; confine yourself strictly to the narrative of *facts*; and recollect, above all, that even if the thing that infests you be, you seem to suppose, a reality with an actual independent life and will, yet it can have no power to hurt you, unless it be given from above. Its access to your senses depends mainly upon your physical condition – this is, under God, your comfort and reliance; we are all alike environed. It is only that in your case, the *paries*, the veil of flesh, the screen, is a little out of repair, and sights and sounds are transmitted. We must enter on a new course, sir – be encouraged. I'll give tonight to the careful consideration of the whole case.'

'You are very good, sir; you think it worth trying, you don't give me quite up; but, sir, you don't know, it is gaining such an influence over me: it orders me about, it is such a tyrant, and I'm growing so helpless. May God deliver me!'

'It orders you about – of course you mean by speech?'

'Yes, yes; it is always urging me to crimes, to injure others, or myself. You see, Doctor, the situation is urgent, it is indeed. When I was in Shropshire, a few weeks ago' (Mr Jennings was speaking rapidly and trembling now, holding my arm with one hand, and looking in my face), 'I went out one day with a party of friends for a walk. My persecutor, I tell you, was with me at the time. I lagged behind the rest: the country near the Dee, you know, is beautiful. Our path happened to lie near a coal-mine, and at the verge of the wood is a perpendicular shaft, they say, a hundred and fifty feet deep. My niece had remained behind with me – she knows, of course, nothing of the nature of my sufferings. She knew, however, that I had been ill, and was low, and she remained to prevent my being quite alone. As we loitered slowly on together, the brute that accompanied me was urging me to throw myself down the shaft. I tell you now – oh, sir, think of it! – the one consideration that saved me from that hideous death was the fear lest the shock of witnessing the occurrence should be too much for the poor girl. I asked her to go on and take her walk with her friends, saying that I could go no farther. She made excuses, and the more I urged her the firmer she became. She looked doubtful and frightened. I suppose there was something in my looks or manner that alarmed her; but she would not go, and that literally saved me. You had no idea, sir, that a living man could be made so abject a slave of Satan,' he said, with a ghastly groan and a shudder.

There was a pause here, and I said, 'You *were* preserved nevertheless. It was the act of God. You are in His hands and in the power of no other being; be therefore confident for the future.'

X

HOME

I made him have candles lighted, and saw the room looking cheery and inhabited before I left him. I told him that he must regard his illness strictly as one dependent on physical though *subtle* physical causes. I told him that he had evidence of God's care and love in the deliverance which he had just described, and that I had perceived with pain that he seemed to regard its peculiar features as indicating that he had been delivered over to spiritual reprobation. Than such a conclusion nothing could be, I insisted, less warranted; and not only so, but more contrary to facts, as disclosed in his mysterious deliverance from that murderous influence during his Shropshire excursion. First, his niece had been retained by his side without his intending to keep her near him; and, secondly, there had been infused into his mind an irresistible repugnance to execute the dreadful suggestion in her presence.

As I reasoned this point with him, Mr Jennings wept. He seemed comforted. One promise I exacted, which was that should the monkey at any time return, I should be sent for immediately; and, repeating my assurance that I would give neither time nor thought to any other subject until I had thoroughly investigated his case, and that tomorrow he should hear the result, I took my leave.

Before getting into the carriage I told the servant that his master was far from well, and that he should make a point of frequently looking into his room.

My own arrangements I made with a view to being quite secure from interruption.

I merely called at my lodgings, and with a travelling-desk and carpet-bag, set off in a hackney carriage for an inn about two miles out of town called 'The Horns', a very quiet and comfortable house, with good thick walls. And there I resolved, without the possibility of intrusion or distraction, to devote some hours of the night, in my comfortable sitting-room, to Mr Jennings' case, and so much of the morning as it might require.

(There occurs here a careful note of Dr Hesselius' opinion upon the case, and of the habits, dietary, and medicines which he prescribed. It is curious – some persons would say mystical. But, on the whole, I doubt whether it would sufficiently interest a reader of the kind I am likely to meet with to warrant its being here reprinted. The whole letter was plainly written at the inn where he had hid himself for the occasion. The next letter is dated from his town lodgings.)

I left town for the inn where I slept last night at half past nine, and did not arrive at my room in town until one o'clock this afternoon. I found a letter in Mr Jennings' hand upon my table. It had not come by post, and, on enquiry, I learned that Mr Jennings' servant had brought it, and on learning that I was not to return until today, and that no one could tell him my address, he seemed very uncomfortable, and said that his orders from his master were that he was not to return without an answer.

I opened the letter and read:

Dear Dr Hesselius,
It is here. You had not been an hour gone when it returned. It is speaking. It knows all that has happened. It knows everything – it knows you, and is frantic and atrocious. It reviles. I send you this. It knows every word I have written – I write. This I promised, and I therefore write, but I fear very confused, very incoherently. I am so interrupted, disturbed.

Ever yours, sincerely yours,
Robert Lynder Jennings.

'When did this come?' I asked.

'About eleven last night: the man was here again, and has been here three times today. The last time is about an hour since.'

Thus answered, and with the notes I had made upon his case in my pocket, I was in a few minutes driving towards Richmond, to see Mr Jennings.

I by no means, as you perceive, despaired of Mr Jennings' case. He had himself remembered and applied, though quite in a mistaken way, the principle which I lay down in my *Metaphysical Medicine*, and which governs all such cases. I was about to apply it in earnest. I was profoundly interested, and very anxious to see and examine him while the 'enemy' was actually present.

I drove up to the sombre house, and ran up the steps, and knocked. The door, in a little time, was opened by a tall woman in black silk. She looked ill, and as if she had been crying. She curtseyed, and heard my question, but she did not answer. She turned her face away, extending her hand towards two men who were coming downstairs; and thus having, as it were, tacitly made me over to them, she passed through a side door hastily and shut it.

The man who was nearest the hall, I at once accosted, but being now close to him, I was shocked to see that both his hands were covered with blood.

I drew back a little, and the man, passing downstairs, merely said in a low tone, 'Here's the servant, sir.'

The servant had stopped on the stairs, confounded and dumb at seeing me. He was rubbing his hands in a hand-kerchief, and it was steeped in blood.

'Jones, what is it? What has happened?' I asked, while a sickening suspicion overpowered me.

The man asked me to come up to the lobby. I was beside him in a moment, and, frowning and pallid, with con-

tracted eyes, he told me the horror which I already half
guessed.

His master had made away with himself.

I went upstairs with him to the room – what I saw there I
won't tell you. He had cut his throat with his razor. It was a
frightful gash. The two men had laid him on the bed, and
composed his limbs. It had happened, as the immense pool of
blood on the floor declared, at some distance between the bed
and the window. There was carpet round his bed, and a carpet
under his dressing-table, but none on the rest of the floor, for
the man said he did not like a carpet in his bedroom. In this
sombre and now terrible room, one of the great elms that
darkened the house was slowly moving the shadow of one of
its great boughs upon this dreadful floor.

I beckoned to the servant, and we went downstairs together.
I turned off the hall into an old-fashioned panelled room, and
there standing, I heard all the servant had to tell. It was not a
great deal.

'I concluded, sir, from your words, and looks, sir, as you left
last night, that you thought my master seriously ill. I thought
it might be that you were afraid of a fit, or something. So I
attended very close to your directions. He sat up late, till past
three o'clock. He was not writing or reading. He was talking a
great deal to himself, but that was nothing unusual. At about
that hour I assisted him to undress, and left him in his slippers
and dressing-gown. I went back softly in about half an hour.
He was in his bed, quite undressed, and a pair of candles
lighted on the table beside his bed. He was leaning on his
elbow, and looking out at the other side of the bed when I
came in. I asked him if he wanted anything, and he said no.

'I don't know whether it was what you said to me, sir, or
something a little unusual about him, but I was uneasy,
uncommon uneasy about him last night.

'In another half-hour, or it might be a little more, I went up again. I did not hear him talking as before. I opened the door a little. The candles were both out, which was not usual. I had a bedroom candle, and I let the light in a little bit looking softly round. I saw him sitting in that chair beside the dressing-table with his clothes on again. He turned round and looked at me. I thought it strange he should get up and dress, and put out the candles to sit in the dark, that way. But I only asked him again if I could do anything for him. He said, "No", rather sharp, I thought. I asked if I might light the candles, and he said, "Do as you like, Jones." So I lighted them and I lingered about the room, and he said, "Tell me truth, Jones; why did you come again – you did not hear anyone cursing?" "No, sir," I said, wondering what he could mean.

'"No," said he, after me, "of course, no"; and I said to him, "Wouldn't it be well, sir, you went to bed? It's just five o'clock"; and he said nothing but, "Very likely; good-night, Jones." So I went, sir, but in less than an hour I came again. The door was fast, and he heard me, and called as I thought from the bed to know what I wanted, and he desired me not to disturb him again. I lay down and slept for a little. It must have been between six and seven when I went up again. The door was still fast, and he made no answer, so I did not like to disturb him, and, thinking he was asleep, I left him till nine. It was his custom to ring when he wished me to come, and I had no particular hour for calling him. I tapped very gently, and getting no answer I stayed away a good while, supposing he was getting some rest then. It was not till eleven o'clock I grew really uncomfortable about him – for at the latest he was never, that I could remember, later than half past ten. I got no answer. I knocked and called, and still no answer. So not being able to force the door, I called in Thomas from the stables, and together we forced it, and found him in the shocking way you saw.'

Jones had no more to tell. Poor Mr Jennings was very

gentle, and very kind. All his people were fond of him. I could see that the servant was very much moved.

So, dejected and agitated, I passed from that terrible house, and its dark canopy of elms, and I hope I shall never see it more. While I write to you I feel like a man who has but half waked from a frightful and monotonous dream. My memory rejects the picture with incredulity and horror. Yet I know it is true. It is the story of the process of a poison, a poison which excites the reciprocal action of spirit and nerve, and paralyses the tissue that separates those cognate functions of the senses, the external and the interior. Thus we find strange bedfellows, and the mortal and immortal prematurely make acquaintance.

CONCLUSION

A WORD FOR THOSE WHO SUFFER

My dear Van L., you have suffered from an affection similar to that which I have just described. You twice complained of a return of it.

Who, under God, cured you? Your humble servant, Martin Hesselius. Let me rather adopt the more emphasized piety of a certain good old French surgeon of three hundred years ago: 'I treated, and God cured you.'

Come, my friend, you are not to be hippish. Let me tell you a fact.

I have met with, and treated, as my book shows, fifty-seven cases of this kind of vision, which I term indifferently 'sublimated', 'precocious', and 'interior'.

There is another class of affections which are truly termed – though commonly confounded with those which I describe – spectral illusions. These latter I look upon as being no less simply curable than a cold in the head or a trifling dyspepsia.

It is those which rank in the first category that test our

promptitude of thought. Fifty-seven such cases have I encountered, neither more nor less. And in how many of these have I failed? In no one single instance.

There is no one affliction of mortality more easily and certainly reducible, with a little patience, and a rational confidence in the physician. With these simple conditions, I look upon the cure as absolutely certain.

You are to remember that I had not even commenced to treat Mr Jennings' case. I have not any doubt that I should have cured him perfectly in eighteen months, or possibly it might have extended to two years. Some cases are very rapidly curable, others extremely tedious. Every intelligent physician who will give thought and diligence to the task, will effect a cure.

You know my tract on the cardinal functions of the brain. I there, by the evidence of innumerable facts, prove, as I think, the high probability of a circulation arterial and venous in its mechanism, through the nerves. Of this system, thus considered, the brain is the heart. The fluid, which is propagated hence through one class of nerves, returns in an altered state through another, and the nature of that fluid is spiritual, though not immaterial, any more than, as I before remarked, light or electricity are so.

By various abuses, among which the habitual use of such agents as green tea is one, this fluid may be affected as to its quality, but it is more frequently disturbed as to equilibrium. This fluid being that which we have in common with spirits, a congestion found upon the masses of brain or nerve, connected with the interior sense, forms a surface unduly exposed, on which disembodied spirits may operate: communication is thus more or less effectually established. Between this brain circulation and the heart circulation there is an intimate sympathy. The seat, or rather the instrument of exterior vision, is the eye. The seat of interior vision is the nervous tissue and brain, immediately about and above the eyebrow. You remember how effectually I dissipated your pictures by the simple application of iced eau-de-Cologne. Few cases, however, can be treated exactly alike with anything like rapid success. Cold acts powerfully as a repellent of the nervous fluid. Long enough continued it will even produce that permanent insensibility which we call numbness, and a little longer, muscular as well as sensational paralysis.

I have not, I repeat, the slightest doubt that I should have first dimmed and ultimately sealed that inner eye which Mr Jennings had inadvertently opened. The same senses are opened in delirium tremens, and entirely shut up again when the overaction of the cerebral heart, and the prodigious nervous congestions that attend it, are terminated by a decided change in the state of the body. It is by acting steadily upon the body, by a simple process, that this result is produced – and inevitably produced. I have never yet failed.

Poor Mr Jennings made away with himself. But that catastrophe was the result of a totally different malady, which, as it were, projected itself upon that disease which was established. His case was in the distinctive manner a complication, and the complaint under which he really succumbed was hereditary suicidal mania. Poor Mr Jennings I cannot call a patient of mine, for I had not even begun to treat his case, and he had not yet given me, I am convinced, his full and unreserved confidence. If the patient do not array himself on the side of the disease, his cure is certain.

The Bishop's Ghost
and the Printer's Baby

Frank R. Stockton

Around the walls of a certain old church there stood many tombs, and these had been there so long that the plaster with which their lids were fastened down had dried and crumbled, so that in most of them there were long cracks under their lids, and out of these the ghosts of the people who had been buried in the tombs were in the habit of escaping at night.

This had been going on for a long time, and, at the period of our story, the tombs were in such bad repair that every night the body of the church was so filled with ghosts that before daylight one of the sacristans was obliged to come into the church and sprinkle holy water everywhere. This was done to clear the church of ghosts before the first service began, and who does not know that if a ghost is sprinkled with holy water it shrivels up? This first service was attended almost exclusively by printers on their way home from their nightly labours on the journals of the town.

The tomb which had the largest crack under its lid belonged to a bishop who had died more than a hundred years before, and who had a great reputation for sanctity; so much so, indeed, that people had been in the habit of picking little pieces of plaster from under the lid of his tomb and carrying away as holy relics to prevent diseases and accidents.

This tomb was more imposing than the others, and stood

upon a pedestal, so that the crack beneath its lid was quite plain to view, and remarks had been made about having it repaired.

Very early one morning, before it was time for the first service, there came into the church a poor mason. His wife had recently recovered from a severe sickness, and he was desirous of making an offering to the church. But having no money to spare, he had determined that he would repair the bishop's tomb, and he consequently came to do this before his regular hours of work began.

All the ghosts were out of their tombs at the time, but they were gathered together in the other end of the church, and the mason did not see them, nor did they notice him; and he immediately went to work. He had brought some plaster and a trowel, and it was not long before the crack under the lid of the tomb was entirely filled up, and the plaster made as smooth and neat as when the tomb was new.

When his work was finished, the mason left the church by the little side door which had given him entrance.

Not ten minutes afterwards the sacristan came in to sprinkle the church with holy water. Instantly the ghosts began to scatter right and left, and to slip into their tombs as quickly as possible, but when the ghost of the good bishop reached his tomb, he found it impossible to get in. He went around and around it, but nowhere could he find the least little chink by which he could enter. The sacristan was walking along the other side of the church scattering holy water, and in great trepidation the bishop's ghost hastened from tomb to tomb, hoping to find one which was unoccupied into which he could slip before the sprinkling began on that side of the church. He soon came to one which he thought might be empty, but he discovered to his consternation that it was occupied by the ghost of a young girl who had died of love.

'Alas! alas!' exclaimed the bishop's ghost. 'How unlucky! who would have supposed this to be your tomb?'

'It is not really my tomb,' said the ghost of the young girl. 'It is the tomb of Sir Geoffrey of the Marle, who was killed in battle nigh two centuries ago. I am told that it has been empty for a long time, for his ghost has gone to Castle Marle. Not long ago I came into the church, and finding this tomb unoccupied, I settled here.'

'Ah, me!' said the bishop's ghost, 'the sacristan will soon be round here with holy water. Could not you get out and go to your own tomb; where is that?'

'Alas, good father,' said the ghost of the young girl, 'I have no tomb; I was buried plainly in the ground, and I do not know that I could find the place again. But I have no right to keep you out of this tomb, good father; it is as much yours as it is mine, so I will come out and let you enter: truly you are in great danger. As for me it does not matter very much whether I am sprinkled or not.'

So the ghost of the young girl slipped out of Sir Geoffrey's tomb, and the bishop's ghost slipped in, but not a minute before the sacristan had reached the place. The ghost of the young girl flittered from one pillar to another until it came near to the door, and there it paused, thinking what it should do next. Even if it could find the grave from which it had come, it did not want to go back to such a place; it liked churches better.

Soon the printers began to come in to the early morning service. One of them was very sad, and there were tears in his eyes. He was a young man, not long married, and his child, a baby girl, was so sick that he scarcely expected to find it alive when he should reach home that morning.

The ghost of the young girl was attracted by the sorrowful printer, and when the service was over and he had left the church it followed him, keeping itself unseen. The printer found his wife in tears; the poor little baby was very low. It lay upon the bed, its eyes shut, its face pale and pinched, gasping for breath.

The mother was obliged to leave the room for a few moments to attend to some household affair, and her husband followed to comfort her, and when they were gone, the ghost of the young girl approached the bed and looked down on the little baby. It was nearer death than its parents supposed, and scarcely had they gone before it drew its last breath.

The ghost of the young girl bowed its head; it was filled with pity and sympathy for the printer and his wife; in an instant, however, it was seized with an idea, and in the next instant it had acted upon it. Scarcely had the spirit of the little baby left its body, than the spirit of the young girl entered it.

Now a gentle warmth suffused the form of the little child, a natural colour came into its cheeks, it breathed quietly and regularly, and when the printer and his wife came back, they found their baby in a healthful sleep. As they stood amazed at the change in the countenance of the child, it opened its eyes and smiled upon them.

'The crisis is past!' cried the mother. 'She is saved; and it is all because you stopped at the church instead of hurrying home, as you wished to do.' The ghost of the young girl knew that this was true, and the baby smiled again.

It was eighteen years later and the printer's baby had grown into a beautiful young woman. From her early childhood she had been fond of visiting the church, and would spend hours among the tombs reading the inscriptions, and sometimes sitting by them, especially by the tomb of Sir Geoffrey of the Marle. There, when there was nobody by, she used to talk with the bishop's ghost.

Late one afternoon she came to the tomb with a happy smile on her face. 'Holy father,' she said, speaking softly through the crack, 'are you not tired of staying so long in this tomb which is not your own?'

'Truly I am, daughter,' said the bishop's ghost, 'but I have no right to complain: I never come back here in the early morning without a feeling of the warmest gratitude to you for having given me a place of refuge. My greatest trouble is caused by the fear that the ghost of Sir Geoffrey of the Marle may some time choose to return. In that case I must give up to him his tomb. And then, where, oh where shall I go?'

'Holy father,' whispered the girl, 'do not trouble yourself; you shall have your own tomb again and need fear no one.'

'How is that?' exclaimed the bishop's ghost. 'Tell me quickly, daughter.'

'This is the way of it,' replied the young girl. 'When the mason plastered up the crack under the lid of your tomb he seems to have been very careful about the front part of it, but he didn't take much pains with the back where his work wasn't likely to be seen, so that there the plaster has crumbled and loosened very much, and with a long pin from my hair I have picked out ever so much of it, and now there is a great crack at the back of the tomb where you can go in and come out, just as easily as you ever did. As soon as night shall fall you can leave this tomb and go into your own.'

The bishop's ghost could scarcely speak for thankful emotions, and the happy young girl went home to the house of her father, a prosperous man, now the headprinter of the town.

The next evening the young girl went to the church and hurried to the bishop's tomb. Therein she found the bishop's ghost, happy and contented.

Sitting on a stone projection at the back of the tomb, she had a long conversation with the bishop's ghost, which, in gratitude for what she had done, gave her all manner of good advice and counsel. 'Above all things, my dear daughter,' said the bishop's ghost, 'do not repeat your first great mistake; promise me that never will you die of love.'

The young girl smiled. 'Fear not, good father,' she replied. 'When I died of love, I was, in body and soul, but eighteen years old, and knew no better; now, although my body is but eighteen, my soul is thirty-six. Fear not, never again shall I die of love.'

Canon Alberic's Scrap-book

M. R. James

St Bertrand de Comminges is a decayed town on the spurs of
the Pyrenees, not very far from Toulouse, and still nearer to
Bagnères-de-Luchon. It was the site of a bishopric until the
Revolution, and has a cathedral which is visited by a certain
number of tourists. In the spring of 1883 an Englishman
arrived at this old-world place – I can hardly dignify it with
the name of city, for there are not a thousand inhabitants. He
was a Cambridge man, who had come specially from Toulouse
to see St Bertrand's Church, and had left two friends, who
were less keen archæologists than himself, in their hotel at
Toulouse, under promise to join him on the following morning. Half an hour at the church would satisfy *them*, and all
three could then pursue their journey in the direction of Auch.
But our Englishman had come early on the day in question,
and proposed to himself to fill a notebook and to use several
dozens of plates in the process of describing and photograph-
ing every corner of the wonderful church that dominates the
little hill of Comminges. In order to carry out this design
satisfactorily, it was necessary to monopolize the verger of the
church for the day. The verger or sacristan (I prefer the latter
appellation, inaccurate as it may be) was accordingly sent for
by the somewhat brusque lady who keeps the inn of the
Chapeau Rouge; and when he came, the Englishman found
him an unexpectedly interesting object of study. It was not in

the personal appearance of the little, dry, wizened old man that the interest lay, for he was precisely like dozens of other church-guardians in France, but in a curious furtive, or rather hunted and oppressed, air which he had. He was perpetually half glancing behind him; the muscles of his back and shoulders seemed to be hunched in a continual nervous contraction, as if he were expecting every moment to find himself in the clutch of an enemy. The Englishman hardly knew whether to put him down as a man haunted by a fixed delusion, or as one oppressed by a guilty conscience, or as an unbearably hen-pecked husband. The probabilities, when reckoned up, certainly pointed to the last idea; but, still, the impression conveyed was that of a more formidable persecutor even than a termagant wife.

However, the Englishman (let us call him Dennistoun) was soon too deep in his notebook and too busy with his camera to give more than an occasional glance to the sacristan. Whenever he did look at him, he found him at no great distance, either huddling himself back against the wall or crouching in one of the gorgeous stalls. Dennistoun became rather fidgety after a time. Mingled suspicions that he was keeping the old man from his *déjeuner*, that he was regarded as likely to make away with St Bertrand's ivory crozier, or with the dusty stuffed crocodile that hangs over the font, began to torment him.

'Won't you go home?' he said at last; 'I'm quite well able to finish my notes alone; you can lock me in if you like. I shall want at least two hours more here, and it must be cold for you, isn't it?'

'Good heavens!' said the little man, whom the suggestion seemed to throw into a state of unaccountable terror, 'such a thing cannot be thought of for a moment. Leave monsieur alone in the church? No, no; two hours, three hours, all will be the same to me. I have breakfasted, I am not at all cold, with many thanks to monsieur.'

'Very well, my little man,' quoth Dennistoun to himself: 'you have been warned, and you must take the consequences.'

Before the expiration of the two hours, the stalls, the enormous dilapidated organ, the choir-screen of Bishop John de Mauléon, the remnants of glass and tapestry, and the objects in the treasure-chamber, had been well and truly examined; the sacristan still keeping at Dennistoun's heels, and every now and then whipping round as if he had been stung, when one or other of the strange noises that trouble a large empty building fell on his ear. Curious noises they were sometimes.

'Once,' Dennistoun said to me, 'I could have sworn I heard a thin metallic voice laughing high up in the tower. I darted an enquiring glance at my sacristan. He was white to the lips. "It is he – that is – it is no one; the door is locked," was all he said, and we looked at each other for a full minute.'

Another little incident puzzled Dennistoun a good deal. He was examining a large dark picture that hangs behind the altar, one of a series illustrating the miracles of St Bertrand. The composition of the picture is well-nigh indecipherable, but there is a Latin legend below, which runs thus:

Qualiter S. Bertrandus liberavit hominem quem diabolus diu volebat strangulare. (How St Bertrand delivered a man whom the Devil long sought to strangle.)

Dennistoun was turning to the sacristan with a smile and a jocular remark of some sort on his lips, but he was confounded to see the old man on his knees, gazing at the picture with the eye of a suppliant in agony, his hands tightly clasped, and a rain of tears on his cheeks. Dennistoun naturally pretended to have noticed nothing, but the question would not go away from him, 'Why should a daub of this kind affect anyone so strongly?' He seemed to himself to be getting some sort of clue to the reason of the strange look that had been puzzling him all the day: the man must be a monomaniac; but what was his monomania?

It was nearly five o'clock; the short day was drawing in, and the church began to fill with shadows, while the curious noises – the muffled footfalls and distant talking voices that had been perceptible all day – seemed, no doubt because of the fading light and the consequently quickened sense of hearing, to become more frequent and insistent.

The sacristan began for the first time to show signs of hurry and impatience. He heaved a sigh of relief when camera and notebook were finally packed up and stowed away, and hurriedly beckoned Dennistoun to the western door of the church, under the tower. It was time to ring the Angelus. A few pulls at the reluctant rope, and the great bell Bertrande, high in the tower, began to speak, and swung her voice up among the pines and down to the valleys, loud with mountain-streams, calling the dwellers on those lonely hills to remember and repeat the salutation of the angel to her whom he called Blessed among women. With that a profound quiet seemed to fall for the first time that day upon the little town, and Dennistoun and the sacristan went out of the church.

On the doorstep they fell into conversation.

'Monsieur seemed to interest himself in the old choir-books in the sacristy.'

'Undoubtedly. I was going to ask you if there were a library in the town.'

'No, monsieur; perhaps there used to be one belonging to the Chapter, but it is now such a small place –' Here came a strange pause of irresolution, as it seemed; then, with a sort of plunge, he went on: 'But if monsieur is *amateur des vieux livres*, I have at home something that might interest him. It is not a hundred yards.'

At once all Dennistoun's cherished dreams of finding

priceless manuscripts in untrodden corners of France flashed up, to die down again the next moment. It was probably a stupid missal of Plantin's printing, about 1580. Where was the likelihood that a place so near Toulouse would not have been ransacked long ago by collectors? However, it would be foolish not to go; he would reproach himself for ever after if he refused. So they set off. On the way the curious irresolution and sudden determination of the sacristan recurred to Dennistoun, and he wondered in a shamefaced way whether he was being decoyed into some purlieu to be made away with as a supposed rich Englishman. He contrived, therefore, to begin talking with his guide, and to drag in, in a rather clumsy fashion, the fact that he expected two friends to join him early the next morning. To his surprise, the announcement seemed to relieve the sacristan at once of some of the anxiety that oppressed him.

'That is well,' he said quite brightly – 'that is very well. Monsieur will travel in company with his friends; they will be always near him. It is a good thing to travel thus in company – sometimes.'

The last word appeared to be added as an afterthought, and to bring with it a relapse into gloom for the poor little man.

They were soon at the house, which was one rather larger than its neighbours, stone-built, with a shield carved over the door, the shield of Alberic de Mauléon, a collateral descendant, Dennistoun tells me, of Bishop John de Mauléon. This Alberic was a Canon of Comminges from 1680 to 1701. The upper windows of the mansion were boarded up, and the whole place bore, as does the rest of Comminges, the aspect of decaying age.

Arrived on his doorstep, the sacristan paused a moment.

'Perhaps,' he said, 'perhaps, after all, monsieur has not the time?'

'Not at all – lots of time – nothing to do till tomorrow. Let us see what it is you have got.'

The door was opened at this point, and a face looked out, a face far younger than the sacristan's, but bearing something of the same distressing look: only here it seemed to be the mark, not so much of fear for personal safety as of acute anxiety on behalf of another. Plainly, the owner of the face was the sacristan's daughter; and, but for the expression I have described, she was a handsome girl enough. She brightened up considerably on seeing her father accompanied by an able-bodied stranger. A few remarks passed between father and daughter, of which Dennistoun only caught these words, said by the sacristan, 'He was laughing in the church', words which were answered only by a look of terror from the girl.

But in another minute they were in the sitting-room of the house, a small, high chamber with a stone floor, full of moving shadows cast by a wood-fire that flickered on a great hearth. Something of the character of an oratory was imparted to it by a tall crucifix, which reached almost to the ceiling on one side; the figure was painted of the natural colours, the cross was black. Under this stood a chest of some age and solidity, and when a lamp had been brought, and chairs set, the sacristan went to this chest, and produced therefrom, with growing excitement and nervousness, as Dennistoun thought, a large book, wrapped in a white cloth, on which cloth a cross was rudely embroidered in red thread. Even before the wrapping had been removed, Dennistoun began to be interested by the size and shape of the volume. 'Too large for a missal,' he thought, 'and not the shape of an antiphoner; perhaps it may be something good, after all.' The next moment the book was open, and Dennistoun felt that he had at last hit upon something better than good. Before him lay a large folio, bound, perhaps, late in the seventeenth century, with the arms of Canon Alberic de Mauléon stamped in gold on the sides. There may have been a hundred and fifty leaves of paper in the book, and on almost every one of them was fastened a leaf from an illustrated manuscript. Such a collection Dennistoun had hardly dreamed of in his wildest moments. Here were ten leaves from a copy of Genesis, illustrated with pictures, which could not be later than AD 700. Further on was a complete set of pictures from a Psalter, of English execution, of the very finest kind that the thirteenth century could produce; and, perhaps best of all, there were twenty leaves of uncial writing in Latin, which, as a few words seen here and there told him at once, must belong to some very early unknown patristic treatise. Could it possibly be a fragment of the copy of Papias' *On the Words of Our Lord*, which was known to have existed as late as the twelfth century at Nîmes?[1] In any case, his mind was made up; that book must return to Cambridge with him, even if he had to draw the whole of his balance from the bank and stay at St Bertrand till the money came. He glanced up at the sacristan to see if his face yielded any hint that the book was for sale. The sacristan was pale, and his lips were working.

'If monsieur will turn on to the end,' he said.

So monsieur turned on, meeting new treasures at every rise of a leaf; and at the end of the book he came upon two sheets of paper, of much more recent date than anything he had yet seen, which puzzled him considerably. They must be contemporary, he decided, with the unprincipled Canon Alberic, who had doubtless plundered the Chapter library of St Bertrand to form this priceless scrap-book. On the first of the paper sheets was a plan, carefully drawn and instantly recognizable by a person who knew the ground, of the south aisle and cloisters of St Bertrand's. There were curious signs looking like planetary symbols, and a few Hebrew words, in the corners; and in the north-west angle of the cloister was a cross drawn in gold paint. Below the plan were some lines of writing in Latin, which ran thus:

1 We now know that these leaves did contain a considerable fragment of that work, if not of that actual copy of it.

Responsa 12ᵐⁱ Dec. 1694. Interrogatum est; Inveniamne?
Responsum est: Invenies. Fiamne dives? Fies. Vivamne
invidendus? Vives. Moriarne in lecto meo? Ita. (Answers
of the 12th of December, 1694. It was asked: Shall I find
it? Answer: Thou shalt. Shall I become rich? Thou wilt.
Shall I live an object of envy? Thou wilt. Shall I die in my
bed? Thou wilt.)

'A good specimen of the treasure-hunter's record – quite
reminds one of Mr Minor-Canon Quatremain in *Old St
Paul's*,' was Dennistoun's comment, and he turned the
leaf.

What he then saw impressed him, as he has often told me,
more than he could have conceived any drawing or picture
capable of impressing him. And, though the drawing he saw
is no longer in existence, there is a photograph of it (which I
possess) which fully bears out that statement. The picture in
question was a sepia drawing at the end of the seventeenth
century, representing, one would say at first sight, a biblical
scene; for the architecture (the picture represented an
interior) and the figures had that semi-classical flavour
about them which the artists of two hundred years ago
thought appropriate to illustrations of the Bible. On the
right was a king on his throne, the throne elevated on
twelve steps, a canopy overhead, lions on either side –
evidently King Solomon. He was bending forward with
outstretched sceptre, in attitude of command; his face
expressed horror and disgust, yet there was in it also the
mark of imperious will and confident power. The left half of
the picture was the strangest, however. The interest plainly
centred there. On the pavement before the throne were
grouped four soldiers, surrounding a crouching figure
which must be described in a moment. A fifth soldier lay
dead on the pavement, his neck distorted, and his eyeballs

starting from his head. The four surrounding guards were looking at the king. In their faces the sentiment of horror was intensified; they seemed, in fact, only restrained from flight by their implicit trust in their master. All this terror was plainly excited by the being that crouched in their midst. I entirely despair of conveying by any words the impression which this figure makes upon anyone who looks at it. I recollect once showing the photograph of the drawing to a lecturer on morphology – a person of, I was going to say, abnormally sane and unimaginative habits of mind. He absolutely refused to be alone for the rest of that evening, and he told me afterwards that for many nights he had not dared to put out his light before going to sleep. However, the main traits of the figure I can at least indicate. At first you saw only a mass of coarse, matted black hair; presently it was seen that this covered a body of fearful thinness, almost a skeleton, but with the muscles standing out like wires. The hands were of a dusky pallor, covered, like the body, with long, coarse hairs, and hideously taloned. The eyes, touched in with a burning yellow, had intensely black pupils, and were fixed upon the throned king with a look of beast-like hate. Imagine one of the awful bird-catching spiders of South America translated into human form, and endowed with intelligence just less than human, and you will have some faint conception of the terror inspired by this appalling effigy. One remark is universally made by those to whom I have shown the picture: 'It was drawn from the life.'

As soon as the first shock of his irresistible fright had subsided, Dennistoun stole a look at his hosts. The sacristan's hands were pressed upon his eyes; his daughter, looking up at the cross on the wall, was telling her beads feverishly.

At last the question was asked, 'Is this book for sale?'

There was the same hesitation, the same plunge of determination that he had noticed before, and then came the welcome answer, 'If monsieur pleases.'

'How much do you ask for it?'

'I will take two hundred and fifty francs.'

This was confounding. Even a collector's conscience is sometimes stirred, and Dennistoun's conscience was tenderer than a collector's.

'My good man!' he said again and again, 'your book is worth far more than two hundred and fifty francs, I assure you – far more.'

But the answer did not vary: 'I will take two hundred and fifty francs, not more.'

There was really no possibility of refusing such a chance. The money was paid, the receipt signed, a glass of wine drunk over the transaction, and then the sacristan seemed to become a new man. He stood upright, he ceased to throw those suspicious glances behind him, he actually laughed or tried to laugh. Dennistoun rose to go.

'I shall have the honour of accompanying monsieur to his hotel?' said the sacristan.

'Oh no, thanks! It isn't a hundred yards. I know the way perfectly, and there is a moon.'

The offer was pressed three or four times, and refused as often.

'Then, monsieur will summon me if – if he finds occasion; he will keep the middle of the road, the sides are so rough.'

'Certainly, certainly,' said Dennistoun, who was impatient to examine his prize by himself; and he stepped out into the passage with his book under his arm.

Here he was met by the daughter; she, it appeared, was anxious to do a little business on her own account; perhaps, like Gehazi, to 'take somewhat' from the foreigner whom her father had spared.

'A silver crucifix and chain for the neck; monsieur would perhaps be good enough to accept it?'

Well, really, Dennistoun hadn't much use for these things. What did mademoiselle want for it?

'Nothing – nothing in the world. Monsieur is more than welcome to it.'

The tone in which this and much more was said was unmistakably genuine, so that Dennistoun was reduced to profuse thanks, and submitted to have the chain put round his neck. It really seemed as if he had rendered the father and daughter some service which they hardly knew how to repay. As he set off with his book they stood at the door looking after him, and they were still looking when he waved them a last good-night from the steps of the Chapeau Rouge.

Dinner was over, and Dennistoun was in his bedroom, shut up alone with his acquisition. The landlady had manifested a particular interest in him since he had told her that he had paid a visit to the sacristan and bought an old book from him. He thought, too, that he had heard a hurried dialogue between her and the said sacristan in the passage outside the *salle à manger*; some words to the effect that 'Pierre and Bertrand would be sleeping in the house' had closed the conversation.

All this time a growing feeling of discomfort had been creeping over him – nervous reaction, perhaps, after the delight of his discovery. Whatever it was, it resulted in a conviction that there was someone behind him, and that he was far more comfortable with his back to the wall. All this, of course, weighed light in the balance as against the obvious value of the collection he had acquired. And now, as I said, he was alone in his bedroom, taking stock of Canon Alberic's treasures, in which every moment revealed something more charming.

'Bless Canon Alberic!' said Dennistoun, who had an inveterate habit of talking to himself. 'I wonder where he is now? Dear me! I wish that landlady would learn to laugh in a more cheering manner; it makes one feel as if there was someone dead in the house. Half a pipe more, did you say? I think perhaps you are right. I wonder what that crucifix is that the young woman insisted on giving me? Last century, I suppose. Yes, probably. It is rather a nuisance of a thing to have round one's neck – just too heavy. Most likely her father has been wearing it for years. I think I might give it a clean up before I put it away.'

He had taken the crucifix off, and laid it on the table, when his attention was caught by an object lying on the red cloth just by his left elbow. Two or three ideas of what it might be flitted through his brain with their own incalculable quickness.

'A penwiper? No, no such thing in the house. A rat? No, too black. A large spider? I trust to goodness not – no. Good God! a hand like the hand in that picture!'

In another infinitesimal flash he had taken it in. Pale, dusky skin, covering nothing but bones and tendons of appalling strength; coarse black hairs, longer than ever grew on a human hand; nails rising from the ends of the fingers and curving sharply down and forward, grey, horny and wrinkled.

He flew out of his chair with deadly, inconceivable terror clutching at his heart. The shape, whose left hand rested on the table, was rising to a standing posture behind his seat, its right hand crooked above his scalp. There was black and tattered drapery about it; the coarse hair covered it as in the drawing. The lower jaw was thin – what can I call it? – shallow, like a beast's; teeth showed behind the black lips; there was no nose; the eyes, of a fiery yellow, against which the pupils showed black and intense, and the exulting hate and thirst to destroy life which shone there, were the most horrifying features in the whole vision. There was intelligence of a kind in them – intelligence beyond that of a beast, below that of a man.

The feelings which this horror stirred in Dennistoun were the intensest physical fear and the most profound mental loathing. What did he do? What could he do? He has never been quite certain what words he said, but he knows that he spoke, that he grasped blindly at the silver crucifix, that he was conscious of a movement towards him on the part of the demon, and that he screamed with the voice of an animal in hideous pain.

Pierre and Bertrand, the two sturdy little serving-men, who rushed in, saw nothing, but felt themselves thrust aside by something that passed out between them, and found Dennistoun in a swoon. They sat up with him that night, and his two friends were at St Bertrand by nine o'clock next morning. He himself, though still shaken and nervous, was almost himself by that time, and his story found credence with them, though not until they had seen the drawing and talked with the sacristan.

Almost at dawn the little man had come to the inn on some pretence, and had listened with the deepest interest to the story retailed by the landlady. He showed no surprise.

'It is he – it is he! I have seen him myself,' was his only comment; and to all questionings but one reply was vouchsafed: '*Deux fois je l'ai vu; mille fois je l'ai senti.*' He would tell them nothing of the provenance of the book, nor any details of his experiences. 'I shall soon sleep, and my rest will be sweet. Why should you trouble me?' he said.[1]

We shall never know what he or Canon Alberic de Mauléon suffered. At the back of that fateful drawing were

---

1 He died that summer; his daughter married, and settled at St Papoul. She never understood the circumstances of her father's 'obsession'.

some lines of writing which may be supposed to throw light on the situation:

> *Contradictio Salomonis cum demonio nocturno.*
> *Albericus de Mauleone delineavit.*
> *V. Deus in adiutorium. Ps. Qui habitat.*
> *Sancte Bertrande, demoniorum effugator, intercede pro me*
> *miserrimo.*
> *Primum uidi nocte 12^{mi} Dec. 1694: uidebo mox*
> *ultimum. Peccaui et passus sum, plura adhuc*
> *passurus. Dec. 29, 1701.*[2]

I have never quite understood what was Dennistoun's view of the events I have narrated. He quoted to me once a text from Ecclesiasticus: 'Some spirits there be that are created for vengeance, and in their fury lay on sore strokes.' On another occasion he said: 'Isaiah was a very sensible man; doesn't he say something about night monsters living in the ruins of Babylon? These things are rather beyond us at present.'

Another confidence of his impressed me rather, and I sympathized with it. We had been, last year, to Comminges, to see Canon Alberic's tomb. It is a great marble erection with an effigy of the Canon in a large wig and soutane, and an elaborate eulogy of his learning below. I saw Dennistoun talking for some time with the Vicar of St Bertrand's, and as we drove away he said to me: 'I hope it isn't wrong: you know I am a Presbyterian – but I – I believe there will be "saying of Mass and singing of dirges" for Alberic de

---

1 *I.e.*, 'The Dispute of Solomon with a demon of the night. Drawn by Alberic de Mauléon. *Versicle*. O Lord, make haste to help me. *Psalm*. Whoso dwelleth (xci).

'Saint Bertrand, who puttest devils to flight, pray for me most unhappy. I saw it first on the night of Dec. 12, 1694: soon I shall see it for the last time. I have sinned and suffered, and have more to suffer yet. Dec. 29, 1701.'

The *Gallia Christiana* gives the date of the Canon's death as December 31, 1701, 'in bed, of a sudden seizure'. Details of this kind are not common in the great work of the Sammarthani.

Mauléon's rest.' Then he added, with a touch of the Northern British in his tone, 'I had no notion they came so dear.'

The book is in the Wentworth Collection at Cambridge. The drawing was photographed and then burnt by Dennistoun on the day when he left Comminges on the occasion of his first visit.

Acknowledgements

Robert Aickman, 'The Cicerones' from *Sub Rosa*, reprinted by permission of Artellus Ltd on behalf of the Estate of Robert Aickman

M.R. James, 'Canon Alberic's Scrap-book' from *Collected Ghost Stories*, reprinted by permission of N.J.R. James on behalf of the Estate of M.R. James

Christopher Park, 'The Beckoning Monk', reprinted by permission of the author

Ruth Rendell, 'The Haunting of Shawley Rectory', reprinted by permission of the Peters, Fraser & Dunlop Group Ltd

Every effort has been made to contact copyright-holders. However, the editor and publishers would be pleased to hear from any that they have been unable to trace and due acknowledgement will be made in future editions.